I0657304

A Saint's Letters
from the
Depths of Hell

Ralph Vincent Morales

Halo
PUBLISHING
INTERNATIONAL

Copyright © 2020 Ralph Vincent Morales
All rights reserved.

No part of this book may be reproduced in any manner without the
written consent of the publisher except for brief excerpts in critical
reviews or articles.

ISBN: 978-1-61244-819-0
Library of Congress Control Number: 2020903268

Printed in the United States of America

Halo Publishing International
8000 W Interstate 10
Suite 600
San Antonio, Texas 78230
www.halopublishing.com
contact@halopublishing.com

The publisher and the author are providing this book and its contents on an "as is" basis and make no representations or warranties of any kind with respect to this book or its contents. The publisher and the author assume no responsibility for errors, inaccuracies, omissions, or any other inconsistencies herein.

The events described in this book are based on actual letters that Vinnie Santaniello sent home to his family, as well as on stories that a number of Marines and Corpsmen shared with the author about their experiences in Vietnam during Vinnie's tour in country. Further, the author gratefully used the names of Ned LeRoy, Michael Reagan, John Nunn, Daniel King, Tony Milazzo, and John Chang with their permission. All other names and nicknames utilized by the author to identify Marines in the book are fictional. Furthermore, the names and nicknames of Vinnie's surviving family members who have since passed away are real. The name or names of any of Vinnie's surviving family members that are referenced in this book and that were alive at the time of the publication of this book have been changed. The names of any Santaniello family friends that are referenced in this book and that were still alive at the time of publication have been changed, unless permission was granted to utilize any such names. All other persons and names listed in this book are entirely fictional. Any resemblance to persons living or dead resulting from changes to names or identifying details is entirely coincidental and unintentional.

This book is dedicated first and foremost to the uncle I never knew: Vincent Benore Santaniello. Uncle Vinnie, this book has brought me so close to you. Indeed, in reading your letters to Lillian Santaniello, your sister and my mother, and in speaking to the men who served with you and loved you in Vietnam, I have come to love and respect you immensely. You are more than my uncle, Saint: You are my HERO.

Next, I dedicate this book to my eternal best friend and late mother, Lillian Santaniello Morales. Vinnie's letters to you educated me about the amazing bond of love, trust, and kinship that you shared with him. Surely, his death devastated you. Thank you for the honor of allowing me to carry his name as my middle name. I love you fiercely, Mom, and I miss you every single day.

Of course, this book would not be possible without the love and support of family, past and present. This book is dedicated to my beloved, late grandparents, Rose and Carmine Santaniello; Uncle Vinnie's surviving family members; my siblings, Vinny, Tony, and Rosina; and, last but not least, my wife, Joanne, and our five remarkable children: Mark, Luke, Rebecca, Gianna, and Mateo.

I also dedicate this book to some amazing gentlemen and American heroes who served our country in the Vietnam War. You will come to know and love these men in the pages that follow, but understand that this book NEVER gets written without the memories that they graciously shared with me. Michael "Red" Reagan, John "Doc" Nunn, Tony "Doc" Milazzo, Daniel King, Ned LeRoy, and John "Doc" Chang: Thank you for your service to our country in Vietnam, and thank you for courageously foraging through the recesses of your minds and sharing very personal—

and exquisitely painful—memories of your brother, Vinnie "Saint" Santaniello. You men join your brother Vinnie as my heroes and I truly love you all very much. Semper Fi!

Finally, this book is dedicated to the memories of every single serviceman and servicewoman who has made the ultimate sacrifice while serving in the military to bravely preserve our country's freedom and to the Gold Star families that survive them. The courageous sacrifices of our nation's fallen heroes, and the continued sacrifices and despair of their survivors, serve as the very foundation of America. Such heroes are revered and never forgotten.

ACKNOWLEDGEMENTS

T his book would not be possible without the contributions of the following American heroes and veterans of the Vietnam War: Michael Reagan, John "Doc" Nunn, Tony "Doc" Milazzo, Daniel King, Edward "Ned" LeRoy, and John "Doc" Chang. I am also very grateful to my mother's best friend, Marie Mattia (formerly Marie Graves), who shared her memories of how Vinnie's death impacted everyone back home, especially her next-door neighbor and friend, Lilly, and Vinnie's father, Carmine.

A huge debt of gratitude also goes out to my Georgetown University Class of 1991 classmates and friends, Bill Stewart and Fred Dews. These fellow Hoyas reviewed a very early version of this book and utilized their military backgrounds to offer helpful constructive criticisms, insights, and edits. Additionally, a huge thank you goes out to Suzanne D'Amico and her company, *Inspired by CJA Photography*, for my author photo and for taking the time to carefully photograph many of Vinnie's letters for the cover of this book. Suzanne also tirelessly restored and downloaded the amazing photos of Vinnie that adorn the center of this book. Furthermore, I am very grateful to Rosalie "Roe" Wagenecht (formerly Rosalie Vitale), whom I "met" for the first time well after I finished writing this book. Roe was kind enough to share poignant stories about her relationship with Vinnie and she also provided me with amazing pictures from their time together. I also thank Giang Duong and Mai Tran for providing me with the correct spellings and accent marks for the Vietnamese words and phrases that appear in this book.

Finally, many thanks to Lisa M. Umina and her company, Halo Publishing International, for believing in this story and for providing me with the platform to share my Uncle Vinnie with the world. Lisa, your charisma is contagious and your undying support of, and belief in, this endeavor was incredibly uplifting! Thanks to Halo's editor, Laura Burks for meticulously editing this book to ensure that *A Saint's Letters from the Depths of Hell* was ready for publication. Lisa, Laura, and the entire Halo Publishing team have helped to fulfill my dream of sharing with the world this tragic yet inspirational story of selfless bravery, loyalty, love, and family.

CONTENTS

"FOURWORD"

Foreword One:
Michael "Red" Reagan

A lot of my friends died during and because of the Vietnam War. These were people I had grown up with and people I met while I was there myself. Two of those people died in battle on a fateful day: March 28, 1968.

My unit, Kilo Company, 3rd Battalion, 4th Marine Regiment, had spent the previous year on or near the Vietnam demilitarized zone (DMZ). However, we eventually were moved to the Cam Lo Regional Headquarters. We were told this new area would be a lot safer than the area where we had been, even though it was still near the DMZ. But we were tired, we were short-staffed, and we were hungry for food, mail, and sleep. We needed a rest. For some reason, our platoon was allowed to be the perimeter guard while most of the other units were sent out on patrol. Those patrols are the reason I am able to write this account of that day.

Early that morning, on March 28th, we were hit by both rocket and mortar attacks—a lot of them! We were being attacked with very large rockets because we still were near the DMZ. The hellfire was just dropping out of the sky, with no one on the ground knowing where they would hit. We had holes to hide in but what the enemy liked to do was sneak up on you under their own incoming, catch you in those holes, and kill you. But we knew that, so we were ready to get out, hoping the incoming had stopped, and fight to stay alive. We did that.

Because of the patrols I mentioned earlier, there was a delay in the enemy's attack, which allowed us to get to our wounded. Two of the wounded were people I knew well: Peder Armstrong, from my high school in Seattle, and Vincent ("Saint") Santaniello, from Queens, New York, who was our company driver. Peder was dead and Vinnie was badly injured. "Doc" John Nunn, "Doc" Tony Milazzo, and I went to Vinnie. Unbeknownst to me, I would be reborn by virtue of what transpired that day.

I took Vinnie into my arms and tried to calm him, although it didn't appear to me, as I remember it, that he was feeling a lot of pain. But he was badly injured. Both of the Docs went after him as vigorously as anyone possibly could have, trying to keep him alive. All I could say to him as he lay in my arms was, "You'll be okay." I needed him to know that he wasn't going to be alone! We all knew our battle wasn't over, that this was just a pause and it was going to start again. We needed Vinnie to know that he had our absolute attention. At that moment, my life changed forever!

As Vinnie looked up at me for the last time—I will never forget these words—he said, "Mike, I just want to go home!" He looked right into me, closed his eyes, and died. He went home.

I've since seen that face every day for the last fifty-plus years.

When I began drawing portraits of fallen heroes back in 2004, nearly 7,000 portraits ago, I didn't really understand the importance of that moment in time on March 28, 1968: The moment I was reborn. For nearly sixteen years now, I've been trying to keep Vinnie's wish for a lot of other fallen heroes: getting them home. I know now that that morning in my arms, Vinnie was telling me: We will be doing work one day, and it will change your life!

On April 19, 2014, I had the honor of presenting Vinnie's portrait to his nephew, Ralph Vincent Morales, who was born sixteen months after Vinnie's death, is named for his uncle, and is now the author of this book.

The story you are about to read is the story of a true hero, one who is not dead, but very much alive through the work we are doing! Vinnie is a part of every fallen hero portrait I've drawn or will draw. In fact, sometimes while working I feel that Vinnie is with the fallen hero that I am drawing, just to be sure that I do it right. We will do them right, for every hero we are drawing deserves nothing less!

I will never forget.

Michael "Red" Reagan
Corporal, USMC
3rd Battalion, 4th Marine Regiment
3rd Marine Division, Kilo Company
Vietnam, 1967-1968
Founder of the Fallen Heroes Portrait Project
www.fallenheroesproject.org

*　　　*　　　*

Foreword Two:
John "Doc" Nunn

I've written and rewritten more about me and Vinnie—and more in this story—than I wanted to tell. You would think that writing a foreword about a friend that has been dead for more than fifty years would be easy, right? Well, you'd be wrong if you thought that. In fact, this is one of the more difficult things that I've ever had to do, and that's saying something, as I was a corpsman in Vietnam. I love Vinnie Santaniello. Not *loved*: Vinnie still lives in and with me each and every day, so I *love* him.

I remember how proud Vinnie was of his family back in New York and I especially remember how fond he was of his sister, Lilly.

Lilly always sent Vinnie pictures and tapes from back home and the guys in the platoon were quite *fond* of her! I still remember her tapes: She often recorded herself singing and I vividly remember the guys saying that she had the sweetest New York accent they had ever heard. Vinnie really loved Lilly and we all knew that he spent much of his free time writing her letters. Vinnie and Lilly were more than just siblings. They were best friends.

When I met Ralph Vincent Morales, the author of this book, I told him that I saw some of Vinnie in him. I also apologized to him. He looked confused, so I told him what I've been holding in my heart for half a century: I am sorry for failing Vinnie that day in Cam Lo, Vietnam, after a North Vietnamese Army daytime assault on us. We lost four brothers in that attack. As one of two corpsmen that responded to our fallen brother, I saw that Vinnie was alive but was in a really bad way. My fellow corpsman, Doc Milazzo, and I did everything that we could to save Vinnie.

But it wasn't enough to save Saint.

And I've never forgotten that, just as I have not forgotten that we suffered four deaths, plus another thirteen wounded, on that day.

I mended a lot of injured brothers in the jungles of Vietnam during the war and I saw a lot of death. For some reason, none of those deaths impacted me as much as Saint's death. I have often questioned why I'm still here while he's gone. Vinnie was—and is, to this day — a very special person in my life. I will never forget Saint because he is world-famous, thanks to Michael Reagan.

I began to wear a KIA bracelet to honor Saint shortly after I traveled to Washington, D.C. on November 11, 1984, for the dedication of the statue *The Three Soldiers* at the Vietnam Veterans Memorial—what's known as "The Wall." Fast forward to early 2014, when I got a call from Mike Reagan. He told me that he'd been interviewed by a television reporter about the tenth anniversary of the Fallen Heroes Project and was asked about why he started the project. Mike knew that he began the project to honor an old

Marine brother who died in his arms—the company driver for Kilo Co.—but he couldn't remember his name, so he reached out to me to ask if I remembered the brother's name.

I immediately responded, "Vincent B. Santaniello. Saint."

Mike seemed flabbergasted and immediately asked, "How did you know that?"

I told Mike that I'd been wearing Saint's KIA bracelet for over thirty years. Mike called the reporter back to provide him with Vinnie's name and, within a day, the reporter had found Vinnie's niece, Rosina Morales, and his nephew, Ralph Vincent Morales. The rest, as they say, is history! As my old lieutenant in Kilo Co. used to say during our time in Vietnam, "You can't make this shit up!"

Saint was my friend. Saint was my brother.

I love you, Saint, and I miss you so very much. I'm sorry, brother.

John "Doc" Nunn
Navy Hospital Corpsman
Combat Corpsman
3rd Battalion, 4th Marine Regiment
3rd Marine Division, Kilo Company
Vietnam, 1967-1971

*　　　*　　　*

Foreword Three:
Tony "Doc" Milazzo

It is an extreme honor to be asked to add a little something to the story of a young Marine, Vinnie "Saint" Santaniello. I'm proud to call him my friend and brother.

As a twenty-year-old corpsman in Vietnam (and I was one of the older members of our platoon), I was seeing, doing, and touching things that no one should ever have to see, do, or touch. And that brought a whole new meaning to the word *brotherhood*. Saint and I had known each other since November 1967 and, for whatever reason, we hit it off right away. Maybe because he was a Queens guy and I was, and continue to be, a Jersey guy. We would rib each other about his Rockaway Beach and my Jersey Shore. He even referred to me as a "stone" Italian in a letter that he had written to his sister, Lilly, back in the world. Vinnie and I became close but, really, Saint was close to all of us.

That day, March 28, 1968, will live with us forever. Saint did not need to be at Cam Lo District Headquarters that day; he could've stayed back in the rear as the company driver. However, Saint loved to be with his brothers.

Doc Nunn and I were at different locations on the base when the incoming attack started that morning, and we both were trying to find a safe place. Then we heard "CORPSMAN UP!"—a chilling cry of desperation and exasperation that we heard far too many times during our tours. Doc Nunn and I ran into the incoming mortars and artillery, to see where we were needed, and we ran as fast as we could to get to the area where four of our brothers were down. We learned that three Marines already were dead but that a fourth, Saint, was still alive but severely wounded.

Doc Nunn and I did our very best to save Saint as he lay in Mike "Red" Reagan's arms but, unfortunately, our best just wasn't good enough. After a while, Saint told Mike, "I just want to go home." And then he died. He died in our hands. We sat there for a moment, stunned. After all, this was Saint, our pal, and the guy who had constantly, proudly boasted about how he was going to serve as the best man in his sister's wedding in just a few months.

Reality set in and we had to leave him as others needed our help. But I know that Doc Nunn looked back as we returned to the mayhem because I did, too. It was Saint . . .

I will remember you forever in my heart, my friend. I keep your name on a bracelet that I wear on my right wrist, too.

I love you, my brother, my friend.

Tony "Doc" Milazzo
Navy Hospital Corpsman
Combat Corpsman
3rd Battalion, 4th Marine Regiment
3rd Marine Division, Kilo Company
Vietnam, 1967-1968

*   *   *

Foreword Four:
John "Doc" Chang

Vinnie was my best friend. He still is.

We met in the 1950s. Vinnie and I, along with two other friends, Robbie and Georgie, were a tight little group of childhood friends. We grew up in the city, doing what city kids did. We played stickball, handball, and stoop ball. We sang on the street corner and the neighborhood rooftops. We weren't good, but we didn't care.

I'm first-generation American, half-Chinese and half-French/ English. I was a poor kid from a large family of fifteen children. I was different from my friends, both ethnically and socioeconomically. I worked to help my family, even as a child. I collected bottles, shined shoes, delivered fruit . . . the kinds of odd jobs that people would pay a little kid to do. I spoke differently, too, with an accent that was an odd hybrid of Chinese and inner-city urban.

None of that mattered to Vinnie.

Vinnie taught me about acceptance. His small, tightly-knit family was kind and welcoming. I had my first taste of Italian food at their table, including my first—and my most memorable—bite of Italian bread! In my adult years, Vinnie's mother, Rose, taught me how to make her tomato gravy (she called it *sauce*) for pasta and I make it to this day.

Vinnie was devoted to his family and loyal to his friends. Our lives weren't easy, but we didn't know any different. I remember our times together, with our group of four friends, as the happiest times of my childhood.

When we were called to serve, Vinnie went into the Marines, 3rd Battalion, 4th Marine Regiment, 3rd Marine Division, Kilo Company. He was a rifleman. I was a Fleet Marine Force corpsman with the 1st Battalion, 5th Marine Regiment, 1st Marine Division, Charlie Company. Robbie was a Navy Seabee and Georgie was an infantryman with the Army.

We all went to Vietnam.

Vinnie and I stayed in touch through letters and through our families. After thirteen months in country, I was the first to leave for home.

And then it all fell apart.

It was April 1968. Four days after leaving Vietnam, I was at Dover Air Force Base in Delaware, escorting Vinnie's body home to Jamaica, New York. Mr. and Mrs. Santaniello had requested that of the Marine Corps, which had complied.

Robbie and Georgie made it home after their tours, but both died soon after: Robbie of cancer and Georgie in an automobile accident.

Vinnie is at the center of my happiest childhood memories. And he's at the center of the saddest time of my life. He now resides peacefully in my heart, where he remains forever young. My son carries his name. His photo greets me when I start up my iPad.

I'm grateful that his nephew has paid tribute to him with this book. I think Vinnie would be humbled by the honor. Vinnie was a good kid. A good son. A good man. A good friend. And a damn great Marine.

I miss him every day.

John "Doc" Chang
Fleet Marine Force Corpsman
1st Battalion, 5th Marine Regiment
1st Marine Division, Charlie Company
Vietnam, 1967-1968

CHAPTER 1

ARRIVAL IN THE DEPTHS OF HELL

And don't you worry about me playing hero. My middle name is "Chicken Man." No, that shit ain't for me anyway. I'll probably never see fighting. I have it pretty good so far. So don't worry about me, Sis. I'll be OK. Just say a few prayers for me once in a while.

Excerpt from eighteen-year-old Vincent Benore ("Vinnie") Santaniello's July 21, 1967 letter to his twenty-year-old sister and best friend, Lilly. Vinnie penned this letter while he was stationed at Camp Pendleton, two days before he was set to fly to South Vietnam

*   *   *

*A*ugust 6, 1967. Vinnie was aboard a chopper, also known in military jargon as either a *Huey* or a *bird*, flying over the vastest expanse of nature that the kid from New York City had ever seen. *Holy shit*, Vinnie thought, *I ain't seen this many trees since I went to Central Park with my girl, Rosalie, for her eighteenth birthday last May.*

Vinnie closed his eyes and, as the bird wavered and dipped through the soupy Vietnam fog, he allowed himself to dream—for just a second—that he was back home in Jamaica with his girl, Rosalie, and, of course, with his beloved family: his father, Carmine, a Navy veteran of World War II; his devoted mom, Rose; his kid brother, twelve-year-old Joseph; and, perhaps the one that he missed most of all, his older sister, Lilly. Vinnie was jostled from the serenity of that dream by a sound that he soon would hear in his dreams: the *whump whump whump* of machine-gun fire.

"Hey, Skipper, the fucking gooks are firing on us! Is that LZ ready for us to come in hot? Over!"

Vinnie didn't know the name of the kid who was screaming those words into the radio, but he immediately realized one thing about him: He did not look scared shitless, which perfectly described Vinnie and his fellow greenies as they were about to land in country for the beginning of their thirteen-month tours in Hell! Vinnie sat frozen on the floor of the chopper, his gear strapped onto his back and his M-16 rifle at his side, unable to move, as the returning grunts inexplicably and calmly glanced over their weapons and checked their ammo belts and grenades. Others slept—actually *slept*—as bullets flew past the bird. Vinnie felt many thumps against the craning body of the heavily fortified chopper and he watched guys jump into their familiar spots, to return fire to the invisible enemy far below them.

Vinnie thought, *How the hell can something that looks as serene as these endless treetops, mountain tops, and valleys be so fucking deadly?*

"Hold on, boys, we're going in hot!"

Next thing Vinnie knew, the bird had seemingly stopped flapping its wings. The chopper was going down and going down fast. For a second, Vinnie was overcome with an unforgiving sense of melancholy and doom, as he mistakenly thought that the bird had been shot out of the sky.

I'm gonna die before I even get into the shit down there, he worried before recalling what he had been taught in boot camp: that, after coordinates were confirmed with Marines at the LZ, the choppers would deliberately dive out of the sky, to minimize taking on heavy machine-gun fire. Vinnie swallowed and admitted to himself that he was a little embarrassed at his green mistake. However, his shame receded dramatically when he looked around at the other recruits on the chopper and realized that most of them, including one green that appeared to have shit himself, were equally dismayed at the rapid descent of the bird.

Thank God I rode the Cyclone rollercoaster all those times at Coney Island, Vinnie mused, *or I'd-a shit myself, too, for sure!*

One resounding thud and many jostled bodies later, Vinnie realized that he no longer was a wise-cracking kid from Jamaica, Queens—one of the five boroughs in New York City—who'd graduated from Thomas Edison Vocational High School a little over one year earlier.

No, now he was a U.S. Marine in Vietnam. *Semper Fi!*

"Let's go, greens, move your asses, unless you wanna fucking go home in a bag tomorrow," yelled someone with a couple of bars on his sleeve on an otherwise barely-recognizable USMC-issued uniform. Vinnie looked at the holes and filth all over the lieutenant's shirt and pants and then peered at his own perfectly pressed shirt and pants, before whispering, *"Shiiiiiit!"*

Vinnie then cast a discerning glance at the yelling lieutenant's boots and couldn't understand why, or when, the Corps had issued grey-white boots to the Marines. After all, Vinnie's boots shined a proud black sheen that contrasted quite vividly with the brown muck and soot that seemed to envelop him.

As he walked in a fog—literally and figuratively—from the chopper whose blades still whirred ferociously, a large, black canvas bag, swaying uneasily between two Marines carrying this amorphous cargo, bumped into Vinnie's shoulder. The propellers struggled to slice through the soupy fog that enveloped Vinnie and his fellow Marines as they fastidiously jumped off the chopper and waited for further directions from their superiors. They propped their heavy seabags over their shoulders. But for the scant light that was generated by the burning C-4 cans that were placed inside of helmets that encircled the LZ, as well as the small flashlights that some Marines were shining toward the chopper, the blackness of the area was downright unnerving.

Vinnie struggled to peer through the dark before he realized the sheer futility of such an endeavor. He turned again to try to visualize what those Marines were carrying rather clumsily inside of the canvas wrapping, but he was overcome by a smell that repulsed him. It was a rotting stench that made the NYC subways that he'd been riding just a few months earlier smell like the aromatic garden that his parents meticulously tended every spring and summer, in the diminutive swath of Earth that decorated the front of his home in the concrete jungle. Indeed, Vinnie's home could not have seemed farther away than it did at that very moment.

Vinnie peered harder at the black bag and noticed what appeared to be a foot protruding from its bottom. This foot did not resemble any foot that Vinnie had seen before: It was at least three times as big as he thought it should be. Was it the fog? It sure did look to be ashen and gray.

"Hey," Vinnie innocuously asked one of the Marines, "what the hell *is* that?"

One of the men, tall and impossibly thin, wore an official USMC-issued green t-shirt, which hung on his skinny frame as if it had been clumsily placed on a metal clothes hanger and torn, and filthy green pants that resembled parachutes over his rail-thin legs. This Marine had soulless black eyes; a pockmarked, scarred Caucasian face whose uneven sprouts of wispy hair spoke of a kid who hadn't seen a razor in weeks, if not months; and a helmet-less head that displayed short, yet grimy, brown hair. Indeed, this kid, whose eyes spoke voraciously of a Hell that his mouth never would, did not bother acknowledging the query or the numby who had posed it.

The other Marine, a slender black man who couldn't have been more than eighteen and who came up to his brother Marines' shoulders, had an equally distant look in his eye, but his face was softer than that of the man with whom he shared the unenviable task of carrying this strange cargo. He strained to see the dumb grunt that had had the temerity to question what he and his fellow gunny were carrying.

"Brother," the black man stated with a hint of a Southern twang, "this here will be your dumb white ass if y'all ain't able to look in every direction at the same got-damn time when y'all's in the shit." Then, with a disheartening chuckle, he exclaimed, "Welcome to the Crotch, dude."

What Vinnie didn't know then was that Smitty, the white Marine, and Sharpshooter, the black Marine, had been entrusted with carrying the remains of Steel, a brother Marine from Bravo Company, after Steel had had the misfortune *six days earlier* of stepping on a land mine while he had been proceeding to an LP for a planned ambush on the gooks. Smitty and Sharpshooter had had to hump Steel down a mountain and through the jungle just to reach this LZ, so that what was left of him could be flown back to the world.

Vinnie had been in Vietnam for all of about forty-eight seconds when he realized that he wanted to get the fuck out—*alive*. He mumbled what sounded like *sorry* to no one in particular (or was it to what was left of Steel?) before he clumsily sidestepped Smitty and Sharpshooter as they struggled under the unforgiving weight of Steel's dead body while loading the body bag onto the bird.

Vinnie, still at the mouth of the doorway to the chopper from which he jumped a minute earlier, was pretty certain that he heard the pilot yell, "Let's go! Get the Oleys onto this goddamned Huey so that we can medevac 'em! Are there any more Coors? Load 'em up, 'cause I gotta get the fuck outta here, before I join 'em."

Vinnie soon would become fluent in the unique language that was *Marine-glish* but, at that moment, he was vaguely familiar with the notion that a *Huey* was the helicopter from which he had just disembarked. He had no idea that an *Oley* was a Marine wounded in action, or that *Coors* was radio code for a dead Marine. Vinnie watched tired, hungry, and absolutely filthy Marines struggle to load (*very* unceremoniously, he thought) about six more Coors onto the helicopter, followed almost immediately by nearly a dozen Oleys who either limped or were carried onto the Huey.

All of these men were in various states of disrepair, from shrapnel-induced and jagged lacerations to broken bones and grotesquely missing limbs. Vinnie thought that more than a few of them seemed eerily happy, or relieved, albeit it in a terribly perverse way.

Vinnie's observation proved to be rather astute. A few of those Marines felt relieved to be injured because it meant, at least, a temporary reprieve from the overwhelming madness that was *the shit*—a less fanciful synonym for active combat. Mind you, these Marines were simultaneously wracked with guilt and happiness: They were happy to be leaving the shit behind, even if it only was for a few days, but terribly guilty because they believed that they were abandoning their brother Marines. For many of these war-scarred teens and young men, that guilt never would subside. Rather, it would continue to grow and cascade, weighing upon their psyches for decades to come.

Vinnie watched the Huey literally fall off of the LZ that was precariously perched atop a mountain. That was the manner by which the helicopter could gain sufficient airspeed in order to gain flight and fly back to the relative comfort of a remote command post. Vinnie stood there for what seemed to him be an eternity but was, in actuality, about fourteen seconds before he let out a deliberate sigh and followed the other grunts to the relative comfort of their *hooches*, which were nothing more canvas sleeves, propped up by poles, sticks, or other jungle materials, into tent-like structures. The hooches sheltered "rubber ladies"—that is, USMC-issued mattresses or, more often than not, just sheets that were strewn about the jungle floor. These primitive constructions constituted what would be the Marines' new home for much of the next thirteen months, assuming that they would live to see the end of their thirteen-month tours.

Vinnie lost all sense of time in the blackness of the jungle. He was fairly certain that it was about 11:00 p.m., based on the time that he had boarded the bird for transport to his new home: Kilo Company, 3rd Battalion, 4th Marines, otherwise known as the Thundering Third. At this very moment, Vinnie realized that, when he wrote letters to Lilly and to his family and friends back home, he would have to do what the U.S. government was trying to do when explaining the war back in the world: He'd have to sanitize them. Indeed, if Vinnie were ever to write *truthfully* about the war, much less about what had transpired in the last five minutes, his family and friends would lose their collective mind.

Suddenly, Vinnie was jolted unexpectedly by a sharp lump in his throat. His stomach lurched and his eyes burned. Shocked, Vinnie realized that he was crying spontaneously after the following thought had crept into his mind: *I may never again see Lil, Ma, Pop, Joseph, Rosalie, and my friends.* Valiantly, Vinnie endeavored to short-circuit the self-pity party. *Cut the shit*, he reprimanded himself within the confines of his own mind. *You're an eighteen-year-old man and a fucking Marine and Marines don't cry.* As Vinnie angrily admonished himself and wiped the tears and snot from his face, twenty of his fellow newly-minted Marines also wept in silent shame.

A mortar exploded nearby, shaking the Earth beneath the weeping grunts, as horrific shrieks of pain and calls for corpsmen rose above the din of Vinnie's new reality, the Vietnam War.

CHAPTER 2

JAMAICA, NEW YORK

I sure do remember when we used to fight like cats and dogs. I punched the crap out of you right next to the kitchen's back door. You got some good punches then. And then the time you pushed me down Mrs. Smith's stairs. I fell all the way down and laid on the floor, yelling and crying. I know you remember that, Ratface. You really used to beat the crap out of me when we was younger. But if anyone else tried to hit me, you would protect me. I know why now: I was your private punching bag and you didn't want anyone else to use me (the punching bag). Ha Ha. I know you remember that little red 3-wheeler tricycle that we had: me, you, Richie, and Steven Knell used to ride that thing so much. We used that so much that there was no rubber on the back wheels left. You could hear that bike coming a block away. I remember that you always made me peddle and you would stand on the back and make me ride you around. I can remember how you looked then: a scrawny, boney kid with blue jeans, print blouse, and white-and-black shoes, with wiry, jet black hair in a ponytail. It looks more like a horse's ass. Ha Ha Ha.

B *ack home.* Growing up in Jamaica, New York was a wonderful experience for Vinnie. The neighborhood was very blue collar; all of the neighbors worked diligently for the sake of their families. Whether you were Italian, Irish, Jewish, black, or Hispanic, every man in the 1950s and 60s understood that he was getting up at the crack of dawn, throwing on his work boots, and earning that buck. Vinnie's dad, Carmine, was no different.

Carmine, born on January 1, 1920, was one of nine siblings who grew up in South Jamaica. Carmine was the son of an Italian-immigrant father and a first-generation American mother of Italian descent. Vinnie's paternal grandfather, also named Carmine, had immigrated to the U.S from Avellino, Italy on January 31, 1911. Vinnie's paternal grandmother, Pasquallina La Vechia, whose first name was later Americanized to *Lilly*, was born in Little Italy, in Manhattan. Carmine and all but one of his siblings had the traditional, dark, Mediterranean features of their parents: olive skin, dark hair, and dark eyes. The one outlier was a younger brother named Vincent, or Vinnie. That Vinnie, Carmine's brother, had blond hair and blue eyes, a total anomaly in the Santaniello family. Vinnie was the baby brother in the family and, as such, everyone catered to him.

Carmine Santaniello, Sr., Vinnie's grandfather, was a stern disciplinarian and a carpenter by trade. He taught his kids the value of hard work and he shared his craft with his sons. Vinnie's father, Carmine Jr., grew up in the Roaring Twenties and he spent his formative years surviving the Great Depression of the 1930s. The Great Depression was a very difficult time for Carmine Santaniello, Sr. and his young family, as money was scarce and the kids often had to make due for days at a time with small rations of bread, milk, and water. Further tragedy struck this family, too, as young Vinnie, everyone's favorite baby brother, died at the tender age of five from complications from the flu. The blond-haired, blue-eyed angel's passing devastated the Santaniello family and it impacted

Carmine Jr. so profoundly that he vowed to bestow that name upon his first-born son.

Rose, the mother of Vinnie the Marine, was the oldest of three children, born in New York to Benore Buffa and Rosina Internicola. Benore had immigrated from Sicily in the late 1910s and Rosina had been sent to the U.S. in 1921, on the S.S. *Argentina*, for an arranged marriage with Benore. Rosina's family, like Carmine's, was very blue collar. She stayed home to tend to the kids while Benore worked as a welder in New York City. Benore was exceedingly proud of the fact that he had welded girders that ultimately rose high into the sky and transformed into the Empire State Building which, to him, represented all that was alluring about America. It was a land of infinite promise and endless possibilities, to which the Empire State Building, that wonder of architectural genius, attested.

Rose and Carmine began to date in the late 1930s, toward the end of the Great Depression. Carmine enlisted in the U.S. Navy shortly after the Japanese attack on Pearl Harbor on December 7, 1941. He and Rose secretly eloped before his deployment to the South Pacific theater, where Carmine served as a Seabee carpenter during World War II. Carmine and Rose began their family shortly after his return from the war.

On September 25, 1944, Rose gave birth to her first child, Lillian, who had a light olive complexion, piercing dark-brown eyes, and thick black hair. Rose and Carmine's second baby, a boy, entered the world on September 20, 1946, and Carmine fulfilled his vow from years earlier. He named the child Vincent and gave him the name of his maternal grandfather, Benore, as a middle name.

Coincidentally, Rose and Carmine's little Vinnie was not just the second child in the Santaniello family to bear that name but, like his uncle who had died young, this Vinnie also had fair skin, blond hair, and blue eyes. Carmine hoped that his son would fare better in life than his son's late uncle did.

Rose and Carmine had a second son, Joseph, in 1955, and his complexion and features were more in line with the traditional Italian genes that were shared by Carmine and Rose. With their family complete, the Santaniellos forged their collective lives in Jamaica, Queens.

Carmine continued his trade as a carpenter and he and his brother, Al, began to work together building houses. That business did not pan out, but Carmine stayed in the carpentry business, doing work on people's homes and businesses. Rose, like her mother, and like many women in the 1950s and 60s, stayed home and cared for the kids. Lilly, Vinnie, and, later, young Joseph grew up in a very disciplined home.

Carmine was a stern father who was loving but demanding. He did not take kindly to misbehavior and he'd let the kids know that misbegotten actions would not be tolerated. Rose tended to the kids and took them wherever they had to go, whether it be to school, family functions, or extracurricular activities. Lilly and Vinnie were nearly two years apart in age and were very close as children, especially given that Joseph came along nine years after Vinnie. Lilly and Vinnie were the only kids for a while, and they'd fight one minute and then ride bikes around the neighborhood the next. They shared the same friends and socialized in the same circles.

Of course, growing up in the city and having a disciplined, no-nonsense dad meant that Vinnie and Lilly had tough exteriors. They protected each other and always had each other's backs. Indeed, Vinnie and Lilly seemingly lived by the credo that the only person that could lay a hand on either of them (other than their parents, of course) was the other. Anyone else risked getting an ass-kicking! Vinnie and Lilly were equally protective of their little brother.

Carmine taught his kids about the importance of family and of loyalty to the family, and neither Vinnie nor Lilly ever forgot this critical virtue. Indeed, Vinnie was a good kid that did not have a bad word to say about anyone, but God help the person who dared to try to hurt his younger brother or his older sister. Vinnie didn't stand for such actions, and any transgressor quickly came to understand that the mild-mannered kid was not one to cross. Beneath the gentle, disarming smile was a fierce advocate for and protector of his family's honor.

While family was of paramount importance to young Vinnie, he also had three close friends with whom he shared the bulk of his childhood: John Chang, Robbie Boss, and George Schaeffer. Vinnie, Robbie, and George were friends before any of them had lost their baby teeth; John and Vinnie became friends when John was eleven and Vinnie was a year younger. John, Robbie, and George grew up in South Jamaica, a short bike ride from Vinnie's middle-class neighborhood. Robbie and George lived in a lower-middle-class section of the neighborhood, while John grew up in the slums. All four kids were first- or second-generation Americans: Robbie's parents were Irish, George's parents were from Germany, and John was of mixed heritage. His father hailed from China and his mother had immigrated from the British West Indies.

The boys grew up in an era when expectations for them were very simple and straightforward: attend a vocational school to learn a trade; when you graduate, enlist in the military to serve your country; take up a job in your vocation when you return to the U.S. after your service; then get married and start a family. However, before the boys fulfilled society's mandate, they were just young boys who did the typical things that city boys in the 1950s and early 60s did. They hung out, played stoopball and stickball, went to the movies, checked out the girls, and listened to soul music, including the Four Tops, the Temptations, and the Supremes.

Vinnie, John, Robbie, and George often hung out at the corner deli and sang their favorite songs. Imagine this scene: A dirty-blond-haired, blue-eyed Italian kid; a fair-skinned, black-haired German kid; a red-headed Irish kid; and a relatively-dark-skinned Chinese kid, all standing in front of a corner deli in Jamaica singing their favorite tune, "Silhouettes" by The Rays.

Only in the melting pot that was 1960s Jamaica, Queens!

When the boys weren't singing badly on the corner, they were playing in Goose Pond Park, hanging out on the fields and courts of Jamaica High School, sitting on Vinnie's porch, or going down to the basement of Vinnie's house, where they'd listen to their transistor radios, play shuffleboard, or chat about girls.

Vinnie, Robbie, and George all attended Thomas Edison Vocational High School in Jamaica, while John went to the New York School of Printing, located in Hell's Kitchen, Manhattan. Vinnie studied auto mechanics. From a very young age, he had an amazing knack for, and love of, fixing cars. George also took auto mechanic classes, while Robert took classes in electrical work. John chose the printing school because he believed working a printing press would serve him well once he got out of the service. Of course, John never worked another printing press after he graduated from the New York School of Printing.

The boys also took on any jobs that they could find during the summers. They were paperboys, stock boys, and bottle collectors (which they'd redeem for a whole nickel each at the local grocery store). The boys even worked at a pigeon coop one summer, where they were given the Augean task of cleaning pigeon droppings from massive bird cages. The boys often scooped up their earnings (no pun intended) and bought dinner at a Chinese restaurant on nearby Jamaica Avenue before catching a flick at the local theater.

This quartet was a genuinely nice collection of young boys who didn't get in trouble. The worst thing they did was scale the fence to a local public pool and sneak a midnight swim one summer. The boys had a great time frolicking in the pool until the cops crashed the party. Youth, however, treated the boys well, as they jumped out of the pool and ran away from the police without anyone getting caught.

The youngsters did not drink or do hard drugs (which was becoming more prevalent in the mid-1960s). When they were teenagers and one of the kids experimented with LSD, Vinnie galvanized his other two companions to tell the fourth that they loved him, but if he didn't clean himself up and get off the crap, then he'd get himself extricated from the brotherhood.

The fourth teen quit LSD cold turkey because he realized that his lifelong friends were right and he didn't want to disappoint them.

Vinnie demonstrated his leadership from a very young age and this crisis was no different. Vinnie was loyal to a fault, and he'd bend over backward for a friend, but he wouldn't tolerate abhorrent, self-destructive behavior. Amazingly, Vinnie's peers, irrespective of whether they were older or younger than the tenacious teen, acquiesced to him and did not question his word. Vinnie loved his friends and treated them like family, as that was what his father, Carmine, had taught him.

However, Vinnie also learned another strong lesson from his streetwise dad: Don't tolerate anyone's bullshit.

As the boys approached the latter portion of their high school careers, they were sure of a couple of things: They were going to learn a trade, they were going to smoke cigarettes (like all red-blooded American boys of the early-to-mid-1960s), and they were going to enlist in the military. These boys were the children of men and women that knew firsthand—either from their own life experiences or from hearing the stories of their parents—the hardships of coming to a new land—a land of promise but a foreign land nonetheless. The boys' parents grew up with very little and they bestowed upon their children the virtues of loyalty, respect, dignity, and hard work. The quartet grew up in an era when children respected the edicts of their parents and took parental mandates to heart.

After all, these parents had survived the squalor and hardships of the Great Depression and they adhered to the notion that, through hard work and dedication to family, one could not only persevere, but flourish. America was, after all, a land of great promise and opportunity. Whether one's ancestors had arrived at Ellis Island from Sicily, Italy, Ireland, Germany, or China, they all harbored the same lofty aspiration of achieving new heights in the burgeoning country.

The boys of the early 1960s also were inspired by the country's youthful, handsome president, John F. Kennedy. Vinnie and his cohort were squarely in the generation that took to heart President Kennedy's timeless exhortation during his January 20, 1961 inaugural address to the nation: "Ask not what your country can do for you, ask what you can do for your country."

The United States was assuming the role of champion against the evil empire of the time, the communist Soviet Union. And, for many young men of that era, there was great pride in the notion of joining the armed forces to assist in the valiant fight to keep the communists at bay and prevent them from achieving their goal of worldwide domination.

With that, Vinnie, John, Robbie, and George all began to ponder which branch of the service each of them would join. In those days, the draft was highly controversial, but the boys weren't preoccupied with the stress of whether or not their draft numbers would be drawn. Instead, each of the boys enlisted in the service before his graduation: Vinnie in the Marine Corps, George in the Army, and Robbie and John in the Navy, with the latter enlisting as a corpsman.

"You crazy bastard," Vinnie exclaimed to John, only half-kiddingly. "You're going to be running into firefights to save guys while bullets are whizzing around you!"

"You better watch what you say, Vinnie," John responded, in mock disdain. "You might need me to remove some shrapnel from your ass one day!"

Not missing a beat, Vinnie, the youngest of the quartet, replied, "Just make sure that you guys still are alive when me and my badass fellow Marines come to clean up the mess that you squares create!" The boys all chuckled at Vinnie's wisecrack. Vinnie was seventeen and the other boys were either eighteen or soon-to-turn eighteen, and they all were convinced that they were immortal.

John, Robbie, and George all were deployed to Vietnam in early 1967, a few months before Vinnie. However, before they went off to their respective boot camps, the threesome got together with Vinnie one last time, at his house. The boys laughed, played cards, ate some of Rose's delicious pasta, sang Ben E. King's "Stand By Me" (out of key, of course), and cracked the usual assortment of jokes at each other's expense.

However, as the night was drawing to a close, the boys turned serious and they began to discuss the conflict in Vietnam and the country's growing disdain for the continued conflict.

George asked, "You think the country will treat us like they treated Mr. Santaniello and the other servicemen after V-J Day?"

Robbie answered defiantly, "I don't know, guys. Americans don't seem too happy with this war in Vietnam."

"Yeah, Robbie. A lotta people on TV seem to be against the guys fighting over there," added John, with an air of disdain in his voice.

There was a deliberate pause, as the three older boys waited for the youngest, yet strongest, of the quartet to render his opinion.

Vinnie sensed the palpable quiet in the room and he opted to let the tension grip the three friends by their throats before he spoke. "You guys are freakin' dummies," Vinnie chuckled. The tense air escaped from the room. "We're gonna come home world-beating heroes, boys." Vinnie continued, "You guys better wait for me to get back from 'Nam after yous. We'll all meet up at the corner deli and sing "It's the Same Old Song" to impress the chicks!"

John, Robbie, and George were grateful that Vinnie, ever the practical joker, had effectively dissolved the air of melancholy that was beginning to envelop them. All four young men shared a hearty laugh. And, deep within the recesses of John's, Robbie's, and George's young souls, the three elder teens all hoped that their young friend's predictions would be realized.

*   *   *

"Vinnie," Lilly asked one warm spring day in 1967, "what are we going to do if some wise guy bothers Joseph or me when you're in the service?"

"Are ya kiddin' me, Lil? All yous gotta do is tell Pop and he'll crack some heads for you! And then when I get home from Vietnam, I'll take clean-up duty from Pop!"

Lilly was only slightly sure that Vinnie was joking. She reflected on how much she loved her brother, and how afraid she was that he would get hurt—or worse—while he was so far away, in a strange, dangerous land. Lilly had seen coverage of the war on TV and it seemed like a terrible ordeal.

Vietnam was not a critical issue to Lilly, as she did not have any connection to the conflict halfway across the world. However, that detachment was suddenly replaced with a palpable sense of dread. Vinnie, despite being two years younger than Lilly, was an older brother to both her and Joseph. He was the leader of the siblings and the second man of the family, after their dad.

I can't have anything happen to this kid, Lilly often thought that spring. *My life would never be the same if something were to happen to him. None of our lives would be normal again.*

"You gotta pee again, Lil?" Vinnie would ask as Lilly would abruptly leave, with the excuse that she had to use the bathroom. "Ain't you too young to have bladder problems, granny?" Vinnie kidded as Lilly locked the bathroom door behind her.

"Shut up, you jerk," Lilly said, with a pretentious air to her voice, as if she was joining in the lighthearted moment that they were sharing. Then she'd run to turn on the tap, to muffle her sobs.

Vinnie graduated from Edison High in May 1966 and he was in Vietnam before the end of the summer of '68. However, before he left for boot camp, Carmine and Rose pulled their son aside to share their farewells. Rose, who had lived with a constant fear in the pit of her stomach two decades earlier when her then-new husband was whisked overseas and out of her life to serve in World War II, now had to re-live that terrible time. Only now she was a worried mother, not a new wife.

She had seen the grainy stories from Vietnam on TV, and she knew how bloody and drawn-out the war was becoming. She couldn't bring herself to ponder what her life would be like if her oldest son returned from Vietnam in a casket.

She hugged Vinnie tightly, with tears blurring her son's handsome face. "I love you, Vinnie. Please be careful out there."

Carmine then placed his strong right hand on Vinnie's shoulder and looked his son in the eye before saying, "I'm proud of you, son. You're going to be fine out there. Be careful and we'll see you before you leave for Vietnam."

They hugged, and then Lilly and Joseph shared their goodbyes with the sibling that did not share their physical attributes but, instead, shared a spiritual bond with them, which far surpassed the merely physical realm of genetics.

CHAPTER 3

INITIATION TO THE JUNGLE

But now we're grown up. We're not playing games anymore. Things are for keeps now. You turned out to be a beautiful woman. And me? I don't know yet. I know after I come back from this war, I'll be a man. Life is very funny. You got to live it day by day. And take advantage of everything you can. Now, like you going out with Bobby . . . you would be stupid if you didn't because, after you're married, your life is tied up and it's not your own. It's just like the service: Your life is not yours to decide where to go and what to do. You got to do and go where ever your superior tells you, or what your orders state. So, all I can say is go and do what you want while you got the chance.

My present location is right above Da Nang, it's called Camp Carroll. Chang is down south; I'm north, so there's hardly a chance of meeting him. Although I would like to very much. Well, I got to go now, Sis. Take care. Love ya, Vinnie

P.S. Don't worry about me and keep up the good work of writing. Love ya, Sis.

Further excerpt from Vinnie's August 9, 1967 letter to Lilly.

Vinnie and Lilly's relationship changed dramatically from the time that they were beating each other up as kids to the time that Vinnie was about to depart for the service. Vinnie had grown up into a strong young man, both mentally and physically, and Lilly had matured into a street-wise, savvy, beautiful young woman.

Vinnie's blond hair darkened as he got older. It was closer to brown than it was to blond, but his eyes remained a crystal-clear, striking blue that saw right through you when you peered at them. Prior to joining the Marines, Vinnie wore his hair in the style that was fashionable during the 1950s and early 60s: short on the sides and the back, longer hair on top greased to the side with a slight pompadour. Of course, staying consistent with the era in which he grew up, Vinnie always was clean-shaven.

He maintained an average five-foot-eight frame that gracefully carried a sinewy, yet muscular, 160 pounds. He had a light complexion and grew into a chiseled jaw with distinct cheekbones. By the age of seventeen, Vinnie knew that he had a future in auto mechanics. He was average when it came to traditional scholastic achievement, but he was unparalleled when it came to knowing his way around every component of a car or motorcycle. Indeed, Vinnie earned some cash on the side during his high school years by repairing neighbors' cars.

Succinctly put, Lilly grew into an absolutely gorgeous woman. She no longer was the skinny, tomboy-ish, olive-complected young girl with bushy eyebrows who frequently wore her long, jet-black hair in pigtails. By the spring of 1967, the twenty-year-old Lilly was quite attractive: The long, black hair that she had maintained in the fashionable, stylish beehive for a number of years was now cut short and sexily combed to the right, so that her hair tumbled gently over the right side of her forehead, obscuring her right eyebrow and just kissing her eyelashes. The back of her hair was neat and shoulder-length. Lilly wore fashionably dark eyeliner that, combined with her impeccably thin, manicured eyebrows, sensuously accentuated her large, dark-brown eyes. Lilly's skin was majestically smooth and supple, complete with prominent, high cheekbones, a subtle nose, supple lips, and a rounded chin.

Lilly's olive complexion and subtle, yet very complementary, facial makeup gave her an exotic likeness to the theatrical depiction of the lovely Cleopatra. Lilly stood a petite five-foot-three and she flaunted her curves and thin, shapely legs in the stylish miniskirts and form-fitting blouses that were exceedingly popular amongst the young ladies of her era.

Lilly wasn't all good looks, though. She was very street-smart and savvy, as a result of growing up in Jamaica. She didn't take any nonsense from the guys who often hit on her and she was quick to speak her mind, even if it meant dropping a few F-bombs to accentuate her point. Upon graduating from Jamaica High School, Lilly began to work as an office manager and receptionist for the Social Security Administration. She was an affable young lady who was befriended by many in her office. She had no airs about her; what you saw was what you got, and she really didn't concern herself with whether or not others liked her.

Vinnie and Lilly each possessed very strong personalities, and that is why they fought so often as kids. However, as they each matured into their late teens, they developed a fierce love for— and loyalty to—each other. They respected each other greatly and would stand up for each other without hesitation. Of course, this being the 1950s and 60s, Vinnie adopted the traditional role of protector and he treated Lilly like his little sister. Lilly embraced this status enthusiastically, in stark contrast to her acerbic reaction to potential suitors.

*　　　*　　　*

Da Nang, Vietnam. Vinnie was not far from the DMZ, and his asthma afforded him the opportunity to spend time *in the rear,* which was military jargon for being out of combat. Happily, Vinnie didn't have to live in the makeshift hooches that littered the jungles and hills throughout South Vietnam. Vinnie found his new home to be an ironic twist upon his old one. New York was known as the concrete jungle and Vinnie had been transported from that jungle to an authentic one. Vietnam was a confounding maze of dense bamboo, scorched rice paddies, elephant grass, and miles of impossibly profound jungle, littered with vertigo-inducing steep mountains, and what the grunts called *hills*, makeshift mounds that the Marines would build or cultivate from pre-existing rock and then defend in frequent, bloody battles with the enemy NVA (North Vietnamese Army).

The funny thing about the jungle, Vinnie thought, is that everything that he learned in schools about them led him to believe that he always would be hot as hell under an unforgiving sun, but that wasn't the case at all. It rained frequently in South Vietnam and when it was not raining, a dense, soupy, omnipresent fog hung over the world like a bad dream.

Vinnie loved *Peanuts* cartoons and he especially enjoyed drawing Charlie Brown and Snoopy. When the young Marine first traversed the thick Vietnam fog, he felt like a sullen Charlie Brown, walking around with a thick cloud of sadness suspended just above his round, bald head. Vinnie mused that he could unsheathe his USMC-issued Ka-Bar knife, which the grunts used to cut bamboo and thick sugar cane, to slice through the seemingly impervious fog.

In addition to the suffocating fog, Vinnie found that he often was cold. The constant rain seeped into the Marines' fatigues and permeated their bones. That obstinate chill was nothing like Vinnie had ever experienced, even during the coldest winters that NYC had to offer. *Ain't this some shit,* Vinnie thought. *Who'd have thought that I'd be freezing in a jungle . . . in August?*

Of course, jungle life was such that when the rains ceased and the incessant fog lifted, the intense heat over the South China Sea was unrelenting. This meant that the Marines' previously wet clothing would dry, only to receive a fresh soaking from its wearer's severe perspiration. Then, once the blazing sun finally set behind the zenith of any one of the countless mountain ranges, the suffocating blackness of night returned, which was accompanied, of course, by nail-biting cold. The day's copious amounts of perspiration that contributed to the return of the bone-deep chill.

And so went the cycle for the average grunt.

There were times when Vinnie spent the night with a platoon out in the jungle, or on a hill because his jeep's headlights were either too flaccid to pierce the dark or weren't working at all, and he marveled at the fact that he could not see his hand directly in front of his face, no matter how long he allowed for the pupils of his blue eyes to adjust. Vinnie amused his fellow Marines by observing that the authentic jungles of Vietnam could take a cue from the concrete jungles of New York and "get a couple of fucking street light poles!"

As the Kilo Company driver, Vinnie's primary responsibility was to drive his superiors—the lieutenant, or the Two (the battalion intelligence officer), or the Three (the battalion operations officer)—from HQ in Da Nang down the Marine-built Highway 9 to any of the various CPs or platoons in the region. Vinnie also brought C-rations, artillery shells, fresh uniforms, grenades, repaired rifles, refurbished boots, and other supplies to his buddies out in the field.

However, Vinnie's most precious cargo, and the one that made him immensely popular with the grunts out in the shit, was mail from home. It was the men's one connection to the world and a semblance of sanity in their increasingly insane existence. Vinnie brought the Marines a reprieve, even if fleeting, from the suffocating stress that was their daily grind in the jungle. They read their letters from home with more enthusiasm than they took in food and water—which often was in short supply for these overworked and highly stressed grunts—because the letters returned them to times and places for which they all fiercely yearned. The comforts of home. Vinnie was a type of dope dealer to his brother Marines and the letters in his satchel were the dope. When the men took a hit from the letters, their minds relaxed immediately and they hallucinated about being back home with Mom and Pop, or with their girlfriends or buddies or pets, or even in their goddamned beds

. . . they knew that *anything* was better than their current miserable existence.

"Hey, lookie here, it's Santa Claus, with his bag of gifts for all the terribly bad boys of the Thundering Third," announced one wise-cracking Marine that had befriended Vinnie. This Marine, nicknamed Red thanks to his thick red mane, always greeted Vinnie with a bear hug when he arrived. The kid from Jamaica represented home to the kid from Edmonds, Washington. Red, known as Michael Reagan back in the world, hailed from a Seattle suburb. Vinnie often joked that Red, a corporal here in the jungle, wouldn't last five minutes in big, bad New York City, almost three thousand miles from where Mike lay his head each night back home. Red had patches of sunburn on his otherwise milky-white face and arms. His perpetual five o'clock shadow was the brunt of many jokes because it grew out red and thick, not wispy like those of many of his peers. Mike stood a few inches short of six feet tall but he was strongly built, with his forearms resembling those of Popeye the Sailor Man.

"Red, you sure that you're twenty-one and not fifty, you old, hairy bastard?" Vinnie asked one day.

"That ain't a nice way for a Saint to speak, now is it?" Mike replied. And instantly, a nickname was born. Vinnie no longer was "Mailman" to his brother Marines; he now was Saint, a play on his last name.

Vinnie's Marine Corps superiors developed a fondness, too, for Saint because he was a miracle worker when it came to the company's jeeps. The USMC was using Korean War-era jeeps and the old, battle-scarred jalopies were showing their age. Vinnie was an automobile savant and he always had his head under a hood, or his body under a vehicle, working his healing magic to get the sputtering vehicle to continue the arduous task of driving through and across uneven, irregular, and unforgiving terrain. Thus, when the lieutenant or the platoon commander needed to get from HQ in the rear to a specific platoon that was guarding a hill miles away, they both knew that Saint would get them there expeditiously.

The old vets recalled being delayed in getting to the field because the aging jeeps became stationary targets for incoming mortars. Captain Foggo, who was on his third tour in Vietnam, regaled Saint with stories of how the company's jeeps often were parked far away from HQ for fear of being struck with shrapnel created from a lifeless jeep with a dormant carburetor that had met its unexpected demise from a wayward mortar. Saint chuckled, "Shit, all those babies need is a loving hand to bring them back to life! This company ain't never gonna lose another clunker with me here." Foggo nodded approvingly.

*　　　　*　　　　*

Hi Greenie, how are you? I hope you're not riggering anymore. As for me, I'm just fine. The temperature here is pretty high today. It didn't rain in the last few days. Believe it or not, I got today off. They gave us one day of rest. I couldn't believe it: We thought the war ended when they told us, but it didn't. Right now, I'm watching the engineers fix a road: It's the only thing interesting to watch here.

When I come home, I won't have any manners and my language will be atrocious. We slop down the food like pigs and talk like the devil himself. I have to really watch myself when I get home after 13 months of being over here and then going back to the world. It will be one big jump. Like comparing a three-wheel bicycle to a brand new Cadillac car. All of us often talk about it and just laugh thinking about the way we'll act when we get home. Is little Joey getting any bigger? I'll bet he'll really be grown when I get home. I sure hope that time does fly by. Well. I got to go now. Love ya, Sis.

Vinnie

Excerpt from Vinnie's August 31, 1967 letter to Lilly

Fuck. Fuck. Fuck. Fuck.

Damn, Vinnie mused, *these boys sure do curse a lot! I've only been here a couple of weeks and I've heard the F-word more during my short time here than I did in the first eighteen years of my life!*

The Marines transformed the word *fuck.* In fact, they used it in each of the eight parts of English speech. Marines cleverly utilized the heretofore-forbidden four-letter word as a verb, a noun, a pronoun, an adjective, an adverb, a preposition, a conjunction, and an interjection! The *really* clever (or the really fucking stressed) Marine could use the word in each of its eight forms in the same sentence. Vietnam was many things, Vinnie thought, but he never thought it would be so educational.

"Hey, Saint," yelled John "Doc" Nunn, a corpsman from Pennsylvania who had been in the shit for a while before Vinnie had dropped in a few weeks earlier, "you gonna eat that fuckin' slop or not? Pass that caviar down here if you ain't, 'cause I sure as hell will put it to good use!"

Vinnie had just made a food run one steamy October morning to yet another hill. The men surfaced from their foxholes, as if they were Pavlov's dogs, after hearing the familiar rumble of Vinnie's jeep while he still was a couple of football fields north of their platoon. Doc Nunn, a string-bean-thin twenty-year-old Caucasian, had sunken cheekbones that spoke of multiple tours. His sullen eyes lurched deep beneath his brow and his unkempt brown hair was tucked haphazardly beneath his filthy green cap.

The distant look in Doc's eyes told the tale of too much pain, anguish, and catastrophic injury to possibly be processed by a single human brain and its nervous system. Nonetheless, Doc was able—at the moment, anyway—to compartmentalize the gruesome visuals of broken and missing limbs, organs, and body parts, to push them into the far recesses of his mind. This uncanny ability to repress the pain, the anger, and the palpable, overwhelming sadness served Doc Nunn well during his time in 'Nam, but what of the untold price to be paid down the line should Doc survive this hellish experience? Well, that was a problem for another day, as Marines in Vietnam lived in the nanosecond, as opposed to in *the moment*.

For now, Doc Nunn was a foul-mouthed man who had the utmost respect of his brother Marines. Whenever enemy mortar or AK-47 rounds were speeding at the Marines with bad intentions, and as our boys' return fire of equally deadly caliber littered the air, corpsmen like Doc Nunn ran into the shit to tend to their injured brothers.

A person does not know pure, unadulterated fear until that person is trying to place an IV line into the flailing arm of a semiconscious, delirious, eighteen-year-old kid whose small intestines (and is that *thing* his spleen?) are splayed across his flak jacket and onto a corpsman's pants in the middle of a jungle monsoon while artillery rounds whistle precariously close to that corpsman's skull and exploding mortars test his precision and skill in placing the line, all while the ground shakes under the repercussive force of the explosions.

Marines were the toughest warriors in the Vietnam War and *they* thought that the corpsmen were "fucking crazy" to do what they did. Yet the Marines quietly revered these men. Indeed, the word *brave* was too underwhelming an adjective to adequately describe the corpsmen. Of course, any Marine worth the jungle rot on his face would never admit to such sentimentality while in the shit.

*   *   *

As for Chang, he sees enough action. Like you said, he sees the worst because he has to work on these wounded Marines. As for me being by the DMZ, I'm about 25 miles south of it. Con Thien is about 2 miles south of it. When I was in Con Thien, it was really getting bad at the end of August, beginning of September. We got out of there and boy, was I glad. The only thing we had to worry about is when we got hit by mortars and artillery rounds. But now, I'm in Cam Lo. Boy, is this place nice. It's like there was no war going on here because we don't get hit here; maybe once a month and sometimes not even that. See, where I was, there are NVA (North Vietnamese Army), they're regular soldiers. They're not VC (Viet Cong), the VC are farmers who run around with a rifle at night and then plow their fields during the day. The NVA are soldiers, not farmers. The Marines kick the shit out of the NVA but the only threat to the Marines is the artillery, but it's not like it's told back in the world. There's not always fighting going on. It's like little spurts of fighting here and there, unless the Marines are on a big operation like "Hickory" during the summer. 1st Bn. 5th Marines are not up here—that's what Chang's in—unless they're at Phu Bai or they just moved up to Dong Ha. Phu Bai and Dong Ha are both nice places, not too much action. During the monsoon, all the action slows down to almost a complete stop. Don't worry about me, I'll be coming home in A-1 condition.

I got your birthday card, it was the nicest thing I could've received. Did you get mine yet?

Excerpt from Vinnie's September 20, 1967
letter to Lilly, on his nineteenth birthday

"Doc, you mangy bastard," Vinnie replied to Doc Nunn's plea for his grub, "you'd eat the insides of this C-rat can even if I just took a shit in it!" Luckily for Vinnie, he ate fairly regularly as the company driver because he often was back in the rear, at HQ, so he didn't go days without consistent meals like many of his brothers out in the jungle and on the mountains. Saint gladly surrendered his *caviar* to Doc.

"Thanks, Saint," replied Doc, "I'll save your Yankee ass if you ever step on a nail or something, you fucking rear-loving mailman!"

The boys were sitting outside of their hooches in the vicinity of Qua Nang one early afternoon, oblivious to the rain that was steadily falling on them. By now, the boys were fully inured to the nearly daily ritual of being soaked. Vinnie had driven some supplies from H&S to the platoon's CP and the skipper's orders permitted him to stay there for a couple of days because the platoon had incurred a couple of Oleys in a brief skirmish with the NVA earlier in the week. Four riflemen had been medevaced out of the jungle and the company didn't expect more than two of them to come back after getting patched up on the Navy ship that was docked in Okinawa, Japan.

"Goddamn gook snipers," lamented Tony "Doc" Milazzo, an Italian-American like Vinnie, who hailed from northern New Jersey. "They took out Floozy and Moonshine at the LP and then they hit Jones and McMahon while they were trying to rescue the first two." Charles "Floozy" Mulholland and Timothy "Moonshine" Jackson had stationed at the LP at the northern-most reach of the platoon perimeter in Qua Nang. Marines who got this nerve-wracking assignment had the responsibility of watching and listening for any suspicious movements or sounds in front of their position. Of course, these men bore immeasurable responsibility. The lives of the twenty to twenty-five men in the platoon literally depended on their keen ability to see the unseen and to hear that which barely emitted a sound.

Unsurprisingly, the Marines did not envy a brother's LP assignment. It brought an entirely new appreciation to the art form of paranoia. Try listening for an enemy movement while sitting in high elephant grass in a monsoon. Better yet, try to ascertain if that rustling that you *think* that you hear a couple of meters ahead of you is just another jungle breeze, a snake, a tiger readying its pounce, a sniper ready to blow a hole through your head, or a just a figment of your paranoid imagination. And how do you discern what exactly is in the brush a few meters away when it's pitch-black out?

Floozy and Moonshine were crouched down in the elephant grass at the LP three days earlier, after night had fallen, with mud smeared over their jungle rot-pocked faces to camouflage their lily-white skin. Moonshine had the radio strapped to his back, which he feared made him the easiest target in the jungle. Although he had the volume turned down to the barely audible level, that sound might as well have been a bugle blowing "Taps" in the dark jungle. Meanwhile, Floozy had his rifle at the ready and was giving himself a massive headache trying to see in the dark.

"You think there are any gooks out there?" whispered Moonshine, as the soft murmurs of the radio crackled, as if in harmony with his voice.

"Those fuckers are everywhere, 'Shine," replied Floozy as he allowed his mind to wander back to the previous week's three-day reprieve of R&R in Sydney, Australia. Floozy dreamily thought of the cute red-haired girl he'd met in a bar Down Under.

The four seconds that Floozy Mulholland thought of the girl—*Was her name Daisy or Rachel?*—was all that it took.

Perched in a tree about 150 yards east of the dreamer and the radio man was a Vietcong guerilla with a sniper rifle. His foot slipped on a branch and the audible consequence of his sloppiness should have alerted Floozy that danger was imminent, but he was too preoccupied with being a typical nineteen-year-old kid and not a fully cognizant warrior. He missed his chance to take out the danger and alert his brothers in the platoon.

The sloppiness was not exclusive to the Americans, however. The young Vietnamese man's slight slip in the tree caused him to pull the trigger of his pistol prematurely, and thus the bullet that was intended to tear through Floozy's right eye and brain, thereby killing him instantly, instead penetrated his clavicle and left shoulder, shattered bone and shredded muscle and tendon but failed to extinguish his life.

Floozy was no longer sharing a moment with the cute redhead. Rather, he was shrieking in excruciating pain. Moonshine, completely caught off guard and not sure what the hell was happening at first, instinctively grabbed his radio and began barking into it. The sniper fired a shot at the radio man, but his balance was off and in the second that he had to re-aim and shoot, he could only strike Moonshine in the rear of his right shoulder as he barked into the radio and tended to his wounded compatriot.

The dark, foreboding jungle, eerily silent a mere two seconds earlier, now was alive with an unmitigated, bloodthirsty vengeance.

Two Marines and Doc Milazzo sprinted toward the LP. The grunts repeatedly had to stop and drop into the brush to avoid incoming artillery but Doc Milazzo was undaunted in his mission to get to his fallen brothers because their lives literally could be in his hands. Milazzo knew exactly where the injured men were, based on Moonshine's radio transmissions, and he was oblivious to the fact that he literally had no cover for a number of seconds as the other Marines flanking him were somewhere behind him, dropping, rolling, and reassessing the invisible landscape ahead of them.

As he approached the injured Marines at the LP, Milazzo felt the heat of a round whiz perilously close to his left carotid artery, followed a split second later by a loud, pained, "Fuuuuuuuuck!"

Doc Milazzo knew immediately that one of the grunts (later identified as Jones) behind him took the bullet that had been intended for him. The thought that he'd need therapy for this realization dawned on Milazzo for a brief second as he knelt beside Floozy and shoved gauze into the gaping hole where his left collarbone used to be, but the thought got buried with all of the other stressors that Milazzo confronted daily. The second grunt arrived moments later and he asked Milazzo what he could do to help.

"Don't get fucking shot," was Doc's visceral reply.

Doc directed the injured Moonshine to radio the platoon commander at the CP and ask for a fire team to be dispatched to them to provide cover as they hauled ass back to the relative safety of their lines. The injured Marine followed Doc's command, albeit in excruciating pain, as Milazzo tended to the considerable hole in his upper back. Within a minute, four additional Marines arrived. McMahon took a bullet to the calf on the way down, and Doc would have to tend to him, too, on the way back to the CP.

One of the Marines saw the flash of the sniper's weapon up in the tree and the young warrior instinctively unleashed a motherlode of high-explosive grenades from his M-79 that hurtled in an arc through the humid air before crashing with deadly intention into the tree that served as the VC sniper's previously surreptitious, murderous perch. The men heard a series of loud explosions, followed by truncated squeals, the rustling of leaves, and a loud thud.

"Fuck you, you motherfucker," whispered Johnson, the Marine who had unloaded his weapon into the unsuspecting tree.

"They're *dee-deeing*, Skip. should we hunt them down and kill 'em?" asked one of the late arrivers to the LP. Dee-deeing was a play on the Vietnamese expression *didi mao*, which means "go away." The Marines adopted this phrase and used it when the enemy deserted a fight and endeavored to leave quickly.

"Negative," came the commander's voice over Moonshine's radio, "get back here before we take any more hits. Over." The fire team helped carry the seriously injured Floozy back to the CP while Moonshine, Jones (who had taken Milazzo's bullet in his thigh), and the Marine with a bullet in his calf limped back with the others through the high elephant grass and hot, spent shells.

Milazzo recounted this firefight to Saint a couple of nights later. Vinnie was surprised by his initial instinct of regret at having missed this battle. The men seemed to have a perpetual supply of adrenaline and they both abhorred and craved the heat of battle. This contradictory attitude perplexed and repulsed them. None would speak of his feelings, of course, but the angst of the unexplained lust and disdain for hardcore battles kept the men amped even during the rare moments when they were permitted to rest.

Vinnie subtly shook his head, as if to clear it of the guilt that accompanied his ephemeral remorse over having missed the gunfight with the invisible sniper. He remarked, "Doc, you stone Italian, you. How the hell are we gonna be able to walk down the streets of our homes after we get back into the world?"

"You're the Saint," Milazzo replied, "everyone loves your ass, so you ain't gonna have no problems, man!"

"I don't know, Tony," responded Vinnie, despondently and deadly serious, "we are here to kill everything that moves and doesn't look like us. We kill, and we watch our friends fucking get killed, and if we're lucky enough to get outta the shit and go back into the world, we're supposed to just go about our lives as if nothing happened. Does that sound about right, Doc?"

Milazzo opened his mouth, as if to reply, then tightened his jaw, exhaled through pursed lips, lowered his head and peered up at Saint through misty eyes.

"I don't know, Saint." And then as his voice lowered as each word deliberately left his lips, with the last word barely being audible: "I . . . don't . . . fucking . . . know."

Vinnie reflected on those profound words for a few seconds before breaking the somber silence. "It's gonna be one big jump to return to normal back in the world, Doc. I just hope time flies by, man." With that, Vinnie turned and said, "I'm gonna go to my hooch, pal."

"Why," asked Doc. "we're having a good talk."

"I gotta write a letter to my sister, Lilly."

"You ain't telling your sister what's *really* going on here, are you, Saint?"

"Hell no, Doc. Are you kiddin' me? She'd have a heart attack if she knew what actually was going on right before my eyes."

Milazzo shook his head approvingly and then picked up a vial of reddish-brown medicine. "Yeah, Vin, see this bottle of iodine? I use it to clean wounds and kill all the dirty shit that can mix with your insides and get it all infected." Vinnie turned to look at Milazzo and his lips curled up into a knowing smirk. "Make sure your letters are like iodine and sanitize the truth, Saint. You don't wanna make your sister and your family sick with worry."

With that, Vinnie hustled over to his cramped and damp hooch, got some USMC-issued stock paper, a pen, and a flashlight and began to spin a yarn for his sister. Vinnie was thankful that it was dark because he didn't want anyone to see him crying as he wrote fiction to his pal Lilly.

CHAPTER 4

SAINTLY DUTIES

Rosalie wants to get married as soon as I get home from the 'Nam, but I changed my mind. I got too much to see and do when I get out of the Marines. I'm too young to think about marriage. She just insists on getting married. I feel like I have a rope around my neck and she keeps on pulling me toward an altar. Bullshit. Not me. I am going to be a playboy for a few years and make up for all that I missed over here. The only thing that Rosalie sees when she sees me is wedding bells.

Over here, you worry about a few mosquitos biting you. You got spiders (as big as your fist), snakes, mosquitos that sound like helicopters when they come by your ear. And also billions of ants and flies. The flies annoy the shit out of you during the day and the mosquitos during the night. We got good mosquito repellent, though; it keeps them away from you. The ants are really outrageous. We have elephant ants that are as big as the first joint of your thumb. If you sit down or lay down on the ground, the ants overrun you. What I don't like is they crawl up your leg. See, over here, we don't wear underwear (draws) and it's kind of funny when you drop your draws and start slapping ants. See, the reason we don't wear draws is that it's too hot and if you wear them you get all sweated up and they become "Indian draws" ("they sneak up on you and wipe you out").

It gets very cold at night. Last night, I wore an undershirt and 2 regular shirts before I got warm. During the day, you usually don't wear a shirt. Right now, it's 4:30 p.m. and it's just at a comfortable temperature. 12 noon is the hottest part of the day. A nice cool breeze is blowing now.

Thanks for sending me cigarettes, but you really don't have to. Every once in a while, we get a Px truck and I buy a carton or two for $1.40 (eat your heart out). Plus, we get SP packs and they contain cigarettes that were donated by people back in the world (the States). We get a SP pack about every 4 days.

Whoever gets a package splits it up with everyone in his platoon (12 men). You can send me canned fruit like you did in your other package, just send 2 or 3 cans in each package. There's one thing that you really can send me: Sophia Loren. OK, yea. Ha Ha. Well, you can't win all the time. The guys here are all fine and the moral is fine. But between you and me, we all could use a couple of Sophia Lorens. But what can you do? I'll make up for it when I get back.

Mama could even send me some homemade cookies. As soon as I get them, they're eaten up in 10 minutes.

Excerpt from Vinnie's September 1, 1967 letter to Lilly

"Hey, Red, how the hell can you sit and draw so much shit with all these damn bugs crawling around you?" Vinnie marveled at Mike Reagan's ability to draw so well, almost as much as he marveled at Mike's ability to sit still and draw as the gigantic ants crawled around like they owned the hooch.

"Saint, when I draw, I become one with my art so that I don't hear the bullshit all around me. I forget about the leeches that are trying to suck every ounce of blood outta my body. And please don't get me started on those mosquitos. Those fuckers are nearly as big as pterodactyls!"

Vinnie liked to draw, too, but he drew Charlie Brown and Snoopy, neither of which became one with him, so he continued to hear the cacophony of lunacy that surrounded him. Conversely,

Mike was drawing real life out in Vietnam: fellow soldiers, rifles, and jungle scenes. Mike's right hand was like a magic wand. It created amazing, life-like works of art.

"Whatcha gonna do with that magical right hand of yours when you get back in the world, Red?"

Reagan responded to Vinnie's query after a considerable delay, as if to soak up the question and truly reflect on its meaning before responding,

"Maybe I'll draw some really bad Snoopy cartoons, Saint."

Vinnie playfully threw a C-rat can at Mike. "You Picasso sonofabitch!" The boys then laughed before Mike resumed drawing his Ka-Bar, situated next to a grenade.

* * *

The Marines were outside on a rare sunny October day with no rain and no humidity. There had been no hostilities for at least three or four days and the guys were throwing a baseball around. Vinnie had driven down from H&S with his boss and they joined the fray.

"Hey, look, fellas," said Doc Nunn, "it's Mickey fucking Mantle."

Vinnie laughed. "You're just saying that because I'm dirty blond with blue eyes and I'm from New York, Doc. You know I'm not a big ballplayer."

Another one of the Marines, Bobby Dowd, an eighteen-year-old black kid from Oklahoma, jumped into the conversation. "My pop played ball with The Mick back home before he came up with the Yanks. Said that The Mick could do things that the other ballplayers couldn't dream of doing."

"Yeah, well, out here, we're all doing things that we couldn't dream of doing when we were back in the world," continued Dowd, likely reflecting on the fact that they were expected to kill, often gratuitously, for thirteen dark months of their lives.

Vinnie noticed the dark tone in Bobby's voice and tried to let some air out of the taut balloon. "Bobby, please don't tell me that you're wearing drawers!"

"Yeah, I am. Why do you ask, Saint?"

"Because no one wants to hear you bitching again about your Indian drawers sneaking up your ass and taking your balls as POWs."

The whole platoon broke out in hearty laughter. Saint was a regular riot with the boys and they really enjoyed his company when he drove up from the rear.

A few remarkably quiet days later, Saint returned to the platoon in his loud, cranky jeep and he jumped out with a dusty green satchel that was filled with letters. "Jones. Reagan. Jackson. Mercerio. Nunn. Givens. Henderson. Harvey. Milazzo. Sanchez. Williams. Regents. McCoy."

Vinnie yelled out the names as if it were roll call back at boot camp. But now the Marines, with cigarettes hanging from their lips like James Dean or Marlon Brando, hoped to hear their names so that they could open the envelopes to find the familiar, comfortable cursive of Mom, Grandma, Pop, and their siblings, or even the random paw print of a family pet. Some of them took long, exaggerated sniffs of the letters because they swore they could *smell* home on the letters. Many of the men bear-hugged Saint after he called their names and delivered their precious cargo. Vinnie got the same reaction from each of the platoons he serviced. He truly was like the Santa they'd all revered a mere decade earlier as children.

One day, Saint brought mosquito repellent and the boys reacted to the chemicals as if he were delivering a holy elixir. Those mosquitos were pesky bastards and, boy, were they persistent. You'd smash one and his sister would bite you; kill two and his three enormous friends were nibbling on your ass. The repellent worked fairly well until yet another monsoon rain washed it off, or until it was slicked off by the men's perspiration. Saint also brought malaria pills for them to put in their drinking water, to avoid dysentery.

Vinnie was their one-stop shop for all things happy. He brought letters from home, repellent to keep the brazen and impossibly large mosquitos at bay, and the occasional manna from heaven itself: care packages of fruit and candy, which came from good people around the world.

*　　　　*　　　　*

Hi, Greenie, how are you doing? Fine, I hope. I'm OK. I got some medicine for my asthma and it went away so I'm in A-1 shape again. It's been raining for three days now. "I Hate the Rain." I got four months of rain to look forward to . . . ain't I a lucky guy? The place here hasn't changed, it still stinks. I can't wait till I get out of the Marine Corps. I wish I was a draft-card burner now. Ha Ha. Have you seen the guys in the neighborhood? You know, George, Richie, and the others. Are they still fooling around with that shit? I'd rather be here than be home fooling around with that shit.

When I was in school, I couldn't keep up with my grades, no less stay at home. If it wasn't for Mama, I would've never graduated high school. They should have written the diploma in Mom's name because she earned it. Ha Ha!

How did you like that dollar bill I sent you? Keep it for good luck.

When I go on R&R, I'm going to have a blast. It's going to be "wine, women, and song." I haven't seen an American broad since I've been here. But there are American women stationed in Da Nang. Well, Lillian, I got to go now, honey. Love you, sis.

Vinnie

Excerpt from Vinnie's September 17, 1967 letter to Lilly

Vinnie's asthma had been kicking his ass in Vietnam's humid monsoon season. The days could get up to as high as 120-degrees

Fahrenheit while the nights dipped down to as chilly as fifty. These conditions did not lend themselves to easy living for an asthmatic. In fact, Vinnie's asthma, in part, was the reason why he was delegated the vital duty of being the company driver. Well, that and the fact that Vinnie was a world-class mechanic who serviced the old jeeps like no one had since the Korean War.

Vinnie's days typically began at the H&S in Dong Ha. The Dong Ha HQ was built up after April 1967. Prior to that time, being at HQ still required digging and living in a foxhole, so it was no different than being out with a platoon except for one critical detail: The foxholes down in the jungle tended to feel the wrath of the Vietcong's artillery and mortars a hell of a lot more than HQ did back in the rear.

Between April and October of 1967, Dong Ha HQ progressed from foxholes and trenches to bunkers and tents, then to reinforced tents (tent poles with strong backs, that is, two-by-four wooden frames under the canvas), and finally to complete metal buildings. The larger units situated at HQ consisted of metal buildings, inside of which the Marines would work on vehicles and equipment, but their living conditions were the same.

HQ held ample support facilities for the Marines, including artillery. Battle logistics for the 3rd Battalion originated at Dong Ha HQ, which also provided administrative support for the Marines deployed in the field. C-rations were divvied up in HQ for the men out in the jungle, the hills, the mountains, and wherever else Vinnie could navigate his jeep.

Dong Ha also was the site of the *de facto* database that monitored critical records, such as the numbers of confirmed enemy kills and of Marines who were injured, killed, and/or missing in action. HQ also served as an ammo dump, a silo that stored critical ammunition. Of course, the storage of highly explosive ammo occasionally had unexpected, negative consequences: The ammo dumps occasionally exploded. Of course, every round of ammo is precious when Marines are deep in the shit, so while the exploding ammo dump may have looked as awe-inspiring as a Fourth of

July fireworks show, it created a plethora of red-faced officers who demanded answers.

Vinnie lived in a large general-purpose tent, known as a GP, that housed approximately twenty-five men. The GP was equipped with cots and rubber ladies (inflatable mattresses) and sleeping bags. The tent was surrounded by sandbags and foxholes in case of incoming rounds. Vinnie often sat outside on the sandbags to write letters to Lilly, as well as to his other family and friends. One of the perks of staying in the rear was that Vinnie did not have to consume C-rats very often. Instead, he had the pleasure of eating in the comparatively luxurious mess hall, where he enjoyed actual cooked meals. The company office was a section in the tent with a desk and an EE-8 field phone, a phone that was attached to a landline and had a crank on the side, which could get to a Marine switchboard that would connect to the outside world.

When Vinnie began his day at HQ, he would pack up his jeep with mail and supplies for his daily morning runs to Cam Lo. However, he could not make his trip down Route 9 until after the roads were swept. Every morning, the engineers swept the roadway for mines using handheld metal detectors. These devices were large, with circular bases that attached to packs on the engineers' shoulders. The engineers meticulously and methodically swung the base across the road in front of them to ensure, as best they could, that the roads were not hiding deadly, jeep-piercing explosives. Clearly, the engineers were tasked with an exceptionally stressful responsibility. If their equipment failed to detect a mine, or if the engineer failed to sweep the base just another few inches, such processes were met with devastatingly gruesome consequences.

Vinnie typically made one trip late in the morning to the field, when he would transport the mail, boots, utilities, "special goodies" (beer, real food), and replacement men. Indeed, Vinnie was promoted to lance corporal by virtue of the fact that he performed each of his duties exceptionally and maintained an impeccable appearance. In the rear, a clean, crisp uniform, when combined with polished brass and boots, impressed the hell out of the officers and often resulted in promotions.

As for my asthma, here's the scoop: It battered me only a couple of times, so I kept on complaining to the doctor. So that is why they gave me this job driving a jeep in Dong Ha. All I do is drive and sit in my tent when I'm off. Go to the movies (1920 flicks, Ha Ha) at night. I really got the life compared to before. Since I've been here, I feel great. I got a rack to sleep on and a beautiful tent to sleep in. It's a large, two-man tent and I have a footlocker to keep all of my gear in. I can take a shower every night. It's just great. I got plenty to tell all of you when I get home about 'Nam. I got some real wild war stories about Con Thien from when I was up there.

Excerpt from Vinnie's October 23, 1967 letter to Lilly

My sister always says everyone's asking for me. I want to thank all of you for thinking of me. I am stationed in Dong Ha and I have been here for about a week now. I was in Con Thien for 1.5 months and then Cam Lo for 1.5 months. Things have been quiet here lately. Con Thien has cooled down lately. I hear it's making pretty big news back in the States.

I am the new company driver. I drive a jeep for the supply sergeant and I also drive the first sergeant wherever he wants to go. I will be stationed in Dong Ha for the rest of my tour (10 months). I've been in 'Nam for 3 months and a week, and I'll apply for R&R at the beginning of next month. I'll probably get it in December and I'm going to Taipei. I heard from my friend that went there that it is really great.

The weather here is crazy, it doesn't know what it wants to do. It will rain for a week straight then, the next day, the sun will come out like summer. Right now, it's starting to get cold. It's about fifty degrees outside right now. It was very nice meeting all of you when I was on leave. I hope that we can get together again when I get home from here.

Excerpt from Vinnie's October 23, 1967 letter to Lilly's officemates

The inclement weather made the responsibilities of company driver quite challenging: The monsoon rains created mounds of slick mud that made the otherwise-benign task of driving quite cumbersome and stressful. Vinnie often had to regain control of the jeep after it skidded off the main road. Saint would not have been as skittish if all he had to do was regain control of the jeep and resume the mundane task of driving down to the platoon. However, skidding off of the road, even temporarily, could result in injury or death if the jeep detonated a mine that the engineers had not detected. Furthermore, there were occasions when Vinnie's jeep skidded through the thick mud and came to a sudden stop against a tree in the jungle that lined the Marine-cleared Route 9.

One time, First Sergeant Bryant and Vinnie were in a driving rain, taking supplies from HQ to a platoon, when Vinnie had to veer suddenly. The sheets of gray rain obscured the rear portion of an elephant that was standing ahead of the oncoming jeep and to Vinnie's left, foraging on something in the bush that line the road. Due to the heavy rain, Vinnie did not see the elephant until he was approximately twenty-five feet from the great beast. Vinnie instinctively thrust his foot upon the brake and, predictably, the jeep began to skid along the unforgivingly muddy road. Vinnie immediately turned into the skid, trying to avoid striking the elephant while simultaneously hoping to avoid having the jeep slide into the bush or flip over. Vinnie avoided the elephant and the vehicle did not flip over. However, the combination of the unsteady terrain and the sheer physics involved caused the jeep to veer off the road and into dense elephant grass.

Shaken but uninjured, the Marines realized that they would have to somehow push the jeep about fifteen feet out of the bush and back onto the road while sheets of heavy rain descended relentlessly upon them.

Vinnie and the first sergeant, who was only three years older than Saint, cast a discerning glance at each other and the look in their eyes said, *Shit, do we have to get out of this jeep in the pouring rain, slip and slide in this fucking mud, and possible land directly on a goddamn land mine that will tear us in half and send us home in bags?*

The Marines hopped out of the jeep with apprehensive steps onto the muddy terrain. Vinnie broke out the drying agent that was kept in the jeep for just these occasions and applied an ample amount around the stuck tires. Bryant then got into the driver's seat, placed the jeep in first gear, and gently depressed the gas pedal while Vinnie pushed the vehicle from behind. Mud splattered all over Vinnie as he slipped and flew into the air and landed, hard, on the ground.

First Sergeant Bryant winced as he waited to hear a terrible explosion but the only thing he heard was, "Shit! I just swallowed a gallon of fucking jungle mud!" Relieved that they still were alive, Bryant and Vinnie chuckled at their good fortune. The two Marines then improvised a way to release the jeep from the mud's grip with a combination of bamboo, dirt, elephant grass, and sheer ingenuity on Vinnie's part. (Ironically, Vinnie attributed his ability to free the jeep to his experience with myriad New York snowstorms that had caused his friends' cars to become skidding heaps of steel in the unforgiving snow and ice.) The soaked, filthy men then hopped back into their jeep and resumed their mission to deliver much-needed supplies to a grateful platoon.

An ancillary concern during those times on the side of Route 9 was of an equally unnerving nature. The area north of Dong Ha, beyond Cam Lo to the DMZ, had been declared a free-fire zone by the USMC and all civilians in that region had been evacuated. A free-fire zone meant that the Marines were authorized to kill any non-military personnel seen in that region *at any time*. Such zones were established after countless Marines were maimed and killed after innocent-looking Vietnamese people—often women and children—appeared in the region and asked the Marines for help.

The Marines would let their guard down to assist the needy Vietnamese and, in the midst of their vulnerability, the "innocents" would detonate the crude, homemade bomb vests that were hidden beneath their clothing, causing catastrophic injury, and often death, to anyone in the vicinity of these acts. The USMC educated the Vietnamese locals for weeks before the policy was announced and the Marines assisted in their evacuation. Once the policy was put into effect, the Marines were ordered to assume that any locals were there to kill them. And they were ordered to act accordingly.

Vinnie was not alone in being unnerved by this policy. He often would play with the Vietnamese kids in the countryside and around the lakes and ravines surrounding Dong Ha HQ. In fact, some of Vinnie's favorite pictures of his tour in Vietnam up until that point depicted him with Vietnamese children. However, Vinnie learned that the Vietnam War introduced merciless anarchy to warfare. The NVA and the Viet Cong guerrillas instituted a win-at-all-costs approach and if that meant that women and children had to be used as pawns in the throes of war, then so be it.

Vinnie did not understand why the NVA would render women and children so vulnerable by devaluing their lives, but he had lost friends in Con Thien to such a practice, and he did not want to lose any others, much less lose his own life. Reluctantly, he knew that he could not hesitate to take up his weapon and kill anyone who did not belong in the free-fire zone. He had not been taught this ruthless mindset in boot camp, back in the world.

War, indeed, was Hell.

*   *   *

On another occasion when the monsoon-induced mudslides caused Vinnie's jeep to career off a road within the free-fire zone, Saint and his superior officer were again tasked with the stress-inducing job of getting the jeep freed from the mud's tenacious grip. The two Marines apprehensively stepped from the disabled jeep and, with their M-16 rifles at the ready, scanned the area as best they could through the unforgivingly loud rain. Failing to see any human lifeform whatsoever, they placed their rifles back in the jeep and undertook the cumbersome task of getting the jeep back on the road. Vinnie had taken a step toward the rear of the jeep, to begin excavating it, when he heard a distinct click emanate from under the pressure of his boot.

Vinnie screamed, "Shit! Clear . . . *CLEAR!* It's a fucking *Bouncing Betty!*"

A Bouncing Betty was a deadly landmine that the Germans introduced during World War II and that the Viet Cong employed during the Vietnam War. The Bouncing Betty was a canister of intricate explosives, filled with ball bearings. The canister had a cylindrical lever atop it that was only a few inches high. The lever had three small, thin prongs sprout from its top and these prongs acted as the tripping mechanism for the landmine.

The canister and lever were buried below the ground so that only the three virtually invisible prongs were exposed above the ground. When the prongs were depressed, or disturbed in any fashion, an audible click occurred before an intricate series of charges within the lever and the canister caused it to be propelled upward like a mini-rocket, going through the ground in which it had been buried and roughly three-to-four feet above the ground, before it violently exploded within approximately three-to-four seconds from the time that the prongs had been disturbed. This explosion propelled the hundreds of ball bearings within the canister—in all directions, at great velocities, and with deadly intention.

Fearing that this was that moment that every Marine dreaded yet never acknowledged amongst his brothers—an unnerving obsession with the unavoidable time of their bloody, painful demise—both men frantically scrambled in the mud, in a futile effort to get away from the mine. The boys were simultaneously slipping in the mud, like something akin to the fictional Wile E. Coyote fostering the energy required to speed after the elusive Road Runner, and counting silently in their heads, knowing that they had roughly three or four seconds to get as far away as possible from the concussive force of the imminent blast, as well as from the body-shredding shrapnel that would follow. After what seemed like a lifetime of inefficaciously running in place, the unnerved, panic-stricken Marines jumped behind a large rock approximately five feet away from the detonating Bouncing Betty.

The men clenched each other in a tight crouch, waiting for the piercing explosion, but nothing happened. Vinnie, with his forehead clenched up in a wrinkled fury, nervously held up four fingers to his superior, seeking confirmation that four seconds indeed had elapsed since the terrifying click of the land mine and the officer nodded affirmatively. Still, the boys remained behind the rock, barely breathing, for at least another ninety seconds before they cautiously emerged from their defensive position.

Vinnie knew exactly where he had stepped, so he slowly approached the site and immediately realized that he had unknowingly stepped on a branch of bamboo and the resulting crack was mistaken for the *click* of an activated Bouncing Betty. Relieved beyond belief, the men released the primitive reaction that all good Marines repeated after cheating the grasp of the Grim Reaper: "FUCK!"

They proceeded to free the jeep and then continued on their way to Cam Lo, where a platoon of twenty-five men was relying on them to complete their mission.

"R-and-fucking-R can't come soon enough for me," Vinnie exclaimed after a profound sigh.

"Fuck yeah, Saint," was the sufficiently succinct response.

Vinnie was uncertain as to what was going to kill him first: the fucking war itself or the terribly unforgiving nature of the anxiety that the war was causing him.

CHAPTER 5

GROWING UP
IN 'NAM

I received two letters and the Christmas card and the article about Con Thien. I also got the tape from you; the tapes are coming so fast that I can't play them that fast. Pop has gone news-crazy. That's all that is on those tapes. I like hearing about Con Thien and places where I've been, but I hate to hear that bastard's (President Johnson's) voice. In one of Pop's tapes, he started taping the news about Con Thien and he shut it off and put on music instead. Boy! I don't know. Tell him to slack off on the news. Limit it to what's happening around the DMZ because that's near us, 12 miles from here.

That article about Con Thien in the New York Times *was very good. The one in* Life *was good, too. But, as far as Marines calling it a place of angels . . . never happens. The Vietnamese call it that. The Marines call it everything BUT that. And what we call it starts with an "f", with an "up" at the end of it. You know what I mean. I'll never forget that place as long as I live. A lot of guys got blown away (killed) up in Never Never Land. And a lot of gooks got it, too.*

The article in Life *is about the 3rd Bn. 9th Marines at Con Thien. 3/9 was the battalion that relieved us, 3/4, in Con Thien. But if you look at the pictures in* Life *and look at the Marines, we were very much the same as them, only we were up there for 52 days and they were up there for 30 days. It's a big difference. They rotate battalions up there and, right now, it's 1st Bn. 1st Marines up there. After we'd spent 52 days up there, they came up with an order that the battalion rotations in Con Thien are limited to 30 days.*

Mom really made me laugh when she commented in one of her letters after she received the NVA pack (that I sent to her). She said, "The owner of the pack must be dead." Ha, ha. I really got a laugh out of that, but that's just like Moms. Who cares that he died? He's the enemy. I hope Mom doesn't wash the pack because I'm pretty sure that the back of the pack has his bloodstain on it. It was hard to tell because the pack was stored for a while.

Excerpt from Vinnie's December 1, 1967 letter to Lilly

C on Thien made the Vietnam War personal to Vinnie. In short, this 158-foot-high hill, which actually was comprised of a cluster of three smaller hills, was a virtual killing field. Vinnie and his Marine brethren lost too many Marines in the conflicts that erupted on a seemingly daily basis—not to mention the multiple men who were medevaced from the area, but only after they had been violently separated from critical bodily appendages that previously made them whole. Local religious missionaries called Con Thien the "Hill of the Angels" due to the plethora of men on both sides who met their grisly demise while engaged in fierce battles to defend—or take, depending on your allegiance—a muddy, shell-hole-scarred hill.

Vinnie technically was assigned to the rear, but he spent many days in the shit in Con Thien. After all, it wasn't like he could simply amble to his jeep and drive down jungle "roads" when there were mortars and artillery zipping and exploding literally everywhere. Vinnie unloaded his rifle's magazine and threw his fair share of grenades during his time on the hill. If the platoon needed supplies, it was his mission to hump down the hill with a fire team, find his jeep (if it still was in one piece), and haul ass back to the relative sanity of HQ back in Dong Ha, only to stock up and drive back to Hell.

The Hueys couldn't run missions to Con Thien because of the real risk that the birds would be shot out of the sky or would crash into the side of a mountain while navigating the skies and trying to avoid NVA surface-to-air missiles. Saint often was the Marines' only hope to get chow, replacements, or crucial ammo re-supplies, and his brothers never ceased appreciating Vinnie's selfless loyalty to them.

He risked getting killed ten different ways to Sunday during his brave runs, yet he never wavered and never said no.

Brother Marines often thought to themselves that Saint was fucking crazy because he'd be driving through Con Thien— fucking *Con Thien!*—with a jeep full of ammo. One direct hit by an intentional round or a wayward mortar, and Vinnie would be blown halfway back to Jamaica, New York.

Con Thien was the driving force behind the dehumanization of the enemy in Vinnie's eyes. If a Marine acted counter to his training by pondering the notion that who he had been called to kill was a fellow warrior, just one on the other side of the ring, then the duty would become mentally arduous and exceedingly stressful. However, if a Marine acted in accordance with his training and experiences in the bush, then the NVA soldier or Viet Cong guerilla would be permutated in such a way that the guerilla became, in a Marine's subconscious, not on par with him. As such, firing a bullet into the skull of the amorphous *enemy* was easier, if not noble.

The nineteen-year-old Saint watched as his friends were felled by the arms of the enemy and he could not allow himself to think that the NVA soldiers were caught in the identical quagmire as Vinnie and his brother Marines. Such a thought process was not a healthy way of thinking for the Marines. Thus, instead of allowing sympathy to permeate his soul while in Vietnam, that segment of

Vinnie's psyche was suppressed. He was a United States warrior and the enemy, despite being Saint's age, if not younger, and equally aghast at this unforgivingly deadly plight, could not possess any redeeming qualities. Who cares if the enemy died? *Besides*, thought Vinnie, *they don't give a fuck when they kill my friends.*

War is Hell and death is the collateral that we put down for the privilege of serving our country.

*　　　*　　　*

"Hey Vinnie!," said the sultry young voice of a beautiful young lady from back in the world, "how the hell are ya doin', big brother? We really miss ya *heyah* at home and we can't wait to see ya again real soon!"

Vinnie leaned against his bunk at H&S back in Dong Ha, cast a furtive glance at his immediate surroundings to confirm that no one was scoping him out, and then allowed himself to break down and weep quietly. Lilly, his older sister who playfully referred to Vinnie as the older sibling because of the role of protector that he assumed back home, sent Vinnie myriad cassette tapes of her stream-of-consciousness thoughts. She sometimes included recordings of their parents and younger brother, which made Vinnie equally happy and devastated because he missed his family immensely. *If I get ho—* . . . when *I get home*, Vinnie quickly corrected himself as he continued his internal thought and a promise to himself, *I'm gonna make sure that I make my family proud! Mama and Pop worked so damn hard for us, so I'm gonna bust my ass to make sure that I repay them someway, somehow when I get the hell out of this shit.*

Vinnie played Lilly's tapes for the other Marines and they got an absolute kick out of listening to this beautiful woman. Vinnie also showed them pictures of Lilly, but he sternly warned them that he'd plant his boot so far up their asses that they'd choke on his shoelaces if they so much as *thought* anything disrespectful about his beloved sister. One brother Marine, Billy, chuckled loudly in response to this warning, incorrectly assuming that Saint was just bullshitting the guys. After all, this Lilly was a hot broad and the boys hadn't seen a woman that beautiful since they were back in the world.

The stoic, ice-cold stare; balled-up fists; and pursed lips on Vinnie's face that met Billy's ill-considered laugh belied his nickname of Saint and assured the suddenly panic-stricken Marine that Lilly's "big brother" most assuredly was *NOT* kidding. Vinnie retained this hardened posture as he took a few deliberate steps toward his startled brother Marine.

"Whoa, whoa, Saint," stammered Billy, as he held up his hands, splayed palms facing out. "I—I—I meant no disrespect. It was jus– just a stupid joke. I'm sorry." Vinnie unfurled his fists and ceased approaching the cowering Marine, but he didn't release his soul-piercing stare for quite a few seconds more.

Billy was the last Marine who dared to disrespect the revered Lilly.

Red and Doc Nunn couldn't get over Lilly's over-the-top New York accent. Doc was from Pennsylvania, so he had some experience with *Noo Yawk*-speak. Conversely, Red, from Edmonds, Washington, had never heard a real New York accent. In fact, as he often joked, the closest thing to an authentic New York accent that Red had encountered was Lucy Ricardo from *I Love Lucy*. Vinnie found that hilarious.

"Vinnie, your sister is beautiful, but are you sure that you're related to her?" asked Doc, in an obviously joking manner, "after all, she looks like Sophia Loren with her olive skin, dark hair, and dark eyes. And then there's you, ya ugly blond-haired, blue-eyed mutt!"

The platoon burst out in laughter, a rare sight in the combat-torn region of Cam Lo. Vinnie laughed so hard that tears streamed down his face. Vinnie's fair complexion, light hair (the boys jokingly called it blond despite the fact that it was closer to a light brown), and piercing blue eyes stood in stark contrast to Lilly's Mediterranean look. Vinnie also did not have such a distinct New York accent. In fact, he spoke more in the "aw, shucks" manner of Wally Cleaver, from *Leave It to Beaver* fame, and less in the gruff, street-wise manner of Tony from *West Side Story*.

"Hey Milazzo, you stone Italian, come here, I have something for you," said Vinnie to his Jersey buddy, Tony "Doc" Milazzo. Vinnie knew that Tony would greatly appreciate the latest tape that Lilly had sent him.

"Your sister's quite a swell doll, Vinnie," Tony said, "I'm gonna marry her when I'm outta here to make sure that I can bust your chops for the next fifty years, pal!"

"I don't think my family needs any more stone Italians, Milazzo," countered Vinnie. "Besides, why would my lil' sis wanna get hitched to a square like you?"

Tony good-naturedly punched Vinnie in the shoulder and Vinnie proceeded to thrust the cassette tape into the beat-up, archaic tape deck that served as one of the men's few portals to the world. That dusty old machine had cranked tunes from Sinatra to Elvis to the Four Tops to the Commodores. Of course, Vinnie made sure that it also played the sometimes off-key singing of the less-well-known Queens crooner Lilly Santaniello!

Vinnie pressed the *play* button and the dingy speaker crackled with the voice of an angel, albeit one who sang Van Morrison's just-released "Brown Eyed Girl" with a distinctly nasal twang.

Doc Milazzo was beside himself. "Did you put Lilly up to that, Saint?" he inquired.

After all, Lilly *was* the brown-eyed girl!

"Naw, my sister simply is very hip and she knows all the groovy tunes!" replied Saint.

"Hey, fellas, c'mere," yelled Tony, "come listen to this!" Billy, the scared Marine; Red; Doc Nunn; and about twenty other brother Marines crawled out of their hooches, stopped digging their holes, paused writing their letters back home, and even quit cleaning their rifles. They traipsed through a steady rain over to Vinnie, who was perched upon a large rock. His cassette player was perched on the rock, too, underneath a canvas canopy.

There, they joined in singing with their favorite gal, someone that they had never known and someone who they'd never meet, but a gal they felt they'd known all their lives, thanks to the miracle of cassette tapes.

"Man, it's like she's right here with us even though she's a world away, thanks to these here cassettes," marveled one Marine.

"Yeah," agreed another, "what could they possibly invent next to make communication even more personal?"

One of the Marines suggested the *Dick Tracy* two-way wristwatch and the men howled with laughter.

"That's just fantasy, boys," said a kid nicknamed Socrates because he was the cerebral member of the cast of playful clowns, "it ain't never gonna happen in our lifetimes."

With that, the Marines sang harmony between the raindrops with their lead singer, their long-distance sister Lilly, who came crackling in oh-so-sweetly through the speakers of the cassette player. Lilly sang "live" from Jamaica, Queens, all the way over to another nondescript hill in Cam Lo, Vietnam.

Van Morrison had no idea how profound the Marines in the shit found his lyrics to be. And singing them with the beautiful Lilly, a clandestine dream girl for many of these homesick boys, seemed like a perfect fit.

Lilly often sent Vinnie tapes that detailed her life's events, from the mundane tasks she did as a receptionist and secretary in the New York State Social Security Office, to the delicate travails of her love life. Indeed, nothing was off-limits. And as the quasi-big brother, Vinnie was not shy about dispensing advice. *Should I go out on a date with Sam, or John, or [fill in the name of the guy who was enamored with Lilly]?* often was met with rebukes from Vinnie that included such descriptive adjectives as *jackass*, *idiot*, and *shithead* to accentuate his point. Vinnie would get lost within the confines of his own mind when he read his sister's letters; or listened to his hero, his father, read the news; or laughed as his mom told him about chasing after his dog, Apache.

The letters and tapes gave Vinnie a sense of peace in his chaotic world that thrived on death, maiming, and disorder. Indeed, Vinnie allowed himself to get far away from 'Nam every time he sat down to enjoy a letter from Lilly, or from any other member of his family or his friends. Whereas 'Nam brought Vinnie anxiety and spontaneous bouts of rage, anger, constant dread, and fear of death at every turn, the letters from home transported Vinnie away from such madness, to a wonderful place, deep within the recesses of his very soul, which forbade the encroachment of the morass of death, decay, and destruction that constituted his war-torn reality.

* * *

You know, no wonder all the Marines go crazy and assassinate people. You're taught to kill from the day you join the Marines and then you come over here ('Nam) for 13 months and they expect you to be a civilized person when you get back in the world.

Excerpt from Vinnie's December 28, 1967 letter to Lilly

* * *

In a private moment, Vinnie felt a fleeting tinge of guilt about sending the dead NVA soldier's backpack home to his mom, but then he saw a buddy screaming in agony while a corpsman searched for the young man's missing right arm amidst the mud, blood, and mortar shells of rounds that brother Marines had fired at the enemy and Saint's guilt evaporated back into his subconscious.

After surviving and rotating out of Con Thien, Vinnie and his buddies gathered back in Cam Lo on the evening of December 30,

1967, with some beers and stale potato chips, to recount some of the insanity that they had withstood for fifty-two days, which seemed like fifty-two years. They talked about those tense moments when they were in the shit and honestly believed that a bullet would tear through their brains at any second. Vinnie talked about the time when he was driving back to the base of the hill when a round smashed through the windshield of his jeep and lodged in the passenger seat where Lieutenant Gaglio had been sitting just seconds earlier. Red talked about watching his grenade blow a gook apart. Docs Nunn and Milazzo shared so many stories of cheating death while tending to injuries that a Hollywood producer would reject the tales as a script because they seemed too surreal.

The war stories waned as the beer ceased flowing and, after a deliberate pause, Keidinger, one of the grunts who survived Con Thien with *only* minor flesh wounds caused by shrapnel, mused that the boys from 3/9 got all the glory in *Life* magazine while he and his brothers from the Thundering Third, the 3rd Battalion 4th Marines, did twice the amount of time in that shithole than they had.

"We shoulda been on that cover," cried Keidinger, "not them!"

"C'mon, Keeds," interjected Vinnie, "that ain't fair. Those guys saw a *helluva* lot of combat on that hill. And anyways, why the hell would any respectable magazine want ass-face Dunn on its cover?"

The boys roared with laughter at Doc Nunn's expense. Without missing a beat, he good-naturedly retorted, "We can't all be blue-eyed pretty boys from New York City like you, Saint!"

*   *   *

Hi, stupid! How's it going? I hope fine. As for me, I'm just fine. I haven't been doing too much driving lately so I got a lot of time now, so I usually work on the jeep. I just put a muffler on it and, boy, what a difference. You can't even hear the engine anymore. I used to get headaches when I drove the jeep all day but not anymore.

Something is wrong with the mail over here. I haven't gotten a letter in 5 days. All I got was a tape, a newspaper, and a package. No letter mail at all and I know that all of you are writing me. I guess the post office is taking an R&R break after all that Christmas mail. I'll probably get 20 letters all at once. I hope they straighten it out soon because I can't wait to get a letter from someone.

Tell Mom that I got the three pairs of socks. I have to go pick up a lieutenant at the disbursing office. He told me to pick him up at 11:00 and right now it's 10:45. I'll probably be chauffeuring him around all day. I'm going to go pick him up and I'll bring this with me. I'll just finish writing this letter when I am waiting for him.

. . . Well, I'm at the disbursing office and the lieutenant ain't here yet. He's probably lost somewhere. He's a real boob. He's a second lieutenant, an officer, and he's about 21 years old but he looks about 17.

Last night, I had a groovy dream. It was about me and you and I just came home from here. I didn't call up, I just walked into the house and you were the only one home. Pop was working, Joseph was at school, and Mom was shopping. Well, you were just ready to go to work and I walked in. You were so shocked, all you said was, "You're home." Boy! I wish that dream came true! But, some day, I will come home.

In one of your letters, you said that one of the guys at your office said that you should have some of the girls write me and you said I'm writing 3 already and you also said how many can I handle. Well, I'll let you know after I come back from R&R, okay? Ha Ha. And I'm not writing 3 girls, I'm writing 5. Not constantly, more or less on and off. But if you have some good-looking, available girls in your office, I'd like very much to write them. Because when I come home . . . well, anyway, you let them write me. It's nice to receive letters from different people once in a while. That's a good excuse, ain't it? You can show them a picture of me and if they're not interested, too bad for them! But if they are, tell them to write and they'll receive a response from me. Now, you don't say anything about this to Rosalie and don't give me a lecture in your next letter, either. Because I ain't engaged like some girl I know who still messes around. Get the picture? Okay, you better have some good-looking girls write and I don't mean old married women. Ya hear, ugly?

Well, Lil, I guess I said enough for now. You must think I'm crazy but if you were over here for 5½ months, you'd be a nut, too. Well, take care and be good.

Love, your brother, Vinnie

P.S. Don't forget to tell Mom about the socks and also don't forget to have some good-looking chicks write because if you don't, I'll get mad and then when I come home I'll put you over my knee and spank you. Ha Ha. Take care and write. Hey! Do you got the wedding date settled yet? If so, let me know, okay?

Vinnie's January 4, 1968 letter to Lilly

The Thundering Third was stationed on a hill in Cam Lo for New Year's Eve 1967 and Vinnie made sure to drive down from H&S to celebrate with his mates. There was a mutual understanding amongst the warriors on both sides of the DMZ that neither side would attack each other on this holiday evening. Thus, the Marines were much more relaxed than they'd otherwise be and were interacting as if they were hanging out in Times Square as opposed to in Hell Central. Vinnie made certain to bring a bevy of cigarettes and booze from H&S (his superiors assured him that they were "looking the other way" as he packed up his jeep) and the boys greeted him like a conquering hero. Saint was greeted with hoots, hollers, pats on the back, and hugs. There even were unconfirmed rumors that one or two kisses were planted on Vinnie's pretty-boy mug when he arrived with cold beers and smokes.

A few beers into the revelry, Vinnie yelled to Doc Nunn, "Hey, Doc, how many girls are writing to you from the world, you freakin' squid?"

"Saint, I have more girls than Elvis and Sinatra COMBINED, you stinkin' mailman!"

"You ain't nearly so groovy, Nunn," Vinnie replied. "Remember, I pick up all of the letters from yous guys and I deliver letters from back in the world to everyone, and I can't recall bringing you any letters, except from your old lady! A'course, *I'm* getting letters from chicks all over New York City because the ladies love me!"

The deafening chorus of laughter drowned out the litany of good-natured F-bombs that were exploding like mortars out of Doc Nunn's mouth. When the laughter died down to a dull roar, the grizzled, experienced corpsman cracked wise on Saint by issuing a good-natured warning, "You better not need my help if you're ever stuck in the shit, ya wiseass!"

"Don't you worry none, Doc," Vinnie replied, "I ain't getting my ass fulla shrapnel anytime soon." The boys continued to smoke and drink as if they would never get another chance to do so (which would prove true for all too many of these celebrants) and the last grunt stumbled into his hooch for shut-eye as the sun was beginning its slow ascent over the eastern mountaintops.

New Year's Day, 1968. "Happy New Year, boys! May we all get out of the shit in one piece and back in the world to greet all the groovy chicks who are waiting for us back home," exclaimed Keidinger, who fancied himself as something of a rock star. Vinnie crawled out of his hooch, the unexpectedly blazing January sun temporarily blinding him as his eyes adjusted to the light. After a couple of sneezes, Saint noticed Keidinger milling around, swishing the remnants of warm beer in his mouth before accentuating the effort with an exaggerated gulp.

"Hey, Keeds," Vinnie softly called out to his pal, "you ever have any dreams about back home?"

"Hell yes, Saint! I dream all the time about being back home in L.A., hanging out with my best friend, Mike, and my girl. Y'know, I'm getting short here and the shorter I get, the more intense my dreams, Vin."

"I tell ya, Keeds, I still got another seven months to go, but I'm already dreamin'! I dream about my girl, Roe, every so often but I dream about my family more than anything."

"I hear you, man," Keidinger said, "I know that you're missing your kid sister, Lilly. Man, can that doll sing. I wish that I could sing like her!"

Vinnie squinted unnecessarily and looked up at the sun, as if to excuse the tears that were streaming down his face. "Fuckin' blinding sun," Vinnie muttered unconvincingly.

Keidinger knew what was going on, so he looked away, to give Vinnie the impression that his tears went unnoticed. "Yeah," Vinnie continued, "I dream of Lilly a lot and I hope that she's doing fine without me, her guardian angel, protecting her from the assholes trying to get up her skirt."

Saint's mood darkened and he angrily kicked at the rocks in front of him, layered in dried mud, causing a few to skip a couple of yards ahead of him. A plume of dust rose up in response to Vinnie's angry boot and the resulting cloud invaded Vinnie's throat, causing him to choke for a few seconds. Keidinger threw his canteen of water toward Saint, who gratefully took a swig, cleared his throat, spit out the remnants, and continued, "I just had a dream that I showed up back home in New York to surprise my family. My sister was the only one who was home, and the look on her . . . face . . ."

Vinnie abruptly went silent as his throat was overcome by a wave of heaves. Vinnie tried to quickly compensate for the melancholy and yearning that had overcome him by gesturing to the canteen, but he realized that no amount of acting was going to mask what had just happened.

Keidinger, usually a relentless kidder and pain in the ass, glanced around the perimeter to ensure that no one was watching, placed his arm around the crestfallen Saint's shoulder, and whispered in his ear, "We've all fuckin' been *there*, Saint. Don't hang your head in shame, man."

Between gasps, Vinnie replied, "All she said was, 'You're home, Vinnie, you're home,' before she hugged me tight and told me how much . . . how much she . . . she missed . . . me." More tears and a heartier hug came from the surprisingly sympathetic Keidinger. Vinnie *hated* himself for breaking down, despite his friend's heartfelt compassion. "That dream's gotta come true, Keeds. I gotta make it home to my family 'cause they need me."

Vinnie paused to take a deep breath and then he continued in a barely audible, choking whisper, "And I need them."

"Happy New Year, Saint. This is the year that our dreams will come true. We're both getting outta the shit this year and we'll both be home with the people that we love so much."

"Happy New Year, Keeds. When I get back home, I'll get my sister and some of my buddies and we'll haul ass to hang with you and Mike in L.A." Keidinger began to walk away, but Vinnie grabbed him by the arm. "Hey, man," Saint stuttered while looking ashamedly at his dusty boots, which were in dire need of a Marine shine, "thanks for . . ."

Keidinger cut off his humbled friend. "Don't worry about it, Saint. Don't worry about it." With that, Keidinger returned to form: running around, annoyingly waking up terribly hungover Marines from their own dreams about places exceedingly distant from the jungle they currently called home.

CHAPTER 6

LOVING YOUR BROTHERS AND YEARNING FOR WOMEN IN 'NAM

Over here, you don't see any girls. All the girls you see are the Vietnamese and they are not my type. I saw a beautiful American girl in a paper and she looked like a girl that I used to go out with named Mary Nardone. I just fell in love with her (infatuation).

Being over here makes you susceptible to becoming infatuated with a woman. You fall in love with the first girl you meet, either on R&R or when you go home. That's why so many of these guys get married on R&R. Like right now: I've been here for 6 months and I'm lonely for a woman's presence, just her being in the same room. I'd just like to sit down and talk all day to a woman because I haven't talked to one for 6 months. I'd like to do other things also but we won't discuss that because it has nothing to do with your problem. Well, Lil, that's all I can say or suggest to you. I hope you did learn a lesson for yourself. Your little brother, Vinnie, alias "Dear Abby." Be a good little girl from now on. Ha Ha Ha.

Excerpt from Vinnie's January 4, 1968 letter to Lilly

The irony of being in the Crotch for a number of weeks or months was that the Marines developed a profound sense of love and respect for each other. Indeed, it was understood that every kid out in the shit would risk his life to save his brother Marine. Vietnam taught these guys a lesson that the civil rights movement back home had been trying to accomplish for the better part of twenty years: to look beyond a fellow American's skin tone and accept him or her as an equal under the law. In Vietnam, the Marines weren't black, white, yellow, or brown to the enemy. Indeed, to the enemy Vietnamese, the Marines were only three colors: red, white, and blue. The Marines learned that their skin color was totally irrelevant to whether they lived or died. Instead, the colors of the flag under which they fought so fiercely made them targets for death. Therefore, the Marines suspended their personal convictions when it came to race and bought into the notion that, at least while the boys were in 'Nam, their race and their creed was the USMC. This belief bonded the brother Marines and inspired them to engage in great feats of bravery for each other.

When Vinnie had first arrived in Vietnam, he couldn't fathom risking his life for a stranger, even if the stranger was a fellow Marine. Now, six months into his tour, he couldn't imagine *not* doing just that if the situation were to call for it. After all, he had witnessed dozens of brother Marines running into a hail of hot artillery just to pick up an injured brother who needed assistance.

Vinnie himself had been involved in one such mission. He joined a team of five Marines that ran down into the jungle one early morning, in the pre-dawn hours, to recover a brother who had been injured at an LP. The radioman who accompanied the injured Marine, initially shaken that his brother Marine had been shot while sitting just a few feet from him, had quickly regained his decorum and gestured to a region of lower ground distal to the LP, to gain the advantage of more obscurity and better cover. He then grabbed his injured brother and together they scrambled to the new, safer location. The radioman, in an intentionally low, muffled voice, informed the platoon over the radio that his partner was injured and he shared their new coordinates.

Vinnie heard that the Marine serving as the lookout had taken at least a round or two in his shoulder, near his chest, and Vinnie recognized that the radioman transmitting this information sounded scared. Vinnie and the rest of his brothers ran toward the coordinates the radioman provided. The men thought it was a sniper hit, which both exhilarated and scared the shit out of Vinnie. He heard the sounds of exploding mortars and weapons firing nearby but, amazingly, Vinnie gave no thought to getting hit. Instead, he was focused only on finding his ambushed brother and getting him out of danger, by any means necessary.

It took Vinnie and the other Marines a long time to travel the relatively short distance of roughly two hundred yards to the LP. *I walked a mile to Edison High School in a fraction of the time that it's taking me to get to these guys,* Vinnie thought as he intermittently ran, crawled, stopped, listened, and slowly jackknifed his way through the bush. *Of course,* he continued as he made his way through thickets of elephant grass, *I didn't have sixty pounds of gear strapped to my body while holding a rifle and trying not to get shot when I was walking up 168 Street to Edison!* Vinnie surprised himself by chuckling silently at his own observation.

Upon arriving at the LP, Vinnie found the radioman pressing a dirty t-shirt against a bloody hole in his partner's upper chest. The kid was wheezing heavily, but the corpsman who accompanied them, the incomparable Doc Nunn, reassured the scared grunt that he'd survive to be with his girl again. The injured Marine, Smitty, a black kid who was barely eighteen, told Vinnie and the other Marines that the shots had come from a single sniper that he believed was perched in a tree roughly one hundred yards to the north. The men coordinated their escape plan while propping up the injured Marine in preparation for their retreat back to the safety of their platoon. Two gunnery sergeants who had accompanied Vinnie and Doc were to cover Vinnie as he and Doc supported the injured Marine on the way back to safety. The Marine who remained with the radioman would also cover their retreat back to the platoon. On the count of three, the two gunnies opened fire on the tree. If they were wrong about the source of Smitty's wounds, they'd all be dead in about three or four seconds.

One of the gunnies shot a grenade from his M-79, which the Marines called a "Blooper" because it made a nondescript *bloop!* sound when it fired, and watched as it sliced through the air in a parabolic trajectory toward the tree. Vinnie mused at how peacefully silent the grenade flitted through pink-and-navy-blue dawn sky—it reminded him of a small beach ball floating through the air—before it detonated with a fury against the targeted tree. Another *bloop!* sound ensued roughly ten seconds later, followed by a second explosion. A third and final *bloop!* pierced the chill of the early morning air ten seconds thereafter, followed by one final, intense explosion.

When the third and final round hit its mark, Vinnie, Doc, the injured Marine, and his fellow lookout all made a beeline for the cover of the jungle. Again, if the boys were wrong about their belief that they were facing a single sniper, then they were dead because there was no way that the injured Marine could duck, dodge, belly crawl, and deftly maneuver through the thicket of tall elephant grass. And Vinnie and his brothers sure as hell were not going to leave their injured brother behind. Vinnie heard a series of cracks. Were they rounds smashing through some nearby bamboo? He could not tell. All he knew was that they had to keep moving forward and hope the two gunnies would catch up. If not, then they'd be circling back to see what had happened.

Minutes later, the two gunnies caught up to Vinnie, Doc, and Smitty.

"They got him!" one of the gunnies exclaimed with a tone of adrenaline-tinged furor that surprised Vinnie.

"Fuck that gook," came a wheeze-filled reply from Smitty, the man with a hole in the front of his upper body, with a smaller version to match on his back. The two gunnies then flanked the four men, one in front and one in back, to act as cover until they all made it safely back to the platoon area.

Once back inside the platoon perimeter, there were a few back slaps and words of gratitude before arrangements were made to get Smitty medevaced the hell out of there. He'd lost a lot of blood, as Vinnie's crimson-tinged flak jacket could attest, and he was getting light-headed and delirious. Doc Nunn gave him as much morphine as the syringe could shoot out and then he added an IV line for good measure. Smitty soon became high as a kite as a result of the morphine and began to mutter about some broad he'd met on R&R a couple of weeks before, back in Sydney. "I'm gonna marry that chick when I get outta the shit!" Smitty stated with loopy conviction.

"Good for you, Smitty. Hey, what's the lucky lady's name?" Vinnie asked.

The injured Marine opened his eyes, his brow curling into a series of maniacal furrows. Finally, after an awkwardly long pause, Smitty exhaled and revealed, "I can't remember her name right now, but I'll never forget that face, or what we did together over R&R. I love her, I tell ya, and she loved me. We said that we were going to get married. Once I get patched the fuck up, I am going right back to Sydney and hooking up with . . . shit, I still can't remember her name . . . and we're going right to the church near her hometown. Yeah, we picked out our church! And we're getting married!"

"Congrats," said Vinnie, "can I be the best man? I hear the broads in Sydney are mighty groovy, and, boy, can they swing! I could use some good lovin' right about now!"

The Marines laughed because they all felt Vinnie's pain. After all, none was older than twenty-two. They all were in their prime, so to speak, and they all were holed up in a hot-and-cold, messy jungle, with the closest women being either in their dreams or in magazine centerfolds that tantalizingly dangled from the makeshift walls of their flimsy hooches. Many of the guys talked publicly in a confident fashion about what they yearned to do with women. In the privacy of their own thoughts, all that a majority of them wanted was a woman to open up to, to share the maddening anxiety, fear, and spontaneous rage that had gripped so many of them during their tours in 'Nam. They desired a woman who would hug them, kiss their foreheads, and tell them that everything was going to be all right. Indeed, these young men missed and fervently desired a very special kind of woman. For many of them, they missed their mamas.

> *Sorry that I haven't written you for a while, but there's not too much to say. I'd like to change my R&R to Sydney, Australia. I hear the chicks in Sydney really swing! Yeah! And they dig on Marines. The guys that went over there said that the broads really treat them good. If I'm not able to change over, it won't really matter as long as I get out of here and will be around some chicks for a while. You know how it is. Ha Ha.*

> *P.S. I miss all of you "Greenies" very much.*

Excerpt from Vinnie's January 19, 1968 letter to Lilly

Shit, Vinnie thought to himself, *Lilly has no freaking idea how it is.* Unless you were experiencing firsthand the insanity that was Vietnam, you had no idea what was going on there. The closest one could get to actually being there was to look at the chilling imagery and reports from embedded reporters, on the nightly news, but even that did not give you a full flavor of experiencing actual combat. Sometimes, Vinnie himself felt that he did not have a full grasp of what was going on in 'Nam, and he was living it! The Marines were government-trained killers and they were expected to annihilate the enemy. Vinnie re-read the line in his letter to Lilly about not having much to say and chuckled disgustedly to himself.

> *Lilly, I've got so much crazy shit about this place that I want to—need to—tell you, but I can't,* he thought. *If I told you everything that I've seen and done over the last few months,* Vinnie mused, *you wouldn't sleep 'til I walked through the front door in August!*

R&R. Other than the word *fuck,* this phrase was the most popular collection of letters amongst the Marines in the bush. In fact, the men talked about R&R almost as much as they talked about girls. Often, R&R and girls were discussed simultaneously because they often coincided. The grunts were ready for their R&R well before the required thirty days in country that established their eligibility. They dreaded going out on recon missions when R&R was imminent, and not because they were afraid of getting killed. Hell, that could happen at any moment. No, they dreaded going on a recon mission because it could interfere with, or eliminate, their R&R altogether. R&R could take place in Hawaii or Sydney, Australia—preferred destinations for many—but often, it was in closer places like Tokyo, Hong Kong, Manila, China Beach, or Bangkok.

Once the boys got their orders for R&R, they were pulled out of the bush. They returned to the base to shower and turned in their weapons and gear. They then were flown to either Tan Son Nhut, Cam Rahn Bay, or Danang, where their jungle fatigues would be checked in before eventually boarding a "freedom bird" —a commercial jet—to their approved R&R location. The men exchanged their MPCs (military payment certificates) for U.S. dollars before those dollars were exchanged for the local currency if they had a foreign destination. The Marines were required to rent civilian clothing from a local service (for a considerable, but returnable, deposit) and an approved hotel room.

The Marines, predictably, sought out female companionship at their R&R locales, and certain places more than accommodated the single, yearning young men. Hong Kong and Bangkok offered women to the Marines as part of a legal service: The Marines entered into contracts with local bars and literally rented women for their time there. Sydney did not offer this type of service, but this destination nonetheless was known amongst the Marines as a place where the ladies wanted to date active servicemen. Vinnie desired Sydney for this very reason, but he instead got R&R orders for Tapei, Taiwan. Initially, he was upset, as he had received so many glowing reports about Oz, but Taipei provided all the spoils that a nineteen-year-old single kid with a lot of downtime and an oppressed libido could ask for. Vinnie met a young lady there named Jo-Jo, who cared for all his needs.

Jo-Jo even spoke broken English, so Vinnie was able to pour out his soul to a woman for the first time since he had left the States. *I don't care if she only understands seventy-five percent of what I'm telling her,* Vinnie thought, *at least she is listening to me.* Saint was amazed at how good it felt to have someone actually listen to him. Vinnie told Jo-Jo about the terrible fear that he had of dying—not because it would mean the end of his life at nineteen but because of how his death would devastate his family. He also told her about all of the death and destruction that he had seen since arriving in Vietnam and how it was giving him occasional panic attacks and fits of anger. Vinnie told her that he couldn't understand why these things were happening and he questioned what he could do to stop them.

In Vinnie's vulnerable state, Jo-Jo was the most wonderfully perfect, loving woman in the world, a sentiment that many of his brother servicemen shared with their own R&R *Jo-Jos.* That's what being in 'Nam did to these young guys: They were so tightly wound that the slightest reprieve from the madness precipitated heights of euphoria that were otherworldly. The men's spirits soared exponentially when the reprieve included female companionship as an added bonus.

*   *   *

Well, I've been back from R&R for 4 days and I'm hurting. I wish that I was back to that good, loving woman. Between you and me, I had everything—and I mean everything—at my fingertips. Whatever I needed, I had. And I had it the way I wanted it. I sure do miss it now.

Things up here are starting to get active. I guess the nice weather brought them out. It hasn't rained in a few weeks now. Richie told me that he got a tape from you. You know, at least fifty guys listen to that tape. So don't act stupid on it or say anything that will embarrass me. Your best bet is to send them prerecorded tapes or just records from the radio. You don't know Marines—you can say something on a tape and they'll twist it around and it will wind up an embarrassing situation. Don't get too friendly with these guys because it's not like it is in the States. He can be dead the next day and it will affect you strongly. But not me, that much, because you get kind of used to it over here. What I'm trying to say, for example: Tommy. Do you get what I mean? So, don't get too friendly, Lil.

I haven't received a package from you in a while. What's wrong: Do you need money for the postage? Ha! Do you get the hints? I remember when I was up at Con Thien, I used to get a package once a week and now it's once a month if I am lucky. Seems like you're worried more about the other guys than your own brother. Ha Ha. Only kidding.

Well, Lil, I got to be going, so take care.

Love, your brother, Vinnie

P.S. Say hello to everyone for me.

Vinnie's February 2, 1968 letter to Lilly

Today I got two letters from you, they were written the 13th and 14th. It was real funny to hear what Mom said about having a girl stay with us for a week. It's true. I had this girl named Jo-Jo. She was 20 but she looked about 17. She was real cute and we enjoyed ourselves. I had her the first night I got to Taipei. During the day, we'd do a little sight-seeing or go shopping downtown. I'd let her handle the money and she wouldn't let anybody try to beat me out of money. She saved me a lot and then, at times, she cost a lot, but I really enjoyed myself. We would all go out to dinner (4 couples) and then go to a night club, or the movies. And the nights. Yeah! I'll enclose a picture of the both of us. And you'd better send it back to me. We just got a couple of new guys today. And I just picked up a pamphlet of Disneyland scenes. It really brings back real nice memories of all the great times that I had while I was at Disneyland. If I get a chance, I'm going to go back to Disneyland when I hit California on my way home from here. You wouldn't believe how beautiful that place is. You should try to visit it on your honeymoon. Did I ever send you pictures of me at Disneyland? If I did, let me know: I'm pretty sure I took three or four rolls of film of Disneyland and sent them home to yous.

I got a letter from John Chang today. He said he got a purple heart in January. I'm glad he only got a small cut in his hand for it. He's really getting short. He has only about 40-50 days left. I got about 155 days left. But it's still going fast for me. I'm sure glad that John is going home soon. When I was on R&R just before I left Da Nang, I met a guy in John's outfit, 1/5, and I asked him if he knew a John Chang. So he said, yeah, I know Doc Chang. And the guy even came from South Jamaica. I found out because he said, "You must come from Jamaica." I said, "Yeah." He then told me he came from South Jamaica. I tried to go and see John but I had only a few hours to go see him and get back and I didn't know where to start and I didn't have any gear, no rifle or helmet. So John was about 20 miles outside Da Nang. I sure wish I could go see him before he leaves. Maybe I might be able to go see him before he leaves. Well, Lil, I got to get some sleep now.

Love, Your Brother

P.S. Don't forget to send the picture back. Also, 2 negatives are enclosed. Give them to Mom and tell her that I forgot to put them in my last letter. The negatives are of me, Bobby J. O'Hare, and Richie Williams.

Undated letter from Vinnie to Lilly

As soon as R&R had begun, it was over, or so it seemed to Saint. *That was the best vacation of my life,* he thought. *When I get out of here, maybe I'll go back for a bit, just to see how Jo-Jo is doing.* Vinnie knew deep down that this was simply a war-induced, hardcore infatuation. *I'll just figure this shit out for sure when I get home after the war and I have plenty of time to hash things out,* he reasoned. Vinnie was proud of himself for having the maturity to postpone making serious, life-altering decisions because the war required one-hundred percent of his attention.

After all, a distracted Marine often was a dead Marine.

Besides, Vinnie thought, *what's the rush? I've got the rest of my life to figure out my future.* Ironically, as Vinnie daydreamed about his wartime infatuation, Jo-Jo, she was back in Taipei, pretending to listen to another serviceman's forlorn war stories while knitting him a special pillow.

Vinnie was happy to write to Lilly about his hometown pal, John Chang. He reminisced about the infamous "corner deli quartet" that would sing every summer day and evening before heading to Vinnie's basement for more innocent shenanigans. John was special to Vinnie, who held him in very high esteem, especially because Saint's parents thought he was a quality person. Carmine and Rose knew John's background and knew how hardworking his parents were, and how much discipline they instilled in their fifteen kids, so they knew that John was a quality young man.

Doc Chang had been in 'Nam for nearly six months by the time that Vinnie arrived and he was hopeful that he'd be able to fulfill a promise that the boyhood chums had made to each other before John left: They'd do everything that they could to see each other if they were in the same general vicinity in Vietnam. There was one caveat, though: The friends weren't allowed to travel to see each other unless they had a combat helmet and a rifle.

"I know we're best pals and all," John innocently said back then, "but I don't love you enough to take a bullet to the head while trying to see you, and you shouldn't, either!" Vinnie shared a hearty laugh with John at that time, but he nonetheless interlocked pinkies with John to complete the sacred pinky-swear on this promise. Now, it could not be broken, lest the boys wanted to willingly commit a sacrilege and defile their friendship.

Vinnie and John Chang wrote multiple letters to each other and these letters were not sanitized. Rather, they were raw, emotional, sickening, and exhilarating. Both John and Vinnie felt a certain sense of relief that they were able to share events and feelings with which both young men could empathize. Vinnie's heart pounded in his chest when he first read that John had received a Purple Heart. Of course, the nausea that instantly followed was alleviated when Vinnie learned of the relatively "minor" nature of John's injuries. He'd taken shrapnel to his left hand as rounds whizzed about him and he rendered aid to an injured brother in the field.

Vinnie wrote to Doc Chang immediately after he read John's letter:

John, you can't afford to get seriously injured so close to your freedom. You're so short that it would be a damn shame if you weren't able to get home as soon as you were able after getting your orders. I hope that we're able to see each other before you leave this hellhole, pal! I just wish I was able to go home with you! Ha Ha!

Love, your brother, Vinnie

*   *   *

The morning after his return from paradise (R&R) brought Saint down from his cloud of euphoria and back to his bleak reality. He had to load up his beat-up jeep that had the terribly loud muffler (*I'll have to fix that soon*, he thought) and get down to the Marines on Cam Lo Hill. Upon arriving there, the men greeting Vinnie like a conquering hero: "Saint's back!," "Hey there, lover boy, you look tanned, rested, and ready!," "Is that jungle rot on your neck, or are you just happy to see me?," "Did you ever get your girl's *last name* or did you figure that it was gonna be Santaniello soon enough?"

Yeah, the boys really had missed Saint! "You buncha miserable assholes," Vinnie good-naturedly chided his brothers, "don't be jealous of my fucking great R&R!"

"Enough about your dream girl, Saint. We all had one of those on R&R! We wanna hear from the real dream girl of Cam Lo Hill: your sister, Lilly!" exclaimed Saint's pal, Richie Williams, who hailed from a rural Pennsylvania town. "Any more tapes from her, man?"

"You're lucky that Lilly likes you, Richie, otherwise I'd punch you square in your face for disrespecting my sister," Vinnie said, without concealing a big smile on his face.

Richie laughed. "Hey, can I help it if your sister has great taste in guys, particularly me?" Lilly knew how sad and lonely the boys were in 'Nam, so, with Vinnie's blessing, she began to record herself singing songs, or simply sharing encouraging thoughts, and mailing them to Vinnie's brother Marines. She had made tapes for Red, Doc Nunn, Doc Milazzo, Richie, Brucie, and Keidinger. In fact, Lilly made a couple of tapes for Tommy, a kid of Irish descent who hailed from Orlando, Florida. Tommy had arrived in the bush on the same day as Vinnie and he became good friends with Saint during their time in country. Tommy had cousins in New York and he and Vinnie agreed to make it a point to meet both in Orlando and New York City after their time in Vietnam, to become acquainted with each other's families.

Tommy wrote a couple of letters to Lilly and even sent her pictures from Vietnam. Many of the pictures contained candid shots of him with Vinnie, each looking tough while holding grenade launchers, or having fun with local Vietnamese kids, or simply looking homesick and ready to leave that Hell behind them. Lilly took a liking to Tommy, and she sent him more letters and tapes than she did to the other Marines. Tommy often climbed a huge tree on Cam Lo Hill that extended up about fifty feet. This tree, which Tommy called "the thinking spot," had a vast number of enormous branches, many of which easily supported the weight of ten to fifteen Marines.

Tommy frequently ascended the tree and sat on one particular branch that extended a good twelve feet above the ground. He dubbed this branch "Tommy's Turf" and he often sat there to "contemplate life," as he put it. This tremendous tree faced a mountain range roughly three hundred yards due east and Vinnie joked that Tommy might as well call the branch "Tommy's Tombstone" and place a bullseye on his chest for the NVA snipers to aim at, because there he was vulnerable to the precise aim of those remote, silent assassins.

Tommy laughed. "Those fuckers have better things to do than shoot a guy just minding his business up in a tree, Saint. Stop being so fucking paranoid."

One evening, Tommy climbed the tree and sat on "Tommy's Turf" to read a letter from Lilly while using a weak penlight. Vinnie and others had yelled at Tommy for using a flashlight while sitting on the tree branch in the past, telling him that he was compromising their position and safety. So, on this evening, the smitten Marine resorted to using a penlight that emitted virtually no glow and therefore would be, in his estimation, a more prudent and safer choice of illumination.

Tommy lost himself in thought as he read about Lilly excitedly writing about meeting Tommy and his family after he and Vinnie came home from Vietnam. *Lilly's one groovy chick*, Tommy thought to himself as he navigated Lilly's carefully crafted cursive. *It sure would be swell to meet this little pistol from New York!*

Tommy then turned his head and inhaled in anticipation of yelling to Vinnie that he was going to marry Lilly, even though she was engaged to some Puerto Rican named Ralph, when a stealthy bullet drastically altered those plans. The round made virtually no sound—it hurtled through the air at a frightening speed—but for a couple of quick, tearing sounds as it sliced through tree leaves on its deadly, unforgiving path to finality. The sniper's round smacked into Tommy's face with such force that it knocked him off the branch and fifteen feet west of its base. The deadly round tore through Tommy's right eye and brain stem, instantly extinguishing the flame of his life right after he read that Lilly could not wait to meet such a good-looking kid from Orlando. Tommy's blood mixed with the ink of Lilly's letter, obscuring her words of hope with the sickening crimson consequences of war.

Vinnie heard a rifle shot from within his hooch, followed by a loud thump and rustling of leaves. *Oh, shit! Oh, no. Oh, no. Oh, no,* Saint thought, with a growing pit of despair in his stomach. He stuck his head out of the hooch and exclaimed in a loud whisper, "Tommy? Tommy? You okay?" No response. *He would've heard me if he was* . . . Vinnie didn't allow himself to complete the thought. Instead, he crawled through the dark, in the direction where he heard the thump. Vinnie suddenly and unexpectedly came upon Tommy's still body.

Saint knew.

Still, he used his hands to feel for Tommy's head and when he encountered it, his hands slipped right off the unseen, slick blood that was pulsating from the small hole that used to be Tommy's right eye. Still, Vinnie got close to Tommy's ear and whispered, "Tommy? Tommy? Fucking shit, Tommy, what did we tell you about this?" Vinnie noticed that Tommy's body was on top of the penlight that he had been using and Vinnie immediately extinguished the sickly glow with a crushing blow from his right fist, for fear that the sniper would be setting his sights on another illuminated fool.

Vinnie knew that Tommy no longer was among the living. He dragged Tommy's body by the shoulders, away from the tree and into his hooch, which was obscured by large rocks and elephant grass. Vinnie then barked out the refrain that made all the grunts cringe: "CORPSMEN UP!"

All Vinnie told Lilly in a letter a few days later was that Tommy had stepped on a land mine one morning and died instantly. It was a necessary, white lie that God surely would forgive.

Lilly cried when she read the letter. She was twenty-one and engaged to be married but she still wasn't that far removed from being an emotional teenager who did not deal well with death. She cried a long time, in her room, for Tommy that night, as she held his picture tight against her chest. A wave of nausea suddenly overcame Lilly as her chest convulsed in repressed sobs. She came to a sickening revelation while mourning Tommy's sad death: She realized that she may never again see her beloved brother alive. The tears flowed even harder and Lilly instantly grabbed her pen and paper and wrote a letter to Vinnie about how much she loved him and how sad she was that Tommy had died.

When Vinnie received Lilly's letter, he noted the irony of it being streaked with tears that had obscured some of her words, much like Tommy's blood had streaked Lilly's letter to him, causing some of those words to become obscured, too. Vinnie had saved Tommy's letter from Lilly because it was the last thing that Tommy was thinking about when he died. Vinnie did not have the heart to destroy that letter. However, he had to warn his sister about getting too close to another Marine.

Marines loved each other and died for each other often, but they were conditioned to repress any feelings of loss when a brother died, lest the mourning grunt allow himself to be distracted, thereby punching a ticket to join his dead comrade in the great beyond.

That's not to say that the Marines weren't affected by the death of a brother. Scores of Marines cried themselves to sleep during the rare times that they could catch more than a catnap here and there. However, in the heat of the battle, a good Marine could not afford to flinch if a brother went down in his presence. You got the body to (relative) safety, because no brother was to be left behind to be violated by the enemy, but you never lost sight of the bigger picture. One of the Marines, Fred Hughes—nicknamed Father Fred because of his devout Catholic beliefs—had Matthew 8:22 inscribed on his helmet: "But Jesus told him, 'Follow me, and let the dead bury their dead.'"

The Marines lived by a derivative of this biblical verse. Many a Marine asked Father Fred what the inscription meant and when he quoted the gospel story to them, no further explanation was required. The boys knew: It was a sobering, yet poignant, reminder of the plight of the Marines in Vietnam.

CHAPTER 7

WAR IS HELL

I've been seeing the guys just about every other day. I'd like to tell you more about my job of driving It may sound nice for me to be in the rear. But the truth is I'm in the rear just to work out of the rear to bring all the supplies and mail, etc. up to Gio Linh.

I'll tell yous all about it when I get home and then it will all be laughed at as the past. You know me.

Well, the guys are all fine I have been spending a couple of nights with them this month. Sometimes I stay overnight to bring someone in the next day. Kilo Co. is not in the field, they are standing lines inside the perimeter of Gio Linh.

The war is getting a little hotter but Kilo Co. hasn't had a KIA (a brother killed in action) since Con Thien. That's almost 6 months. We're a lucky company, so don't worry about me or the boys too much. I know someone has been praying for us. The Marines have been making a lot more contact with the enemy than usual because the heavy rains have gone. Now it's easier for them (the NVA) to move their troops. Well, all I can say is WAR IS HELL.

Listen, do me a favor: Tell Mom not to worry too much about me. And don't aggravate her or make her worry. You know how mothers can be. They worry about the least little shit imaginable. Do your best to make things easier on her, like help her with her work once in a while.

I sent mom a few dollars to buy herself something for her birthday. You know Mom will try to sneak it into my bank account. You tell her that I would feel really bad if she didn't get herself something.

I sure wish I remembered her birthday was in Feb. while I was on R&R but it never really came to my mind. Don't forget to tell her it would really hurt me if she didn't spend the money on herself.

I'm finished helping out your problems. For all I care, you can write or date every guy in the 3rd Marines Division. You'd probably fall in love with every one of them. You're so stupid. Ha Ha. Well, that's a girl for you. Can't make up her mind.

Take care and please do what I said about helping Mom out. You're a doll and I love you even though you're still a little girl. Ha, ha.

P.S. Happy Valentine's Day, Sis. I got your card, thanks . . .
K CO *is the same as if you say* Kilo Co.

*   *   *

"The last couple of nights on Cam Lo Hill have been close calls," Corporal "Red" Reagan exclaimed. He had seen his share of death since coming to 'Nam in March 1967.

"Fuck yeah," said Doc Nunn, "I've seen more death and pain than anyone should have to see in *three* fucking lifetimes, much less a single tour in this shithole." Doc bristled at his words, not realizing their profundity.

"Hey, Doc, do you know why I draw so much?" asked Red.

"Uh, 'cause you're hoping to get a fucking internship with Michaelangelo?"

Mike Reagan laughed at his pal's chutzpah. "You crazy sonofabitch. I paint because it brings me peace, man. This place,"

Mike then gestured outward with his right arm, pencil clenched between his magical fingers, "is crazy. We don't know what the fuck we're fighting for. We get crazy orders that make no fucking sense, but we have to follow them so that we don't get court-martialed. We kill the fucking gooks, they kill some of us, we take a hill, fortify it, and then leave to take another hill, only to have to fend off gooks that are firing at us from the very hill that we fortified so damn well. How is that for a kick in the ass, huh? I get so damn angry when I think about all this, but my art helps me exhale, man. It's like the pent-up anger and fucking frustration escapes through the fingers of my right hand as I draw something, anything. I feel so at ease with a pencil in my hand and a sheet of paper in front of me, Doc. As wrong as this fucking war seems at times, drawing and creating art feels so right to me."

"That was pretty deep, Red, but war is fucking Hell, brother. It ain't a fucking art class, Mike. Your drawings are damn good and I'm sure that your art will find a purpose once you're back in the world. I betcha that you'll touch a lot of lives with that amazing hand of yours one day, man, but for now, how's about we make sure that you don't catch a mortar in your goddamn forehead because you're too busy drawing fucking lagoons and shit, huh?"

"You're a regular Socrates, Doc, you know that?" Red chuckled, balled up a piece of paper and aimed at Doc. "Incoming, you goddamn squid!" Red mimicked tossing a grenade at Doc by hurling the balled-up paper in his direction. The paper struck Doc in the forehead. "BOOM!" exclaimed Mike in an exaggerated tone. "Don't mess with artists, Doc, we never miss our mark!"

Vinnie entered the hooch where Doc and Mike were chatting as Mike threw the paper at Doc. "Red's right, Doc. He took out at least half the gooks' platoon last night with a handful of frags. He had the golden touch . . . them gooks didn't stand a chance!"

Mike gave Vinnie a pained smile; he knew that he had had no choice but to kill the NVA who were holed up in a trench that he and his fellow Marines had dug a few weeks earlier, only to abandon it on orders from the bosses so that they could take another hill. Red knew the intricacy with which the Marines had dug that specific trench. It was a work of art, pun fully intended. Of course, you don't need to be very careful in destroying good art. All it takes is a couple of grenades, good aim, and a little luck. Mike had had all of those in spades during the battle the previous evening.

Mike's platoon got orders to take a specific hill, one that they had fortified and defended six weeks earlier. That was the norm for the grunts in 'Nam: The war was a battle of contradictions. The men would risk death, and many would get injured and maimed, all in the name of defending a piece of land in the middle of the jungle, only to be told to leave that hill and move on to another, equally useless hill, and fortify it to the hilt with barbed wire, mines, and fortified trenches.

War, indeed, is Hell. But, oftentimes, it is just fucking stupid.

Mike and the boys in the platoon were dismayed at the order to re-take the hill. They all agreed that they would not have done such an amazing job fortifying it so expertly if they knew they were doing it for the benefit of the enemy. They also knew that the NVA would be dug in and protected while they were like sitting ducks at the base of the hill. It made no sense, but they were Marines. As such, they would never accept failure as even a remote possibility. What was impossible for mere mortals was not only possible, it was *expected, goddamn it*, of the Corps.

The plan was to storm the hill at 0200 hours. Mike would lead a group of twenty-five men to the southern edge of the hill, while Keidinger directed another group of twenty Marines on the western front of the hill. Doc Nunn accompanied Mike's men while Doc Milazzo accompanied Keidinger's crew. Bravo Company was humping through the jungle to join Red's and Keidinger's men and they were expected to arrive by 2300 hours. Their mission was to take out the eastern portion of the hill. The men had the advantage of knowing that no trenches, mines, or barbed wire were located on the northern region of the hill because it was too steep and dangerous to have men placed on it, but they also figured that the gooks would try to dee-dee the hell off the hill on the northern slope, so ten men would be stationed there to take out the fleeing NVA. The leadership of this mission believed that the hill had roughly forty to fifty enemies in the trenches. If their estimates were off, then the Marines stood to take quite a hit because, while they were well-armed and equipped with a knowledge of how the hill was defended, they still were very exposed compared to the dug-in NVA. If the Marines were right about the estimated enemy on the hill, then they would be able to call the hill home again.

The Marines were ready to roll out through the jungle to prepare for what they expected to be a nasty fight with the enemy. A reflective air of apprehension permeated the boys in their hooches. More than a few of the grunts quietly questioned whether this would be their last night alive. Dozens of the Marines took the quiet time before beginning the latest mission to write letters to moms and girlfriends. In a few weeks, dozens of families would receive letters filled with more *I love you*s then they'd ever received in the past. It made more than a few parents feel a sense of dread and a small minority of them, unfortunately, would have that dread realized.

As Vinnie sat in the hooch, he was torn. The skipper said that as the company driver (and mechanic), and as a result of his asthma, he could stay in the rear and avoid this mission, as it had the distinct possibility of being a bloody conflict. There was a significant part of the young Marine that wanted to accept the offer to stay back and stay safe. In fact, he yearned for that opportunity. *How many other guys wouldn't take the skipper up on that offer?* Saint reasoned to himself. Vinnie actually rose from his rubber lady and began to walk to the skipper's hooch to advise him that he was going to accept the offer to stay behind. However, as he walked along the jungle floor toward the skipper, he overheard a distinct mumble emanating from the hooch to his left. Vinnie silently peered in and observed his friend, Williamson, kneeling at the foot of his mattress, eyes moist and shut tight, aggressively kneading the rosary beads that adorned his hands. The kid was repeating the litany of *Our Fathers*, *Hail Marys*, and *Glory Be*s that is required when praying the rosary. Vinnie reversed his course, returned to his hooch, sat on his mattress, opened his pack to remove some paper and a pen, and began to write.

Dear Ma and Pop,

First of all, everything is swell here. Me and the boys all are fine and wondering what all the fuss is back home about what's going on here in 'Nam. I just want you all to know how much I love you and how much I can't wait to see yous all when I get home at the end of the summer. Mama, I want you to cook me the biggest dish of your famous spaghetti and meatballs when I get home, OK?

Vinnie was joining his brothers to retake the hill. He loved his family, but he had an obligation to his brothers here, like Williamson, and he couldn't bear staying behind while they were risking their necks for him.

"Hey, Mike, you ready?"

Red turned to his questioner and was surprised to see that it was Saint. "I thought you were supposed to be in the rear. Why are you down here in this shit, Saint?"

Holding the gold crucifix that hung from the thin gold chain around his neck, Vinnie stated in a solemn tone, "I got my good-luck cross on, Mike, I ain't gonna get hit with it on. Besides, I didn't want yous guys havin' all the fun without me here!"

"Just stay low and don't get hit, Saint. Who the hell else is going to deliver our letters from the world if you ain't here to give them to us?"

With that, Red and Saint heard the radio transmission that confirmed that Bravo Co. was in position. It was time. Red and Keidinger looked at the maps one last time to ensure that they had the coordinates memorized. The teams then went over the different hand signals and code words that would be transmitted over the radios just in case they had to engage the enemy. A few *Our Fathers* and dozens of *Hail Marys* later, and after the order to proceed with the mission was issued by the platoon commander via the company commander and the senior NCOs, the men were ready to set out in the dark, through the jungle, ready to kill if necessary, all for the good of taking back a hill that they called home a few weeks earlier.

The NCOs first ran through a litany of checks, including ensuring that magazines were locked and loaded, the men were wearing their helmets, canteens were topped off, all necessary equipment was accounted for, and—the all-important check—making certain that the men taped down any metal, to ensure that superfluous noise was minimized as best as possible.

Once the NCOs completed their checks, Vinnie went out with Mike's team while Keidinger and his boys began the hump through the high elephant grass to get to their position in time for the coordinated strike. The third arm of this squad, comprised of men from Bravo and Kilo companies, began their slow march onto the hill, from multiple sides of the hill. The boys had to walk slowly and methodically through the jungle. Any misstep could set off a mine or some other booby trap, and then the boys would be ambushed. Of course, the company had men remaining at the bases of the hills, responsible for the company's mortars in case a firefight with the enemy ensued. These men were prepared to respond in kind with a barrage of heavy artillery if needed. Additionally, the bases of the hills were fortified with men armed with M-60 machine guns to supplement the mortars.

Johnny Jones, nicknamed Johnny Bravo, was the point man for Mike's team. The point man was responsible for leading a column of Marines on a mission. It was known to make even the bravest Marine squirm: The assignment not only meant that he was responsible for notifying the men behind him of possible dangers ahead, but it also meant that he'd be the first one hit in a firefight.

Johnny Bravo never shied away from this responsibility. He reveled in the role, as crazy as that sounded. Keidinger's point man, Ronald Nicholson, a short, light-skinned black eighteen-year-old from Minnesota, was a reticent fellow who was generally quiet and shy but was an accomplished musician. When he played his guitar for the men, he morphed into another character altogether. The boys joked that the short, unassuming kid turned into a right-handed version of Jimi Hendrix when he played his guitar. Indeed, the kid was a prodigy on the instrument. It was as if the guitar became an extension of his own body when he played it. One night, around Christmas, Nicholson took out his guitar and began performing "Purple Haze," a single from the popular Hendrix album, *Are You Experienced.* The opening riff stopped the boys in their tracks; the funk literally dripped from Ronald's fingertips.

"That's the theme of this fucking war, Nicholson!"

"Sing that groovy funk, Ronnie," came another appreciative grunt.

*　　　*　　　*

It was 0130 hours. Vinnie thought to himself that it felt like they had been walking for dozens of miles but, in reality, they had only gone a little less than a mile. They took deliberate steps and plenty of pauses. The men had dozens of pounds of ammo and gear on their backs, yet they were expected not to make much more noise than a small lizard traipsing through the jungle. The jungle was dark and quiet at night. Too quiet to expect the Marines to be so damn quiet, thought Vinnie.

Like many Marines that night, Vinnie was very aware of his breathing. *Am I breathing too heavily? Will the gooks hear my breathing and open up on us? What if my breathing is the reason why parents back home hafta bury their sons?* Fear and paranoia had no bounds in Vietnam.

Vinnie's thoughts were interrupted by a signal coming down the column of men from Johnny Bravo and instantly, like a chain of human dominoes, the line of Marines began to quietly descend onto their bellies, with their M-16s positioned at the ready. Vinnie gulped and thought of Lilly as he steadied his rifle ahead of him. He began to think that he should've stayed in the rear—he felt some difficulty breathing and he wasn't sure if it was his asthma acting up or simply his nerves acting up. The thought was fleeting, though, because Vinnie understood the mantra that a distracted Marine was a dead Marine.

On the night of the planned ambush, Nicholson led Keidinger's team out to the hill and his column of men followed him, en route to the base of the hill. The radio man for Keidinger's team overheard the progress of the other three teams and he learned that Bravo Co. was making slow, but steady, progress to their station. The path to the western base was about one-and-a-quarter miles and Keidinger and the squad believed that it would take the column of men roughly two-and-a-half hours to traverse that small distance through the thicket of jungle and suffocating pitch blackness. Ronald had to rely on his senses of hearing and smell as he led the group of men through the tall elephant grass. At one point, he thought that he may have heard something. Was it an NVA sniper? A patrol from the other side? A tiger? One of his own men behind him? A figment of his imagination? Nicholson wasn't sure, but he did what he was trained to do and signaled to those behind him to hit the deck, which they all did.

Seconds passed, and nothing happened, so Nicholson gave the signal to get up and continue. The fallen dominoes resumed their vertical positions and stepped forward, carefully and deliberately. It was 0145 hours. Keidinger knew from the radio that Bravo Co. and Red's teams were in position to begin the assault and they were awaiting confirmation that the other two teams were in place. Nicholson felt a bead of sweat begin its slow descent down the side of his head, around his mouth and through the stubble on his chin. Suddenly, he heard a sudden creak some distance ahead of him, followed by what sure as hell sounded like muffled breathing.

The boys were very close to their final destination when all hell broke loose.

Nicholson smelled the malodorous scent of unwashed flesh and instantly he knew: They were walking into an ambush and he began the rudimentary process of notifying the men behind him of his observation by tugging three times on the thick nylon cord that connected him to the man behind him. However, before the message could be conveyed, he heard the sickening sound of metal clanging against rock and hardened mud.

Ronald screamed, "GRENADE TO THE LEFT!"

And with that, he dove to his right, blindly clawing ahead of himself for any cover that he could find as he crab-walked as quickly as he could to avoid what he knew was about to fill the air in a matter of seconds.

Nicholson found a ditch and burrowed his head as far into the mud as possible. The deafening explosion that followed sent a wave of heat over him with a loud *WHOOSH!* The men stationed strategically at the bases of the hills opened up on a precise region of the hill with their M-60s, as the NCO had instructed earlier. The men knew from their own history on that hill where the enemy would be dug in and they knew from their maps and planning coordinates where the enemy was in relation to their position. That is where they sent their M-16s, M-60s, and mortars.

The artillery fire sounded like sheer chaos, but the men discharged their weapons in accordance with the superiors' orders and the NCO's plan. Nicholson resurfaced from his muddy fortress and realized that all he had was a small hole in his left leg: A superficial shrapnel wound that burned like hell but one that wouldn't debilitate him. Bloodied, but unbowed, he opened up with his M-16 on the area where he sensed the NVA point ran for cover.

Bullets were flashing through the thicket of jungle all around Keidinger's team. One kid caught a round square in his lower leg and he fell in a pained heap.

"CORPSMAN UP!"

And, just like that, Milazzo sprang into action. Like a superhero in a familiar comic book, only without the cape and bulletproof skin, off he ran toward the sound of the screaming Marine. Milazzo felt the heat of the unseen rounds whizzing about his head as he crouched and ran faster than any human being should be able to. He stumbled upon the injured warrior and immediately placed a towel in his mouth so that the Marine could bite down on it, in an effort to stifle his screams of pain, before the corpsman began to tend to the young man's wounds.

Milazzo, barely twenty, refused to allow his mind to wander, refused to consider the notion that a bullet could find its mark between the intersecting lines that made up the crucifix on his helmet and could end it right then and there. He had an injured brother who needed his help. Therefore, his own silent, internal cries for help would have to wait for another day. Did he ever get used to having to try to push intestines back into a cavity that extended clear through a man's body? Well, no, but that image simply got shoved back into the dark recesses of his psyche, a debt to be repaid well into the future, if it would be repaid at all.

The NCO called in coordinates for an airstrike and, within minutes, the men on the hill felt and heard the forceful thumping of approaching choppers, ready to unload all sorts of hellfire from above. Red's team hit the dirt as incoming rockets swooped down from not-so-high in the sky. The Huey gunship unloaded its machine guns and twenty-millimeter cannons on the southern side of the hill. The night sky was illuminated in a rather shocking array of reds and yellows as the deployed armament greeted the Earth and any unlucky inhabitants in the target zone.

Mike gave thanks that the fog, which had seemed omnipresent for the last month, actually lifted earlier that evening, which allowed the gunners aboard the Hueys to visualize the Marines' illumination flares, as well as the direction of the Marines' heavy artillery that was striking down below to complete their mission. Johnny Bravo barely waited for the soot to settle back down to the battle-scarred, weary Earth before he began his own assault on the hill. Johnny knew that the Hueys' hellfire may have softened the NVA entrenched on the hill, but it would not have taken them out completely. That was the Marines' job. Johnny sprang into action because he surmised that the enemy soon would load up their .51-caliber machine guns in an effort to shoot the punishing Huey out of the sky.

Johnny sprinted forward and began to ascend the southern terrain of the hill. Red and his team followed closely behind. The competing cacophony of automatic machine-gun fire—the *pop pop pop!* of the Marines' M-16s versus the distinctly different *crack crack crack!* sound of the NVA's AK-47s—rang in Red's ears as he continued running toward the fortified southern range of the Marines' old hill. Mike's eyes were open as wide as an owl's as he moved forward in accordance with the NCO's plan and pursuant to his memory of what the hill looked like on this side. *If the gooks changed up the terrain*, he thought, *I'm gonna run right into my death.* Yet, he continued to run toward where he remembered the trenches were located.

Vinnie and a number of others remained at the hill's southern base, as per their orders that night. They were positioned behind a rock that protruded rudely from the trampled grass and crushed bamboo at their feet. The rock resembled a huge middle finger, as if Mother Nature was not-so-subtlety flipping off the warriors who were wreaking as much havoc on her greenery as they were on each other. Their orders were to take out any NVA soldier they saw on the side of the hill, or any that were trying to dee-dee away.

Shit, if I told Lilly about what I'm doing, she'd lose her mind. And forget about Mama! Vinnie forced those uncomfortable thoughts out of his mind and focused solely on the task at hand. Ironically (or was it pathetically sad?), the thoughts of his mission to kill brought him more solace than thoughts of his own family.

The radios crackled with screaming requests for, and transmissions of, updates, as well as with the feedback from rockets, mortars, artillery and rifle rounds whizzing all over that hill like it was the Fourth of July. Seconds elapsed into minutes as the firefight continued. The NVA had roughly thirty men positioned on the hill, so the Marines' estimate had been a little light. Keidinger's and Nicholson's teams, although caught by an ambush, recovered quickly and began to get the upper hand on the enemy despite the less-than-auspicious start to their mission. The Marines on the northern side of the hill completely surprised the fleeing NVA troops and massacred them while they futilely sought refuge.

"Picking off dee-dees on night-night. Over!"

"Loco Cocoa, Kilo Two. Over!"

Vinnie heard Mike say over the radio that he saw a few NVA disappear on the side of the hill where he recalled building some elaborate trenches that twisted around the tree roots that looped in and out of the Earth like a subterranean snake.

"I'm gonna frag them, clear the area. Over!" Mike's voice came over the radio full of piss and vinegar. Mike ran up to a tree into which he remembered having carved some crude drawings, pulled the pins from three M- 26s that were clipped to his utility belt, and flung them purposely with his magical right hand, up and over his shoulder in rapid succession, like very high hook shots in basketball. Mike was aiming for the trenches that he believed were roughly twenty feet above him and a few feet inland, along the ledge of the hill.

If I can just land one in that trench, it should take out the guys that ran into it. If I'm really lucky, I'll get one in there and another one to rattle around, close to the other trench that we built to house some ammo, he thought. Mike knew that if he failed with his M-26s, then the boys behind him were likely to take significant casualties. The NVA were fairly well fortified up in their hill. None of the three frags came rolling back down at Red, which he took as a moral victory. *At least the fucking frags are heading in the right direction*, he thought. Six seconds after lobbing the third and final grenade, Mike pressed his head against the tree, closed his eyes tight, gritted his teeth, and waited for the crescendo of sound and fury to commence as he rapidly uttered a *Hail Mary.*

The first explosion startled Vinnie. He expected the second and third in rapid succession based upon Mike's radio man's warning that Red had tossed three frags up the side of the hill, but the third blast was a sound that Vinnie had not heard since he landed in 'Nam.

"What the fuck was *that*?!" he exclaimed.

A torrent of gravel rained down on Mike's helmet, although the thuds upon the steel dome were inaudible to Mike because the ringing in his ears intensified with each of the three blasts. The concussion of the third blast knocked Mike from the safety of his tree and about ten feet beyond the perimeter that was set up at the southern base of the besieged hill. Mike lay there, temporarily stunned and unable to move, before he regained his bearings and moved, albeit in an uncoordinated fashion.

Keidinger came over the radio, "Kilo Five, this is Kilo Two, what the fuck just went boom up there? I didn't know we called in a B52 mission, over." Bravo Company radioed a similar query, as did the men that were based strategically on the northern side of the hill: "The Charlies stopped coming over the side of the hill after that last blast. Anyone reading this? Over."

Finally, Mike's radio man handed the radio to Mike and he slurred the following: "Fucking ammo dump . . . I fragged their ammo dump. Over."

Everything got real quiet after Mike threw the three grenades up the southern side of the hill. One grenade had landed in the trench that he had helped dig, which could hold five to six Marines. It contained then eight NVA soldiers who were so badly shredded by the concussive blast of the first grenade that it was impossible to discern where one body ended and the next began. A fleeing NVA soldier had inadvertently kicked the second grenade as it bounced along the hill, which propelled it another fifteen yards toward the eastern perimeter of the hill before it detonated in the midst of three other filled trenches, killing four NVA soldiers and grievously injuring a handful of others. The third grenade had struck a tree and rolled into the trench that served as the NVA platoon's ammo dump. The explosive force of the resulting blast killed scores of enemy soldiers and perforated a few eardrums among Mike's comrades.

When the sun rose over the hill a few hours later, the carnage was apparent. Three Marines had made the ultimate sacrifice and five others were injured. But the NVA was wiped off that hill, due to the well-coordinated efforts of the grunts and some incredible bravery, luck, and ridiculous precision by the artist himself, Mike "Red" Reagan.

The Marines had re-taken the hill, but there was no celebrating. They had to retrieve the bodies of their fallen brothers and bring them to the makeshift LZ, where they would be met by Nicholson and the rest of the injured Marines and be medevaced out of Hell. Doc Nunn stumbled upon the LZ, covered in the blood of one of the boys who had had a mortar take out a third of his body. Doc shrugged his shoulders, sighed heavily, looked at Saint and Mike with a melancholy gaze and murmured loud enough for them to hear, "War . . . is fucking Hell." Vinnie nodded and then felt something suddenly grab at his neck.

"Shit," he exclaimed as the gold chain and crucifix slid down his chest, "my good-luck cross broke."

CHAPTER 8

LIVING IN
THE MOMENT
IN VIETNAM

Right now, we're listening to Hanoi Hannah on the radio. Man, she is a real nut. She talks so much and it's all bullshit. It's a real goof to listen to. Well, the company moved from Gio Linh yesterday. The 3rd platoon is here in Dong Ha right now. The 1st and 3rd platoons are standing lines at a compound about 2 miles from here: It's just off Highway 9.

Lil, I want you to do me a favor. I am enclosing my cross and chain. It broke on me. I want to have another clasp put on it and also have the cross put back on the chain. Tell him to reinforce where the clasp and chain connect. (1) Have the links replaced or tightened. (2) Have the clasp replaced. (3) Have the cross put back on the chain. The condition of it looks like it went through a war. But the fact is, it did. No lie. I want you to have it repaired and send it back to me as soon as possible. This cross means a lot to me, it saved my life many times. So send it back as soon as possible. I really appreciate you doing this for me.

Well, Lil, I got to be going now. So take care, and congratulations, Sis.

Love, your brother, Vinnie

P.S. PLEASE send the cross back as soon as possible. Love You, Sis.

Vinnie's February 24, 1968 letter to Lilly

W hen one is compelled to live not in the moment but in the nanosecond, it's amazing what becomes important to a young combatant. Some kids kept pictures of their moms, girlfriends, or other loved ones in the pockets of shirts or flak jackets or secured in helmets. Others would sew special pockets in their shirts to keep a letter from a loved one over their hearts, and still others would carve loved ones' names into their weapons. Vinnie was no different. He knew that he could be snuffed out at any second, a world away from the people who loved him and whom he loved back. So, in order to help him keep his sanity, he, too, needed something that would give him the belief that he would survive this nanosecond and then the next. That was his golden crucifix and chain.

Vinnie was raised as a Catholic and, while he may not have been devoutly religious, he spent a little less than half of his life—eight years, to be exact—in Catholic schooling, so the vitality of Jesus Christ was something that resonated within him deeply. Thus, the symbolism of the crucifix, which embodied the notion that Jesus voluntarily subjected himself to terrible suffering, torture, pain, and a grisly death, all for the sake of those who believed, was quite compelling to a young Catholic thrust into the epicenter of cruel suffering. Vinnie really came to believe that the cross around his neck was a magical, mystical protector that could protect him from the horrific death that he had seen befall so many brothers and enemies alike. He needed the cross back and the only person he trusted to repair it and send it back pronto before he died without it was his beloved Lilly.

One warm Sunday morning in late February, Vinnie, Milazzo, Nunn, Reagan, and a few others gathered around their makeshift breakfast table: a massive, charred, and jagged rock that somehow had a relatively flat surface. While eating some concoction out of C-rat cans and drinking instant coffee that was very unlike the heavenly Chock full o'Nuts coffee from back home, they tuned in to Armed Forces radio to try to get a little taste of back home. Instead, they had the pleasure of tuning into Hanoi Hannah.

> *How are you, GI Joes? It seems to me that most of you are poorly informed about the goings of the war, to say nothing about a correct explanation about your presence over here. Nothing is more confused than to be ordered into a war to die, or to be maimed for life, without the faintest idea of knowing of what is going on. Isn't it clear that the war-makers are damning your lives while pocketing huge profits?* [1]

This wasn't what the Marines wanted to hear just a few hours after a terribly bloody battle with the NVA over a goddamn hill in the middle of the fucking jungle. Some of the Marines wondered if Hanoi Hannah wasn't just some North Vietnamese propagandist trying to mess with them but, instead, was actually the voice of reason. Freaking propaganda machine in the North. It was having an impact on some of the Marines' self-esteem, even if they didn't want to admit it. And you know what they say: A chain is only as strong as its weakest link. Well, some of the links in the chain of Marines were withering under the duress of the war.

The youthful American warriors who were deep in the shit heard about the vitriolic backlash from back home regarding their valiant war efforts, especially as it pertained to the controversial Tet Offensive, a recent, bloody skirmish that weighed heavily upon the psyches of the Vietnamese and Americans alike. Indeed, the young men heard the stories from loved ones back home, as well as from the relentless North Vietnamese propaganda machine that infiltrated the Armed Forces' collective efforts to stymie it. The deleterious effects of such psychological warfare actually had a more compelling impact upon the young men than the physical

---

[1] ThatVoiceAgain. "Hanoi Hannah." Film date: unknown. YouTube video, Duration: 4:56. https://youtu.be/-dFqGz_fXgE

toll that this bloody war exacted upon their bodies. It fostered sentiments of self-loathing and doubt in the hearts and minds of an alarming number of American combatants. Sadly, the negative reactions to the U.S. efforts in Vietnam resonated in the ears of stressed, mentally and physically fatigued young warriors.

Vinnie,

Hanoi Hannah is saying some really terrible things about what you guys are doing over there. I know it's not true, but all we see on TV are terrible scenes from over there and she's saying that our military is killing women and children over there without a care. I just wish you were home already, Vin, and away from all of the craziness. Promise me that you are safe and that you are not killing little kids, OK?

Vinnie cried for a good ten minutes after reading this note from his beloved Lilly. He reminisced about the advice that Doc Milazzo had given him regarding the manner in which he was to write home. He had to sanitize his letters' content and not let his family know the true horrors of the war, lest they worry themselves to an early grave, and he knew that he'd have to tailor the narrative. He'd tell Lilly that Hanoi Hannah was nothing more than a raving kook, talking shit to turn the world against what the Marines were doing here. And he mentioned nothing of the free-fire zones or the sheer terror that he felt about the feeling that Hannah just may have been telling the truth about the *war-makers*.

"Hey, Red, you're getting mighty short, ain'tcha?"

Mike turned to Vinnie and said, "Yeah, I get to go home in April."

Vinnie digested Red's statement, pondering the fact that he had to stay in Vietnam until November. He sighed with longing and dread. "Wow, that's pretty swell that you get to go home in just a few weeks, Mike. I wish I was going home in April, too."

Red chuckled. "This place'll do that to you, Saint. But, just remember: You're going home to a good family. You have good people at home who love you and will protect you from all the bullshit that's being said about us back home. They'll help you move on from the craziness that you've seen and experienced here and they'll help you forget about 'Nam."

Vinnie whistled long and loud before exclaiming, "Red, the only thing that'll make me forget about this godforsaken place is death itself and even then I'm afraid that I'll have nightmares in Heaven about the shit that we've gone through here!"

"Well, then I guess that neither of us is gonna forget about this shit because we're both going home, Saint. We're both getting the hell out of here, pal."

Vinnie picked up some tools to fix his jeep for the umpteenth time since he had begun driving it to and from Dong Ha H&S. He turned again to Mike, "What do you want to do when you get home, Red?"

"Dunno, Saint. I really like to draw, so maybe I'll use the GI Bill to enroll in art school and try to put my ability to good use back home in Edmonds."

"What is Washington State like, Mike?" Other than his time in the service, Vinnie had never traveled outside of New York and New Jersey, and Vietnam made him curious about what the rest of the world looked like.

"Well, I'd imagine that it's nothing that you're used to seeing, city boy!" Mike chuckled. "There's lots of trees and open spaces, fresh air and lots of the Northern Pacific to enjoy! It does rain a lot where I live, but you get used to doing stuff in the rain and the sound of the rainfall is very relaxing."

It rained a lot in Vietnam during the torrential monsoon season that had just ended. Vinnie and Mike looked at each other after the latter remarked on the peaceful nature of the rainfall in the Great Northwestern U.S.A. and laughed without saying a word.

They laughed because they both realized how much the monsoon rains here stressed them out—the loud rain drowned out the sound of the tubing that acted as an unintentional warning signal of incoming mortars. Your ears often were your best friends in Vietnam because the sounds of the jungle, both natural and man-made, often were harbingers of things to come, and sometimes those things came very fast and with lethal intentions, so every second counted. Often, the difference between living and dying was contingent on one's ability to hear and react. Loud noises, like sheets of falling rain, obscured the sounds of the jungle and eliminated valuable seconds of reaction time.

"You know what the grooviest thing about living in Washington is, Saint?" Vinnie glanced up at Mike and hunched his shoulders upwards, in an *I dunno* gesture. "You can drive to Alaska in less than a day!" Vinnie's eyes widened. He remembered when Alaska became a state just six years earlier, when he learned as a seventh-grader at Presentation of the Blessed Virgin Mary that Alaska was closer to the Soviet Union than it was to the continental United States. Vinnie recalled how he marveled at that fact in school and he asked his teacher, Sister Mary Louise, how long it would take to get to Alaska. He remembered the nun's playful response, "Oh, Vincent, Alaska is too far to even think of ever visiting. The closest that you'll ever get to Alaska is in your textbook, young man."

And now, just a few years removed from the docile nature of that classroom, Vinnie was standing in a jungle in Vietnam, more than eight thousand miles away from that Jamaica, Queens parochial school, and he was talking to a buddy who just told him that he could *drive* to Alaska from his home in Washington in less than a single day. Wow!

Saint turned to Mike and said, "What're you gonna tell me next, Red, that you can drive to Santa in the North Pole, too?"

"Well, now that you mention it," said Mike, "I've been to North Pole, Alaska a couple of times, and it's set up as Christmas all year round."

Vinnie feigned throwing a socket wrench at Mike and laughed heartily. "Stop shitting me, Red. Do you think that I'm a gullible fool from Kansas or something?"

Mike rolled his eyes and sighed. "Nope, you sure ain't a gullible fool from Kansas, Saint. You're just an ignoramus from New York who thinks if it ain't in the big, bad city, then it doesn't exist. Tell ya what, when you get home, give me a call, and I'll get you out to Edmonds one day. We'll hop in my car and head up the coast, through Canada and into Alaska. And you can get your mama and Lilly a nice Christmas souvenir from North Pole, Alaska."

Sonofabitch, thought Vinnie, *there really must be a North Pole in Alaska*. "Yeah, well, when I get home, I'm gonna go straight to the public library and check the Encyclopedia Britannica to see if you're shitting me. And if you are, I'm gonna visit you in Edmonds just to kick your lying ass!"

*   *   *

A couple of weeks had passed since Vinnie wrote to Lilly about his lucky cross and she had yet to return it to him in repaired condition. War can have peculiar effects on even the strongest people, mentally and physically, and Vinnie was not impervious to the nerve-wracking nature of combat. Saint was never the superstitious type back in the world, but now, alone in the jungle and constantly combatting the sickening thought that every breath could be his last, Vinnie resorted to every trick in the book to maintain a positive outlook. If that meant that he had to believe in a lucky cross to heighten his chances of surviving this second, and the next, then dammit, that's what he'd do.

Vinnie looked around the platoon and realized—for the first time, amazingly—how many of the guys who were either in country when he had landed or had arrived with him were no longer there with him. Wistfully, Saint reviewed the names and faces of the last seven months in his mind and, much to his dismay, realized that he was one of the more senior grunts in 'Nam. Vinnie reminisced on his time in the shit, particularly his time in Con Thien and the Tet Offensive, and concluded that he was lucky to be alive. *Musta been the cross*, Saint concluded.

His mind then wandered to that hurtful, desolate place that he tried like hell to shun, but it was unavoidable: Vinnie thought about all the guys who he'd seen grotesquely maimed and killed. Saint had seen more unfathomable injuries and killings over the last seven months than he had anticipated when he was back in boot camp. And the instructors had told the grunts in training back then to expect to see a lot of death. Vinnie began to rattle off the names of the KIAs and the injured that he knew personally.

It took Vinnie roughly eight minutes to complete naming the brothers who did not get to leave Vietnam on their own terms. And it took him almost twenty minutes to stop crying. *Semper Fi.*

"Hey, Milazzo, c'mere for a sec."

Doc Milazzo sauntered over to Vinnie, expecting him to good-naturedly make a blue joke about their mutual Italian ancestry, as Vinnie was a relentless kidder with an acerbic wit.

"Okay, Saint, what do you have in store for me today?"

Vinnie cast a bewildered glance at Milazzo, as his mood was somber and far removed from the jovial Vinnie to whom Doc was accustomed. He did not comprehend that Milazzo was setting himself up for the typically good-natured Santaniello roast. Vinnie was not smiling and his blue eyes looked stressed.

Doc Milazzo, a street-smart kid from North Jersey, flicked a cigarette at Vinnie and then lit his own before lighting Vinnie's, too. "What's wrong, *paisan?*"

Vinnie looked askance at the mountains that extended forever before him, then looked down and shook his head back and forth. "We're going to the beach when we get home, right, Doc? I'm taking you to Rockaway Playland and you're taking me to the Jersey Shore, right?"

Doc Milazzo, sensing what Vinnie really was asking, said, "Yeah, of course. Besides, we gotta compare our moms' cooking. I got ten dollars that says Mama Milazzo's sauce will kick the ass of Mama Santaniello's sauce!"

Vinnie chuckled. "My mama's meatballs can't be beat, Doc, so that ten dollars is as good as mine!" The boys shared a long, hearty laugh with each other, and they appeared to be fine on the surface but, for both young men, a maelstrom of fear percolated underneath.

If the boys lived, surely this storm would take decades to confront, much less overcome.

*   *   *

It's a shame that Aunt Rita's nephew got hit, but up here, getting 2 Hearts isn't a rare occasion. What's a rare occasion is not having a Purple Heart. I came so damn close to getting them. But what really protected me is the fear that if I did get hit and Mom found out, she'd go nutty. I was always afraid that Mom would get scared to death. That's why I can't get hit. You can get a Purple Heart as long as you got a wound inflicted by the enemy and there's got to be proof, like shrapnel or an obvious wound. For instance, my buddy got a piece of shrapnel in his lip; it was taken out and four stitches were put in and he got a Heart for that. But his mother got a telegram that her son got a shrapnel wound in the face. They didn't say how bad or little it was. So his mother was worried until she got a letter from him explaining what happened and how small it was.

All the guys are alright. They're still back here and they'll be rotating with the 2nd Platoon any day now. I'm pretty sure Richie got his picture back. If not, it's probably in the mail.

Love, your brother, Vinnie

Excerpt from Vinnie's February 27, 1968 letter to Lilly

"Hey, Saint," yelled Jackson, a new guy from Las Vegas, Nevada who'd arrived in Vietnam roughly two weeks earlier and fancied himself as a comedian. "I tripped over a gook's body a couple of days ago, fell down and scraped my knee. Does that qualify me for a Heart?"

Vinnie looked over at Jackson, who stood roughly six-foot-one and was a strapping 225 pounds. Jackson, a black man, had the typical haircut of a new Marine, high and tight, and his dark, round eyes and dark-chocolate complexion belied his age of twenty. Jackson looked like he wouldn't need to shave for at least another ten years; he sported virtually no facial hair. He also had a faint tattoo on his right forearm: It read "MOM" in huge, scripted letters that bent over an exaggerated heart shot through with an arrow.

Vinnie cast a quick glance at Red and Doc Nunn, two fellows whose time was getting mighty short in country, whistled, and then set his sights on Jackson. "Jackson, you've been in the shit for all of five minutes and you're already looking to get a Heart? And one for a little booboo on your knee, to boot, huh? Let me tell ya something: If you get a Heart, a letter is sent home to let them know that you got a Heart for being injured in action here in 'Nam. 'Cept that letter won't explain that you got a minor flesh wound that required some iodine and a Band-aid. Hell, your mama will think that you're lying on a gurney somewhere with your guts oozing out. You wanna put her through that, green?"

Jackson's smile quickly evaporated and was replaced with a grimace.

Vinnie sensed Jackson's mood change and he softened considerably. "Listen, Jackson, we all were green when we got here, but this place'll teach you one lesson real quick: It ain't the movies, where the hero gets the medals, the girls, and the glory. Here, every one of us would die for each other—hell, plenty have already died for me in my eight months here—but we all know that getting a medal often means that you ain't never gonna see that medal. It'll arrive home to your mama . . . shortly after your funeral."

Jackson's face became a picture of regret. "Sorry, Saint, I didn't mean no disrespect."

"No disrespect taken, Jackson. I felt the same as you when I got here last year. But you know what I learned immediately?"

"What's that, sir?"

"First off, Jackson, I *work* for a living, so don't ever call me 'sir.' You and I are brother Marines. We ain't officers sitting behind a goddamn desk, so neither of us are 'sirs.'"

Jackson nodded affirmatively.

Vinnie continued, "Next, you gotta understand that, in Vietnam, you should earn a medal for every second that you're able to survive, brother."

And with that, a mortar exploded in the distance. Saint and the boys who had been in the shit for months didn't flinch, but Jackson dove for the nearest foxhole.

"Welcome to 'Nam, Jackson," chimed in Doc Nunn, "you poor sonofabitch!"

Vinnie re-read his letter to Lilly and he considered crossing out the part about coming close to getting a Purple Heart. For the most part, he still was sanitizing his letters to protect his family from the truth about how death lurked behind every shadow and beyond every horizon. Death was one sniper's bullet, one wayward mortar round, one accurate rocket launch away from becoming a reality. That sobering reality never could be expressed to his parents or siblings. No, variations of the "everything's fine" mantra would have to be repeated until he could tell everyone the real truth about the chaos of the war.

Yeah, I'm sure that everyone will understand why I was lying to them in my letters, he thought. *I'll tell 'em that I couldn't be square with them outta concern for their own well-being. I can't have my family worried sick about me.*

Despite his agitated hesitance, Vinnie opted to leave the language in the letter to Lilly. His reasoning: She was too green to understand the meaning of his words—that is, how close he had come to becoming a casualty, or worse, as a result of this goddamn war. Besides, Vinnie thought there was a chance that she'd show the letter to a good-looking chick in her office and she'd be impressed with Vinnie's valiant prowess. After all, Vinnie still was only a few months beyond his nineteenth birthday.

One morning in late February, Vinnie awoke in his bunker at Dong Ha H&S at 0400 hours. He had the benefit of taking a nice warm shower, his first in a couple of weeks, and he thought of how good it felt to wash the filth of the jungle off of his body. He looked in the slab of scratched, yet still reflective, aluminum that was nailed to the wall in the makeshift bathroom and he was shocked at the face that was staring back at him.

I don't even fucking recognize myself. Vinnie was naturally thin, but his face looked gaunt and forlorn. He noticed darker circles under his eyes that hadn't existed before and slight crow's feet at the corners of both baby blues. His forehead was creased ever-so-gently with the lines of a teen who has capitulated to the throes of a painfully bloody and mentally taxing war. Vinnie's eyes, once bright and piercing, had dulled as they had witnessed the overwhelming, incapacitating human suffering of both friend and foe.

The next thing that Vinnie noticed was the jungle rot on his face. Jungle rot was the infection caused by exposure to the microbes and filth that abounded in the jungle. When a dearth of hygienic opportunities is combined with ever-present mud, mosquitos, and incessant tearing of the skin on sharp bamboo and elephant grass, jungle rot will appear. Indeed, when the need to defecate and urinate like animals in the wild was combined with the constant rubbing of one's face with hands so vile that the devil himself wouldn't dare to shake them, the gross, pus-filled ulcers abounded upon the bodies of these young men with significantly compromised immune systems.

Shit, thought Vinnie after he took a good, hard look at his once-handsome face in what amounted to a beaten-up frying pan doubling as a mirror, *how the fuck are Rosalie and the chicks back home gonna want to go steady with a face like this?* Vinnie's complexion, once smooth and pink, was now pockmarked with red blisters, both open and closed, as well as the scars of jungle rot that Vinnie had picked open—thereby exacerbating the pre-existing infections—when he surrendered to the fits of intractable itchiness that befell him if he wasn't otherwise preoccupied with combat.

Vinnie eventually ceased muttering about how the jungle was robbing him of his good looks. He proceeded to get dressed in fresh combat fatigues, with polished boots (he refused to throw away his well-worn, nearly white boots that had been issued in Marine-polished black, of course) and a soft hat. Saint prepared to bring a number of materials to the platoon down in Cam Lo by organizing the following in his jeep: two boxes of mail (HQ had not received any mail in about a week due to heavy fighting in the region), a few thousand rounds of M-16 and M-79 ammo, a few cartons of cigarettes, some small bottles of rum and vodka that Lilly had mailed to him, a couple of *Playboy* magazines, and as many t-shirts and pants in assorted sizes and conditions that he could find. The guys appreciated it when they could change their tattered outfits out in the shit. Many of them hadn't showered in weeks, so a fresh pair of jungle fatigues was the next best thing to a warm shower.

After loading the jeep and getting confirmation that the engineers had swept the roadway for mines, Vinnie climbed into his tin box of a jeep, cranked it up, and put it into gear. The engine made a terrible gasping sound before turning over, and the vehicle rumbled so violently that Vinnie couldn't hear or feel anything except his jeep. *I'm gonna hafta get under the hood of this damn jalopy some point soon because I don't wanna get stranded in the middle of Highway 9, or on the bridge, and become a sitting fucking target for the gooks*, Vinnie thought. He released the clutch and depressed the gas pedal, causing the jeep to suddenly lurch forward. Vinnie was on his way back to the boys in Cam Lo. The engine was kicking rather forcefully as Vinnie shifted gears. *I really have to fix this jeep before it gets me killed.*

Vinnie arrived at Cam Lo with his loud jeep. The engine backfired when he pulled into the platoon area, startling some of the greener guys congregated there. The Marines laughed and lauded Vinnie as a conquering hero once they realized that the jeep, as opposed to an AK-47 blast that signaled an enemy ambush, was the culprit behind the unexpected explosive sound.

"Saint's here!"

"Hey, mailman, gimme my *Playboy* magazine!"

"You got more rum? I love your sister, Saint. God bless her!"

"Smokes, smut, and letters from Mom. What could be better?"

"Saint, what the fuck is wrong with that jeep of yours? Get under the hood and fix that hunk of junk already!"

Yeah, thought Saint, *I really gotta fix this goddamn jeep.*

CHAPTER 9

GETTING SHORT AND DREAMING LONG

Hi greeny, how is my baby sister doing? I hope just fine. As for me, I'm doing fine. I have gotten quite a few letters from you today.

So you are getting Rosalie a job where you work. She doesn't know what the hell she wants. She's still a child. She gets on my nerves sometimes. I know what you're going to say: She has it rough. If she has it rough, what do I have it?? All she wants to do is have me marry her to take her away from her father. Well, I'm no Prince Nightingale. So what I do now is let her talk until she's blue in the face about marriage and just ignore her. Now I'm going to warn you: If you conspire with her against me, I'll just stop writing the both of you. I know just how you girls work, so don't try nothing. I can tell whenever you do by the change in attitude in the letters. And I know you have been doing a lot of talking to her, so just stop playing Cupid or Miss Matchmaker. Just let Rosalie show her true self. I just promise her something to stop her from nagging and haunting me like engagement as soon as I get home. I'm not playing her on because I do like her, but I'm not being pushed into a corner. See, little sister, a man changes when he's in war. Now there's a lot of things that I want to do and see before I even think of marriage. It's like this: A girl knows as much about how a man changes at war as a man knows what it's like for a woman to be in labor. So it's really hard for yous to understand. All I can say is that I'm going to have to straighten Rosalie out when I get home. It will be easier to put her in her proper place in person. The way I feel right now is that when I get back to the world I'm going to get back in circulation with the girls. But you never know, my mind might change. Well, enough about me and Rosalie. How are you and Ralph doing? You can expect about three of my friends for your wedding. Well, Lil, it's kind of late and I got to get some sleep, so take care.

Love, your ugly brother, Vinnie

P.S. I love and miss all of you very much. Only 5 more months to go.

Vinnie's February 29, 1968 letter to Lilly

*F*ive. More. Months. Vinnie exhaled and allowed himself to do something that Marines are trained to never do: He looked ahead to what the future held for him after he returned home from Vietnam. *Just five short-ass months,* he thought. *I'll be back home for good with Ma, Pop, Lilly, Joseph, and the dogs, Apache and Queenie, in just five months. Holy shit, I can't wait! I can't wait to see Rosalie again, even though she's been a pain in the ass in her letters recently, asking me if we can get married as soon as I get back. Shit, part of me doesn't wanna get married, but part of me does. After all, this fucking war has made me a man, and a man needs to settle down and start a family. I'll figure all that shit out once I get home. It sure will be swell to be with my girl, Rosalie, again, even if she is on my back with this marriage shit.*

Vinnie, like many of his young brethren, was conflicted about what was in store for him when he returned home. He knew from letters back home that the country seemed to hate the returning veterans more than they seemed to hate the enemy, and that infuriated him. *They have no fucking idea what we face over here.* He could get a job as a mechanic. No, before he did that, he had to travel a lot. He needed to get out to L.A. to party with Keidinger. Vinnie needed to hang with those boys and then he'd get in touch with Red and head up to Washington to see him. *I'll make Mike draw a picture of me in uniform for Lilly. She'd find that pretty groovy.* Vinnie really liked Mike and looked up to him as an older brother. That being said, Vinnie resolved that he'd make sure that he and Mike traveled up to Alaska. And there sure as hell had better be a North Pole there, with a bunch of Santas and Christmas trees, or else Vinnie would show Mike what happens to bullshitters in Jamaica, Queens. Vinnie chuckled to himself after this thought flitted through his mind.

Yeah, I definitely gotta travel before I begin working like Pa. Vinnie idolized his father, Carmine, as he had taught Vinnie the essential values of hard work and commitment to family. Vinnie understood that, once he finished traveling like a vagabond around the U.S. of A., he had to settle down and work his ass off to benefit his family. That's the only way that he knew. *Maybe I'll get to Minneapolis to catch up with Nicholson, too.* The war had transformed Vinnie, or so he believed. The experiences in 'Nam—the good, bad, indifferent, cruel, bloody, and everything in between—taught Vinnie valuable life lessons and forced him to become a man sooner than he had anticipated.

The people back in the world could never understand the perspective of the men who returned stateside after doing their thirteen-month tours in hell. To too many people back home, the men returning from the war were dirty, baby-killing bastards, not conquering heroes. This wasn't World War II and there was no V-J Day. Troops weren't kissing their babes in the middle of Times Square. Instead, the men returned from Vietnam and awkwardly tried to assimilate themselves back into society as Joe Q. Public, as opposed to GI Joe.

The returning vets had no outlets for their anxiety and fits of anger. Instead of being welcomed with open arms, many of the men were spat upon and reviled. Vinnie and the grunts in 'Nam were well aware of this treatment back home and this knowledge served to only exacerbate their repressed anger and frustration.

Vinnie figured that he'd have to sneak back into his own country, after spending thirteen months surrounded by suffocating squalor and death while serving the very citizens who would rather stone him than thank him for his service. *What a country*, he thought.

Many of the Marines in Vietnam confronted the same quandary that Vinnie faced when they began to allow the thoughts of "getting short" invade their thoughts. Again, the lesson of Vietnam was that if you allowed yourself to contemplate anything more than the immediacy of that very moment in time, then you were all too vulnerable to getting killed. Still, these were eighteen- to twenty-one-year-olds, and despite the fact that the war was making them men before many of them were ready, many of them could not help themselves when they reflected on being back home with family, friends, and girlfriends. Hell, for a good number of the boys, dreams of taking a long, hot shower in a clean and private bathroom were surpassingly more satisfying than any dream of being back with Suzie, Barbara, Jenny, or Kathy.

In 'Nam, some of the Marines whittled on a stick when they were getting short. The other Marines understood this custom and the greens looked with envy and longing at a brother's short-timer's stick. Each Marine carved his stick, anywhere from three to five feet long and two inches thick, in a different way, but the basics were the same. The Marine would mark each passing day by cutting away that portion of the stick that represented one less day in the shit as the final day drew near. Eventually, the stick would get smaller and smaller as a Marine's time in Vietnam grew shorter. Vinnie wouldn't dare create a short-timer's stick because he was not short enough. However, the notion that he could soon begin to carve one brought a relieved smile to his weary face.

Vinnie also was giddy over the fact that he was going to be granted leave to attend Lilly's wedding in August 1968. Lilly, unsurprisingly, chose Vinnie to be her best man and that made him so proud. "Hey, Doc," shouted Vinnie to Doc Nunn, "I'm going to be the best man in my sister's wedding! Can you dig that? I'll be sporting my dress blues and crisp white pants and I'll instantly be the sharpest-looking guy in the church!"

"That's pretty groovy, Saint," replied Doc, "but I got one question for you: Do you think those dress blues will compensate for that fucking jungle rot on your face, you pretty city boy?"

The boys broke out in good-natured laughter at Doc's joke, and even Vinnie couldn't help but chuckle at his own expense. "Maybe I won't come back here, you asshole," joked Vinnie, "and then I'll be the shortest guy in the whole platoon. How 'bout that, Nunn?"

"I'll be sure to testify against your wop ass at the court-martial proceeding, Saint. I got a lot of shit on you that'd get you a good, long sentence in the clink!"

Turning serious for a moment, Vinnie told Doc Nunn how thrilled he was to be the best man. "I gotta come up with a good speech, John. You know how special Lilly is to me . . . it's gotta be perfect for her."

"I'm sure you'll be fine, Saint. Your sister's a real doll and it's clear as day that she means the world to you. You're gonna hit that speech right out of the park, brother!"

Vinnie knew that he would do just that. He certainly didn't lack confidence and he spent a few minutes every night jotting down ideas for the speech.

"Hey, Red, Milazzo," Vinnie turned to his other two buddies, "what do you guys think: dress blues or greens for Lilly's wedding?"

"Blues," replied Red, without hesitation.

"Yeah," responded Doc Milazzo, "blues are real classy and the greens look like fucking puke! How are you gonna impress your girl, Rosalie, and all the other chicks at the wedding, if you wear those puke-greens?"

Dress blues it is, thought Vinnie, but he concluded that he would write to Lilly and ask for her thoughts on the subject. After all, it was her wedding, and as much as he thought dress blues would be perfect, he'd wear the ugly greens if that is what Lilly chose. *I sure hope she chooses the dress blues*, Vinnie thought to himself.

I'm gonna be an uncle soon! And soon after that, I'll be a dad, too! Holy shit, this war can't end soon enough for me. I have so much that I want to do back in the world! Vinnie's excitement over his sister's wedding also served as a reminder to the young man that he was growing up, and growing up quickly. He was amused by the fact that his parents soon would be grandparents, yet was he confident that they would be fantastic grandparents who would love and spoil their grandkids. He also contemplated being an uncle and he was hopeful that Lilly's kids would like him. Unsurprisingly, Vinnie concluded that he would protect Lilly's kids and make sure that they behaved and respected the family.

Vinnie's daydream was rudely interrupted by Captain LeRoy's voice. Vinnie no longer was back home in Jamaica, New York, playing with his first niece or nephew on the stoop of his house while playfully chiding Lilly about how she'd lost her girlish figure thanks to her pregnancy. Instead, he was back in his bunker in Dong Ha, with mosquitos the size of the large peanuts sold at Yankee Stadium swarming around his face. The sweet smell of the mimosa tree that was located in the very modest, but immaculately maintained, garden in the front of Vinnie's house was supplanted by the omnipresent scent of petroleum and burning organic matter. Vinnie blinked a few times and his beautiful sister, Lilly, faded into the recesses of his mind and was replaced by the square-jawed mug of the Kilo Company commander. LeRoy, a tall, skinny white man from Idaho was not much older than Vinnie—he was twenty-two—but he was on his third tour in Vietnam and was well on his way to being a lifer in the Crotch, so he might as well have been forty which, for the youthful Saint, was akin to being old and decrepit.

Edward "Ned" LeRoy towered over Vinnie. He was six-foot-two to Vinnie's five-foot-eight, but he didn't weigh much more than Vinnie. Both men were thin by virtue of their inconsistent diets out in the jungle, but they still ate like kings compared to the platoons that were permanently humping around the hills and jungles of

South Vietnam. Indeed, the fact that Vinnie and Captain LeRoy operated out of the rear entitled them to regular meals in the mess hall, if they weren't out in the field. Of course, given the incessant rate of attrition of the Marines, Ned and Vinnie found themselves out in the jungles much more than in the relative comforts of H&S in Dong Ha.

Ned had a very polite, Midwestern demeanor, and the men really respected the fact that he didn't carry himself with an air of superiority. He was a regular guy like them, albeit with brass on his collar. Now, this was the military, so the grunts accorded Captain LeRoy the respect that he had earned as their superior, but he didn't flaunt his accomplishments and rank to the boys out in the field and, in return, the boys would willingly jump on a grenade to save his life. When you're forced to live in the nanosecond like these Marines were, a humble "man of the people" leader like Captain LeRoy is greatly appreciated and loved.

"Hey, Saint, we have an order to bring some arty down to Cam Lo; the boys are under a lot of heat because the nice weather has brought the Charlies out to play and we're getting low on RPGs, HEs, and frags, as well as grub for the boys. So load up the jeep because we're departing at 0515 hours."

"Yes, sir," came Vinnie's obedient response. Vinnie began loading the jeep for the twenty-minute trek down Highway 9 to Cam Lo and he noticed that LeRoy looked distracted. "What's up, sir?"

"Saint, you ever wonder about being a lifer in the military?"

"No, sir, I haven't," responded Vinnie. "I couldn't see myself doing this for much longer, much less for the rest of my life, sir."

LeRoy scrunched his lips together, causing his forehead and left eye to furrow inquisitively. "Y'know, a lifer in the military isn't doomed to live in the shit his whole life, Saint. You can work stateside on a base, too."

"Are you trying to convince me to re-up, sir?"

"You're a good man, Saint, and a fucking great Marine. You'd bring honor to the Corps, Santaniello."

"Thanks, sir, that means a whole lot coming from you, but I just want to survive the next five seconds, and the five seconds after that. I can't get too concerned about what I'm gonna do with the next twenty minutes of my life, much less the next twenty years, sir!"

So, ironically, Vinnie quietly contemplated his post-Vietnam future while packing hundreds of pounds of artillery and weapons that were poised to bring mass destruction and death to young Vietnamese soldiers who were the same age as Vinnie and equally hopeful of escaping the madness that was the Vietnam War.

CHAPTER 10

DRIVING TO LILLY'S WEDDING IN AN OLD JUNK BOX

Rite now, I'm finishing up the puzzle you sent me. I got seven mistakes spotted so far. I got nine so far. Man, this puzzle isn't too easy. (1) No air hose on cab; (2) barrel was missing bottom and top half of band; (3) the truck on the sign was missing a wheel . . . I'll give you the two other answers if I get them at the end of the picture. I got to rest my eyes. You know, if you keep looking at the pictures, they start to look like they are moving. So I figured it was time to rest my eyes. I just finished eating chow and I came back to relax for a while. At 3:00 I'll be going out to the field. I got some mail and stuff that has to go out. It started raining yesterday and it's still raining. The weather is very damp. Right now, I'm sleeping in a tent by myself. We got all the company's seabags in this one tent and I moved into it. It's real comfortable. Usually, it's about 20 men to a tent and it's always kind of crowded but now I got plenty of room for myself.

I wish that you'd stop cursing in your letters. That language is my everyday vocabulary: I'm a Marine and a man and it's to be expected from me. But you're a beautiful young woman and it's not very nice at all. Believe me. I hope I haven't embarrassed you. I'm not meaning to but I'd just like to set you straight on it. I'm speaking to you as your little brother to my little sister. OK, Sis?

Yesterday my jeep broke down. The rear axle broke and we were about ½ a mile from the gate to Dong Ha. An army truck in front of me stopped and asked me if I needed any help. So I told him I would need a tow into Dong Ha by 3/4 area. So I pulled out this rope that I keep in my jeep for just such an occasion and he towed me back and they fixed it for me. I picked it up this morning and it's just fine now. We're still waiting for the new jeeps to get here, we're supposed to get them between January and March, but we'll probably get them just after I rotate (go home). We still got these old junk boxes, but they're better than walking. Right now, the jeep that I have is the second-best jeep that our motor pool has, out of about 4 or 5 that are running. Hold on a while, while I try to finish the puzzle.

No more, I'll try again later on. . . . You're not as smart as you think, typing this letter, because what happens if your boss walks in while you're typing? He knows you don't use orange paper for your work, especially your orange paper: It's real cute and the envelope with the flower is beautiful. It's a nice set of stationary.

About me getting a government job: Well, I got one and it's not too shattering. In fact, it stinks. Listen, did you get the chain and cross that I sent you to have repaired for me? Let me know.

The Marines that are fighting at Hue are the 1st Marine Division. The Marines that are at Khe Sanh are the 1st Bn. 26th Marines, 2nd Bn. 26th Marines, and the 3rd Bn. 26th Marines. There's three battalions of guys holding the perimeter.

I have gotten a few sad letters from Mrs. Price. She is so sick over her son's death. She said to me, "Every time I go to Jamaica, I look at Paul's grocery store and I wish all you boys were standing there like you used to." I read that and I had to walk out of the tent. I didn't want my buddies to see me cry. I went and put cold water on my head and face. It made me feel better. She said that she's trying to get permission to have Barry's body brought up to New York to rest. It's really sad to think of what she's going through. The only reason I fear death over here is because I couldn't see Mom going through the same thing. It's so sad.

Listen, Lil, here's what I want you to do. I'd like you to send some nice red or yellow roses to Mrs. Price's house and have them write, "To Mrs. Ann Price; from my brother, Vinnie; signed, Lillian Santaniello." I know that they'll cheer her up a little because she likes me very much and thinks of me as one of her boys. So please do that for me and don't forget to sign your name on them because she might think that I'm home if you don't. Then you write and tell me how much they cost you and I'll send you a money order for the amount. Well, Lillian, I got to be going now. So take care and say hello to everyone for me.

Love, your brother, Vinnie

P.S. I Love You, little sister of mine.

Vinnie's March 2, 1968 letter to Lilly

"Hey, Saint," called Daniel King, a grunt from Maine who'd arrived shortly after Vinnie and become a mainstay in the Thundering Third, "you got any more of them puzzles that your sister sent you from home?" Lilly sent Vinnie puzzles to do when he wasn't busy figuring out the puzzle of life, Vietnam War-style. The puzzles were duplicate drawings of scenes—nature, a big city, or a sporting event, to name a few—and you had to find a series of hidden items, or subtle changes, between the two scenes. Vinnie thought these puzzles kept him sharp in the jungle. He made it a point to try to find distinguishing traits of, or changes in, the terrain that he traversed on any given day. Often, Vinnie's uncanny ability to see something that was out of the ordinary in the jungle was lauded by his superiors for keeping his brothers safe.

Vinnie turned to Daniel, who was a white kid with short brown hair, dark eyes, and an oval face. "Of course, I have an extra one that Lilly sent in my last letter. Here ya go." With that, Vinnie provided Daniel with some extra puzzles.

"Thanks, Saint, these puzzles look so easy, but it is so hard to find all of the differences when you're under pressure."

"Sounds a lot like this goddamn war," mused Vinnie, "doesn't it?"

"This war is a big fucking puzzle, Saint," observed Daniel. "If I knew back in '66, when I enlisted, what I know now, Uncle Sam would've had to draft me to get my ass to the bush!"

Vinnie laughed but Daniel winced, as if his thoughts after his last comment physically sickened him. Daniel had joined the service with the understanding that service to one's country was of paramount importance. Indeed, Daniel's grandfather and father had served the U.S. in World Wars I and II, respectively. Daniel grew up in a family that glorified the military and, growing up in Maine, Daniel revered his dad and grandfather. Indeed, the soft-spoken man knew at the age of ten that he would follow in their footsteps.

Daniel enlisted with the Marines as soon as he was legally able to do so, in the summer of 1966, and arrived in Vietnam roughly one year later. He was eighteen, then, stood five-foot-ten, and weighed a strapping 180 pounds. Vietnam had cost Danny about thirty pounds since he'd arrived in country, transforming the shape of his face from oval to long and lean. He had a square jaw, and his skin, once pre-pubescently smooth, was now pocked with jungle rot and sprouts of faint hair. His dark eyes sunk into his head, as if they purposely tried to avert any inquisitor's gaze. Daniel learned at a young age to always be respectful, so he felt obligated to apologize to Vinnie for expressing his reservations about the war.

"Damn, Vin, I'm sorry about that. I should've kept my comments to myself. We all got a job to do here and I would not want you to think that you couldn't count on me to do my job well."

Vinnie was touched by King's brutal honesty. "Hey, Danny, don't you worry yourself about nothing. I know that you'd take a bullet for me if it meant that I'd die if ya didn't. And you know I'd do the same thing for you, brother. That's why we're Marines, dammit!" Daniel chuckled, then kicked at the dirt in a *golly-gee*, humble manner. Vinnie continued, "That doesn't mean that we can't call a spade a spade, Danny, and this sonofabitch war is one helluva fucking spade!"

"You got that right, Saint, you definitely got that right!"

Vinnie whistled through pursed lips before he observed, "I thought these government jobs were supposed to set you up for life, Danny, not steal the life from you."

The boys laughed at the irony of that last observation and, with that, Danny went back to his puzzle to see if he could find what was different in two pictures of (what else?) a jungle. "Well, I'll be damned . . ."

The next day, Vinnie was driving back to H&S when his jeep broke down on him for what seemed like the millionth time in the last week. *This bucket of bolts is on its last legs,* Vinnie thought. *How the hell does the government expect these old junk boxes from the Korean War to survive another goddamn war?* Vinnie was incredulous. He was expected to give his all, including his own life if that's what the situation called for, yet the government couldn't even ensure that the Marines had jeeps that could survive the treacherous roads of the jungle. *It's not like Vietnam caught us by surprise, dammit! FDR never woulda allowed this treachery during World War II, that's for damn sure! And JFK never would've allowed the troops to be neglected like this. That goddamned LBJ, he don't give a shit about us and his ass wouldn't even survive three seconds in the shit.*

Vinnie was thankful that he was with Captain LeRoy during this latest mechanical breakdown. He knew that, if he had to try to fix his jeep alone, he'd be ambushed for sure. A Charlie would be too happy to pump a bullet into the back of Vinnie's exposed head as he leaned underneath the hood of the jeep to repair the latest malady. "This shouldn't take me very long, sir," said the part-time mechanic, part-time company driver, full-time Marine. "I have to re-jigger a few things with the carburetor to get this old relic fired up again."

LeRoy nodded to Vinnie and replied, "Saint, you definitely got the patience of a saint because I would've driven this goddamn unreliable piece of shit into the Cam Lo River!"

"I don't know, sir, I kinda have taken a liking to ol' Bessie here and I don't think she'd appreciate us fragging her!"

LeRoy smiled before countering, "No offense, Saint, but if it's between you or me taking a round to the head, or ol' Bessie getting fragged in the river, I know which option I'm choosing!"

Vinnie nodded in agreement before ducking his head under the hood to tinker yet again with the machinery beneath it.

The image of Vinnie leaning in, under the hood of the jeep, disturbed LeRoy greatly. The officer didn't see a kid fixing a car— no, the man who had seen too much death over multiple tours in 'Nam saw Vinnie only from the waist down. So naturally, he saw an upper body being separated from its lower half by a burst of machine-gun fire from an NVA AK-47 or RPD. LeRoy shook his head forcefully to shake the disturbing imagery from his mind. *Why do I keep having these fucked-up, violent, random thoughts?* the captain wondered. He resumed surveying the field for anyone who didn't look like him or Vinnie in this free-fire zone.

Captain LeRoy became further distressed at the sight of Vinnie working so myopically on the weathered, past-its-prime, government-issued jeep. *I reckon if the engine is running, with Vinnie's head under that hood, he wouldn't hear a goddamn thing,* LeRoy thought. The officer decided that he'd test his theory. He approached Vinnie and prodded him with the butt of his .45 sidearm.

Vinnie extricated himself from the filth of the engine, straightened up in front of Bessie, and peered at the captain. "Yes, sir?"

"Saint, why don't I start the jeep up and then you can dive back in to see if the engine is turning over properly?"

"Good idea, sir," the unsuspecting guinea pig replied. "When I kick up my right leg, that'll be the signal that it's okay to start her up and throw her into gear."

Vinnie leaned back into Bessie's engine as LeRoy backpedaled to the driver's seat. Upon seeing Vinnie kick his right leg up into the air, the captain started up the old battle ax and the engine rumbled to life. The sound of the engine was deafening. LeRoy then exited the vehicle while it still was running and ran about twenty-five yards behind Vinnie. He then began to scream loudly, "TUBING! TUBING! TAKE COVER!"

Every Marine knew that "tubing" meant that mortars would be crashing down on them within seconds and that they had to take cover. However, Vinnie didn't even flinch. He continued to toil away at his beloved jeep. *Goddamn*, thought LeRoy as he ashamedly turned his head away from Vinnie, who remained blissfully oblivious to what had just transpired and continued to work on the jeep.

LeRoy prodded Vinnie a few heart-wrenching moments later. "How's she looking, Saint?"

Vinnie propped himself up from the engine, which now was humming, albeit quite loudly, and wiped a considerable amount of sweat off his brow. He exhaled deeply and then, with a smile of satisfaction on his face, kiddingly pronounced, "Well, sir, it was touch and go there for a while, but I think that the patient is gonna survive!" Vinnie thought that this response was rather clever and he was taken aback when Captain LeRoy not only didn't laugh, but actually grimaced.

"What's wrong, sir? Did we get orders that we are about to engage in another Tet?"

"No, Saint, nothing like that." LeRoy hesitated and looked down in a defeated posture. Vinnie instinctively grabbed his M-16, disengaged the safety, and rapidly cast a series of furtive glances about his immediate surroundings, fully expecting to see an NVA soldier partially obscured in the nearby bamboo, fully poised to blow Saint's brains out.

Vinnie's scan of the territory proved negative, so he once again turned to his superior with an inquisitive look on his weathered face. "Sir, I don't get it. Why the long face? What's wrong?"

"Saint, look at me. I'm a goddamn lifer in the Crotch. I live and breathe the Corps every day of my life and I'm damn proud to call myself a leader of men like you. We go to war with and for each other, we guide each other, we carry each other, we protect . . ."

LeRoy's voice got caught in his throat. The captain took a deep breath, composed himself, and continued. "We protect each other, and we die for each other. The Marines are warriors of the highest order, as we are trained to kill for the honor of the greater good. And we don't ask for a goddamn thing in return. Look at us, Saint: We live worse than fucking animals, in squalor and filth. We don't eat or drink regularly and, when we do, it's shit that a pig would turn up his snout at. We bathe less frequently than the seasons change and we have burned more leeches off our fucking bodies than anyone would care to imagine. Yet, despite all of that, despite all of that goodwill, the government, which sends us out to do the work of the people, the hard work that not many would sign up to do, can't even provide us with satisfactory equipment to do the job that we're trained to do."

Vinnie was caught off guard by Captain LeRoy's rant. The captain was as mild-mannered as Clark Kent, and he resembled the fictitious gentleman from Kansas, too. Vinnie didn't disagree with the captain's assertions, he was just a tad shocked that Captain LeRoy (a lifer, to boot!) would be at odds with his boss, the United States of America.

"Sir," Vinnie began after a lengthy pause, "what exactly are you so pissed about?"

Vinnie could think of about 1,358 things about his experience as a Marine in 'Nam that angered him, so he wanted to whittle down the list, at least a bit, to address the captain's gripes. LeRoy removed his soft Marine hat and thrust his right hand vigorously through his coarse hair. He removed two Pall Malls from his flack jacket, placed one in the crook of his mouth, lit it, then lit the second cigarette and handed it to Saint. Vinnie graciously accepted the smoke, took a long drag, held it for a bit, then released it through his nose and mouth. The billowing smoke resembled the fury of

146

an angry dragon. Vinnie cocked his head to the side and squinted through the smoke at LeRoy, expecting a response.

"Saint, that jeep of yours is a fucking death trap. I was hootin' and hollerin' right behind you as you were fixing it and you didn't hear a goddamn thing. We need a lot of new things out here, including some decent fucking transport vehicles."

Vinnie appreciated LeRoy's concern and, despite his earlier anger at the state of the jeep, he tabled his own rancor and tried to placate his exacerbated superior. "Gee, Captain, the jeeps ain't that bad when you consider what they have to drive in and over every day. I'm careful, sir, and I don't intend to die in a goddamn jeep!" Vinnie laughed as he walked toward the taller LeRoy. He placed his right hand on the captain's left shoulder and squeezed down in a reassuring manner. "The Saint ain't gonna die in a goddamn jeep, sir. Besides, I got a wedding to attend in August and I have a lot of work to do on my best-man speech!"

"You're a good man, Saint, and you'd make one hell of an officer. Promise me one thing, Vinnie. Promise me that you will at least *consider* the possibility of becoming a lifer. We could use more good men like you, Santaniello."

Vinnie paused and looked over at his loud, rumbling jeep before replying, "Thank you, sir. That means a great deal to me coming from you. I will consider that option, sir." With that, the two men jumped back into the jeep and continued back to H&S. As if Vietnam wasn't stressful enough, now Vinnie had to ponder the safety of the very jeep that he had to use on a daily basis. *There are enough ways to fucking die out here*, Vinnie thought to himself over the roaring jeep engine, *this damn jeep should not be one of them.*

*   *   *

"Hey, Red," Vinnie called to his friend, "can you believe the blue language that Lilly uses in her letters to me?"

Vinnie, Mike Reagan, and a few of their friends were sitting outside their hooches in Cam Lo one early March morning. The men were oblivious to the falling rain, as rainfall in Vietnam seemed as ubiquitous as the air they breathed. When the Marines first arrived in Vietnam, the damp environment made them very uncomfortable; their clothes stuck to their bodies and their feet swelled and cracked after being confined in damp, tightly bound boots. Now, a few months into dealing with death, hunger, and thirst, a steady rainfall and sticky uniforms were relative pleasures.

Red wiped the brim of his helmet to clear away the line of water that cascaded across it and dripped constantly over his left eye. He peered over at Vinnie, chuckled, and stated, "Saint, your dad was a squid, and the Marines are under the Navy, so it doesn't shock me in the least that your sister curses like a sailor in her letters to you and us here. After all, it's in her blood!"

"Yeah, Lilly is pretty sore at Hanoi Hannah and the people back in the world who are dumping on us guys here in Vietnam. I'm not surprised that Lilly is supporting all of us here because she's always been loyal to me, but I really wish that she wouldn't use the curses to express herself. That ain't how a proper lady is supposed to speak."

Doc Nunn chimed in at this point. "I dunno, Saint, I find Lilly's use of the F-word to be creative and downright sexy! 'Fuck those hippie-commie bastards,' right, Lil?"

Doc Milazzo laughed and also came to Lilly's defense. "She's got a right to express herself in any fashion that she sees fit to get her point across. After all, a fucking gook bastard is still a fucking gook bastard, no matter if you're a man or a woman, right?"

Again, the boys laughed at the lighthearted nature of the conversation.

"Bottom line, though, she ain't a Marine, and she ain't at war," countered Vinnie in a serious tone. "So she's gotta speak like a prim and proper young woman. We talk like fucking animals because of what we do for a living right now, and it's expected of us.

Lilly works in an office with a bunch of professionals and I'm sure that her boss wouldn't appreciate hearing constant F-words. It just ain't right and I gotta straighten out my kid sister."

Vinnie went back into his hooch and Red, sensing the tension in Vinnie's tone, followed him in a few minutes later. "Hey, Saint," came the gentle, soothing voice, "everything okay, pal? You seemed a little cross back there." Vinnie purposely looked away, turning his back on Mike. "Sorry, Saint, I'll leave you be. Let me know if you wanna share a smoke later."

With that, Mike turned to leave Vinnie to his thoughts, but the forlorn Marine stopped Mike from exiting. "I lost a friend today, Red." Vinnie then tucked his chin into his chest and his shoulders heaved up and down in the all-too-familiar fashion that was very common among a company of tough guys and trained killers.

"Vin, we lose friends practically every day. Hell, it's a near-miracle that you and I still are walking in this shit."

"This was different, Red. I lost someone who was my buddy back home. My pal, Barry Price, was in the Army and I just learned that he was killed in a mission south of here, in Quang Tri. Barry and I used to hang out back home in Jamaica. His mom and my mom are very close. Barry's mom . . ." Vinnie paused to collect himself. "I got a letter from Barry's mom, Ann, this morning, and she told me that she'd gotten the news about Barry. I had no idea and alls I could write to her was how sorry I was."

"Saint, there ain't no rhyme or reason as to why one of us lives while another dies. I used to drive myself crazy early on, wondering why so-and-so had to die while I got to live another second in Hell." Mike paused and stared intently at Vinnie. "And then I realized something: We are in the business of death, Vin. We kill while we try like hell to avoid being killed, day in and day out. That's our reality here."

Vinnie pondered that last statement for a few seconds. "Yeah, I know, but I could practically hear Mrs. Price crying in her letter to me. She really was beside herself, Red." Vinnie leaned into his hooch. The heavy rain was pelting off of the canvas liner that served as Vinnie's shelter. Its sound relaxed Vinnie. "I can't die here, Red."

"What?"

"I said, I can't die here, in country. I just can't."

Mike looked at Vinnie with a quizzical expression on his face. "Why are you talking like that, Saint?"

"Red, my mom would be devastated if I was killed out here. She'd be miserable for the rest of her life. That keeps me going out here, Mike. Well, that and my lucky cross, which Lilly still hasn't sent back to me. The thought of my mom going berserk after hearing that I died is my incentive to stay alive. I don't wanna cause my mom the same heartache that Barry caused his mom."

"Vin, I'd tell you to stop worrying about shit like that, but the bottom line is: You know that all of us Marines worry about dying, twenty-eight hours a day, nine days a week, and 487 days a year." Mike held out his hand, which shook with a slight tremor, as evidence of his astute observation.

"We ain't never gonna stop worrying about dying in this shit storm until we get to rotate the fuck out of dodge, Red," Vinnie replied. *"And not a second before then!"*

Red sensed Vinnie's tension and tried to change the subject to something that Vinnie loved to talk about: his beloved "little sis," Lilly.

"Hey, Saint, how far along are you with your best-man speech?" Vinnie knew exactly what Red was trying to do and he loved Mike for his big heart. Nonetheless, talking about Lilly was much more palatable to him, and thoughts of his sister's impending nuptials brought an air of happiness to Vinnie, so he took the bait and welcomed the diversion.

Vinnie's face brightened as the tension dissipated. "Well, I have a few things written down amongst my papers back in my bunker at H&S. I ain't gonna be too serious and all because that's not my style. I'll tell a couple of tales about my lunatic sister to lighten the mood and then I'll share a couple of groovy jokes to bring the house down."

"Whatever you do," warned Mike, "don't bring up 'Nam. Nobody wants to hear about this bullshit back in the world."

"You ain't shitting me, brother," said Vinnie. "But I gotta tell some stories about you guys. Gee, I really wish you guys were able to come to the wedding. All of yous are practically Lil's stepbrothers by now! She always asks about you guys and says that she's worried sick about each of yous!"

Mike laughed, "Good ol' Lil. I'm not sure if she's a sister to us here in country, or another mom! So what could you possibly share at your sister's wedding about this shithole without making everyone angry or upset?"

"Well, for starters, I'll probably let everyone back home know about this big-hearted redhead from Oregon . . ."

"Washington! You typical, ignorant New Yorker!"

"Whatever," said Vinnie, in jest. "How this big dummy from *Washington* had a really bad farting problem." Mike flung his soaked hat at Vinnie, striking him across his face, and the two young men shared a satisfying laugh.

Doc Nunn, soaked through by the sheets of rain that were falling relentlessly on the men outside of the suddenly crowded hooch, entered to gain some refuge from the deluge. "Hey, brothers, mind if good ol' Doc joins this tea party?"

"Sure thing, Doc," offered Vinnie, "but it'll cost you a couple of cigs!" Doc tossed two Marlboros at Vinnie and nestled between the two Marines under the billowing canvas that heaved under the strain of the pouring rain above their heads. Given the close quarters of this hooch, Doc's soaked clothing seeped into Mike's and Vinnie's relatively dry cargo pants. The men had to shout in order to be heard over the precipitation that angrily pounded the hooch above their heads.

"Ain't this the fucking life, gents?" shouted Doc.

"Yeah," came Vinnie's equally loud response, "I definitely gotta tell stories of all this fucking rain during my best-man speech at Lilly's wedding."

Doc's eyes lit up at the mention of one of his favorite women in the world, despite never having met her. "Is that why you two grunts holed yourselves away in this here hooch, to talk about your sister's wedding, Saint?"

"That's right, Doc. I was telling Red here about my plans for Lil's wedding. You agree that I'd look sharper in my dress blues than in my dress greens, right?"

"Goddammit, Saint," Doc replied gruffly. "If I've told you once, I've told you a thousand times. There ain't nothing more handsome than a clean-shaven Marine in his dress blues and shiny black shoes! Lilly's cute-chick friends—not to mention your main squeeze, Rosalie—are gonna swoon over you like you was James fucking Dean!"

Mike chuckled at Doc's unique brand of speaking and offered, "I can't speak as eloquently as our corpsman here, but I will simply say that dress blues definitely are the way to go, Saint. Now, are you going to arrive in style to the wedding, in a nice stretch limo?"

"I'm hopeful that Ma and Pop will somehow find the money to pay for a nice stretch Caddy, to make sure that we arrive at the church like royalty, but I got a backup plan just in case they can't swing the limo."

Vinnie paused for effect and it worked. Both Mike and John craned their necks at him, giving Saint their complete, undivided attention. "If the limo doesn't work out," Vinnie engaged in another dramatic pause, "then I will fly home that hunk of bolts parked outside and drive up to the church in my old junk box!"

The boys roared in laughter at the thought of such a spectacle.

"Holy shit, Saint," responded Doc Nunn between fits of uncontrolled laughter, "e'rybody in the goddamn church'll hear you coming five minutes before you actually walk through the door, Vin!"

"How's *that* for a dramatic entrance?" Vinnie asked.

"Goddamn," muttered Red, in between fits of laughter. "Goddamn!"

CHAPTER 11

HOT WEATHER AND HOTTER BATTLES

How's it going? I hope fine. As for me, I'm just fine. Only 142 days left before I go home. I'm getting there. I remember when I had 395 days to do and it seems like only yesterday. Today I got my cross and the picture I sent you. First of all, thanks very, very much for having the cross fixed for me. Would you believe this cross went through a war? Yep! No lie. Thanks again, Lil.

About me wearing the blues and everyone else wearing tuxes: We can solve that problem. All the other guys should join the Marines, come over here for 13 months, and then they'll rate blues with the ribbons. I would like to wear blues instead of a tux but it's your wedding, so what you say goes. I'm glad Marie is my partner. I couldn't see Rosalie as mine. She probably would run up to the priest and ask him to marry us while she had me near the altar. Tell Marie that I'm very happy she's my partner; maybe Ro will leave with Ralph's brother. Ha Ha . . . only joking. Tell Ralph to tell his sister I said congratulations to her and her husband. Hey, I was just thinking maybe we can have Rosalie and Albert up on the altar after you and Ralph step off. That would be great; I don't think that Rosalie would mind as long as she got married. Ha Ha . . . Only joking.

Lil, find out if I can wear my blues for the wedding. I'd really like to because if I can't, I ain't going to buy them. But if I can, I'll definitely get them.

Love your brother, Saint

P.S. That cross saved my life so many times. It's enchanted. Well, Lil, find out about the blues. Dress blues are much more dressier than a tux.

Vinnie's March 7, 1968 letter to Lilly

M arch 1968 was an exceedingly hot month in South Vietnam. The rains relented and the sun became unbearably hot, especially for Marines who were lugging dozens of pounds of clothes, gear, and weapons. The grunts' running joke was that the warm weather brought out the NVA. Skirmishes were on the uptick, with fairly routine shelling occurring in and around the hills and regions that were occupied by the Corps. Cam Lo in particular was doubly hot: The scorching sun drenched the boys in their own sweat while they tried like hell to avoid the heat of incoming mortars, rockets, and deadly artillery. Doc Nunn, ever the joker, commented that the incoming ordnance routinely missed the mark because the air was so thick with humidity that it stopped the mortars and rockets dead in their tracks. At one point, Doc Nunn repeatedly scratched the back of his calf in an exaggerated fashion.

"Did one of those monster skeeters bite you, Doc, or has yet another leech taken up residence on your leg?" Vinnie asked.

Not missing a beat, John retorted, "Hell no, Saint, I'm just scratching my balls. This heat has caused them to droop all the way down yonder!"

In 'Nam, any joke that included a reference to a body part, and especially to the groin, was guaranteed to bring the house down. And no one was better at that than Doc Nunn.

One morning in early March 1968, back in Dong Ha HQ, Captain LeRoy advised Vinnie that they had to make a run to Gio

Linh because the boys were getting low on ammo. Gio Linh was a USMC combat base located just south of the DMZ and east of the other killing field, Con Thien. In the early morning, Vinnie and LeRoy began loading up Vinnie's old reliable jeep while the engineers swept the highway for land mines. Three mines were detonated, and "thankfully" one of the engineers "only" suffered shrapnel wounds to his legs.

"The kid's gonna get a Heart for that, sir," commented Vinnie, "but I betcha he'd gladly trade it for all those holes in his legs."

"You ain't kidding, Saint. I tell ya, when greens come over here, they think getting a Heart is a fantastic achievement. Those numbies think it's like getting a letter on their fucking high school jackets!" Vinnie nodded in agreement as Captain LeRoy continued, "They learn real fucking quick that this ain't high school and that a Heart means that you're likely bleeding from a nasty hole in your body. Or that you're dead."

Vinnie and LeRoy knew that the drive to Gio Linh could be lethal, so they enlisted two gunnies from the mess hall to hop in the back of the jeep and act as lookouts, one with a rifle and the other with an M-60. The region between Dong Ha and Gio Linh was a free-fire zone, so the gunnies knew that they were to shoot first and ask questions never in the event that they observed any human life on the road. The gunnies, LeRoy, and Vinnie understood all too well that a tenth of a second of hesitation could mean the difference between life and a grisly death. Marines are not in the business of *wanting* to die. Indeed, it was bad enough that they knew that death was on the menu all too often.

The gunny sitting behind Vinnie was Eugene Pryor, an eighteen-year-old black kid from Alabama. The greenie was quiet, respectful, and had a dry sense of humor. Pryor was joined in the rear of the jeep by John "Yellow" Freeman, nineteen and a native of Oklahoma. Freeman was mouthy and a little too *gunji*, or hardcore, for Vinnie's tastes. Vinnie commented to LeRoy recently that Yellow "thought he was fucking John Wayne in a Western." Pryor and Yellow had both come to 'Nam with reputations of being great marksmen, hence their election to serve as lookouts on the drive to Gio Linh.

Yellow was yapping away to Pryor, who feigned interest in the conversation while swiveling his head to inspect the landscape for snipers or for an ambushing unit of NVA guerillas. "Yeah, I reckon that the gooks won't show their faces this early in the morning, 'less they want a third hole 'tween they're eyes." Yellow laughed and reminded the other three passengers in the jeep that he was the number-one marksman in his class back in boot camp.

Three minutes into the ride, Vinnie had had enough.

"Yellow! Listen, greenie, you gotta understand something. No one gives a fuck what you achieved back in boot camp. NO. ONE. All we care about is that you do your job with honor and that you look out for your fellow Marines. I need to rely on you completely and you need to rely on me just the same. Now do me a favor, please: Shut your fucking mouth and keep your eyes peeled for gooks. Got it?"

"Got it," came Yellow's embarrassed response.

Forty seconds later, all hell broke loose.

Off to his left, Vinnie heard what sounded like a car backfiring, a sound that he had heard thousands of times at home and here in 'Nam from the very jeep that he was driving. However, Saint had been in country long enough to know what that sound really was.

"INCOMING!"

It's only seven-fucking-thirty in the morning, thought Vinnie in the milliseconds after he notified the team of what they likely already knew: They were being attacked. *Why the fuck are the gooks out already?* The unwritten rule in these parts was that neither side wanted to attack the enemy without the cover of night because such an action exposed their position. Once exposed, the aggressor would be rendered susceptible to a counterattack without sufficient time to haul ass out of their position. Of course, if there was one thing that the boys learned during their time in 'Nam, it was that nothing was conventional about this warfare.

LeRoy was to Vinnie's right in the passenger seat. Vinnie took stock of the situation and he was fearful. If any enemy arty made a direct hit on the bounty of weapons and artillery in the back of the jeep, he'd be blown halfway back to Jamaica, Queens from the resulting explosion. At that moment, time froze for Vinnie. No one and nothing moved. Vinnie quickly peered at Captain LeRoy: his jaw jutted out, his eyes were wide open, and his right finger was squeezing the trigger of an M-16. Saint peered in his rearview mirror and was amazed at how composed and calm Pryor seemed despite this being his first firefight. Next, he glanced at Yellow and saw a face of abject terror. *Fuck*, Vinnie thought, *these guys' lives are in my hands right now. I can't let them down.*

The war suddenly roared back to life and the fury of what was happening filled Vinnie's ears. "Yellow, get on the horn and radio in our coordinates NOW. You understand me? Fucking NOW!"

Freeman did as Vinnie instructed. Pryor squeezed out about a dozen rounds in what seemed like a second. Vinnie quickly shifted gears on his ol' reliable jeep and rapidly accelerated down the rocky, dirt-strewn road. "HOLD ON!" he yelled as he quickly veered left and then right to throw off the attackers that seemingly lined the road to his left and right. Vinnie heard what he thought was shattered glass and figured that a headlight had taken a hit. He kept going but he kept hearing the *thud thud thud!* of automatic weapons' fire echoing all around him. *Where the fuck are these gooks?* he thought as he masterfully navigated the rear-heavy jeep down the uneven terrain. Vinnie's fear of blowing up was supplanted with righteous indignation and sheer rage. *I'll run these bastards over before I let them hurt one of my guys*, he thought.

The onslaught was going in slow motion. Artillery rounds were flying all around the heads of the men in the darting, veering jeep. Screaming voices in different tongues were suspended beneath the din of the crackling machine-gun fire. The Marines winced as bullets whizzed in their midst and they all were amazed, really, that they weren't killed during the ambush.

And then it happened.

Amidst all the chaos, a propelled *chi-comm*, a fragmentation grenade used by the NVA, landed in the rear of the jeep. The clinking sound was imperceptible to everyone in the jeep. everyone, that is, except Pryor. The young Marine's eyes widened at the sight of the grenade and he instantly realized that none of his brother Marines had a clue that they were about to die. The grenade was nestled on top of the box of assorted artillery rounds that was to be delivered to Gio Linh. Pryor knew that he had no more than four seconds to do something. He hoped that the *chi-comm* would roll out as Vinnie maneuvered the jeep in a zig-zag fashion, but the damn thing was stuck on the box.

I got about two seconds to act, Pryor thought, *and I ain't got time to reach for the goddamn grenade then rear back and throw it as far as I can before it blows.* Pryor knew what he had to do.

"I LOVE YOU, MAMA!" came the cry from the rear, startling Vinnie, LeRoy, and Yellow. What happened next was a blur. Vinnie noticed a cat-like move through the rear-view mirror: Pryor, in a flash, reached behind him and, in one motion, leapt mightily from the jeep that was traveling at least thirty miles per hour. Time once again stood still for Vinnie as he saw Pryor hurtling in slow motion, high in the air, and getting increasingly smaller as the jeep sped forward. Vinnie looked over his left shoulder and he could've sworn that he made eye contact with his heroic brother before–

The concussion of the explosion rocked the jeep so hard that only Vinnie's ability to steer out of a skid, a skill that he had harnessed while driving on snow-covered streets in New York City, kept the jeep from rolling over into a fiery mess. Suddenly, everything became silent. The enemy gunfire stopped, as did the firing from within the jeep. Vinnie had traversed beyond the ambush zone. And then it hit the stunned men, almost simultaneously. Pryor had been blown up by a grenade, which meant that he must've removed the live *chi-comm* from somewhere in the jeep before he leapt from the jeep to save the lives of his brothers. Pryor, who was in country for all of six days, was dead. And a martyr.

Yellow vomited over the side of the jeep. LeRoy sat in stunned resignation and Vinnie blinked rapidly to ensure that his tears didn't obscure his view of the road as he continued driving to the base. LeRoy grabbed the radio from the shocked Yellow and barked orders to get some Hueys to the region of the ambush so that the Marines could recover whatever was left of their heroic brother, in order to get him home. As he pulled into the combat base in Gio Linh, Vinnie observed two CH-46s flying low overhead toward the ambush zone. Without saying a word, he jumped into another jeep that was parked at the base, barked at Red and Doc Nunn to hop in, and sped back toward the location where Pryor had made the ultimate sacrifice.

The two machine gunners aboard the first CH-46, a twin-rotor assault chopper, were obliterating the periphery of the road where the ambush had occurred. Any NVA guerillas nestled in their holes at this time surely were dead. About fifteen Marines were lowered out of the rear ramp of the second CH-46, under the cover of the weapon fire from the companion bird. Vinnie, Doc, and Red joined the fifteen men in an effort to find their fallen hero. Doc found a leg. Vinnie found a headless torso with mutilated dog tags pressed into the pulpy black flesh that protruded from the vest. The portion of the dog tag that was legible read *PRY*.

The remaining Marines found other parts of Pryor, including his head which, amazingly enough, was intact and still connected to part of his left shoulder. The body was respectfully assembled in a black canvas bag—the bag of death—and placed into one of the CH-46 choppers.

Vinnie, Red, and Doc climbed back into the jeep, without saying a word. As Vinnie pulled away from the scene that would remain seared in his mind for the remainder of his days, he muttered in a rage-filled voice, "Why didn't he just throw the fucking grenade?"

Mike was seated in the passenger seat, and he realized that Saint said something, but he couldn't decipher the words. "Saint," Mike asked gently as he placed his left hand on Vinnie's right shoulder in a comforting manner, "what did you say?"

Vinnie turned his head toward Mike but was looking through him. Mike realized that the look on Saint's face scared him more than anything he had seen thus far in country. Saint's blue eyes, which projected a serenity at all times before this, now were bulging, steely, and fiery. Vinnie's brow was angrily creased in a downward V shape, and his jaw jutted out in such a fashion as to accentuate his pursed lips. Indeed, even Vinnie's nostrils flared in opposition to his rapidly rising chest, as the forlorn Saint heaved in a rapid, shallow fashion.

Vinnie turned his eyes back to the road and began to maniacally strike the steering wheel and dashboard with his right fist as he furiously spat out each word: "WHY . . . DIDN'T . . . HE . . . JUST . . . THROW . . . THE . . . FUCKING . . . GRENADE . . . OUT . . . OF . . . THE . . . JEEP?" Following a deep inhalation, Saint continued, albeit in an exceedingly shallow, breathless fashion, "He didn't have to jump out of the jeep with the fucking thing shoved into his gut."

"Saint!" bellowed the much-less-sympathetic voice from the rear. "Snap the fuck out of it, man! Obviously, Green did it because he believed that there was no other option." Vinnie began to weep. He knew that Doc Nunn was right.

"Let's say he picked up that fucking grenade," Doc continued, "and cocked his arm back and started to throw that motherfucker with all his might over the goddamn DMZ. That fucking grenade would've exploded right there and you, Cap, and the two greens would've blown the fuck up."

Mike glanced at Doc, who was outwardly calm despite the raw edge to his voice, and subtly nodded. "That there green, what was his name?"

"Pryor. Eugene Pryor," Vinnie replied.

"That there Eugene Pryor is a goddamn hero. He sacrificed his life to save three brothers. Don't be mad, brother. Be thankful. Eugene Pryor gave you precious life in exchange for his own. Now, keep your eyes on the fucking road before you drive off a fucking cliff and kill the three of us. Got that, Vincent Benore fucking Santaniello?"

A pregnant pause ensued before Vinnie replied, "I got it, Doc."

The three Marines did not say another word for the rest of the drive back to the base at Gio Lihn. When they arrived, Vinnie went straight to a hooch, without saying a word to anyone. He grabbed a poncho liner, wrapped it around his shoulders, and lay face down upon the rubber lady inside. The men let Vinnie stay there for a couple of minutes to cool down, but they knew that it wasn't safe for him, given the hostilities that had occurred earlier that morning. So Captain LeRoy entered the hooch with Doc Milazzo.

"Hey, Saint," exclaimed LeRoy as he patted Vinnie on the calf, "c'mon now, we got work to do."

"Yeah, Vinnie, it ain't safe for you to be holed up in this hooch, because we expect incoming pretty much any second," added Milazzo.

Now, Vinnie was many things, and Vietnam was changing him by the minute, but the one thing he was not—and not even Vietnam could transform him in such a way—was an insubordinate Marine. Equal parts furious, sad, and delirious, Vinnie respectfully removed himself from the hooch and stood outside in the hot sun, with a sticky mixture of tears, dirt, and perspiration streaking his face and arms.

"PFC Pryor will be honored by the Corps for the valiant sacrifice of his life for the good of his brothers," LeRoy announced to the Marines who had congregated outside of the hooch. As he said this, the bag containing Pryor's remains was wrapped in an American flag and brought to a Huey for the first leg of his long, lonely journey back home. The men in the field instinctively stood at attention, saluting the body bag as it was loaded onto the chopper, and remained at attention until the bird was some distance away.

"Sir, one week ago, Pryor arrived in country and, one week later, he's heading back to the States . . . in parts." Vinnie was distraught. LeRoy and Milazzo tried like hell to comfort the forlorn Marine, but their efforts were unsuccessful, so the only option available was to move on.

After all, the Marine who dwelled on the past *became* the past.

Permanently.

The men began to unload the supplies from the jeep and ensured that every man at the base had fresh C-rats, two canteens of water, and plenty of arty. Once the Marines were re-fortified, Milazzo approached Vinnie and asked, "Saint, you okay?"

"Doc, I got two eyes, two arms, two hands, two legs, and my heart's still beatin', so I'm a'right. I got nothin' to worry about!" Milazzo walked away from the conversation marveling at Vinnie's fortitude. Vinnie walked away from the same encounter wondering why he felt so edgy and angry.

Such was the Vietnam experience in a world before PTSD would be recognized as truly one of the most grievous and long-lasting casualties of war.

CHAPTER 12

GETTING CLOSE TO GETTING AWAY AND A PROMOTION

Dear Lilly,

I'm doing fine. I'm glad to hear that everything is turning out well for your wedding. It really sounds groovy that you got everything set up. Just think, my little sister is going to be a married woman in less than a half of a year. WOW. Man, is time going by fast. Just think, in a few years, you might be a mother and me an UNCLE. It seems like just yesterday that you and me were little kids going to St. Mary's School. And now you're engaged and I'm at war. Boy, did we grow up.

I'm going to have a 10 day extension on my leave, so instead of getting 20 days, I will get 30 days' leave. I'll be home anywhere between the 18th to 24th of August so, don't worry, I'll be at your wedding. That apartment sounds real groovy. It would be real nice if you got the apartment so close to our house. Mom will be really happy if you live so close.

I haven't seen TV since I've been in 'Nam. I seen TV once when I was on R&R and it was in Chinese so it didn't help at all. It will be funny to watch TV when I'm home. I'll probably get hung up on the cartoons.

I've got to get cleaned up. The road is real dusty. It's been real nice weather. The sun is always shining. The weather we're having now reminds me of the first days of summer vacation when we just got out of school a few years ago.

You better not have Pepe home when I come home. I got to dislike that dog: He sounds like a real fairy. He better not bother Queenie while I'm home or else I'll have to do away with him. How is my normal dog, Queen, doing? Is it still as skinny as ever? Say hello to everyone for me and take care. I miss all of you very much.

Vinnie's March 9, 1968 letter to Lilly

Yep, I got my medal and picture back a few days ago. Thank you for congratulating me on my promotion. The raise in pay is $20 a month. Big deal. I haven't received your package yet. Right now, I am warming up a can of vegetable soup that Rosalie sent me.

Tell Marie I don't mind if she's small. Tell her I'll walk on my kneecaps and she'll walk on stilts and then we'll be the same height. Ha Ha. Only joking. Girls should be small, not giants. Tell Marie I'm real proud that she's my partner. Marie's a real good kid. She's like a sister, you know.

Here's what my rank insignia is as LCpl: crossed rifles are added to the stripe, as opposed to PFC, my old rank.

Excerpt from Vinnie's March 10, 196 letter to Lilly

"*Uncle Vinnie.* That's got a nice ring to it, don't it, Stone?" Vinnie asked his pal Doc Milazzo.

"Yeah, Saint, it sounds swell," Doc Milazzo replied, "but why are you so quick to get your sis knocked up? Don't you want her to have a little fun before she starts having a family?"

"Tony, she's gonna be twenty-two in September. What, ya want her to be an old maid before she has her first kid? C'mon, Doc, you and I are Italian, for Chrissake, we don't have our first kids in our late twenties! I better have a nephew or a niece in a couple of years, Stone. Don't you worry, I'll make sure to have you come up to Jamaica from Jersey to visit the family. I'll have the kids call you *Uncle Tony* 'cause you and I became brothers in this shithole!"

Tony chuckled, "You might wanna make sure that your sister is cool with me being *Uncle Tony* before you go and make that official, okay, hotshot?"

"My nephews and nieces are gonna have a whole team of uncles. There's gonna be me; my kid brother, who's barely gonna be older than the kids as he's only turning thirteen in May; you; Red; Doc Nunn; and my buddy from Jamaica, Doc Chang. We all are gonna take care of the pipsqueaks and make sure that they grow up to be good kids!"

"Howzabout we get outta 'Nam and back to the world before we start making such plans, huh, Saint?"

Vinnie chuckled and exclaimed, "Sure thing . . . *Uncle Tony*."

The next morning brought a hard downpour and the boys once again were waterlogged. "If I never see another goddamn rain cloud, it'll be too soon!" exclaimed Doc Nunn. I feel like I've been soaked to the bone for just about all of my time in this joint," Nunn continued, "my skin is so wrinkled and pruney that only an old broad would give me the time of day back home!" The men who were gathered for chow in the mess hall that morning laughed at Doc Nunn, but they all shared in his soaked misery. The Marines had suffered from rashes in their nether regions that would have brought them to their knees in tears back home. But here, where they were exquisitely aware of their own mortality, a terribly itchy, burning rash in one's groin was a welcome alternative to being blown to bits. In fact, most of the Marines considered their terrible rashes to be nothing more than nuisances. After all, the jungle rot and the scars from relentless leeches competed with the rashes, and they often won the battle.

The heavy rain also reduced the chances of being engaged with the NVA because it obscured their ability to plot an attack and carry it out with the precision that would be necessary to thwart any chance of a counterattack by the American forces. As such, a rainy day was like a snow day from school. The guys got to be lazy and take it easy—relatively speaking, of course. The men congregated under a large makeshift canopy and lit up little balls of C-4s, composition C-4 plastic explosives that the men often used to heat up coffee and C-rat cans. A couple of C-rats that contained beans and some mystery meat were thrown on the white-hot C-4 flame, as was a canteen of coffee.

"It's like Thanksgiving in March!" exclaimed one hungry Marine.

Vinnie, Docs Milazzo and Nunn, Red, Dennis, Captain LeRoy, and three other grunts who had just recently joined them in the Crotch were beneath the canopy. In addition to the C-rats, Vinnie was heating up a can of Campbell's soup, sent by Rosalie from back home. In the shit, it was akin to caviar.

The three green grunts could tell that the other Marines had been in the shit for a long time by how they spoke, by the weariness of their eyes, and by their tattered uniforms. One of the greens, Gerard Duffy, from Port Washington, New York, was the most inquisitive of the trio. He wore round spectacles over his blue-gray eyes and he had short, brownish hair that looked like it would be more wispy than thick were it not for the standard, high-and-tight, Marine-issued buzzcut. Duffy had a thickness to him that gave away his status as a green, for no one who'd been in the shit for a long time could have possibly kept on so much weight. He still had some home cooking on his bones and the boys would be sure to work it off him.

"Hey, Duff, get on the back of the line, you bastard. The front of the line is reserved for real Marines," chided Vinnie. Duffy smiled sheepishly and sauntered to the rear of the collection of Marines who were huddled around the glowing C-4, waiting for their slop to be served up. A few minutes later, the boys were sitting under the canopy, eating their meal.

Duffy looked at the men who clearly had been in country for a while and he realized that they all had "a look" about them that he couldn't figure out. Not misery, per se, but a look of . . . what was it? Exasperation? Despair? Fear? Frustration? Emptiness? Duffy couldn't put his finger on it, but it was very unsettling to him. *Am I gonna look like that, too, after a while?* Gerard bristled at the thought and took in another unsatisfying mouthful of slop.

In a couple of months, Duffy would learn the answer to his query. The boys had the look of death in their eyes. They had seen too many of their buddies die—and die horrifically—right before their eyes. They had carried too many mangled bodies and body parts, for hours and often days, until they could be disposed of at an LZ. High-volume exposure to death, especially in a war as protracted and unpredictable as Vietnam, had a certain way of killing pieces of the souls of the living. And that manifested as a specific look of death in one's eyes.

"Hey, Duff, when you're done chewing that shit in your mouth, let me know if *Looney Tunes* and *Tom and Jerry* still are popular cartoons on TV back in the world," asked Vinnie in a cheerful tone.

Vinnie allowed his mind to wandered for a split second, back to those lazy Saturday mornings when he'd awaken later than usual and saunter into the living room from his bedroom. Still sleepy-eyed, he'd emerge from his room, which was directly behind the small living room, and trudge toward the small black-and-white TV positioned on top of a small wooden table that Carmine had custom-made in his shop in the basement. Vinnie would pull a knob to turn on the TV, adjust the metal clothes hangers that doubled as TV antennas, and manually twist the stubborn dial to channel five, which was home to many of Vinnie's favorite cartoons. He'd then plop down onto the couch and revel in watching a bunny use a rifle to blast away at any number of God's creations.

Vinnie realized that his mind had wandered all the way across the globe and that he wasn't paying attention to Duffy's answer. Duffy's mouth was moving: ". . . and that's what's popular right now, Saint."

Fuck, I have no clue what the green just said. How the hell do I not look like a total idiot now? "Hey, you don't get to call me Saint until you've been in at least one firefight, or when you've been in country for three months, whichever comes first, green!" *Damn, I'm clever!*

"Fucking Saint. He asks a question and then doesn't even listen to the kid when he's answering it," joked Doc Nunn. Leave it to the jocular Doc Nunn to call out his pal for not listening.

Vinnie shot an angry glance at Doc before shaking his head and exclaiming, "Fucking Doc. The goddamn gooks are more trustworthy than that snake in the grass!" All of the fellas laughed, even Duff and his two fellow greens.

Doc Milazzo chimed in, "Yeah, Doc Nunn is like that bulldog on *Tom and Jerry*. What's his name? Oh, yeah, Spike! Spike always gets his ass kicked at first by a random iron, or a shotgun, but then always finds a way to give Tom a beatin' by the end of the cartoon!"

"So what you're saying, Stone, is that Nunn always gets the last word in, huh?" asked Vinnie.

"Goddamn right!" replied Nunn, before Milazzo could answer.

"Excuse me, Saint," asked one of the greens, Diego Montañez, a tall, dark-skinned kid with thick, jet-black hair and a roundish face that was offset by a square jaw. Montañez hailed from San Antonio, Texas and he was of Mexican heritage. He spoke with an accent that was part southern drawl, part Spanish-inflected. "Why do you call Doc Milazzo *Stone*?"

"Good question, green," replied Vinnie, "it's because he's a stone Italian. I mean, look at him. It's as if he just fell off the goddamn boat! If he wasn't a Marine, he'd be in the mafia!"

The ensuing laughter was deafening.

"Well," Milazzo interjected, "at least I got enough guns and artillery to fill that role!"

The boys continued to laugh in a good-natured manner. This is how the Marines often passed the rare downtime that they had: They took tongue-firmly-in-cheek pot-shots at each other. It made the madness of war just that much more tolerable.

"Hey, buddy," Red said as he gestured toward Montañez, "what's your name?"

"Diego Montañez, from San *Antón*, Texas."

Mike's eyes widened. "Oh, shit! We are gonna have fun with you, Montañez!"

More raucous laughter, followed quickly by a reassuring word from Mike: "Don't worry, Montañez. You'd have a problem if we DIDN'T make fun of you!"

"Hey, Montañez," interjected Vinnie, "how ya like that dog food that we made ya for breakfast?" Diego responded with an uneasy smile. He knew that Saint and the guys had been in country for a long time and he figured that they all had to be slightly crazy by this point in time, so the notion that they'd find it funny to surreptitiously feed dog food to an unsuspecting new grunt was not beyond the realm of possibilities.

Diego immediately began chewing much more slowly and he cast darting glances to the left and right to ascertain where he may spit the slop without causing any "shrapnel" to splash on the otherwise-filthy long-timers. Saint and his buddies immediately noticed Diego's reaction and they silently, but playfully, made eye contact with each other and took glee in the Texan's discomfort.

After what seemed like an eternity, Saint blurted out, "Don't worry, Tex, everything's groovy with the grub. Besides, we need you strong to watch our backs out here in the shit and, if you're too busy looking for a place to barf your brains out, then you're o f absolutely no use to us!"

170

The consternation immediately drained from Diego's face and his jaw slackened considerably. "Thank you. I would never let my brothers down," came his measured response. That impressed the Marines mightily and Montañez immediately became one of the boys.

"Hey, Tex," began Vinnie, with a nickname that became Diego's moniker from that moment on, "you got any pets back in the world?"

"Why, yes, we do! I live on a ranch back home so we've got plenty of farm animals, but my favorite pets are my three Rottweilers. Those dogs would tear the shit out of an attacker but they are gentle as bunnies with me and my family."

Vinnie mused, "Farm animals, huh? Yeah, we don't see many pigs and cows back in New York City where I'm from, Tex! But I have three dogs, too: Apache, a German shepherd; Queenie, a golden lab; and Pepe, my mom's little poodle. Apache is just like one of your Rotties. She'd tear apart anyone that tried to hurt one of us Santaniellos. Queenie had a loud bark, but she wouldn't hurt a fly. Now, Pepe . . . Pepe is a little pain in the ass. He's no bigger than a goddamn football, but he barks in this annoying, high-pitched tone that drives me crazy! I gotta say, I miss Apache and Queenie, but that goddamn Pepe . . . not so much!"

The light-hearted revelry was interrupted suddenly with a gruff, "Santaniello, get in here, on the double!" Captain LeRoy had barked the order from inside of the main tent that served as the base of operations in Cam Lo. Vinnie was startled by the sudden order and the other boys looked quizzically at each other as Vinnie rose immediately and hustled toward the tent. Duff, Tex, and the other greens looked petrified at the sudden change in the mood.

Vinnie approached the tent, which was actually quite large. It was considered a full bunker, as it was built up with concrete walls, had rudimentary electric power, a secure telephone line, and a very small fridge. Of course, given the importance of this bunker, it was fortified heavily by hundreds of sandbags, stacked ten-high around its perimeter. As he climbed over some rocks to approach the entrance to the bunker, Saint recalled how much back-breaking effort he and the boys had put into fortifying this "fortress" a few months back.

"Yes, sir?" came Vinnie's respectful response as he observed LeRoy, standing over the table with the secure telephone line, phone still in hand. LeRoy placed the handset back on its base and turned to Vinnie with a serious look in his eyes. *Holy shit*, thought Vinnie, *what the hell did I do wrong?* Typical paranoid military thinking: The Marines—and probably everybody else in every other branch of the military immediately—assumed the worst when any of their members were suddenly called out by a superior.

"Saint, sit down here for a second," LeRoy placed the handset back on the telephone base and gestured for Vinnie to sit in a makeshift chair located next to a table that was adjacent to the phone.

Vinnie, with uneasy nervousness rising from the pit of his stomach, strode toward the chair and sat down.

"Sir?" Vinnie made eye contact with his superior. Saint's blue eyes pleaded silently with LeRoy to let him know what he had done wrong and how it would impact the rest of his tour here in Vietnam. *Holy shit, if I did something that causes me to miss out on being the best man at Lil's wedding, I'll lose my goddamn mind!*

"Santaniello," started LeRoy, his voice seemingly rising with each syllable–

Oh, God, thought Vinnie, *this ain't gonna be good!*

"–you've been with me since you arrived here last fall, right?"

"Yes, sir," replied a despondent Saint.

"We've been through a lot, haven't we?"

"Yes, sir, we definitely have. And it's been a real honor to serve under your command, sir." *Oh, boy, did that sound desperate and corny*, thought Vinnie.

LeRoy, whose face was partially obscured by the shadows cast by the dull sources of light within the tent, turned to Vinnie and said, "Well, in light of all that you've done for the Corps in general, and for your brothers in the Thundering Third, specifically, I thought that it would only be right to promote you to lance corporal. Congrats, Saint!"

"Goddamn, Skipper," Vinnie breathily exclaimed after releasing a long, exaggerated sigh, "I thought that I was getting court-martialed after the way that you called me in here!" Vinnie then broke into a smile. "Why'd you do that, sir?"

"Because I like you, Saint. You're a good Marine. Sorta like what you did to that green, Montañez, a few minutes ago, right?"

"Touché, Skip. Touché!"

LeRoy turned serious for a moment. "Saint, I told you before that I thought you'd make a good officer, a good Marine Corps lifer, and this promotion is further evidence of that. I hope that you'll consider this after your twelve-and-twenty is done."

Vinnie didn't really know how to respond. It felt good to be recognized, and even better to get a promotion, but all he could think of was getting the hell out of this shithole and back to his family and friends a world away. "I will consider that, sir. Thanks for the promotion, Skipper. That means a great deal coming from you."

With that, Vinnie saluted Captain LeRoy and then walked toward the bunker's exit.

"Saint," LeRoy called as Vinnie was about to walk out into the pouring rain, "you're a good fucking Marine."

Vinnie stopped in his tracks, turned from his waist and then turned his head around, toward his left. He re-established eye contact with Captain LeRoy and nodded his head as he said, "Thank you, sir. Ya know, I learned from the best!"

And with that, Vinnie hopped out of the tent, over the rocks, and through the monsoon, back to where his brothers remained congregated.

"Ya need a good lawyer, you mafioso bastard?"

Leave it to Doc Nunn to show true compassion in such an uncertain scenario. All of the Marines who had been horsing around with Vinnie had tensed up when the captain had called him into the main bunker. Of course, no one said anything after Vinnie departed, but no one moved from their spot, either, until Vinnie re-emerged from the mysterious encounter with the skipper. Red gave Doc Nunn a half-hearted punch in the chest and shoved him aside as Saint returned to his cronies.

"You okay, brother?" asked Red, with genuine empathy for his friend.

Vinnie, ever cunning, realized immediately that the crowd of concerned Marines was as equally paranoid as he was and automatically assumed that he, a model Marine by all accounts, somehow had fucked up. Vinnie looked down and kicked at the ample mud that was gathering around them as a result of the rain.

"Shucks, fellas, I just wanna say what a real treat it's been to be with you fine fellas all these months," Vinnie began, "but . . ." He followed with a dramatic pause, a bow of his head, and a tear-wiping gesture with his right thumb and index finger.

"Goddamn," muttered Milazzo, "they're gonna shitcan Saint!"

Tex, who had just met Saint moments earlier, got a pit in his stomach, thinking that he was doomed to fail in the service if a quality guy like Santaniello was getting hammered by the bosses. Even the irrepressible Doc Nunn was beginning to wonder if his joke had been in poor taste.

"But . . . now you fuckers are gonna *have to* take orders from me, 'cause I've been promoted to lance corporal!"

174

There was an audible gasp, like air being released from a tire. The tension that had built to a fever pitch dissipated and was replaced with unadulterated glee and admiration.

"Yeah, Saint!"

"Congrats, brother!"

"Groovy news, for sure!"

"Great news!"

"I still ain't gonna listen to you, ya greasy New York bastard!"

Vinnie didn't have to look around to realize who made that last comment. "I love you, too, Nunn, ya goddamn hillbilly! Now, go dig me a goddamn hole, will ya?"

The boys circled around their promoted colleague and gave him respectful pats on the back. Red quickly held up his cup of slop, in the gesture of a toast. Daniel King clanked on the side of his aluminum cup to get everyone's attention and Doc Nunn burped very loudly (and for quite a long time, too) to quell the din.

"A toast," began Mike Reagan, "to a fine Marine and a good man. Our very own Vincent Benore Santaniello, the best fucking company driver in the Corps!"

"Cheers, Saint!"

"Yeah, pal!"

"*Salud!*" exclaimed Milazzo, the stone Italian Vinnie respected greatly.

"Congrats to our Saint," exclaimed Captain LeRoy. "There was no one more deserving of such an honor. Saint, what you did in commandeering that jeep during the ambush last week was incredible. You saved us, man."

The sting of Pryor's valiant decision to die so that Vinnie, LeRoy, and Yellow could live had impacted Vinnie profoundly.

Deep down, the firefight and Pryor's death haunted him, and he unfairly blamed himself for Pryor's death. Vinnie's face tightened upon hearing LeRoy's words, and his easy smile was supplanted by a pained grimace.

"I shoulda done something to save that green Pryor. He was killed on my watch, Skipper."

"Saint, you drove a piece-of-shit, broken-down jeep down a goddamn minefield and through a fucking ambush. There ain't nothing more that you could've done to save our asses. If it weren't for you, that jeep would've flipped over and blown up, killing all of our sorry asses!" LeRoy meant business when he said this. His eyes widened to a nearly impossible width. "You deserve that promotion, Saint. You're a great fucking Marine, and I'm proud to serve with you. Pryor did what he did because he knew that you would've done the same thing for him."

Doc Nunn realized that Vinnie was about to break down again, so he jumped in as only he could. "Okay, motherfuckers! Do you sonsabitches know what this little promotion really means for ol' Saint here?"

Everyone peered through misty eyes at Doc, anxiously awaiting his response so as to break the profound tension that was enveloping them.

"Why, twenty more U.S. fucking dollars a month in salary and a couple of crossed rifles below the stripe on his sleeve, of course! Saint is a fucking Rockefeller now! Next month's allotment of booze, smokes, and girlie magazines is on Vinnie's dime! Let's hear it for Saint!" Nunn yelled out, "Hip hip!"

"HOORAY," came the collective response from the boys, once again relaxed and laughter-filled.

Doc Nunn repeated, "Hip hip!"

"HOORAY!" yelled the boys in obedient unison.

Doc had done it again.

As the men all yelled and cheered, Saint sidled up to Nunn and kissed his filthy face. Vinnie then placed his lips close to Doc's right ear, directly underneath his battle-scarred helmet, and whispered, "Thanks, Doc. I owe you one."

Doc winked at Vinnie, who nodded in return, before the boys proceeded to prop him up on a couple of shoulders and gleefully parade their new lance corporal around the base for an impromptu parade.

I still should've done something to save Pryor, Vinnie thought as he took a guilt-filled trip around the base while hoisted on the men's shoulders. *His blood will always be on my hands.*

HIP, HIP, HOORAY!

CHAPTER 13

ANXIETY IS A CONNIVING, RUTHLESS BITCH

I got two letters from you today. I was glad to hear from you. I also got a letter from "Doc" (John Chang). He is just fine. He is getting short: He has between 25-37 twenty-five and thirty-seven days left in 'Nam. I'm glad he's going home. At least I won't have to worry about him anymore. Bruce is doing alright for himself: It's pretty safe where he is. John—"Doc"— told me to hurry up home because there'll be a few drinks sitting on the bar in the Monument Tavern. Doc is a great guy. He's the most trustworthy guy that I know. He is like a brother to me. When he comes home, I want you to give him the King treatment. Doc really has seen the war over here. Not like those guys who spent their time in Da Nang. I'll really feel a lot better when he gets home.

So, our little brother's mug wasn't in the newspaper yet. It probably takes a few days before it gets in it. By now, you have probably seen it in the paper. But it really doesn't matter if it's in the paper; we all know that he won first place and that's all that counts. I am really proud of him; he's really a smart kid.

I really haven't gotten your package yet. No lie. The last letter that I got was dated the 8th of this month. The other one was dated the 6th. I'll probably get your packages sooner or later.

Well, here's the news on the war up here. Well, enough about the war. Ha Ha. That was some helluva report. Ha Ha. What can you do. Sorry 'bout that, Sis.

Well, little sister of mine, your marriage date is coming up sooner and you must be getting nervous. Ha Ha. I'm only trying to make you nervous. I'm in a joking mood tonight.

Well, today I traveled 79 miles. I went to Cam Lo and back to Dong Ha four times. My jeep was giving me some engine trouble and we couldn't spot it. But yesterday we found out what it was and it's running fine now. We still haven't gotten the new jeeps yet. We'll get them when the war is over. I bet you.

You know the way Mom writes, she's really worried sick over me. Mom worries sick over me. Do me a favor, Lil: Teach Joseph to be grateful for what he has and what Mom and Dad do for him and his benefit. I know you realize how good our parents are to us. It's hard to bring up and teach a little brother how to be and what to avoid and stay away from. I want you to start by teaching him how to do things for himself. It's really hard for me to teach Joseph all this by writing to him. Here's what I want you to start at: Teach him to clean up his own mess. For instance, to clean up his clothes that he throws on the chair, bed, floor, or wherever he throws it. And if he still leaves that damn bathroom like he used to. I remember I used to go in it after he finished taking a bath and it was like it took a direct hit by a 140-mm rocket. I would clean it up before Mom would see it. It's really sickening that Mom has to be a nurse to him. Don't worry: I'll be coming home in 4 ½ months. You know, I used to feel real proud of myself when I finished cleaning up the bathroom after bathing. I know Mom wouldn't have to do it. And I know it pleasured her and helped her along. Now, I don't want you to baby him. I want you to teach him to take care of himself, to be capable of doing something without Mom having to clean up after.

If the both of you kicked in and helped Mom out, it would really make Mom feel good and even more I'd feel real good and proud.

Well, Lil, I got to be going; I got a whole mess of letters to write tonight.

Love your brother, Vinnie

P.S. Don't worry, I'll be coming home in 4 ½ months . . . Well, little sister of mine, take care. I love and miss all of you very much.

Vinnie's March 16, 1968 letter to Lilly

For what seemed like the first time since he'd gotten to 'Nam, Vinnie had some time to himself. He had just finished his fourth and final run to Cam Lo and he was exhausted, both mentally and physically. The drives to and from Marine bases typically involved transporting at least a small cache of arty and there was always the chance that the jeep would be attacked, like in the ambush that had cost the Thundering Third the services of a brave Marine, PFC Pryor. In fact, ever since that ambush and the concomitant brush with death, Vinnie experienced an unexplainable (to him, anyway) debilitating anxiety every time he had to make a run. Vinnie would experience extreme shortness of breath and he'd break out in a terrible sweat whenever his superior told him to gear up the jeep for another run. Vinnie blamed his stubborn asthma for the inability to breathe and attributed the sweating to the oppressive jungle heat that was pounding all of the men. However, deep down, Vinnie knew that the ambush and Pryor's death—Vinnie saw Pryor's body blow apart, after all—was the cause of his bedeviling anxiety.

And this realization brought Saint great shame. The badass Vinnie Santaniello from Jamaica, New York, a car whiz back home and the universally praised and beloved company driver for his brothers here in Vietnam, was afraid to get in his jeep and perform his duties.

What a fucking sad excuse for a Marine, Vinnie chided himself. *You're not worthy of your brothers' praise and trust.* And so was the internal torture that Vinnie endured quietly and ashamedly.

Vinnie was physically exhausted, too, because while he forced himself to drive the jeep up and down this tiny piece of Hell, he also had to load and unload the jeep while often taking time to get under the vehicle to repair the latest piece of machinery to fall from its chassis. Drenched in the sweat that was the byproduct of his own anxiety and the unforgiving sun, Vinnie trudged into his hooch back in the rear, emphatically plopped onto his rubber lady, and engaged in something that always brought him great joy. He began to write a letter to Lilly.

"Well, here's the news on the war up here." Vinnie's stopped writing after that sentence. *I really need to tell Lilly about what's going on here*, Vinnie thought to himself. *She deserves to know the truth and I can't keep lying to my best friend back home.* And with that, Vinnie began to tell Lilly the real story about Vietnam. He told her about Tet, when he'd witnessed an incredible amount of suffering and dying on both sides of the war. He wrote about the time he'd thought he had stepped on a land mine when his jeep had gotten stuck in the mud. And he wrote about Eugene Pryor and the overwhelming guilt and anxiety that the ambush had caused him. Vinnie spent a good hour writing the letter before falling asleep with the pen in his hand, the paper under his face, and dried tears on his cheeks.

"Hey, anybody seen Saint?" Doc Milazzo inquired of the group of Marines sitting under trees, behind rocks, and anywhere else that they could find precious shade from the unforgiving heat of the sun.

Blake Connors, a twenty-year-old fair-skinned kid from South Dakota and one of the grunts who had arrived with Pryor, looked up at Milazzo and replied, "I seen him go into his hooch about an hour ago, and he ain't come back out yet."

"Thanks, Connors," replied Milazzo. "I'll go wake his ass up."

Milazzo entered the hooch and saw Saint sprawled on the floor, with the letter to Lilly exposed under his head. Tony read the letter and was slightly appalled and moderately angry. *Why is Saint telling his sister about what's really going down here in 'Nam?* he thought.

She's gonna be sick every day now until Vinnie gets back for her wedding in August.

Tony gently patted Saint on his left shoulder until he awakened. "Hey, Saint, you fell asleep, pal, and you were drooling on this here letter to your sister. I moved it from under your face so you wouldn't ruin it."

Vinnie was groggy until he realized that Tony had taken his letter while he was asleep. Once that realization hit Vinnie, his senses sharpened and he peered intently at his pal from Jersey.

"Stone, you read the letter, didn't you?"

The words stung Milazzo like a defendant hearing a jury return a guilty verdict and he could not bear to make eye contact with Vinnie, whose accusation both appalled and emboldened the corpsman. "I didn't intentionally read it. I took it out from under your wet mug so that it wouldn't get soggy. A couple of words then caught my eye and I realized that you were telling your sister shit that she doesn't need to know."

Vinnie was furious. "You had no fucking right to read that letter, Tony. That was between me and Lilly," Vinnie spat angrily, "not you!"

Tony knew that he had violated his brother's privacy by reading the letter, but he stood his ground, albeit apprehensively, as he saw the anger furrow into Vinnie's creased brow and taut jaw. "Saint, listen, man. You can't send your sister that letter. You love that girl more than anything, right?"

Vinnie stared intently, his lips sealed tight, with nary an acknowledgment that Milazzo had posed a significant question to him.

"Look, I know you love Lilly more than you love your own life, man. The shit you put in that letter would crush your sister. She'd cry herself to sleep with worry over you and your safety here.

"Vietnam is madness, pal. We're here to kill and to avoid being killed. That's what we are: Fucking Marine killers, and we're damn good at it. You and I understand what our mandate is here in fucking Vietnam and we accept it. But," Milazzo paused as he noticed Saint's face soften, ". . . but a young girl shouldn't have to know that THAT is her beloved brother's reality every second of every fucking day, Saint."

Vinnie unfurled his fists and rubbed his sweaty brow while turning his back to Milazzo.

Saint reached into his pocket and removed one of his favorite treasures, a picture of him and Lilly taken in his backyard in Jamaica. The picture was taken right after he had completed boot camp. He had leave and had flown back to New York to see his family again before he left for Vietnam. Vinnie was in full uniform: all khaki, including a tie. He was proudly wearing the National Defense Service medal and ribbon that he'd received after completing boot camp. Vinnie'd graduated from boot camp as the top grunt in his class—something that he never boasted about here, unlike that mouthy Yellow—and he was damn proud to share that news with his family back in his modest Jamaica, New York home.

Vinnie peered at the pic and laughed. He was wearing his official Marines cap and he dreamily recalled Lilly's reaction when he'd told her what the Marines called the cap: a *piss cutter*! Lilly was drinking a can of Pepsi and she choked so hard with laughter when Vinnie revealed the name to her that she had soda streaming from her nostrils. *Shit*, Vinnie thought, *that was so damn funny!*

Vinnie stared harder at the picture and he realized that Queenie, one of his dogs, was running across the shot as he and Lilly posed happily. Vinnie was holding a cigarette in his right hand as always and his left hand was wrapped around his "kid sister's" waist. Lilly wore a cheetah-print skirt that was all the rage back in the late 1960s and she wore her hair in an attractively short fashion.

Vinnie and Lilly. Lil and Vin. They were inseparable back when life was much less complicated and scary. *I look like a fucking baby*, thought Vinnie as he absentmindedly stroked the newfound crow's feet at the corners of his eyes. *I wonder if I could ever return to the groovy, worry-free kid that I was back in the world. The kid in this picture is long gone and he has been replaced by*—Vinnie paused, peered into his scratched aluminum mirror, and saw the eyes of a stranger—*THIS!*

Milazzo watched intently but dared not speak. His brother was in great distress. Vinnie, alone in his thoughts for several minutes, suddenly remembered that his pal was still in the hooch.

"Goddammit, Tony. You're right," Vinnie exclaimed as he trudged toward the corpsman. "I can't let Lilly know what's going on with us Marines here in 'Nam because the news would scare her. And forget about my mom's reaction if she learned about the craziness that is Vietnam."

Tony put his arm around Vinnie and squeezed his shoulder. "You're doing the right thing, Saint," said Tony. "Lilly and your mom would not be able to handle the brutality that you wrote about in that letter and they'd be worried sick until the second that you finally walked through your front door."

Vinnie's shoulders slumped under the weight of Milazzo's arm and he became noticeably less tense. "Sorry for snapping at you, Stone. After all, you were right. That letter woulda caused nothing but *agita* for my mom and sister."

"It's alright, chum. We're *paisans*, and us Italians are known to get a little hot under the collar every now and then!"

With that, the two friends and brothers shared a hearty laugh, followed by Vinnie landing a mock punch to Tony's right shoulder. "Finish that letter and then get the fuck out of this hooch. It's blazing hot in this thing."

As he walked out, Tony glanced at the picture that Vinnie had been looking at; he had absent-mindedly placed it on the table next to the mirror.

"Your sister's a fox, Saint. You better not ever let her outta your sight 'cause I just might come up to the city and show her what a real man looks like!"

Tony began to laugh as Vinnie reached for a pillow on his rubber lady and flung it at Milazzo's head. "Get the fuck outta here," Vinnie laughed. "I ain't never taking my arm from around my sister's waist, to make sure that dirty bastards like you don't get within a hundred yards of this here fine young lady!"

Tony feigned abject fear as he hooted in an exaggerated fashion before scampering out of the hooch. Vinnie smiled. He then peered at the picture one more time, kissed the image of Lilly, and placed it back in his pocket, right above his heart, but not before he whispered, *I love you, Lilly, and I only want the best for you. I'll protect you 'til the day that I die.*

With that, Vinnie took the first draft of his letter and re-read it. As luck would have it, the first paragraph of page three was where Saint began his scary recounting of what he had experienced thus far in Vietnam. Vinnie paused for a couple of minutes and then slowly tore up pages three through seven and set them ablaze with a match. He then took another sheet of paper, whispered under his breath, *I'm sorry for lying to you, Lil, but I can't make you and Mama sick with worry over me until I get home. I promise to tell you the truth about this fucking war when I get home.* And, with that, a lying Saint began to write anew to his beloved sister.

"Well, here's the news on the war up here. Well, enough about the war," he began writing. "Ha Ha. That was some helluva report. Ha Ha. What can you do. Sorry 'bout that, Sis." *It's for your only good,* Vinnie thought, and then he continued to write the homogenized letter to the woman he'd spent most of his teenage years protecting. Why would this one instance be any different, albeit from the other side of the world?

Saint emerged from the hooch with his freshly written letter, dated March 16, 1968 and sealed in a USMC-issued envelope. He'd make sure that the letter went out with that day's mail.

"There he is: the fucking hermit of Kilo Company!" The voice bellowed from behind a cluster of Marines huddled under the shade of a tree, but Vinnie didn't have to peer through the faces of the dozen or so young men obscuring the identity of the wise-ass who'd cracked wise at Saint.

"Ha, ha, very funny, Doc. Why don't you show your face so I can shoot a slug up your fucking nose?" Vinnie said this with a smile, of course, and the other Marines roared in response.

"It's fucking hot enough out here, Saint. Shut yer trap so that we aren't punished with more hot air!"

Doc Nunn was on a roll, and Vinnie paid him his dues as only a veteran Marine could: "Try not to trip over your saggin' balls when you come out of hiding, you goddamn squid!"

Nunn emerged from the boys with a cigarette dangling from the corner of his mouth. He sauntered up to Vinnie and began to slowly and playfully circle him, as if he was sizing up his brother for a fight. Doc removed the cigarette, blew a plume of smoke in Vinnie's face, and then put his lips close to Saint's left ear.

"You *awright*, pal?"

Vinnie looked into Doc's squinting right eye, thought to himself that Nunn eerily resembled an emaciated Popeye the Sailor Man, and winked at him to convey that all was as well as could be expected for a nineteen-year-old kid who desperately was trying not to die before he could leave this hellhole for home, to be the best man at his sister's wedding.

"Saint, Captain LeRoy asked that I accompany you on your trip out to Cam Lo tomorrow morning," said Montañez.

Vinnie cocked his head down and peered at the young Marine from Texas. Vinnie liked the kid's moxie and thought that he'd develop into a trusted leader of Kilo Company, assuming that he wasn't killed first. Vinnie feigned annoyance and whined ironically, "Fucking Cam Lo *again?!* I made four goddamn trips there just yesterday, Tex. What the hell could those greens possibly need back there?"

Tex smiled uneasily, for he was *fairly* certain that his company driver, mentor, and idol was pulling his leg. "Well, I would venture to guess that the Marines need more ammo. There've been lots of reports of the gooks making inroads down by the DMZ." Tex was smart and he did his homework.

"Don't get all *gunji* on me now, Tex," replied Vinnie. "Most guys who *want* to be heroes get their wish, but it becomes a *death wish*, green, and we've had enough dyin', ya hear me?"

Vinnie immediately thought of Pryor and the look in the young Marine's eyes before the bright light and deafening explosion obliterated his life. The vision of Pryor's body blowing up—a vision seared in Saint's mind, despite his fastidious efforts to suppress it—caused Saint to unconsciously jerk his head to the side and downward, as if to turn away from Pryor's violent death.

Montañez knew that being *gunji* was akin to being too gung-ho about the war. And the guys who had put in hard, harrowing months in the shit really despised the greens who came in country all gung-ho, often oblivious to the fact that they were there to replace the grizzled veterans' dead friends. The last thing a guy who was long in his tour and had lost more buddies than he'd care to admit needed was a bigmouth *gunji* who thought he was going to be Captain America.

Armed with that knowledge, Tex did not speak again. He made sure to show deference to his superiors by allowing them to dictate what was done and how it would get done. Saint knew exactly what Tex was doing and he was very happy to realize that Montañez got it, that he knew his role as a new Marine in Kilo Company.

"Okay, Tex, let's not keep the captain waiting."

And with that, Vinnie and Montañez departed to Captain LeRoy's bunker, to learn their latest orders.

Upon arriving at the bunker, Vinnie noticed his pal, Michael Reagan, standing with LeRoy, shooting the breeze.

"Hey, Red, what's the good word, pal? You getting outta this dump any time soon?"

Vinnie knew that Mike was short, *real* short, and that he just *had* to be allowing himself to think about getting back to the friendly confines of Edmonds, Washington. Red chuckled at Vinnie's comment and noted that he'd be shipped off to Japan in about a month to spend the last four weeks of his thirteen-month tour far enough away from the hellhole that was 'Nam.

Vinnie immediately thought of his childhood friend from Jamaica, John "Doc" Chang, who also was getting really short here in 'Nam.

"Red, you'll probably see my buddy from home, Doc Chang, when you're spending your last week in paradise over in Japan. Make sure you tell that lucky bastard that Saint says hello. Then, tell him that I also said to keep an eye on my sister until I get home over the summer."

"I'll be sure to look for Chang while I am being fed grapes and fanned by some foxes, Saint," came Red's sarcastic, good-natured response.

Chang is such a great guy, Vinnie thought to himself. *I'm happy that he survived 'Nam and is heading back home. It sure will be nice to stand outside the corner store again with him and the fellas, singing songs and drinking cold soda! Shit, I can't wait to get back home for good!*

Vinnie turned his attention back to Mike Reagan. "Hey, Red, what exactly will you be doing with my buddy Chang over in purgatory for a month before you are paroled from the Corps?"

Reagan pondered the question for a moment and then said, "I think we'll be shining boots and washing dishes. You know, only the most dangerous shit is reserved for the bravest Marines in this here Vietnam War."

Vinnie chuckled and Tex merely gazed at Red, wondering what would be going through his own mind when he got so close to getting out of Vietnam that he could taste it.

"Hey, Skipper," Mike called out to Captain LeRoy, "would you mind if Vinnie and I take a little walk before I help him and Tex load up that goddamn jeep?"

"Absolutely not, Red. Just be back by 1800 hours, got it?"

"Sir, yes, sir!" Mike turned to Tex and said, "We'll be right back, green. How's about you begin to load up Saint's jeep with some fresh linens that are stored in the boxes over there?" Mike gestured to some nondescript wooden boxes located outside of the bunker.

"Will do." And with that, the obedient Tex was off to perform his duty. Once the two young friends and brother Marines were alone, Mike patted Vinnie on the shoulder and gestured with his chin to proceed out the rear of the bunker.

"What's going on, Red. Why are you so serious?" Vinnie asked.

Mike squinted at Vinnie for a long time before he exhaled and said, "I don't know what I'm gonna do if I get outta here alive, Saint. All I've known is killing and avoiding getting killed for the last year. When I go back home, what am I supposed to do? What is my destiny?"

"Whoa, Red. That is some deep shit, man. All I think about is what kinda sauce my mom is gonna make over the meatballs and pasta that will greet me when I walk through the front door of my house in a few months!"

Mike gave a pained smile, and then he pressed on. "Do I go to school? Do I get a job? Do I get married? Here, I never have to worry about what I'm going to do because I've always got orders; every fucking second of my life is accounted for. But, back home, there is no gunny or officer barking out orders to me. Then what?"

"Then you adjust to your old way of living, Mike. You'll be back home, pal. You'll have what every fucking guy in this shithole wants, what every guy dreams of: being back home." Vinnie whistled and slapped his leg in reaction to his own observation. "Mike, I want to go home in the worst way. I miss my family, I miss my friends. Hell, I even miss my girlfriend who wants to get married nine fucking seconds after I get off the plane at JFK!"

Mike chuckled and looked Vinnie square in the eye. "Saint, I'm scared, man. The truth is that I'm scared. The irony is that I'm not scared about my job here in Vietnam and this is the scariest shit that I have ever seen. I'm scared of going back to being Michael Reagan, U.S. citizen."

Vinnie squeezed Mike's shoulder. "Pal, we're all scared of what's waiting for us back in the world. But ya know what? Whatever is waiting for you and me back home, it can't be no worse than a fucking gook looking to blow our heads off with a machine gun or a grenade. I'll take my chances trying to find a job over trying to stay alive on a battlefield!" Mike hunched his shoulders and shook his head in a resigned fashion, causing Vinnie to turn deathly serious. "Mike, look at you. You're well-spoken, respected by everyone in the company, and you're educated. You're gonna land a great job, marry some great broad, and have yourself a wonderful life. I believe in you, man. But ya know what? If that doesn't pan out, you will do something like go back to school to be an artist. I've seen your sketches, pal, and that's some serious talent you have in that right hand of yours!"

Mike was genuinely humbled by Vinnie's sentiments. "Saint, I really appreciate the kind words of encouragement, but the real truth of the matter is that all the guys here look up to you, me included. You're funny, you speak with that strange *Noo Yawk* accent, and you're the bravest guy in the company. Every single guy in the company knows that you'd take a bullet for them without thinking twice."

"What accent?" Vinnie laughed and put his arm around Mike's broad shoulders. "Listen, Red, me and you, we seen a lot—probably too much—during our time in country. We seen many of our brothers die and we've probably sat up at night wondering how we still were alive in this fucking madness. But we are here for a reason, buddy. There is a reason why we ain't dead yet, and there's a reason why you're going home in a couple of weeks.

"You made it, Mike. You survived this shithole. There's gotta be a reason for that."

Vinnie looked around the platoon and noticed that they were alone in the jungle. He marveled at the deafening silence that was enveloping them and he thought that he couldn't remember if he had ever previously had such a quiet moment during his time in 'Nam.

Vinnie completed a visualization of his immediate surroundings, including an instinctive glance into the distant trees for any sniper movement, before he continued speaking from the heart.

"I don't know if you believe in God or Jesus—and I ain't the most religious guy around—but I do, and I believe that we all have a purpose in life. God gives everyone a chance to do something great. We don't know when that chance will come, or what we will have the chance to do, but we all get that shot. Many of us are too goddamn preoccupied to see when that chance comes and we blow it. You, Mike? You ain't gonna blow that chance. It may come next month, or next year, or maybe forty fucking years from now, but it's gonna come for you. And when it does, you're gonna be ready. And you're gonna be great."

Mike hugged Vinnie and Saint hugged Red right back.

"You're gonna get outta here, too, Saint. We're all gonna go home and put this shit far behind us. And then you're gonna fly across the country and hang out with your boy from Edmonds, Washington. We'll hit Seattle and then, I promise, we'll drive up to North Pole, Alaska and visit Christmas land in the summer!

"You're a good man, Vinnie. Thanks for the pep talk. I can't wait to see what greatness God and Jesus have in store for you!" With that, Mike glanced at his watch and noticed that it was a few minutes to six. "C'mon, pal, let's get back to camp before LeRoy has our asses court-martialed! I'll help you pack that tin can before we head back to Cam Lo."

Vinnie extended his hand toward Mike. Red grabbed Saint's hand and they exchanged a firm handshake before they turned and walked back to the camp. Two brave Marines, walking side by side, mutually scared of what their futures held but cautiously optimistic that, when their time for greatness presented itself, they would be prepared to seize the opportunity.

CHAPTER 14

143 MORE DAYS TO GO IN 'NAM, BUT WHO'S COUNTING?

I haven't written to you for a while. I have been meaning to but I just never got around to it. Well, the weather here has been just like our summers in NY: It's just at the right temperature. I have started to get a nice tan again. Yesterday, me and a few of my buddies went swimming at the Cam Lo Bridge. Boy, was the water great! Most of the river is usually very shallow, about 3 ½ feet deep. But there are parts the Seabees dug out just for the guys to go swimming and it is great. You walk out 6 feet and it's way over your head . . . you can swim or dive into the water and there's always a lot of guys there. The river runs right through the middle of the perimeter while you're swimming. So you're always inside the perimeter while you're swimming. The guy I was with, "Doc" Tony, comes from Patterson, NJ. He's a stone Italian. Me and him get along good. We're always talking about NY and NJ: He always talks about Wildwood and I talk about Rockaway. Lil, if you ever seen a bunch of mental cases you would've seen all of us when we were swimming.

Well, yesterday was eight months in Vietnam for me and, man, am I happy. I can remember when I was up at Con Thien like it was only yesterday and that was when I first came over here and joined the company at Con Thien. Right now, the company is at Cam Lo district headquarters. It's real nice here, at least I think. I'm living with the company again. I like it much better when I live with the company than when I live in Dong Ha. I still go back to Dong Ha once or twice a day to pick up mail, supplies, etc. I live in this bunk that is as big as my room and there's seven guys living in here, counting me. It's a real groovy bunker. It's even painted inside and has a concrete floor. It has lights and outlets in it but there's no electricity because the generator is broken down.

Listen to this: In Cam Lo village, there are these stands where the people sell candles, clothes (like I sent yous) and a lot of other little things. Well, there's this girl about 12 or 13 and I buy my candles from her. She's a real doll and I believe that she likes me. What she did was crochet me a pillowcase and gave it to me. It's the cutest thing. Her name is Susie and she made it like this:

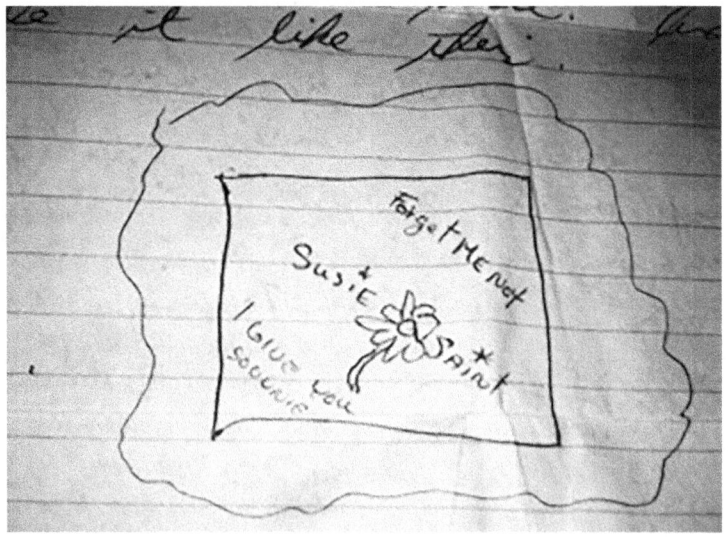

It is really groovy. I'm going to send it home to save it. She talks English pretty good. As soon as I get to send another package home, I'm going to put it in it. Or I might end up sending it separate

before I wind up losing it. You'll really like it, but when Rosalie sees it, she'll get jealous. Ha Ha. That will be a laugh.

Well, Lil, I got to go up to Cam Lo Hill right now. Take care.

Love, your brother, Vinnie

P.S. Say hello to everyone for me.

First of two letters Vinnie wrote to Lilly on March 23, 1968

Hey little sis,

I went into Dong Ha a few hours ago and I also picked up the mail for the company. I got four letters: 1 from Rosalie, 1 from our family, and 2 from YOU. They were real nice letters and they made me very happy. First of all because I'll be able to wear dress blues for your wedding and second of all because you're such a doll to let me wear them. If any of the other guys want to wear dress blues, tell them to join the Marines and then they will rate to wear them. Ha Ha.

You tell my other little sister Marie that I'll be more than happy to be with her all night if John's not there. Me and her will definitely have a good time. She is a real great girl. She's just like a sister to me. About Johnny getting drafted, well, I really feel sorry for him because he's married. But if he was single there would be nothing wrong with him going into the service. Tell Marie not to worry because the chances of him coming to Vietnam if he's in the Army are very, very slim. But if he gets drafted into the Marine Corps the chances are very, very good. If he can, he should join the Navy for 3 years or the Seabees for 2 years. But he might not be able to get either one. But they're both about the safest outfits to join. Just tell him I said "good luck."

I can't wait for John [Chang] to get the hell out of Viet Nam. He's in a pretty bad place. Bruce said he's been skating since he joined the Marine Corps. Just tell him to keep those planes in the air. They're saving a lot of lives up here.

Hold on, the Px truck is here.

. . . I just went out to the Px truck and there was about a million guys on line already. See, a truck comes by with cigarettes and shaving and writing gear and we buy it off the truck. It only has the needs that I mentioned, no luxury stuff like soda, etc.: There's been no soda or beer for us Marines for about 2 ½-3 months. But the Seabees got it, the Air Force people got it (that's in Dong Ha). All they give the Marines is ammo and hard times. That's why I hate the Marine Corps. We used to get 2 cans of beer and 2 of soda about twice a month. But like I said before haven't gotten it for 2 ½-3 months. And when we do get it we have to pay for it. Boy, is it a big joke. Let me get off the subject before I start getting pissed.

So, Bobby Kennedy is going to run for president. He definitely can't sell us down the drain more than Johnson did. I just hope that we get someone that helps every one of the Americans over here and back home in the U.S.A. and the heck with helping every other country under the sun. A 143 days left for me and 181 days left for you.

Love ya, Lil!

Your big brother,
Saint

Second of two letters Vinnie wrote
to Lilly on March 23, 1968

"Hey, Stone, let's go take a swim in the river under the Cam Lo Bridge!" Vinnie loved to swim in the big hole that the Seabees dug out for the Marines to blow off some steam. Of course, it was not actually a river; it was basically an incredibly large version of the inground pools that Vinnie recalled seeing at the fancy houses on Long Island when he took the Long Island Rail Road to Jones Beach during the summer.

"Shit, Saint. You shoulda been Aquaman because you can't get enough of that damn pool," replied Doc Milazzo. "Gimme a minute to get my trunks on so that I can join you at the Jersey Shore, 'Nam-style."

"Rockaway Beach, not the Jersey Shore, Tony. How many times I gotta correct you?"

Milazzo chuckled at Vinnie's brash statement and went into the large bunker that he'd been sharing with Saint, Doc Nunn, Red, Tex, and Daniel King. Tony emerged seconds later and took a running leap into the refreshing water while simultaneously shouting in his distinctively loud voice, "CANNONBALL!"

Tony leapt right into the midst of Vinnie, Doc Nunn, Red, and Tex, and the boys in the pool scrambled to avoid being crushed by the incoming Milazzo. Tony landed with a great splash and the ensuing concussion of waves splashed mightily into the faces of the Marines who were enjoying the coolness of the river.

"Goddammit, Milazzo, you Jersey mobster. Now all the shit is coming up from the river floor. Why couldn't you just dive in like a normal person?" bemoaned Doc Nunn, who simply was trying to float on his back but had to stop because of the dirt and seaweed that was rising to the surface of the water. Tony laughed and then made an exaggerated kicking motion to splash copious amounts of water into Doc Nunn's weathered face.

Vinnie, Red, and Tex were engaged in a fun game of Monkey in the Middle; Vinnie and Red were tossing an old football that Tex had brought from home. Tex tried to intercept the wayward tosses. Milazzo looked at the boys frolicking and entertained the notion of crushing Saint from behind with a vicious sack that would've made Dick Butkus proud, but he opted against such tomfoolery because he didn't want Vinnie to go crazy on him.

He hasn't been the same since Pryor's death and that jitteriness will only get worse if I pound him unexpectedly, thought Milazzo before he opted to continue swimming close to Doc Nunn.

"Hey, fellas," yelled Red, "we're just like the Kennedys playing football on Thanksgiving, right?"

Vinnie laughed, "Yeah, and hopefully, Bobby can get elected president and rescue us from here!"

Tex noted, half-mockingly, "C'mon, chums, President Johnson is a Texan and he'll do the right thing by us, now won't he?" The Marines were flabbergasted until they realized that the native Texan was being facetious. LBJ wasn't exactly a popular figure with the boys in the service.

"That goddamned Johnson," bemoaned one of the boys in the pool, "he don't give two shits about us Americans in this here shit!"

"And he wouldn't last three seconds here if he ever had the balls to show himself," said another.

"Okay, fellas," exclaimed Vinnie, "that's enough of your Hanoi Hannah-ing, ya hear? Let's get back to having some fun without the politics!"

With that, the boys resumed their aquatic adventures.

All of the boys except for Doc Nunn resumed frolicking and playfully tackling each other in the water as they fumbled for the pigskin. Nunn was especially exhausted this morning and was intent on floating blissfully on the glistening surface of the river. Doc was floating about twenty yards west of the boys when Daniel King, who was sunbathing on the "shore," looked out at the prone Doc on the water and noticed a long, thick, green object that appeared to be a belt floating slowly in his direction.

Daniel yelled out, "Hey, Doc! The belt from your shorts must've come loose. Swim over and get it before we're all treated to the unpleasant sight of your narrow ass!"

Doc yelled out while still floating on his back, "I'm wearing my trunks, jackass. There ain't no belt holding them up." Daniel quickly re-focused on the object in the water and realized that it was no belt. A cacophony of sound then interrupted everyone's fun.

"Snake!" Daniel screamed out the warning and Doc Nunn instantly tried to prop himself onto his feet, only to realize that he had floated beyond the shallow end of the pool as his head bobbed under the water. The bamboo viper snake, a deadly, venomous beast native— albeit rare—to these parts continued to swim slowly and graciously toward its bumbling prey.

"Oh, shit!" Doc screamed, followed by a screeching yelp that would've shattered any glass within a hundred yards. Doc began to swim toward Vinnie and the boys, all of whom had escaped the pool and were running toward the shore.

"Fuck, fuck, FUUUCK!" bellowed Doc Nunn. He frantically waded toward the shallow end in an attempt to escape sure death from the fangs of the encroaching bamboo viper snake that was quickening its deadly pace.

Doc finally was able to stand in the water, but the quick ascent of the river bottom caused him to trip and fall face-first into the river. The snake, sensing its prey's vulnerability, poised itself to strike the helpless young man.

CRACK! CRACK! CRACK!

The boys back on the shore instinctively ducked and Doc, who had emerged from the water, froze with his head just inches above the surface. He heard three quick splashes inches away from his head and began saying an *Our Father* because he figured that he was good as dead: If the venomous snake didn't kill him, the ambushing gooks would. Resigned to his fate, Doc Nunn peered toward the shore and, astounded, realized that there were no gooks, just a Saint, legs bowed and back arched forward, with his hand wrapped around his .38, from whose barrel smoke wafted peacefully up into the humid Vietnam air.

Doc peered to his right, remembering that the bamboo viper was about to strike. He no longer saw the snake. Rather, he no longer saw a single snake. Instead, he saw pieces of the obliterated remains of what had been the deadly animal, floating listlessly a few yards from his head. Vinnie had jumped out of the water, grabbed the .38 from the holster that was affixed to his fatigue pants, and fired at the snake, saving Doc's life.

"Holy shit," Doc Nunn muttered repeatedly to himself as he walked through the waist-high water to the shore.

"How the fuck . . ." spat out Doc Milazzo in stunned amazement. Red was speechless; he simply shook his head, not believing what he had just witnessed. Tex still was in a defensive crouch, not realizing what had just materialized before his fellow Marines. And Daniel King still was at the opposite end of the pool, lowering his arm, as he realized that he still was pointing out to Doc what had been the deadly snake just seconds earlier.

"What?" Vinnie asked in a cocksure manner. "I didn't earn these rifles on my sleeve by just being the goddamn mailman, you buncha clowns! I finished first in my class back in boot camp as a marksman, fellas!"

Vinnie turned to Nunn, now sitting on the dirt adjacent to the pool, still looking out at the last piece of the snake that hadn't sunk down to the pool floor just yet. "You're welcome, you lousy, good-for-nothing! Your little squeal there gave me a friggin' headache, pal!" The boys laughed at Doc's good fortune and marveled at Vinnie's amazing kill. "One thing, boys: This stays here. Nobody says nothin' about this to nobody, got it?"

One by one, the Marines assured Vinnie that his heroic feat would never be divulged to the company. Doc Nunn trudged over to Vinnie, still sopping wet and panting deliriously.

"Thanks . . . for . . . saving . . . me. You . . . wop mother . . . fucker!"

"Good ol' Doc," reflected Tex. The other Marines roared.

"That's enough swimming for me," said Red, "let's get some chow." And with that, the Marines walked back to the camp, as if nothing special had transpired, and proceeded to prepare their meals over burning balls of C-4.

The next morning, Captain LeRoy gave Vinnie his orders for the day. He was to drive his jeep north from Cam Lo to Dong Ha.

Once there, Vinnie was to load up the jeep with rounds, food, some fresh clothing, water, and many grenades before joining a convoy of military vehicles that was going to travel along Highway 9 to Gio Linh. LeRoy also ordered Daniel King to accompany the company driver, as the drive could be long and tedious.

The convoy was to consist of an Army M42 "Duster," a small armored vehicle that resembled a tank, with two anti aircraft cannons on top, manned by three GIs. There were a couple of other Army vehicles in front of the Duster and Vinnie's jeep took up the rear, about thirty feet behind the M42. Of course, the engineers had swept Highway 9 for mines, and other booby traps, before the convoy proceeded on its mission to Gio Linh. The engineers had not uncovered anything in their morning sweep, so Vinnie and Daniel were fine, knowing that they could bullshit about anything while following the Duster up Highway 9 to Gio Linh.

The convoy set off from Dong Ha to Gio Linh at 0500 hours that morning. Vinnie and Daniel admired the Duster ahead of them. The vehicle moved on tracks, like a tank, and it was well-fortified with the dual cannons and an M-60.

"I would love to see that beast in action," commented Vinnie. "Those sonsabitches up on top would take out any of the gooks' birds if they dared try to take us on!"

Daniel chuckled at Vinnie's observation and noted, "Yeah, I would not want to be on the receiving end of one of those rockets!"

Vinnie drove at a leisurely twenty miles an hour to keep pace behind the Duster. He and Daniel nonetheless scanned their perimeter because the enemy could emerge at any time from the bush that lined the roadway. Daniel had his M-16 locked and loaded on his lap for the trip to Gio Linh and he was ready to discharge it at a moment's notice. Vinnie had his left hand on the steering wheel and his right hand nestled around his .45-caliber handgun for good measure.

The Marines were about halfway to Gio Linh when they noticed a herd of elephants to their left. Vinnie and Daniel marveled at the wondrous creatures and Saint cracked that one of the beasts' droopy faces and stringy hairs on his trunk reminded him of Doc Nunn.

"You're right, Saint, except for one important difference. That beast don't smell half as bad as Doc!" The young men shared a hearty laugh about Doc Nunn's hygiene.

Vinnie chimed in, "That was pretty damn funny, Danny. Poor Doc would kick your ass if he heard you sa—"

The thunderous explosion sucked the air out of Vinnie's throat mid-word. A rain of dust and gravel was instantaneously thrust into the men's faces. Vinnie's eyes widened as he peered through the dusty downpour. Saint's mouth agape, he exclaimed, "HOLY SHIT!" at the sight before him.

The M42 Duster, which had been plodding along thirty feet ahead of Vinnie's jeep just two seconds earlier, was propelled upward, like a rocket taking off. Vinnie initially questioned whether an errant rocket had struck the vehicle, but that suspicion was immediately replaced with the realization that the engineers who'd swept Highway 9 earlier missed this spot and the mine buried here. Vinnie's eyes followed the Duster—a vehicle that weighed multiple tons—rise like a balloon at a local street fair while pieces of the vehicle began to cascade down. Time stood still as Vinnie watched this unfold before his eyes and his mind drifted, ever so briefly, to the Fourth of July fireworks celebrations that he and his family attended each summer.

Time accelerated and Saint was back in the present. He looked to his right and he saw Daniel grimacing and bleeding from lacerations to his face. He was still alive, albeit with a look of terror fixed on his face as he endeavored to shield his eyes from the descending shards of metal. Vinnie tasted blood in his mouth as he quickly realized that what goes up must come down and there was a multi-ton Duster that was not going to stay suspended in mid-air for much longer. Saint instinctively made a hard steer to the left, causing the jeep to lurch suddenly out of the path of the ill-fated tank. As the jeep responded uneasily to Vinnie's quick steering, Saint heard a loud thud, almost like a crashing sound. He peered out toward the hood of his jeep and saw what appeared to be part of an arm roll off the hood.

Stunned, Vinnie and Daniel each peered around the perimeter of their quivering jeep and noticed other body parts raining down around them, along with pieces of twisted, hot metal. The Marines then looked up while shielding their eyes with their forearms. The remains of the duster were rapidly descending back to Earth roughly sixty yards to their northeast.

Vinnie and Daniel each flinched and braced themselves for impact. The sound of the impact of the Duster was sickeningly loud. Daniel's right eardrum burst and blood began to trickle from his ear. The concussive force actually lifted Vinnie's jeep a couple of feet off of the ground and, upon reacquainting itself with Highway 9, the jeep skidded terribly. Again, only Vinnie's astute handling of the vehicle prevented the jeep from careening into the hapless, dismembered, and smoldering M42 carcass, or into the trees that lined the roadway. Vinnie parked the jeep about a hundred yards from the charred M42 and he and Daniel instinctively hopped out of the jeep and sprinted toward the Duster.

Vinnie arrived at the charred M42 first and called out to no one in particular, "The driver's dead!"

What could be seen of the driver's head was impaled grotesquely against some metal protrusion within the cabin. The metal bore into the soldier's helmet and tore through the right side of where his forehead and right eye had been located. Two men located behind the driver were unconscious but groaning. The guns atop the tank were twisted and broken like pretzels and the GIs that were manning them were gone. There was no trace of these men but for a foot and lower calf torn away from the remainder of a brave soldier's mutilated body, intertwined with the remnants of the guns.

Daniel and Vinnie were joined by other members of the convoy, from the vehicles that were ahead of the doomed Duster. Those men were calling in coordinates of the incident and they had radioed for some Hueys to swoop in to remove the dead and injured. As Marines, Vinnie and Daniel were commissioned to stand guard over the remains of man and machine until the birds landed. Saint and Daniel, each with an M-16 locked and loaded, stood guard over the grisly scene until help arrived roughly an hour later. Neither Vinnie nor Daniel said anything to each other over the course of that hour, but the panting of their breath and their repeated murmurings of *fuck*, *holy shit*, and *goddamn* spoke volumes.

Every rustling of the elephant grass that lined the roadway caused a nervous twitch and a knee-jerk cocking of their rifles. When the Hueys finally arrived, Vinnie turned to Daniel and stated, "That was the longest fucking hour of my life."

"You got that right," responded Daniel as the two shaken Marines walked back to the dusty, dented, but still operable jeep and proceeded to complete the five-minute drive to Gio Linh.

The two Marines were silent for the remainder of the trek, as each nervously feared that another mine was lurking unseen on the roadway ahead of them, waiting to deliver the same disassembling blow that befell their comrades. Vinnie drove one-handed the entire way. His right hand bounced between the steering wheel and the stick shift on his right while his left hand clasped vise-like upon—and never released—the crucifix that dangled around his neck.

When Vinnie pulled into the camp at Gio Linh, he released his grip from his crucifix and exhaled loudly as his forehead descended slowly upon the steering wheel. Vinnie gritted his teeth, clenched his eyes shut, and fought back bile in his throat and tears in his eyes, before he grabbed the cross once more and whispered, "Thank you, Jesus, for allowing me and Danny to arrive here safely."

Daniel missed this excruciating moment for, as Vinnie pulled into the camp and brought the jeep to a stop, Daniel thrust his head back and peered upward before closing his eyes. He was exhaling and saying, to no one in particular, "Holy fucking shit."

The boys at the camp knew what had happened and they gave Daniel and Vinnie their space. No one said anything to them as the dazed and bloodied Marines trudged toward a medical bunker to receive attention for their wounds before taking long, hot showers. Vinnie leaned against the makeshift wall as the hot water cascaded down the nape of his neck and continued down the crease of his spine. The sensation of the warm water crashing onto the back of Vinnie's head slightly alleviated the knot of tension that caused his head to throb. Alone with his thoughts, Vinnie wept as he pondered his own mortality yet again.

Sadly, like many of his brothers in Vietnam, Vinnie could not help but repeatedly envision his own grisly demise. Indeed, Vinnie struggled with the notion of death tremendously since he'd watched that green, Pryor, blow up during the ambush. *Why am I still alive? Why did those Army guys die today only thirty feet ahead of me while I survived with just a couple of holes in my face? When will my luck run out?* And so went Vinnie's private torture. He stayed under the hot water for quite some time and, for the first time, began to doubt that he'd make it out of 'Nam alive, much less make it to Lilly's wedding in August.

I've had so many close calls, Vinnie lamented. *My luck's gotta run out at some point.*

CHAPTER 15

LUCK, DON'T FAIL ME NOW!

Hi little sis, how are you doing? I hope just fine. As for me, I'm just fine. Only miss all of you very much. Well, I have eight months and four days in 'Nam already. I got 16 letters today and 7 of them were from you. Wow. I owe you all kinds of letters now. I got one letter from Pop that was dated the 20th of February. I'll try to answer most of the questions that you asked me, but I'll probably forget a few because there were so many letters that I read all at once. Well, first of all, I think you're a doll. OK, here goes.

About my hair: A couple of my buddies cut it for me. I didn't shave the sides. It started to spread through the company, but then the captain put a stop to it. With your hair like that, it's much cooler and easier to wash and keep clean during the summer. Plus it looks groovy over here. The village people would look at me like I was crazy, or an animal. It was funny.

When I was up at Con Thien, we used to have rats in all of our bunkers. At night, when we were asleep, they'd jump down and crawl on you. It happened to me 2 or 3 times. I used to freeze when they were on me. Then I'd run like hell out of the bunker. I killed one that got me pissed off because he attacked me. I stayed up all night with my bayonet on my rifle and I stabbed him when I saw him and pinned him to the wall. He let out a scream and I ran out of the bunker with the rifle and bayonet and the rat still stuck into the wall. After he finished screaming, I went in and got it out.

All the guys here are just fine. I'm living out with the company. I really like living here. There's more to do and you're always with your friends. And you can go around looking unshaved and no one says anything to you. In Dong Ha, the people thought they were stateside.

About the war over here: Yes, we are killing a lot of gooks, but I guess they exaggerate a little when they have it in the news. We killed I-don't-know-how-many thousand this year alone. When I say WE I mean the entire American forces over here. But in any war, you're going to take casualties on your side. That's to be expected. The belt I got was off a friend. The gooks I seen were too rotten to take the gear off them. Most of the fighting over here is man-to-man. They call it a firefight when both sides shoot it out and call in artillery on each other. But bombing and gunships and artillery and other ordinances help a great deal. I hope that I satisfied your curiosity.

Vinnie's March 26, 1968 letter to Lilly

A few days had elapsed since the mine incident along Highway 9, and Vinnie had made several roundtrips to and from Dong Ha HQ over that time. Every trip in the jeep was a harrowing experience for the forlorn company driver. Vinnie cringed at every pothole and he flinched every time that he ran over a rock that jutted out of the uneven roadway.

The worst experience, by far, was when the jeep would backfire, which it did more than Vinnie could tolerate. Indeed, Vinnie nearly drove the jeep into the bush on one occasion when his dilapidated vehicle jerked and backfired violently. Vinnie was alone in his jeep on that particular occasion, and his jeep was loaded with artillery that was intended for Cam Lo. There were too many firefights in that region of Vietnam and too few available Marines to allow for a couple of gunnies to accompany Vinnie on this particular trip. Vinnie was flabbergasted that he was made to drive with all of the obvious ammo stored in his jeep, but he wasn't about to bitch about his predicament because insubordination was not in his DNA. Besides, he knew that Captain LeRoy had no viable alternatives, as he was being squeezed by his superiors on manpower.

As Vinnie drove alone down Highway 9 that morning, his jeep stocked to the brim with deadly explosives, a backfire hurled his mind into a chaotic frenzy. The jeep lurched as a consequence of the violent kickback of its taxed engine. Vinnie's heart rate doubled and he instinctively steered hard to the left to avoid what he imagined was a land mine that was prepared to blow him into indecipherable chunks of pulpy flesh. The jeep, which was as unstable mechanically as Vinnie was becoming psychologically, did not respond as well as Vinnie would've liked to the sudden movements, and it began to careen uncontrollably toward a thicket of dead tree trunks that jutted out of the scorned, angry jungle that crept toward the roadway.

Vinnie saw the pockmarked trunks getting increasingly closer and he, for a split second, saw his broken, limp body wrapped grotesquely around the inanimate relic of a peaceful time from long ago. Eerily, the vision of his own death brought the young Marine an awkward sense of peace before he shook the vision out of his mind and replaced it with thoughts of Lilly, Rose, his kid brother, and his beloved father, Carmine.

Fuck that, I ain't dyin' on them. They need me, goddammit! And with that, the suddenly courageous Marine regained control of his metallic steed when it was just a few feet from the trunk. He jammed on the brakes and released the clutch. The weight of the ammo in the rear of the jeep made the relatively sudden stop much less graceful than it otherwise would've been, but the vehicle screeched to a stop about ten feet from the ditch that contained an unforgiving tree trunk. Dust abounded and Vinnie choked on the residue that arose from the roadway as a result of the angry friction caused by his jeep's locked tires. Vinnie's face was chalked with the color of the reddish-brown road. He furiously wiped his eyes and brow, but he smeared the clay with his sweat to unintentionally mimic the camouflage face paint that he and his Marine brothers wore when heading out on a mission.

Saint sighed and realized that he was grasping the crucifix around his neck. *Jesus is watching over me, for sure,* he thought. He eyeballed the area to ensure that there were no gooks nearby and to check that no ammo had been thrown from the rear. Satisfied that his cargo remained tied down securely, the rugged, filthy, and still-slightly-jittery Marine re-engaged the clutch, reversed the jeep back onto the roadway, and resumed his solo mission.

When he arrived at Cam Lo, Vinnie was met by three Marines who helped him unload the secured ammo from the jeep. Tex, Red, and the Docs Milazzo and Nunn saw Vinnie's clay-covered face and immediately thought that he had encountered an ambush on the way in to camp. Vinnie read the looks on their faces and was confused by the ubiquitous look of consternation. However, one glance into the mirror in his bunker explained everything: Vinnie looked as if he had bathed in mud. His face was caked with red clay. Saint actually laughed to himself as he washed the layers of muck off of his face. Vinnie left the bunker and saw that his friends were nervously peeking at him.

"Guys, no need to worry," Vinnie exclaimed clearly and loudly. "I had a little spinout on the way here and the jeep kicked up some dust. That's the story, for real!"

The guys bought the story, or so Vinnie thought. In reality, the guys had seen so much, and their nerves were frayed so desperately, that they accepted the story if for no other reason than their fragile psyches could not withstand yet *another* brush with death.

"GODDAMMIT!" Vinnie was outside the bunkers, having a smoke while leaning against a large, moss-covered rock, when he was momentarily startled by the exasperated exclamation of a familiar voice. "These sonofabitch rats are gonna drive me crazier than the fucking gooks," ranted a fed-up Doc Nunn.

Vinnie chuckled as he heard a series of crashes coming from Doc's bunker. He jogged over to the opening of the bunker that he shared with Doc when he wasn't stationed in the rear, at Dong Ha HQ. Red, Doc Milazzo, Danny King, and Tex were sitting inside the bunker, delighting in Doc's follies. Saint, who was disgusted by the filthy rodents, did not enter the bunker. Rather, he poked his head in and began to serenade the flabbergasted Doc Nunn.

"Who's the leader of the club that's made for you and me? M-I-C—K-E-Y M-O-U-S-E!"

The Marines who had gathered inside the bunker let out a collective roar. Saint's sense of humor had a habit of reducing the men to tears, given the heartiness of their laughter. This occasion was no different. Here they were, young men anywhere from eighteen to twenty-one years of age. Instead of going to school, or hanging out with girlfriends and buddies in a carefree setting back home, they were deployed to a foreign land amidst a perplexing, deadly war. Indeed, each of the men was petrified that he was going to be the next serviceman to be removed from a battlefield in a black canvas bag of death. Yet, here they were, laughing uncontrollably as one of their beloved brothers sang the theme song of a TV show that was exceptionally popular during their not-so-distant youth: *The Mickey Mouse Club*.

Only in Vietnam.

A pillow hurtled through the opening of the bunker and Vinnie demonstrated the reflexes of a wily fox, darting away from the tumbling projectile and allowing the pillow to strike an unsuspecting Red square in the mouth as he was laughing.

"*Ugghhh*, yuck," exclaimed Red. "Doc, your pillow tastes like fucking shit. Have you ever washed the goddamn thing?" Red began to expectorate repeatedly amidst a series of gags, which elicited even further laughter. The beleaguered rat, sensing an opening to escape the enraged Doc Nunn, darted out of the bunker, running over Vinnie's right foot in the process.

"Oh, shit!" Vinnie squealed as the other men, all of whom had experienced angry enemy gunfire, immediately retreated—as if this confused rat posed a greater threat than the NVA guerillas did at Con Thien.

For a few seconds in the quagmire that was Vietnam, a rare hilarity ensued. A scurrying rat made a throng of battle-hardened men scurry, which, in turn, increasingly frightened the stricken rat. Thus, the rat would dart to its left, which scared the shit out of one of the Marines, causing him to dart in the opposite direction. The rat then stopped dead in its tracks and reversed direction, which caused yet another Marine to fall, in his haste to escape the heretofore-unknown deadly powers of the nine-inch-long rodent. This cat-and-mouse routine ended when the rat saw an opening and, like a running back plowing through a hole in the thicket of men that comprise the offensive and defensive lines of a football game, it ran to pay dirt, escaping into the jungle that enveloped the camp.

"What a bunch of pansies you guys are!"

Saint peered from behind the tree where he was standing to see Doc Nunn shaking his head in mock indignation. The guys emerged from their defensive positions and the laughter began, initially as a slight murmur and rising to a piercing din of sound. Of course, Doc Nunn had set off the panic in the camp by howling in his bunker at the sight of the hungry rodent.

"Saint, remember that time in Con Thien when you saw a fucking Mickey in your hooch? Goddamn, you took care of that critter good that night, brother!"

Tex, who had missed the chaos that was Con Thien, turned to Vinnie and asked, "What's Doc talking about?" Vinnie shuddered in disgust before his face softened and he chuckled. He placed his left palm against his forehead and then slid it up through his coarse hair, which appeared much darker than its natural color thanks to the omnipresent soot and dirt of the camp.

"Let me tell ya, Tex. I hate rats! Back home, the rats roam the streets and the garbage outside of the apartment buildings in my neighborhood. Plus, there are more rats than subway cars in the New York City subways. They're disgusting creatures and they make me sick!"

Red laughed and retorted, "That's all well and good, Vin, but I think Tex wants to know about your little friend in Con Thien, not your neighbors in New York City!"

Tex turned to Red, nodded affirmatively, and then glanced to his left to cast his widened eyes upon Saint.

"First of all, green, ya gotta understand that Con Thien was an absolute shithole. I ain't never seen more bodies—gooks and good guys—than I seen in Con Thien." The men in this group of Marines who'd survived Con Thien all reflected on their own personal, hellish recollections of the "City of Angels" before further repressing those sickening memories and returning their attention to Saint.

"You'd go into your bunker at any odd hour to try to get a few winks of sleep in on the rare occasion that it was—well, I can't say *safe* because it never was safe to let down your guard in fucking Con Thien—uh, *okay* to lay down in your hooch after crazy firefights with the gooks. I can't tell you how many times I climbed into the hooch and collapsed onto my rubber lady, only to feel the hooves of these fucking rats climbing over me!"

"Uh, Saint, rats ain't got hooves," Milazzo interjected.

"Fuck you, Stone. Who's telling the goddamned story, you or me?"

Vinnie and Doc Milazzo each laughed and Vinnie continued his tale.

"Anyways, the first time I got overrun by a rat in Con Thien, I almost died. The fucking thing came out of nowhere after I had collapsed onto my rubber lady and I was just about asleep. I felt something heavy on my leg and I figured that my canteen or my M-16 had moved while I was asleep, so I paid no mind to it. But then, the heaviness starting moving up my leg, toward my ass, and

I realized that it was not my rifle or a canteen. Thing is, I thought it was dumbass Nunn goofin' on me, so I says, 'Goddammit, Doc, can't you see that I'm trying to get some fucking shut-eye here?' and I don't hear nothin' in response, not even his annoying laugh!"

"Hey, man, go easy!" Doc Nunn interjected before he exhorted Vinnie to continue.

"So, now the heaviness is on my ass and moving up, slowly and uneasily, onto the small of my back. In my head, I'm saying shit like, 'Okay, it ain't my canteen, my rifle, or fucking Nunn. What the fuck is moving up my back?' Then it hits me: I'm in the middle of the fucking jungle and shit's exploding all around me, so the critters that called this shithole home before we lit it up are scurrying for cover, just like we are. So, I realized that there was some jungle critter crawling on me! I began to think: Was it a tarantula, a python, a viper, a fucking tiger cub?"

Vinnie looked around and saw that he was captivating the boys. Their eyes were focused on him, some with mouths agape and others with knowing smiles at the expected climax to the tale.

"I wasn't sure what it was, but I knew that I had to get up and get up quick. The other problem was that we were in fucking Con Thien and the NVA was so close that you could hear them breathing. No shit! We knew that we had to be quiet as a mouse— no pun intended!—at night because the NVA would light us up if they knew where we were. So, I slowly coiled my body and I could feel that goddamn thing on my back jostle a bit, as if it were wondering why the ground was tensing up under its feet. Suddenly, I sprang up as quickly and as quietly as I could and, against my better judgment, I grabbed my flashlight and darted its weak beam all around the hooch in a frenzied burst."

"Saint, you fucking shined your flashlight in the middle of the night?" asked Red, before he continued, "Why didn't you simply install a huge neon billboard above your hooch that said, 'Hey, gooks, plenty of GI Joes platooned right here! Aim your mortars here!'"

The guys laughed at Red, including Vinnie as he forged on.

"At first, I didn't see anything because it was dark as shit in the hooch. I shined the flashlight a second time and then I saw it: the reflection of the damn thing's eyes! I then focused the beam on its eyes and I realized it was a goddamn rat! I didn't catch Mickey that night, and the sonofabitch did the same thing to me the following night, and escaped again. I was ready for the fucker the third day, though. I took a nap in my bunker at about 1645 hours, so it still was light outside. I lay down on my rubber lady with my right hand on my rifle, underneath the unsheathed bayonet. I also put some old peanut butter on a piece of paper on the floor about ten inches from my face. I was ready!

"Sure enough, five minutes into my nap, Mickey is back. I crack open my right eye, as I was laying on my stomach, with the left side of my head resting on my pillow, ready to pounce like a goddamn lion. I watched as Mickey carefully bounced around the bunker until he came to the peanut butter. He stopped and looked around to make sure that he was in no danger before he began to nibble on the peanut butter across from me. Slowly, I tightened my grip around the barrel of the rifle and then *WHACK!* I thrust my rifle so hard and so fast that I thought that I separated my shoulder! I got out of the bed to get a full account of the carnage. The bayonet went right through the fucking rat's belly and came out the other side, where it actually got stuck in the bunker wall next to the rat. The rat was squirming uncontrollably and making some sickening noises, so I hopped up and ran the hell outta the bunker, screaming, before I got sick right then and there. The squad leader came running over, ready to kill whatever was causing me to scream, and when I told him about the rat, he almost killed me!"

"You're a cold-blooded killer, Saint," observed Doc Nunn. "How do you sleep at night?"

"It was the rat or me, Doc, and I wasn't about to let the rat win! I didn't go back in the bunker until the thing stopped screeching. Once I knew it was dead, I pulled out the bayonet. I then grabbed an old towel to sop up the blood before I picked up the dead Mickey."

"What did you do with that disgusting carcass, Vinnie?" asked Doc Milazzo.

Without missing a beat, Vinnie responded, "I stowed it in *your* hooch, Doc!" The boys laughed and then Vinnie concluded the story. "That was the last time I ever had any mice problems in the bunker. The other rodents knew that I was a fucking psycho and they didn't wanna join their brother in Mouse Hell!"

"Some *saint* you are, Saint," joked Red as the other guys joined in some light-hearted razzing of the Mickey murderer.

*   *   *

After a couple of hours of sitting around and BS-ing with his buddies, Vinnie turned in for the night. However, instead of going to sleep on this warm, late March evening, Vinnie opted to write a letter to his sister. He was feeling nostalgic about old times and guilty about sending his sister such antiseptic letters.

He thought back to that day the previous August, right before he left for his tour in 'Nam. He was back in Jamaica, Queens after finishing at the top of his class in boot camp and he officially was a U.S. Marine. He had gotten his orders and knew that he was headed to Vietnam to kill the enemy, protect democracy and the American way, and to be forever loyal to his brother Marines while in combat. Indeed, Saint would hear the mantra *NO Marine gets left behind . . . EVER!* in his sleep.

Vinnie allowed his mind to wander back to that time before he was shipped to Southeast Asia, back to when he flew home to surprise his family for a final goodbye before heading to Vietnam.

"Oh, Vinnie," said Mama Rose through a sea of proud tears, "you look so handsome in your uniform! Promise me that you'll stay safe and don't try to be a hero over there. We are losing too many good boys in this war and it seems like there's no end in sight!" Rose's black hair, peppered with grey, was styled in a short bob with a stylish flip in the front, from left to right. Her hair curled upward at the nape of her neck. Her thick, black-framed glasses rested on the bridge of her nose and the color of the rims offset her olive complexion, which was streaked with salt stains as a result of her crying fits after Vinnie had surprised them a few hours earlier.

Rose's red-rimmed eyes, abrupt breathing pattern, choppy speech, and general inability to maintain her composure spoke of a mother who was being involuntarily separated from her offspring. Vinnie was Rose's first son and, while he looked handsome and brave in his USMC khakis, she couldn't shake off the manifest dread that her eighteen-year-old baby was being shipped off to the worst war in the history of the world, and as a US Marine, to boot. *My baby*, Rose thought, *is a trained killer now and he's going off to a faraway country where the enemy will be looking to kill him!*

This sobering reality devastated Rose.

"Vinnie," Pop's authoritative voice was unmistakable, "I'm proud of you, son. You done good in boot camp and you're gonna be a helluva Marine. You're going to do great things over there in 'Nam and the boys there are gonna respect the hell outta you because of the type of man you've become."

Saint revered his dad and those words remained with him well after they were spoken.

"Thanks, Pop. Just make sure that you take care of Apache, Pepe, and Queenie for me while I'm over there, okay?"

Vinnie and his father Carmine chuckled, before Vinnie got closer to his dad, lowered his voice, and said, "And please take care of Mama. Don't let her worry herself sick over me. I'm gonna be fine. I'll do my duty there like you did for the Navy during World War II right before I was born and then I'll come back home, get a good job, and help take care a' yous. I promise that I won't let yous down."

Carmine placed his right hand on Vinnie's right shoulder, locked eyes with his beloved son and said, simply, "I know, son,

I know. You know how we all feel about you. You could never let us down."

Carmine was not one to show emotion and Vinnie thought that this was as emotional as he had ever seen his dad.

The living room was very cramped, the size of a small bedroom. A pair of two-seater box couches occupied two walls and met at the corner. A small coffee table was located in front of the couches and there was a small dresser across from one of the couches, parallel to the coffee table. A small, thirteen-inch black and white TV was perched atop the dresser. There was barely enough space for one person to navigate between the couches, the coffee table, and the dresser. A china cabinet was located on the far wall, adjacent to the coffee table, inside of which Rose kept a collection of porcelain plates and assorted knickknacks. There were two standing lamps in opposite corners of the living room, but they did not sufficiently illuminate the area, so the room had a slight pallor to it even when both lamps were in use.

The living room led directly to Carmine and Rose's very small bedroom on the left, directly behind the wall against which the TV was propped, and to the kitchen on the right. The fridge was located on the left side of the kitchen, directly at the threshold of its doorless entry. A closet door was located to the right of the kitchen entrance, as viewed when entering from the living room. The closet door opened to a spinning, circular shelf system akin to a Lazy Susan that Vinnie's father, an accomplished carpenter, had built. Rose often baked oatmeal raisin, chocolate chip, and oatmeal-chocolate chip cookies from scratch in the tiny kitchen. She'd place them in empty Quaker Oats cylindrical tins that she would store on the top circular shelf. Vinnie often spun that shelf to reveal the revered Quaker Oats tins. If a quick shake of the tin caused rattling inside, then he and his siblings were in for a delicious score.

The kitchen sink was located catty-corner to the closet and directly across from the fridge, while the washing machine was between the sink and the adjoining stove. The kitchen table was directly across from the washer and the stove. Carmine's chair abutted the far wall and window which looked out into the small, modest backyard. In between the stove and Carmine's chair at the dinner table was a door that led to the back yard.

Carmine had built a small, concrete porch directly outside of the back door. The small ten-by-six-foot porch led to four concrete steps that descended into the thirty-square-foot backyard. Despite being in the middle of a highly populated urban neighborhood, Vinnie's parents liked to garden. So the back yard, despite its very modest size, had tomato plants, strawberry patches, a pear tree, and a cherry tree. Vinnie's father also would put up and take down a four-foot oval pool every summer.

Vinnie turned to Lilly and said, "Where were you, ugly?"

"I was upstairs trying to talk to *Nunu*," replied Lilly, using an old Italian term of endearment that she and her brothers used instead of *grandma*. Nunu was Rose's mother and she lived upstairs, taking up a diminutive room at the top of the steps of the two-story home. Nunu spoke very little English, and her sentences often were ninety percent Italian, three percent English, and of the rest a hybrid of the two. Vinnie laughed at Lilly's comment, as he knew how frustrating it was to try to speak to their grandmother.

"Let me guess. You just nodded and smiled a lot as Nunu spoke, right, you kook?"

"You got that right, baby brother," Lilly said as she walked through the living room, into the kitchen, toward the back door. Vinnie opened the kitchen closet, spun the Lazy Susan, and grabbed the Quaker Oats tin. He then shook the tin, heard the familiar rattle, and pried off the top to remove a fistful of oatmeal chocolate chip cookies. Just then, Lilly gestured toward the back yard as she opened the door and walked out onto the porch.

Vinnie devoured three of his mother's ridiculously delicious cookies before he followed Lilly into the yard. Lilly had descended the four cement steps and was standing next to the pear tree, facing the enormous apartment building that loomed about ten feet beyond the Santaniello property line. Lilly had her back to Vinnie so he presumed that she was angry at him for some reason.

"Hey, Lil, why are you sore, little sis?" Vinnie walked up next to her, but she ducked away and walked a little further ahead.

Lilly was crying.

"What the hell, Lil? You're one tough broad, so why the hell are ya cryin'?"

Lilly chuckled and then wiped at her mascara-stained right cheek. Just a few months shy of her twenty-first birthday, the attractive young woman was crying like a six-year-old.

"Nunu said that you were crazy to go to the war. She said that you're gonna get yourself killed and make Mama sick. I tried to tell her that you were gonna be fine, but she waved me off and called me a stupid little girl." Lilly heaved a little, then caught her breath and composed herself. "She seemed pretty sore that you enlisted in the Marines. I think she's just spooked by what she has seen on TV about the war over there. She doesn't want anything to happen to you."

Vinnie felt terrible that his sister was so conflicted and sad. He had a duty to serve his country, but he didn't want to do that at the cost of his family's mental well-being. "Lil, ain't nothing gonna happen to me over there. I'm a tough kid from a tough neighborhood and I'm definitely coming back home to take care of all a' yous!"

"Vinnie, how the hell do you know that? Really, how can you promise me that you definitely are coming home when so many boys have been killed already over there? I'm scared of losing you, Vinnie. You're my best friend and my biggest pain in the ass. I—"

A rush of emotion sucked the air out of Lillie's lungs and interrupted her ability to speak. Lilly wept. Vinnie draped his arm around his sister's heaving shoulders, pulling her toward him until her head came to rest against his chest. Lilly rested her hands on Vinnie's shoulders and muttered, "I can't lose you over there, Vinnie. I can't see Mama and Pop getting that 'We regret to inform you' letter . . ."

"Lilly, I ain't gonna die, I promise. I'm gonna be safe and smart out there. And if anyone tries to shoot me, I'm gonna blow his ass away first! I was the best shooter in boot camp, Lil. I'm ready for this, trust me."

"Vinnie, this ain't the movies and you ain't John Wayne. How the hell can you promise me anything like that?" Lilly's dark-brown eyes narrowed, and her carefully manicured eyebrows lowered over them like shades on a window. The combination of her eyebrows, her glistening and glowering dark eyes, and her running mascara gave Lilly a very foreboding presence. She glared at her brother, genuinely angry at him. The striking young woman pushed her brother away before she turned her back to him and walked toward the rear of their small yard. Vinnie started to walk after his sister but then stopped, knowing that she was quite angry and heartbroken at the unfathomable notion of losing her beloved brother and best friend.

A few minutes passed without the siblings moving toward each other and without a word being exchanged. Lilly did not turn around at all, keeping her back to him the entire time. The two siblings, who spent their lives constantly talking, laughing, occasionally fighting, and always loving each other, were standing there, without saying a word to each other.

Lilly decided to break the ice. "You gonna write to me when you're over there?"

Vinnie exhaled, thrust his head back and smiled. For a second there, he thought that his sister was going to boycott speaking to him for the remainder of his time in the States before heading to 'Nam. "Of course I will, little sis," replied Vinnie, through a wide smile. "I'll have nothing else to do over there, y'know!"

Lilly, a woman who shared her dad's stubborn pride, hated the fact that she was crying. Nonetheless, she turned to face her brother and was stunned to see that the eyes of the tough kid from Queens were glistening.

"Why are you crying, dummy," she said before she chuckled nervously.

"I ain't crying," Vinnie replied, "the wind made my eyes tear up a little, that's all."

Lilly then reached her arms out, pulled Vinnie close to her, embraced him, and whispered in his right ear, "I love you, you freaking leatherneck bastard!"

"Nunu spooked you for no good reason, Lil. Everything's gonna be groovy over there for me. Remember: I'm a chicken, so I ain't gonna get into no trouble over there, I promise!" Vinnie was trying his best to convince Lilly that he was not going to place himself in peril's way, but he knew that his words were ringing hollow. His boot camp drill sergeant had warned the recruits not to get too close to brother Marines over in the jungle because odds were that the Marine that you called *buddy* today would be dead tomorrow.

Vinnie felt a pit in his stomach as he looked at his disheartened sister and said, "You ain't gettin' rid of me that easily, little sis. Besides, an armed Vietcong soldier ain't got nothing on my feisty, hot-blooded Italian sister!" Vinnie then playfully punched Lilly in the face and she feigned a punch toward Vinnie's gut, causing him to instinctively lurch forward in a defensive posture.

The two youngsters giggled and, for a brief moment, Vinnie wasn't about to go off to a faraway land and into a bloody war and Lilly wasn't a young woman who was contemplating marriage to her current boyfriend, Ralph. Rather, they were the carefree teens who climbed trees, rode bikes, and chided each other unmercifully.

The ephemeral moment brought a welcome reprieve to the melancholy siblings. The lumps in their throats were alleviated and they were able to look at each other without anger, malice, or fear.

"You want one of Mama's chocolate chip cookies, stupid?" asked Vinnie.

"Yeah," Lilly replied, with a barely perceptible air of resignation in her voice. Vinnie heard it, and it saddened him, but he couldn't bring himself to fight with his best friend, especially when he was preoccupied with the notion that this may be the last time that they saw each other alive.

"I love you, Vinnie. Please be careful over there, you chickenshit."

Vinnie hunched over and kissed Lilly on her forehead. "Don't worry, ugly, I gotta stick around to make sure that you don't wind up marrying a goddamn knucklehead!"

Lilly laughed at Vinnie and joked, "Just for that, I ain't naming my first son after you no more. That poor kid is gonna be jinxed by having to carry on your name as his middle name. Ha, ha!"

The two lifelong pals were about to re-enter their house through the back door when Lilly placed her right hand around the crook of Vinnie's left elbow and turned him around. "I want you to promise me one thing, Vinnie."

Vinnie paused and swallowed nervously before replying, "What's that?"

"Don't you ever lie to me in your letters from over there. I know you gotta lie to Mama because she'll have a heart attack if she knows that you're in dangerous situations. But please promise that you won't lie to me."

Lilly's firm grasp underscored her seriousness. Vinnie walked back from the doorway and retreated to the recessed portion of the yard from which they had just walked. Vinnie removed the piss cutter from his head, nervously adjusted his clip-on tie, and ran his right hand through his buzzed Jarhead hair.

"Lil, I don't wanna spook you . . . if I– what I mean is . . ." Vinnie sighed. "I don't want you to spend the next thirteen months worried that my ass is gonna get blown away. I have no idea what's in store for me over there, but I am damn certain that it ain't gonna be pretty! If I tell you everything that I see and everything that I'm experiencing, then it'll be like we're both at war. That wouldn't be fair to you, little sis."

Lilly, full of the sass that Vinnie loved in her, marched right up to her brother, nose-to-nose, looked him dead in the eye, and responded, "Don't you fucking lie to me in your letters."

Shaken, Vinnie stepped back and tried to defuse the situation. "Goddammit, Lil, you speak like you just got outta boot camp! And brush your freaking teeth. Your breath reeks of Marlboros!" With that, Vinnie anxiously walked past Lilly and retreated to the safety of his house.

"Go eat your cookie, you crazy Marine, you. But if I find out that you're lying to me in your letters, I'll poison the cookies that I plan to send to you in care packages!"

Vinnie looked at his sister, and the softness had returned to her eyes, belying the harsh tenor of her proclamation. *Gosh*, thought Vinnie to himself, *she really has turned out to be a beautiful woman. I gotta make it back to protect her from all the jerks out there. I'll apologize for lying to her about the letters that I will write to her from 'Nam. I can't have her worry about me for a year.*

"I promise, Lil, I won't lie in my letters to y–"

BOOM!

Just like that, Vinnie was back in Vietnam. His stressful, yet eerily, pleasant daydream curtailed by a nearby mortar explosion that rocked the camp and resulted in guys scrambling outside, trying to ascertain the extent of the damage from the mortar strike.

"Skipper," Vinnie hollered to Captain LeRoy in the hooch situated next to Vinnie's, "do you need me?"

LeRoy responded, "Everything's under control, Saint. Get some shut-eye."

"Will do," said Vinnie. He took out some paper and a pen to write to Lilly. Vinnie began writing to his pal in his March 26th letter and then he paused a good long while. Milazzo was right about not telling the truth in his letters home. Then he thought back to his promise to his sister while they were together in their back yard last summer. Jesus, that seemed like a lifetime ago.

Shit, Vinnie mused, *I can't lie in every single letter to Lil.* And with that thought, Vinnie retrieved his pen and resumed the letter: *About the war over here: Yes, we are killing a lot of gooks, but I guess they exaggerate a little when they have it in the news. We killed I-don't-know-how-many thousand this year alone. When I say WE I mean the entire American forces over here. But in any war, you're going to take casualties on your side. That's to be expected.*

Vinnie paused and reflected on his words. *I just can't expect that shit to happen to me,* he thought. *Just a few more weeks until I am back home with everyone and then I can forget about all this craziness for a while.* Vinnie heard the pattering of rain smack against the roof of his hooch and the sound calmed him. Vinnie appreciated the false sense of serenity that it provided.

As the rain intensified, Vinnie's mental escape from Vietnam deepened. The troubled young man could feel the tension ebb from his body as his breathing slowed and he slowly fell asleep. However, even sleep was an unforgiving endeavor in the Hell that was Vietnam, for as Vinnie lapsed in and out of a sense of awareness, he was greatly troubled by the notion that he'd been lying to Lilly in his sanitized letters, in contravention of the promise that she'd elicited from him that night in the backyard. The sleepy Saint wavered between consternation and frustration as he recounted many of the letters that he had written to Lilly.

"Well, at least I didn't lie to her in *all* of the letters. That's gotta count for something," Vinnie muttered, half asleep. *Jesus, please forgive me. I lied to protect Lilly from being devastated by the truth.* And with that utterance, the forlorn Saint, with tears streaming down his cheeks and curving around the bend of his taut frown, succumbed to his overwhelming exhaustion and fell asleep.

Saint awakened three hours later to voices outside his hooch. He instinctively reached for his rifle but, recognizing the voices to be his crew of friends, relaxed and took his time to throw some water on his face and brush his teeth before he headed outside.

"Top of the morning, motherfuckers!" was Vinnie's cheerful greeting.

"Well, look which groovy leatherneck decided to grace us with his presence," responded Doc Nunn. "We thought you just were gonna wait for your Prince Charming to come and wake your ass up with a kiss, you lazy, no good, greaseball bastard!"

Vinnie and the rest of the guys—Tex, Red, and Milazzo—all laughed at Doc Nunn's uniquely disarming manner.

"I tell ya, Doc," Vinnie deadpanned, "Hanoi Hannah's got nothing on you!"

"I hate to break up this hippie love-fest, boys," interrupted Captain LeRoy, "but those sandbags aren't gonna fill themselves. We got some bunker fortifying to do today, Marines. The gooks are trying to take Cam Lo Hill and we gotta repel the bastards."

Groaning, the Marines embarked upon the arduous, mindless task of filling sandbags and then using a human chain to get the heavy, clumsy bags to their positions around the exposed bunkers. Tired and still reeling from his disconcerting daydream about Lilly, Vinnie quietly shoveled dirt and sand into the unwieldy burlap bags until they were as hard and as heavy as cement. The bags routinely weighed anywhere from sixty to eighty pounds, so it was not easy to move them from one part of the camp to the other, where they were stacked one atop the other as a life-saving barrier from mortars, hot ammo, and the absolutely-loathed shrapnel.

The guys hated filling and carrying the bags because it was back-breaking labor but, to a man, they all understood and accepted the absolute utility of such a task. The bags they filled today could be the difference between a life-ending hole in the head and just a couple of specks of sand being propelled into one's eyes after hot artillery round pierced the bag, was slowed and stopped before it could continue on its deadly trajectory.

Vinnie was breathing hard as he embarked on hauling his fourth bag. "Goddamn . . . asthma," muttered Vinnie, laboring between breaths. The unremitting heat, combined with the constant lifting and bagging of heavy dirt, was taking its toll on Saint, but he refused to complain and he did not yield in his duties. Instead, the steadfast Marine continued his task without complaining because he convinced himself that *this* specific bag was one day soon going to save the life of one of the brothers in his presence. Vinnie went so far as to use a magic marker he had secured at Dong Ha HQ to place his initials on the bags that he filled: VBS. He joked that every Marine with a VBS bag was going to owe Saint his life one day before they left this shithole.

Tex placed his hand on Saint's left shoulder. The veteran leader and company driver really was huffing now. "Let me fill that bag. Take a break and catch your breath," Tex said in a gentle, concerned voice.

"No . . . fa–faa–f-f-f-uckin' . . . way, green. I–I . . . gotta . . . fin . . . ish this bag."

Alarmed, Tex called over Doc Nunn. "Hey, Doc, come over here and take a look at Saint, he ain't right but he–" Tex's plea to Doc Nunn was interrupted by a loud thump. Tex, Doc Nunn, and the other sandbag-filling Marines turned to see Saint collapse onto his bag, gasping for breath.

"SAINT!" Docs Nunn and Milazzo rushed to their brother in distress, followed by the other Marines.

"Goddammit, you stubborn city slicker. You have a fucking inhaler; use the goddamn thing!" yelled Doc Nunn. And with that, Doc Nunn found the inhaler in the pocket of Vinnie's camo pants, removed the top, shoved it into Vinnie's mouth and pumped three sprays of life-saving mist into Vinnie's mouth and down into his exhausted lungs.

"I know," Vinnie gasped. "Sorry . . . about . . . that." The guys helped Vinnie back to his bunker and gave him a can of C-rats and a canteen of warm water, which was tantamount to a feast fit for a king. Vinnie lay on his rubber lady and concentrated on catching his breath. LeRoy entered the bunker and checked on his loyal Marine.

"You okay, city boy?" he asked.

Vinnie smiled and deliberately inhaled before replying, "Yes, I'm fine," amid a breathy exhalation.

"What happened to you, pal?" asked Doc Milazzo.

"Goddamn asthma," Vinnie replied. "The humid weather and my laziness to use my asthma pump are a bad combination, Stone!"

"Well, do us all a favor, Saint," Doc Milazzo made it a point to peer right into Vinnie's blue eyes. "Don't scare us like that again, okay? We seen a lotta guys die over here but I don't think anyone in the whole damn company is ready to see *you* drop dead on us. *Capisce?*"

"Loud and clear, *paisan*. Loud and clear!" Vinnie then turned to Captain LeRoy and stated, "I'm ready to go back out there and help the boys bag sand. It ain't fair to make them do that work without a senior guy like myself helping out."

Captain LeRoy wasn't surprised at Vinnie's genuine offer to get right back to work after suffering a serious asthma attack, but he was a proponent of the adage that discretion is the better part of valor.

"Oh, hell no, Saint. I ain't letting you back out there for the rest of the day. All's I need to do is call the platoon sergeant and tell him that I let you back out in the heat and humidity to die. I'd be court-martialed! You are going back to Dong Ha for a couple of days to see the medical officer and then to rest up. They have some AC units over there, so you can cool down and take a break for a week or so before you come back here."

Vinnie was incredulous. On the one hand, he actually was getting an unofficial R&R. But on the other hand, he felt terrible guilt over the notion of leaving his brothers out in the field all because he hadn't taken a couple of pumps on an inhaler.

"When can I come back here to be with the fellas, sir?"

Captain LeRoy studied the oversized, completely tattered calendar that hung on the far wall of the bunker for a few seconds, pondered silently for another couple of seconds, and then proclaimed: "Take off an entire week to make sure that you're fine to come back here."

"Red," LeRoy called out, "I want you to take two greens and then drive Saint back to HQ in his jeep, okay?"

"Yes, sir, skip," Reagan replied. LeRoy then returned his attention to Vinnie, who weakly looked up at his superior officer.

"Saint, we'll see you back here in a week."

*　　　　*　　　　*

The drive back to Dong Ha, thankfully, was uneventful. Vinnie actually slept most of the way, which spoke to how ill he truly was, as the drives stressed him out. Once at HQ, Mike and the younger Marines helped Vinnie into an air-conditioned bunker, with Mike throwing Vinnie's duffel bag on top of an actual bed. Mike stared longingly at the bed, as he hadn't seen an actual mattress, box spring and wooden framed-bed since he'd left Edmonds a lifetime ago.

"Wow, Saint. Ain't that something? You have a little cough and the government puts you up like Rockefeller for a couple of days! But if you're shot, or if you lose an arm or a leg, they throw you in a rat hole, place a used Band-aid on your boo-boo, and then send you back to the wolves in a couple of minutes!"

Mike chuckled, and Vinnie laughed weakly. But the comment, benign though it may have been coming from his pal, pierced Vinnie and caused him to be wrought with guilt. He didn't want special favors and he didn't want to be separated from his brothers for so long. The Marines, after all, had a code of honor, and Vinnie understood especially that, as an unofficial leader of the squad, he needed to be out in the field with his brothers.

A goddamn leader can't lead from the rear, Vinnie thought to himself. *I gotta get back to the guys soon.*

"Take it easy, Saint, and don't rush back on account of us, y'hear?" said Red.

"Sure, Mike, sure. Maybe I'll just jump on the next boat from here and sail back to the world when no one's looking. How's that sound?"

Mike smiled, gave Vinnie the thumbs-up sign, and exclaimed, "I'll see you in a week, okay? Don't be your stubborn Italian self and come back earlier, all right?"

Vinnie nodded. Mike, who was sitting on the bed next to Saint, got up and walked toward the bunker door, outside of which the two greens were waiting. Vinnie laid down on the bed after Mike had gotten up. He felt the tension dissipate from his back as the softness of the real mattress offered little resistance.

Mike stopped at the door, his back now to Vinnie. He looked out at the bright, sunny day, then he peered quickly at the two new Marines who were waiting for him. He saw apprehension in the young kids' eyes and thought about how it was not too long ago—and yet it seemed so remote in time—that he was a young, impressionable, scared green. Mike glanced over his right shoulder, back at Vinnie.

"What happens to heroes out here in the shit, Saint?"

Vinnie opened his eyes to meet Mike's eyes. Saint paused deliberately before responding, "They die, pal."

Mike nodded and responded tersely, "Don't try to be a fucking hero, Vincent."

With that, Mike turned and walked out of the bunker. The grizzled vet then walked between the two green Marines who were waiting outside for him. Mike extended his arms as he passed between them and patted their backs as if to say, *Good luck out here, boys. I hope neither of you is killed.* The three Marines boarded Vinnie's jeep for the drive back to Cam Lo. Mike started the vehicle but paused, thinking, *This is Vinnie's jalopy. It'd be disrespectful for me to take it back.*

Mike then shut the vehicle off and announced, "We're taking a different jeep back to camp, fellas."

"Why?" one of the greens asked.

Mike cocked his head to the side as he looked to the kid in the passenger seat. "When you're out here, you learn a couple of things real fucking quick, grunt," Mike said in a soft, reassuring tone that belied the harshness of his words. "First, you learn loyalty. You gotta be loyal to each other. We are all we have out here. No one gives a fuck about us out here, not the government and definitely not the gooks. The only ones that care about you in the shit are your brother Marines.

"You better be ready to die for me because I would die for you, even if I hate your fucking guts."

The kid's jaw tensed as Mike spoke.

"Next thing you gotta learn is that you never take a brother Marine's property. Your rifle is *your* rifle, you know how it works and what makes it work best. If I took your rifle and gave you another rifle, you might think, 'A rifle's a rifle; you pull the trigger and it shoots.' That kinda thinking will get you killed quicker than you otherwise may die. The split-second it takes you to stop focusing on the firefight to look down at the strange rifle is all it'll take for a sniper's bullet to rip half your fucking head from your shoulders." Mike glanced back at the other green who was sitting in the rear of Saint's jeep. The kid was sitting at a perfect ninety degrees. He was seated so rigidly that Mike knew that he had the kid's attention.

"This here jeep is Saint's vehicle. He knows what every goddamn squeak and fart coming out of the engine means. Now,

Saint *probably* would know what to do with any other jeep because he's a genius when it comes to 'em.

"But one second of indecisiveness can lead to an eternity of salvation, if you get my drift."

Mike looked at each of the Marines to make sure they were following him. One of the Marines appeared to be confused, as his forehead was burrowed down, his eyebrows arched slightly upward, and his eyes squinted.

Mike wasn't taking any chances. "The one second longer that Vinnie would take to figure out how to maneuver a strange vehicle would be the one-second difference between life and death for Vinnie." Mike paused before continuing. "And I don't want him dead."

With that, Mike abruptly exited Vinnie's jeep. "Let's go!" he ordered, without looking behind him at the young Marines who still were seated in Saint's jeep. Mike strode toward the motor pool, where other jeeps were parked, and he assumed that the two greens would be scampering behind him, just as small ducklings dutifully, yet frantically, scurry behind their mother. If Mike had peered over his shoulder, that is exactly what he would've seen. Mike eventually received clearance to take a different jeep and he and the greens were back at Cam Lo Hill by sundown on Tuesday, March 26, 1968.

*   *   *

Vinnie awakened the next morning feeling weak but definitely revitalized from the absolute exhaustion that he'd felt a day earlier. He looked around the bunker and heard the loud, panging whir of the air conditioning unit that was propped up on a makeshift window in Vinnie's temporary living quarters.

Shit, I sure could get used to staying here, Vinnie thought. *This is paradise compared to what I've been staying in!* He peered around the bunker and marveled at the modernity of it. There were actual walls, tables, chairs, and, of course, the bed in which he was lying. Vinnie mused that he would've dismissed the bed as an uncomfortable piece of shit a year earlier but now the bed nearly brought tears of happiness to his eyes. He hadn't slept in a real bed since the spring of 1967. *It's been way too long since I've slept in a bed this comfortable!*

Refreshed and happier than he had been in a while, Vinnie stepped outside to warm sunshine. The surrounding roads closest to HQ were not a free-fire zone, so they were lined with huts adjacent to seemingly endless fields of rice paddies that were inhabited by South Vietnamese farmers and their families. Vinnie often frolicked with the kids there during his downtime at HQ and he often snapped pictures with them. The kids seemed genuinely excited to be near Vinnie and they happily posed for pictures with him while yelling, "Hello, GI! Hello!" This time was no different.

On this hot, clear morning, Vinnie observed men, women, and children working in the rice paddies and he recalled how he always observed the locals tirelessly working these fields, irrespective of the weather conditions. The sight of the working children gave Saint an idea, so he returned to his room to retrieve his satchel. Bag in hand, Vinnie walked toward a group of seven young boys, all of whom appeared to range in ages from six to twelve. These specific youngsters were working with one portly man, likely in his forties, who Vinnie assumed was their father. The deep creases that lined the man's weathered face were an indication that he had been working in the rice paddies since he was the age of his youngest son.

Vinnie was wearing green Marine garb, including an ammo vest and green cap, as he walked toward the Vietnamese children in the field. The kids were dressed very raggedly despite the brutal conditions in which they were working. Indeed, one of the boys, who was shoeless, did not appear to be wearing any pants beneath his short-sleeve shirt.

An eight-year-old boy emerged from the group and shyly approached Vinnie. The youngster marveled at Saint's skin, which was much lighter than his, as well as his eyes, whose clear blue color matched the sky and were unlike any eyes that he had seen before. Vinnie warmly smiled at the youngster but he immediately was stricken by the impropriety of the boy's attire: He wore a brown jacket over what appeared to be a long-sleeve red shirt with black denim pants, despite the blazing hot sun. The youngster's six brothers, all of whom appeared older than their precocious brother, albeit not by much, observed Vinnie smiling at the boy and they, too, approached the friendly Marine.

Vinnie had learned some very rudimentary Vietnamese during his prior interactions with the local families, so he tapped on his chest and said, *"Bạn,"* friend in Vietnamese. He then tapped his chest and said, *"Tôi tên Saint"*—"My name is Saint"—in an effort to put all of the boys and their watchful father, who remained in the background, at ease.

The kids smiled back and repeated, "Saint," followed by tapping on their respective chests and enunciating their names. Vinnie clumsily repeated each of their names and the children roared with laughter at his weird accent and his butchering of their names.

Vinnie laughed, too, and then knelt down and opened his satchel, revealing Tootsie Rolls and licorice sticks Lilly had previously sent to him in a care package. He then shared the candy with the youngsters. The young boys smiled and exclaimed, *"Cảm ơn bạn, Saint!"*—Thank you, friend Saint!

The youngsters ravaged the sweets, as they had never experienced such exotic food before this interaction with Vinnie. Saint offered some candy to the boys' father, but he merely bowed slightly and otherwise remained expressionless. The man, dressed in a long black tunic with a burgundy belt and a *nón lá*—the traditional conical hat, made from dried palm leaves, worn by Vietnamese farmers—did not accept Vinnie's gesture.

A convoy of jeeps began to pull into HQ at that moment, and Vinnie noticed that one of the emerging Marines was carrying a camera. Vinnie called his colleague over and asked the young man to snap some pictures of him with the boys. Vinnie intended to send the photos back home to show his family that not all Vietnamese hated Americans. Indeed, the young boys, quite grateful for the delicious chocolate and licorice, continued to thank Vinnie after the Marine took some pictures.

"Gosh, they really have taken a liking to you, haven't they?" said the Marine.

Saint laughed and deadpanned in response, "I sure hope they ain't saying, '*Fuck you*, Saint'!"

Vinnie doled out the last of his prized candy to the grateful children before playfully patting each of the seven boys on the head.

Saint then took a step back and exclaimed in his thick New York accent, *"Chào tạm biệt bạn"*—"Goodbye, friends"—before he patted his brother Marine on the shoulder and said, "Okay, let's go." Vinnie and his colleague then returned to HQ as the young boys, jittery on their sugar highs, returned to toiling in the field of rice paddies under the unforgivingly hot sun.

*　　　*　　　*

Back in his room later that morning, Vinnie heard a muffled sound over the loud air conditioner and it momentarily confused him. The sound continued and Vinnie concentrated on it before realizing that it was knocking. *Oh, yeah, I have a fucking door!* Vinnie marveled, before yelling out, "Yeah, come in!"

A young Marine in a makeshift, white chef's hat timidly entered the threshold of the doorway and stopped, before respectfully exclaiming, "Lance Corporal Santaniello? PFC Smith here. What would you like for chow?"

Vinnie noticed the air of uneasiness that seemingly enveloped Smith and he instantly was compelled to put the young Marine at ease. "Hey there, Smith, the name's Vinnie, but my friends and brother Marines call me *Saint*. How ya doin', pal?"

Smith smiled but thought to himself that he couldn't disrespect a Marine who had been here longer than him—the bars on Saint's shirt denoted lance corporal status—by calling him by his *nickname*, of all things. Further, Smith knew who Saint was. The whole company talked in a reverent tone when they referenced this Marine: Saint was the company driver who refused to stay in the rear, where safety was virtually guaranteed. This was the Marine who fought side-by-side with his brothers and always, ALWAYS did right by his brother Marines.

Golly, Smith thought to himself, *this here man is a celebrity here in the platoon!* Smith looked down and brushed his foot against the dusty floor before raising his brow to sheepishly lock eyes with Vinnie. "Golly, I'm doing swell, thanks for asking. I hope that you're feeling better." Smith paused and instinctively kicked at the floor again before continuing, "It's a real honor to have the pleasure of speaking to an accomplished, well-respected Marine such as yourself."

Vinnie was genuinely touched by the respect that the young Marine was displaying. In fact, Vinnie was humbled and borderline-embarrassed by the deferential manner with which Smith spoke. "Well, that's awfully groovy of you to say, Smith. Say, what's your first name, Private?"

"My name is Matthew Smith."

"Where ya from, Matt?"

"Detroit. Detroit, Michigan."

Vinnie gestured to a chair that was located next to the bed and said, "Why don't you take a load off and have a seat for a few minutes, Matt? I haven't had much company since I was sent here for my make-believe R&R!" Vinnie chuckled.

Smith suppressed a laugh under a conservative smile. "I really shouldn't. After all, I have to cook chow for the company and the Five asked that I take your order, specifically, before I began cooking."

"I understand, Private Smith, but sit down, anyways. I know the Five and he ain't gonna give you a hard time if you tell him that Saint made you stay in his room for a coupla minutes."

Smith obediently sat in the chair, albeit with a modicum of apprehension about disobeying the Five's orders. "How long ya been in the shit, Matt?"

"Ten days."

"Holy shit, you're a genuine green, Smitty! I know you're too scared to ask, so I'll just tell ya: I been here eight months and yeah, it seems like eight *lifetimes*! You become wise to the ways of the jungle—and the ruthlessness of the gooks—real quick out in the shit, Matt." Vinnie looked out of the window to his bunker and, upon seeing the jungle, his mind reflexively drifted to thoughts of explosions and suffocating death.

Private Smith looked at Vinnie peering at the window and wondered why his expression had changed instantaneously. Indeed, Vinnie's brow became furrowed and his eyes, previously wide and steely blue, appeared narrowed and grayish in color as the outer corners of his eyes creased. The private felt exceedingly uncomfortable. Vinnie, realizing that he had allowed himself to mentally wander back into the throes of the war, snapped back into the moment by quickly and gently shaking his head back and forth, akin to a tremor.

He saw the look of consternation on Smith's face. "Sorry 'bout that . . . I kinda had a little daydream there, Private!" Vinnie forced a laugh in an effort to diffuse the awkwardness. "So, do you have any hobbies, Matthew?"

"I love music and I'm a pretty good drummer, if I do say so myself."

"A drummer, eh? That's pretty groovy, Matt. What kinda music do you like to play?"

"Rock 'n roll."

"That's groovy, Matt. I'm more of a blues and soul guy myself, but I'd be happy to sing in your band one day, green, as long as you're playing near me in New York!" The two Marines shared a laugh.

236

"That was a good one."

"You're not going to call me *Saint* or Vinnie, are you, Matty?"

Smith smiled. "Sorry, Saint, I just don't want to show disrespect."

"You're alright, Smitty, you're alright."

"Do me a favor, Matt," Vinnie said as he placed two small tables in front of the young Marine. He then found two crude wooden pointers from the command table in the middle of his temporary room and threw them at the chef.

"Let me see whatcha got!"

Matt chuckled and then pulled up a stool behind the tables and sheepishly began beating on them with the rulers.

The young Marine actually made the rudimentary drum kit sound good as he banged away on a percussionist's rendition of "Break on Through (To the Other Side)" by the Doors. Vinnie genuinely enjoyed Matt's performance and when the kid finished Vinnie stood and cheered before he flung a pair of clean underwear at the drummer.

"Sorry, but I ain't got any chicks' drawers laying around, buddy! That was damn groovy, Smitty. You belong on stage and not out here in the shit. Maybe you can hook up with Jimi Hendrix when ya gets outta here!"

The private was genuinely humbled. "Thanks, Saint. Thanks for giving me the opportunity to play for you."

"What the hell's all that racket over there?" the Five barked from a few bunkers over. Smith turned white with fear but Vinnie just laughed.

"He's a cranky bastard, ain't he? Don't worry, green, I'll take care of this for you."

"Thanks, Saint," Private Smith replied nervously. "Now, what can I get you for chow?"

"I'll take a split-pea soup, but only if you can make it like my mama, Rose, back home." Vinnie winked at Smith and then gestured with his hand to advise the young Marine to return to the mess hall. Smith tipped his chef's hat to Vinnie as a sign of respect and turned to exit the bunker.

"Hey, Smitty," Vinnie called out as the percussionist passed the threshold of Vinnie's bunker.

The young Marine stopped, pivoted on his feet, and faced Vinnie. "Yes?"

"Don't get yourself killed out there, green. I wanna buy your first record, okay?"

The private smiled and nodded before he astutely replied, "You got it, Saint." The young Marine turned and walked to the other side of camp. As he walked, Smith reflected on how impressed he was by Saint. He now understood why the humble, yet brash, vet was so thoroughly respected by the men in camp.

I hope to get to see him again before he goes home, he thought.

CHAPTER 16

DON'T BE A HERO

Thursday, March 28, 1968. Vinnie woke up at 0430 hours. It had been nearly three days since Vinnie had arrived here, feeling half-dead and exhausted after his asthma attack while making sandbags for the bunkers at Cam Lo. Vinnie still felt a great deal of shame and regret for having to desert his brothers out in the jungle. And that guilt only intensified as he peered around his deluxe accommodations in his current digs. Vinnie was living in relative opulence compared to the squalor that his brothers called home back in the shit. Vinnie cast an angry glance about his living quarters before muttering, "I can't stay here another minute. I gotta go back to Cam Lo to be with the boys!"

Vinnie bounced out of his bed and glanced furtively at it, acknowledging that the next time he slept in a bed that comfortable would be when he was home for Lilly's wedding in a few months. *Goddamn, I'm gonna miss that blessed bed!* Vinnie gave himself a moment to reflect on the three glorious nights of sleep that the bed afforded him and, being a disciplined Marine, he immediately made up the bed, boot-camp style, with hospital corners and a four-inch hem. Vinnie repeated a mantra that he heard repeatedly in boot camp—*a perfectly made bed is one that looks like it's never been slept in*—before he looked at the bed and realized that it actually did appear to be a brand-new setup. *I want the next fella that has to call this joint home to feel just swell and welcome when he walks through that door. And nothing says* home *to a tired, injured Marine like a neat, warm bed.* Vinnie then spent the next fifteen minutes sprucing up the room as best he could, so that it felt peaceful and like a home.

Vinnie glanced at the clock on the wall. It was 0452 hours. Vinnie seized the opportunity to take what would be his last shower for a while. Vinnie stripped out of his worn clothing and he was genuinely startled when he realized how disgusting and worn his USMC-issued t-shirt and trousers were. The shirt was pockmarked and the USMC crest along the breast was barely discernible. The knees of his pants were thinner than the sliced cheese that Vinnie's mother, Rose, bought from the local deli, and the smell coming from them would make his dog, Apache, blush. Vinnie tossed the tattered clothes into a canvas laundry sack and instinctively went to remove his underwear only to realize that he hadn't been wearing boxers for so damn long. Underwear was quite overrated for the American boys in Vietnam: They often bunched up and contributed to terrible rashes. They also made great hiding places for leeches.

Saint hopped into the shower and the thrust of hot water startled him as it struck his head and chest. The sound of the water cascading upon Vinnie's head, down the nape of his neck, and to the small of his back was exhilarating. Vinnie marveled at the size of the shower: It was nearly as wide as his shower back home. The shower was so satisfying that the thought of actually staying put, here in the camp, crept into the recesses of Vinnie's mind. But just for a moment.

My boys need me. I can't let the platoon down by staying in this here paradise, he thought.

With that, Vinnie finished his shower, but he hesitated to turn off the water. Instead, he reflected on the fact that he likely would not enjoy another warm, relaxing shower until August, when he was back home for Lilly's wedding. So, he paused to enjoy the calming shower gently pelting his tense body with warmth and security. Vinnie sighed, shook his head, and blinked to channel the water from his eyes and the thoughts of home from the recesses of his mind, before turning off the taps.

Refreshed, Vinnie got dressed and actually put on boxers. The underwear felt soft and comfortable. Saint had requested permission from the captain to recycle his weathered clothes for reinforcements and he'd eagerly swapped his tattered shirt, pants, and vest for new editions when permission was granted. The hardened Marine actually became emotional about the prospect of walking out of the bunker in brand-new clothes. He came to the simple realization that he'd been in 'Nam too damn long. Saint chuckled before thinking, *Merry Christmas to me!*

A sergeant offered to give Vinnie a brand-new set of boots to finish off his new duds but Saint demurred. His shirt and pants meant nothing but his boots? Well, they were another story altogether. A Marine's boots, like his rifle, became an extension of the warrior. Deserting one's boots or one's rifle was akin to turning one's back on a brother Marine in distress and that simply did not happen.

Vinnie looked down at his boots. They were once a pristine, shiny black and were now a barely recognizable, torn, scuffed set of footwear with thinning, battered soles that gasped from the dust, soot, mud, rain, and blood that had long ago spoiled their luster. Vinnie mused that the boots actually looked like a completely different pair from the set that he'd been issued the previous summer. The boots were cracked and torn in more places than Vinnie could count. They looked tired, weathered, beaten, and near death, and Vinnie wouldn't have it any other way. Why? Well, because that exact description could be used for Vinnie and all his brother Marines who had done extensive time in the jungles of 'Nam.

Vinnie knew that his boots had become an extension of his being here in the shit and he knew that both he and his boots had to go back home to Jamaica. Vinnie bent over to place his fantastically clean socks and feet into the decrepit boots and lovingly exclaimed, "Yous guys are coming home with me!"

Fully dressed, Saint realized that he had not yet shaved, so he removed his crisp, clean shirt and retreated to the bathroom, where he cupped hot water onto his face. Vinnie looked up and saw a stranger peering at him. Perplexed for a second, Vinnie actually tried to discern the identity of the familiar stranger looking at him. Then it dawned on him: Vinnie was peering into an actual mirror on the wall in the head. In the previous three days, he had been using the outhouse outside the barracks, as a show of solidarity with his brother Marines.

Holy shit, he thought. *I look like an old man, like I'm forty, for Chrissakes!*

Vinnie knew that he was a good-looking cat before he enlisted in the Marines at seventeen. The ladies' affinity for him back home in Jamaica attested to his rugged, wholesome good looks. He greased his thick, dirty-blond hair back, akin to James Dean, and his steely blue eyes melted many a heart back home. His skin was smooth and supple, a genetic nod to his southern Italian roots. The ladies back home marveled at his smooth face, slick hair, and the piercing nature of his eyes, which were as deep and blue as the Atlantic Ocean that he enjoyed every summer off the Rockaways in Queens.

But that was an eternity ago. The man looking back at him was not that Vinnie Santaniello. That Vinnie was dead and replaced by a haggard old man who'd hijacked the once-ebullient young man's soul.

"God-*DAMN*," Vinnie muttered aloud, "what the fuck happened to me since I got here?" He cast another long, pained glance at the mug in the mirror and slowly exhaled. He quickly resigned himself to the fact that this war had changed him in many ways, including some that he still was incapable of fully appreciating. The smoothness of his skin was replaced by pockmarks of dreaded jungle rot on his chin, his right cheek, and his forehead. He also noticed a series of blackened scars around his eyes, on his neck, along the bridge of his nose, and on his left temple. He had no explanation for them, other than that they were the unintended spoils of war. His hair, once sexy and impeccably neat, was now a matted mess, despite the fact that he had just spent roughly ten minutes trying to wash the muck out of it.

New Marines' hair typically was buzzed barely a shadow above the scalp, but the boys who were getting short typically had long, straggly hair because there really was no opportunity to seek out haircare while simultaneously striving to avoid enemy arty. *Nothing a little Brylcreem shouldn't be able to fix,* Vinnie thought to himself.

Vinnie was most shocked when he saw his eyes and the crow's feet protruding from their corners. Saint could not believe it. His smile before the war had been warm and had accentuated his blue eyes and the smoothness of the skin that surrounded them. Now, his eyelids were squinted, as if Vinnie was in pain, and his eyes looked tired, scared, hurt, and angry. Vinnie noticed that his "smile" now was more of a grimace and the effect that it had on his eyes was equally perplexing.

The creases at the corners of his eyes deepened as he smile-grimaced; they extended as far as his temples. Further, Vinnie's face, once full, with a chiseled jawbone that had accentuated his handsome features, was now taut, too thin, and eerily skeletal. His eyes were sunken into his skull. Equally distressing was the fact that Vinnie's forehead bore newly minted, thick creases.

"Where the hell did they come from?" Vinnie asked aloud. He stared dumbstruck at himself in the mirror for a few seconds before it dawned on him: The stranger staring back at him no longer resembled the young kid who'd arrived in Vietnam the previous summer. Instead, the old man in the mirror more closely resembled Saint's grizzled forty-eight-year-old father. That would have been just fine if Saint was fifty, because his dad was a very handsome fella, but this barely nineteen-year-old teenager did not take much solace in that fact.

Vinnie suddenly reasoned why there were no real mirrors out in the platoons: The USMC didn't want the boys to see how fucking ugly and old the war was making them.

Saint could not get over how different he looked. He was so disgusted, in fact, that he elected against shaving. Instead, he cupped some cold water and splashed it against his face, in a failed effort to symbolically wash away his newfound disdain and angst. The young Marine could not bear to look at what he had become. Instead, he turned his back on the mirror and walked out of the bathroom, riddled with anger and doubt. He somberly paced around the room as he began thinking to himself.

How the hell can I show this mug at Lilly's wedding?

What the hell will Rosalie say when she sees me for the first time?

The questions were coming fast and furious now and Vinnie was bereft of answers. Suddenly, Saint sighed and threw up his hands in exaggerated resignation.

Vinnie reminded himself that the boys out here often said that they could count on him to make them feel better, even in times of despair. *Well*, he thought, *time to help yourself get over this funk*. He exclaimed aloud, "I ain't got time to feel sorry for myself. The boys need me." With that, Vinnie checked the clock on the wall one last time. It was 0900 hours and Vinnie headed down to the mess hall for some chow. "I may be butt-ugly right now," Vinnie muttered under his breath as he walked to the mess hall, "but I can't worry about that now. I need to get back to my guys."

Vinnie dined with Captain LeRoy and a couple of the bosses who led the command from Dong Ha HQ. The men exchanged pleasantries and Vinnie could barely contain his enthusiasm for his imminent return to the platoon. The Marine actually was moderately surprised by his *gunji* attitude. It was as if he was a green arriving in country for the first time, full of piss and vinegar and ready to obliterate the enemy.

"I thought we gave you until tomorrow, Saint. Why are you heading back down to Cam Lo this morning?" Captain LeRoy looked Vinnie up and down after he questioned him. "Let me guess, you wanna show off your new duds, right?"

Vinnie chuckled. "Yes, sir," he responded before thrusting out a dusty boot from under the table and gestured toward it with his right hand before continuing, "new duds."

LeRoy smiled, "Ah, yes, a Marine and his boots shall never be separated. You guys marry your goddamn boots before you marry your broads on R&R!"

Saint and the bosses laughed at LeRoy's observation, for they knew that there was more than a modicum of truth to it! "I just wanted to show the boys what it was like to be clean and showered, with clean clothes, to boot!"

"Then you'd better shave, Saint," LeRoy wryly noted. Turning serious, Captain LeRoy quizzed Vinnie: "You sure that you're up to it, Saint? You were a mess the other day."

Vinnie appreciated LeRoy's sincere concern. "I'm fine, sir. The rest did me good, so thanks for the break, Captain. I'm better now, and I need to get back to the fellas at Cam Lo. After all, they need their Saint!"

LeRoy exhaled and released a sarcastic laugh. "Yeah, but they don't need to resuscitate their Saint on account of his not being able to breathe. Why don't you take another couple of days here in paradise? It wouldn't kill you, y'know?"

Vinnie didn't respond immediately. Instead, he gave LeRoy's suggestion serious consideration. The daily chow (and good chow, at that!); the soft bed; the warm, dry room; the privacy; the bathroom with a real mirror. *Ugh, the mirror!* Vinnie suddenly envisioned the old man in the mirror again and shuddered. He did not want to see *that* again.

"Thank you, sir, that's very nice of you and all, but I don't need the deluxe accommodations anymore, sir. I need to be back in the platoon with the fellas."

"Have it your way, grunt," LeRoy jokingly replied. "We'll head down to Cam Lo Hill at 1130 hours. The men need some more ammo because it's been hot down there while you've been on R&R up here. Intel says that it should be quiet for a couple of days, so it's a good time to bring some reinforcements." The R&R comment was purely tongue-in-cheek but it nonetheless stung Vinnie. He took his duties and his loyalty to his brother Marines ultra-seriously and it genuinely flustered him to learn that his brothers had come under attack by the gooks while he was up here in paradise staring at his ugly face.

"Any Oleys, sir?" Vinnie was genuinely concerned.

Captain LeRoy's eyebrows arched as he rubbed his forehead with his right hand. The captain's green cap slid up his head, revealing a tuft of thick curly brown hair. LeRoy exhaled and exclaimed, "Thankfully, nothing more than a few cuts, bumps, and bruises. You'd've been proud of the boys down there, Vinnie. They even scored a couple of bodies."

"That's swell to hear, sir. Those boys are good Marines," Vinnie paused, "and fucking brave, too."

"That they are, Saint. That they are."

"Ya want me to meet you at the dump with my jeep at 1045 hours to load up the ammo, Captain?"

"That'd be great, Saint. Thanks. I'm giving you shit for being such a *gunji* but, in all seriousness, your presence back at the platoon will lift the boys' morale. They miss you and your pretty-boy good looks!"

"Yeah," replied Vinnie, reflecting on the latter part of LeRoy's observation and reminiscing about the old man that he unexpectedly encountered back in his room. "I'm sure that is *exactly* what they miss about me, sir!"

Vinnie returned to his deluxe accommodations one final time to pack his belongings into his duffel bag. He made certain to snag a few extra shirts, both long-sleeve and short-sleeve, as well as a few more pairs of pants, including pairs for his buddies Red, Doc Nunn, Stone, King, and even a pair for the green, Tex.

He's a swell fella, Vinnie thought, *and he oughta know that I think he's gonna be a fine leader of the platoon one day soon. That'll build up his morale and make this place more tolerable.*

246

Vinnie flung his duffel bag into the rear of the jeep and drove to the ammo dump behind the largest, most fortified bunker at Dong Ha HQ. Saint peered at the beaten up, filthy Timex on his wrist and noted the time. It was 1038 hours. Vinnie hated to be late and he glanced around impatiently for the captain. LeRoy walked up to the jeep at 1045 hours exactly. Vinnie feigned disgust when the captain locked eyes with him before he exclaimed, "You're late, sir!"

"Too bad you can't do shit about that, lance corporal!"

The two Marines laughed and, with that, they each walked toward the ammo dump and loaded enough boxes of ammo to obliterate half of California.

It was 1100 hours. Time to roll.

Vinnie was happy that Mike hadn't taken his jeep back to the hill a couple of days earlier, after he and the greens had dropped Vinnie off. *I know this jeep like I know my best friend, Chang, back home in Jamaica. That was real swell of Mike not to leave me with a strange jeep to drive to Cam Lo Hill,* thought Vinnie. *I'd've been real cross if I had to learn the quirks of a completely different vehicle.*

Saint inserted the key into the ignition and started up his old companion. The engine reluctantly fired up after a few hiccups and pumps of the gas pedal. Vinnie shifted the old bucket of bolts into gear and the jeep kicked and lurched a couple of times like an angry steed before Vinnie tamed the beast and proceeded to HQ to retrieve Captain LeRoy for the drive to Cam Lo. Prior to picking up LeRoy, Vinnie stopped by the mail drop to see if there were any letters for his buddies or for him.

Boy, am I lucky that I decided to stop by here, Vinnie thought. *There must be over five dozen letters here for the fellas! They sure will be happy to see so many letters from home.*

As the company driver and glorified mailman, Vinnie knew the joy that these letters brought to the boys. He knew how ecstatic he became when, in the midst of a crazy war, he received a letter from a loved one. He equated that experience with receiving a gift from Santa at Christmas. It was *that* magical and cathartic.

What I wouldn't give to be back home just nine years ago, nestled in my bed while waiting for Santa to arrive. Seems like Lilly and I were doing that just yesterday . . .

Vinnie packed the letters, including a couple for him from Lilly and the rest of his beloved family, into a crate and secured it between two heavy ammo boxes to ensure that it wouldn't slide or tip over. As Vinnie drove to Captain LeRoy's bunker, a random thought came up.

I wonder if Santa would ever risk bringing toys to the Vietnamese kids who live in the burnt-out huts that litter the perimeter of the road extending down to Cam Lo?

"Morning, Saint. You sure you're ready to leave paradise for a return to Hell?" LeRoy was only smiling slightly when he asked the question. Indeed, LeRoy's comments were a thinly veiled attempt at one last-ditch effort to convince Vinnie to stay behind, at least for one more day. Vinnie understood LeRoy's subtle intentions, and he appreciated the consideration—he really did—but the guilt of leaving his brothers behind while he lived like Caesar here was too burdensome.

Vinnie knew that he could stay here as long as he liked; he had built up enough equity to earn a nice, unofficial vacation. However, that's not how Carmine raised his son, and Vinnie was not going to take such a handout. He was a proud young man, and borderline obstinate, and he was not going to take the easy way out. He had to do what was right and just. He had to return to his brothers in Cam Lo today. Not tomorrow, or the next day, or the next week.

"Yes, sir. I'm ready. Thank you for caring and for your willingness to give me a few more days to recuperate, sir. I really appreciate that. But I owe it to the men down in the platoon to get there and help them out as best I can. It ain't right and it ain't fair to leave them like this, especially if they need reinforcements."

This here Saint is a good fucking Marine, thought Captain LeRoy before responding, "Okay, have it your way, Saint. Let's roll. I'm sure the boys'll be happy to see you . . . in clean clothes, for once!"

Vinnie laughed and threw the jeep into gear. The vehicle lurched even harder than before, causing their helmeted heads to snap backward.

"What the hell, Saint? You trying to break our necks, for Chrissakes?"

"Sorry, sir. She seems a little hostile today. If I hadda guess, I'd say that the transmission's a little sore 'bout not being used for a few days. And a' course, now we're toting a coupla hundred pounds of ammo and a bunch of other shit. That can't be too easy on the transmission, sir. I'll give her a full physical when we arrive in Cam Lo."

And with that, Vinnie chided the jeep for being so rough before he whispered a little tough love to her under his breath: "C'mon, you piece of shit, do us both proud and get us to the hill safely so that I can show you a little tender lovin' care!"

And with that, the two Marines set off from Dong Ha HQ to Cam Lo, along Highway 9. Vinnie slowly drove past a rice paddy and he recognized the same boys to whom he had doled out candy the previous morning. The boys were working the rice paddies with their father, but they immediately recognized Vinnie and began to exclaim, *"Chào bạn, Saint!"*—"Hello, friend, Saint"—as Vinnie waved in response from the driver's seat of his slowly moving jeep. The father looked up at Vinnie from under the brim of his *nón lá* but he did not respond in kind to Saint's enthusiastic wave.

"It's funny how the locals can be so friendly, sir, yet their fellow countrymen a few miles south want to blow our heads off," Vinnie mused.

"Yeah," LeRoy replied as the jeep drove past the farmer, "that has always astounded me, too, Saint."

Vinnie then happily shared his experiences with these same boys from the previous morning. "You really are trying to live up to your nickname, eh, Saint?" Captain LeRoy wryly observed.

Vinnie picked up speed after he passed the happy brothers. The jeep got smaller in the view of the boys' father as the dust that its wheels spit up settled gently against the war-torn, gravelly road. The man turned to his seven sons in the field and said, "I'll be right back."

The father, sweaty and dirty from toiling in the rice paddies, lit a cigarette before walking a short distance to a nearby barn. He spat out his cigarette before entering the barn through a side door. The Vietnamese farmer closed the door behind him and crouched down in the suffocating darkness. He proceeded to crawl on his hands and knees between enormous bales of hay, his fingers clawing at the raw earth below.

The determined farmer counted paces in his head, as the barn was completely engulfed in darkness. Random, weak beams of sunlight snuck through the wooden panels of the roof and sides of the barn, but the beams did very little to illuminate the interior of the humid shack. He peered over his shoulder as his eyes slowly adjusted to the suffocating darkness and he did not see anything. Upon reaching thirty paces, the farmer made a blind left turn and unexpectedly struck his head against a wooden beam that supported the barn.

The blinding pain, coupled with the sudden viscous warmth that trickled down the farmer's forehead, around the contours of his nose, and into the creases of his mouth confirmed that he had cracked open the top of his head and was bleeding. Undeterred, the short, portly Vietnamese farmer remained steadfast in his mission and he crawled on. He turned right after another eight paces and continued his labored approach through the darkness.

Suddenly, the farmer stopped crawling. His right hand clumsily banged against a latch placed surreptitiously below the hay. The bloodied farmer nervously lifted the latch and then fumbled in the darkness until his right hand encountered a concealed walkie-talkie. He instinctively turned the device on before he manipulated a rotary knob to adjust its volume. Initially, a shrill stream of static emanated from the walkie-talkie, but the farmer fiddled with a second knob to adjust its frequency and within seconds he established a staticky connection to a cluster of NVA fighters situated perilously close to Cam Lo Hill.

The farmer that had feigned appreciation for Vinnie's benevolence a day earlier actually was an NVA informant. Walkie-talkie in hand, he began to communicate with the NVA militia over a radio wavelength that had yet to be cracked by American intel.

"The GIs are heading down the road to Cam Lo in a jeep that is loaded with ammunition. If you can hit the jeep, you will destroy their ammo and kill many GIs on the hill."

"Good work. We will advise you of the attack," came the response, transmitted through a wave of static from a fortified location in the vicinity of the DMZ.

The farmer proudly reflected on the good that he had done for his brothers in the North, against the hated U.S.A. *The GIs will not take over our land,* the farmer thought as he placed the walkie-talkie back into its secret location. *The US will not take over our country, steal our culture, and rape our women.*

The farmer believed that his actions were patriotic because they would contribute to a weakening of the sadistic Americans, thereby subverting the enemy's selfish plot to take over the world. The sympathizer, a simple man from the South, of meager means and no education, had fallen prey to a very profound Vietcong propaganda campaign. He firmly believed that his loyalty to the Northern fighters would be rewarded with a better, more comfortable life for his wife and seven kids, all of whom were younger than twelve years of age.

The farmer crawled out of the barn and made his way outside after he had notified the Vietcong fighters of Vinnie's trek down to Cam Lo. The unforgivingly bright sun blinded the man and caused tears to stream down his cheeks. His hands were covered in dirt and caked in blood while the knees of his trousers each bore circular dirt stains. His sons surrounded him upon his return to the field of rice paddies.

"Papa, what happened? You are bleeding and dirty," observed the eldest son.

"Nothing, son. I fell in the barn while searching for a sickle. Now, let's resume our work."

"Father," said the precocious eight-year-old that had approached Vinnie twenty-four hours earlier, "we like that GI that drove by. He is very nice and we hope that he brings us more of those treats next time!" As the boy raved about Saint's benevolence, the expressionless father simply stared past his exuberant son and toward the wake of the departed jeep.

The farmer then trained his cold, steely eyes upon his youngest son and exclaimed loud enough for all seven boys to hear, "The Americans are not out friends. Now, resume your work." The boys were puzzled but they did not question their stern father. Instead, they obediently resumed their monotonous work in the rice paddies.

* * *

Vinnie and LeRoy were ten minutes into their drive to Cam Lo Hill and they still were discussing Vinnie's interactions with the young Vietnamese farmers from the previous morning. LeRoy laughed as Vinnie tried his best to repeat the language the boys used to thank him for the candy. LeRoy, who also had learned simple Vietnamese phrases during his time in country, remarked in jest that the kids really were dropping the F-bomb on him in return for his gesture of kindness.

"Why, those ungrateful sonsabitches," Vinnie said playfully. "They sure as hell had better been thanking me. I gave them my two favorite treats from home!"

Vinnie laughed and then realized that he had not once felt the sense of dread and consternation that he had on previous drives to and from HQ. Vinnie sighed and thought to himself that maybe, just maybe, the tortuous angst of driving on a road where many

Americans had died by land mine had deserted him. Vinnie felt at ease while driving and that made him happy. He was going back to his men a day earlier than planned and he was going to greet them in a jolly mood.

"Damn, Captain," Vinnie remarked, "I am pretty excited about getting back to the boys down at Cam Lo Hill. Am I crazy or what?"

Captain LeRoy laughed before saying, "Uh, I'd say crazy, if you forced me to choose, Saint. I can't believe that you wouldn't want to stay back in paradise and milk the privilege of that arrangement for as long as possible."

Vinnie turned serious. "Sir, there's no way in hell I'd be able to live with myself knowing that I deserted those men in the platoon. I never wanted to leave them in the first place."

LeRoy reassured Vinnie with a firm pat on his shoulder as he shifted gears on his jeep. "I know, Saint, I know. That's exactly why I recommended that you make the Corps a career. You're a genuine leader and the men respect you. You're a natural for the service, Saint. You're loyal, brave, you've got a great sense of humor that keeps the guys loose, and you're down-to-earth."

LeRoy paused for a moment to let that resonate with Saint.

"Oh, yeah, another reason why you'd have a great career in the Corps: You're a little fucking crazy. You need to be a bit crazy to survive this lifestyle!"

"Shit, sir, how can I refuse such a fantastic offer? Where do I sign up?" Vinnie laughed at his brazen response and LeRoy patted him on the back as he enjoyed a hearty laugh as well.

For the first time in a long time, Vinnie felt relaxed. The warm sunshine invigorated him as he navigated the dust-strewn roadway. Feeling brash, the Marine cavalierly arched his chin up, took his eyes off the road, and looked up at the sky. The clear blue skies and scattered, puffy white clouds belied the deadly environs that lurked below the placid vista. Vinnie closed his eyes for a second as he inhaled deeply and soaked in the warmth of the sun.

Ironically, Saint felt a sense of peace.

He thought to himself, *I'll be home soon, and I'm gonna make it a point to look up at the warm summer sky as I walk out of the church after Lilly's wedding. It'll be swell to know that I won't have to worry about being killed by a fucking sniper then!* Vinnie lowered his head and opened his eyes and the rising dust, grit, and unceasing jungle supplanted the much more enchanting image of his sister, aglow in her pristine wedding dress.

Soon . . . that vision will be my happy reality soon enough. In the meantime, it'll be swell to be with the fellas until I get home to my family again, reflected Vinnie as he depressed the gas pedal to get him to his destination that much quicker.

"It sure is groovy that we ain't come across any ambushing gooks on the way down to Cam Lo, ain't it, Captain?"

Those words had barely escaped Vinnie's lips when the jeep suddenly backfired something fierce, causing the vehicle to hesitate before lurching uneasily forward. The heads of the two Marines jerked forward before thrusting back after the jeep jockeyed forward. LeRoy instinctively ducked before he grabbed his sidearm, cocked it and aimed it with deadly intention in the direction of the relentless jungle passing by to his right. The expansive jungle seemingly ran in an endless loop as Vinnie and LeRoy drove to Cam Lo.

LeRoy regained his bearings and realized that he was not being ambushed. Rather, Vinnie's piece-of-shit jeep had backfired and subsequently scared the bejeezus out of him. He exclaimed, "Holy shit, Saint! If we're not killed by this bucket of bolts running over a land mine, we're gonna die of heart attacks after it backfires and scares the shit out of us!"

Vinnie peered over at LeRoy. His shaking hand, still wrapped tightly around his sidearm, belied his attempts to find humor in a tense situation. "I'm sorry, sir," a contrite Saint said to his superior.

"I will get under the hood of this jalopy as soon as we get to Cam Lo and get this vehicle right!"

"Yeah, that's a good idea, Saint," LeRoy offered. "Fix this piece of shit up nice so there's not any more unnecessary drama!"

Vinnie recognized from the terrain that they were just a couple of minutes from their destination. He mused to himself how ironic it was that he was the stoic one during this drive to Cam Lo and that LeRoy was the excessive neurotic.

"We're just a couple of minutes away, sir," Vinnie pointed out to his shaken superior and friend before adding, in half-jest, "you gonna be okay?"

Captain LeRoy, realizing that he still was clutching his sidearm tightly in his right hand, meticulously removed his finger from the trigger of his gun before re-holstering it on the outer half of his right thigh. LeRoy squinted before arching his neck back to bask in the sun's relaxing warmth.

The brightness of the sun caused tears to stream from his eyes and down his cheeks. Of course, tears cascading down a hardened Marine's cheeks are never an acceptable occurrence, so the proud, embarrassed Marine peered over at Vinnie—*Thank God he ain't looking!* he thought to himself—before nonchalantly wiping the tears on his filthy shirt sleeve.

The somber leader then exhaled before saying to the company driver, "Just get us the fuck to Cam Lo Hill in one piece, please, Saint."

"Yes, sir," came Vinnie's obedient response before he depressed the gas a little firmer in an effort to get them to their destination that much quicker.

*　　　*　　　*

"How long ago did we get the farmer's transmission?" The NVA officer was immersed in the thickness of the jungle north of the DMZ. The soldier was covered in grime and soot that spoke of his tenure in this conflict with the American enemy. The NVA saw the United States as a shameful, colonialist power looking to expand its dominion over yet another weak, disorganized, third-world country. Indeed, the NVA felt that the U.S. believed that the North Vietnamese would meekly capitulate to their might. Well, the NVA believed, the hated, arrogant Americans had another thing coming, as its forces were trained to fight in heretofore unseen, unconventional ways. The left sleeve of the inquiring soldier's tattered uniform still bore a number of worn and faded bars that represented his lofty rank amongst his peers.

"Our brother's transmission came through about fifteen minutes ago, sir. The GIs should be arriving at the hill in another five to ten minutes."

"Excellent. Are the mortars and missiles ready for launch over the border at our hill, soldier?"

"Yes, sir. We are ready for the attack on the GIs. We will kill those bastards that wish to take over our land. We will kill those who think of us as weak and submissive." The soldier gestured toward the Soviet-provided mortar launchers and other weaponry that was aimed squarely at the Thundering Third's makeshift base beyond the DMZ. Their fellow warriors were stationed at the ready, waiting for the command to unfurl their deadly fury at the unsuspecting Americans' makeshift base.

"Good, good, good," came the leader's response. "The fools will have no idea that this attack is coming. Besides, they are forbidden from attacking us on the other side of their so-called DMZ, so this will be like hunting a weak goat, or one of its calves." The Vietnamese men laughed at their leader's appropriate analogy before they resumed their positions, awaiting the command to rain a motherlode of destruction on the unsuspecting Marines.

The Vietnamese soldiers grew impatient after holding their positions for nearly ten minutes. "Why don't we destroy the Americans now? Why wait?" asked one soldier.

"Did you not hear the farmer? The Americans are driving south with a truck full of explosives. If we detonate the truck, we will kill or maim every single GI there and then we can take back our land!" observed another.

The leader admonished the impetuous sect of his men and implored them to be patient. "The truck should be arriving in ten minutes. Patience, brothers, for their deaths shall taste sweeter than the finest of wines."

Vinnie and Lilly in the backyard of their
Jamaica, New York home (July 1967)

Vinnie and his father, Carmine, in the backyard
of their Jamaica, New York home (July 1967)

Vinnie and his mother, Rose, in the backyard
of their Jamaica, New York home (July 1967)

Vinnie and then-fiancé, Rosalie Vitale,
in his backyard (July 1967)

Vinnie on the porch of his Jamaica,
New York home (July 1967)

Vinnie in the vicinity of Highway 9,
Dong Ha (circa 1967)

Vinnie at Camp Hill in Gio Linh
(circa 1967)

Vinnie with an M-79 grenade launcher
(circa 1967)

Vinnie and his sea bag
(circa summer 1967)

Vinnie with a group of young Vietnamese
children, next to his jeep on Dong Ha Bridge
(circa late 1967-early 1968)

Vinnie with additional Vietnamese children in
Dong Ha (circa late 1967-early 1968)

Vinnie and Vietnamese children at
Dong Ha Bridge (circa late 1967-early 1968)

Vinnie outside of a bunker-fortified
outdoor shower (circa late 1967-early 1968)

Vinnie in his jeep
(circa late 1967-early 1968)

Vinnie in his jeep
(circa late 1967-early 1968)

Vinnie under the hood of his jeep
(circa late 1967-early 1968)

Vinnie driving his jeep, location unknown
(circa late 1967-early 1968)

Vinnie and his lieutenant in Cam Lo
(October 1967)

Vinnie's Thomas Edison High School
graduation photo (circa June 1966)

Vinnie and "Meatball" at Command Post 3
in Cam Lo (circa late 1967-early 1968)

Vinnie at Rockaway Beach in Far Rockaway,
NY (circa 1966). Credit: Rosalie Wagenecht

Vinnie and Rosalie in Rosalie's Bayside,
NY home (circa Christmas 1966)
Credit: Rosalie Wagenecht

Vinnie and his grandmother, Nunu, in their
backyard in Jamaica, New York (July 1967)

Vinnie in Rosalie's dining room in Bayside,
NY (circa 1966). Credit: Rosalie Wagenecht

Rose and Carmine Santaniello, in their
backyard in Jamaica, New York (circa 1966)

Vinnie and a buddy, seated atop a
bunker in Cam Lo (October 1967)

Vinnie in his USMC dress blues (circa spring 1967)
Courtesy of Rosalie Wagenecht's personal collection

CHAPTER 17

CORPSMEN UP!

"Hey, Captain, the camp is about a mile away. I can see the hills up ahead. The area is so burnt out that the hills stand above everything else." Vinnie's observation was spot-on. Cam Lo Hill was a stronghold of the Marines but it had been taken by force, and that fact was known by all of the veteran Marines. It also was a known fact to the NVA and one for which they wanted vengeance.

"You got here sooner than expected, Saint. How fast were you going?" LeRoy's rhetorical question was greeted with a smile by the young company driver and LeRoy playfully jabbed at his respected brother's right arm.

"Quit it, sir. I'm liable to drive off a cliff or drive over a land mine that'd blow us to kingdom come!" The seriousness of Vinnie's statement was belied by his smile as he spoke the words.

"God forbid, Saint," exclaimed LeRoy. With that, Vinnie's jeep veered into the camp. The men were milling about, enjoying the warmth of the sun and the quiet of the morning.

"Hey, look who's back, fellas!" Tony Milazzo was seated, shirtless, at the forefront of the camp, with his rifle on the ground beside him and his medical kit ten paces hence. He gestured toward the approaching jeep, which was traversing the uneasy gravel of the platoon about a hundred yards to the north.

Milazzo called out, "Hey, boys, the Saint is back from his little R&R up in the rear. That sonofabitch really couldn't bear being away from us for so long!"

Mike Reagan emerged from his foxhole with remnants of shaving cream on his face. "Goddammit! I told Saint not to be a fucking hero by coming back early. He had another day or two in paradise, yet he comes back to this burnt-out, godforsaken hill. What the hell is wrong with him?"

Daniel King interjected, "It's all groovy, Red. We fellas could use a little of Vinnie's personality around here, especially lately." King was alluding to the long, hot days of digging foxholes and shoring up the camp's bunkers with the unforgivingly heavy sandbags.

"Yeah, his ass better not faint again when it's his turn to fill them cocksucking sandbags!" The tenor of the comment made the declarant obvious without the need to see his face. The irrepressible John "Doc" Nunn had emerged from a huge cloud of cigarette smoke. It was akin to a magician whose appearance onstage is harkened by a mysterious shroud of liquid nitrogen.

Vinnie pulled slowly into the camp, carefully navigating around his fellow Marines, many of whom climbed out of their foxholes in joyous anticipation of what their pal was about to deliver. The boys shouted Vinnie's name as he drove through the camp.

"Hey, Vinnie!"

"Look who's back! SAINT!"

"Hey, mailman, you got my girlie magazines?"

"Hey, Vin, ya bring some clean drawers for us poor, dirty suckers?"

"Vincent is back. Ya got smokes and booze in that tin box?"

The jeep lurched suddenly, causing Vinnie and Ned LeRoy to once again bounce around in the forlorn jeep.

"Damn, Vinnie," observed Tex, "it looks like your jeep could've used a little R&R, too!" The comment drew a laugh from the cluster of Marines that had gathered around the dusty jeep.

"Yous sonsabitches missed me a lot, huh?" Vinnie laughed as he shouted that observation and the boys chimed in with a cacophony of responses, most of which concurred with Vinnie's assessment and all of which contained various degrees of vulgarities.

Vinnie hopped out of the jeep and patted Tex on the back. "Good to see you, Tex. I guess you're pretty intent on sticking around these parts!"

Tex was humbled by Saint's words. He looked down and kicked the dirt with his feet before remarking, "Golly, thanks, Saint. It's good to see you, too. Are you better?"

"Better than ever, pal. I'm ready to kick ass and take names. Watch out, gooks: The Saint is BACK!" The boys chuckled. "Okay, enough of the pleasantries. Who wants their mail?"

With that, Vinnie walked to the rear of the jeep as LeRoy exited the vehicle and walked toward the makeshift command center.

As he began to walk away, he turned and asked, "You gonna fix that jeep before it kills somebody, Saint?"

"Yes, sir, I'll get on that right after I give out the mail and supplies."

Mike Reagan, Doc Nunn, Doc Milazzo, and Daniel King descended upon Saint as he began to unload the contents from the rear of the jeep.

"You got a lot of ammo today, huh, Vin?" Mike gestured toward the crates as he asked.

Vinnie nodded. "Yeah, but I got a lot of letters, too, and those'll be better received than more grenades and mortar rounds!" Mike glanced at the crates in the rear of the jeep then looked back at Vinnie and then back at the bag that was filled with letters for the Marines. Mike sighed at the sight and then shot a stern gaze at his friend.

"Why didn't you listen to me, Saint? I told you not to try to be a fucking hero by returning early to this shithole. You said that you understood, yet here you are."

Vinnie had begun the process of organizing the letters in a way that would facilitate an easy distribution for the fellows who were not-so-patiently waiting for their little slice of normalcy in their very abnormal lifestyles.

"I know that I could've stayed back in the rear—it was fucking paradise, after all!—but I just felt like I *needed* to be here with you and the guys, Mike. We're brothers, and it was not fair for me to be back there while all of yous guys were humping on this hill. *Semper Fi*, right?"

Mike looked down and gently shook his head. He raised his head until his eyes met Vinnie's and then he exclaimed, "Oo-fucking-rah!"

Vinnie quickly patted Mike's shoulder, smiled, and said, "Lighten up, pal, and help me give out some of these letters, okay?"

Mike nodded and he and Saint then walked over to a table outside the main bunker in the camp. A throng of Marines swarmed the table, anxious to hear from moms, dads, girlfriends, grandparents, and buddies from back home. Of course, they also wanted to see what goodies Vinnie brought. Like Pavlov's dogs, the boys' collective anticipation rose as they watched Vinnie organize his cargo.

The boys had grown accustomed to the special treats that Vinnie somehow procured from the rear: Tootsie Rolls, Hershey bars, licorice sticks, and, of course, important life essentials such as beer, cigs, and miniature bottles of fancy liquors. Vinnie was the equivalent of Santa Claus to these young men, almost all of whom were just a few years away from the days of innocence when they'd anxiously awaited the real Santa. Amazing what a few short years had done to their sense of reality. Instead of looking forward to unwrapping toy trains, board games, and Lincoln Logs, these young men wanted to get their hands on cigarettes, girlie magazines, and beer, all while hoping to create a distraction from the daily, ultra-stressful grind of trying to kill the enemy while simultaneously trying like hell not to take a bullet between the eyes.

Perspective, indeed.

"Hey, Saint, I'm expecting a letter from my girl back home in Concord. Did you happen to come across it?" Vinnie peered up from the table to see the anxious face of young Gerry Morris. He'd touched down in 'Nam right before Christmas and he looked anxious for a distraction from the chaos.

"I just might've seen something for ya, green," replied Vinnie with his trademark smirk, "but you ain't been out here for but five minutes or so, so ya gotta get in the back of the line!"

The boys howled and, with a shallow *aw shucks*, the younger Marine sheepishly swallowed his pride and trudged to the end of the line.

Vinnie, engaged in about twenty conversations simultaneously, peered into the rather large pile of letters and, as guys continued to plead with him for anything from letters to cigarettes to Tootsie Rolls, he grabbed one letter that was festooned with hand-drawn pink hearts and smelled of overbearing perfume.

"'Scuse me a second, fellas," said Saint as he walked past the desperate, pleading mass of overheated, frustrated, testosterone-driven young men.

"Hey, green!"

No response.

"Hey, New Hampshire," Vinnie yelled again, this time catching Morris's attention. "Don't ever say that the Saint don't love ya! I just don't love ya as much as your artsy girl!"

With that, Vinnie flicked the letter at Morris and he caught it, appropriately enough, against his chest. Gerry broke out into a huge smile.

"Thank you so much, Saint!" He then retreated to a nearby tree to experience the long-awaited letter from the love of his young life. Vinnie watched the young man walk to the tree and smiled, thinking to himself, *The kid's feet ain't even touching the ground as he walks!*

Vinnie then chuckled to himself when he realized that he'd referred to Morris as a kid even though he himself was only ten months older than the greenie.

Vinnie then resumed his post at the head of the table and began to call out guys' names to distribute their mail. This process went on for a few minutes before it was interrupted by a loud, familiar voice.

"Saint, stop being a mailman for a few minutes and come fix this goddamn jeep of yours!"

It was LeRoy and the *no bullshit* tone of his voice convinced Vinnie, and the cluster of guys surrounding him, that he didn't expect to be kept waiting.

"Yes, sir!" came Vinnie's respectful response and, with that, he put the mailbag down, winked at the boys in line, and began to walk toward his cranky jeep.

A few paces into his return to the jeep, Vinnie stopped and turned to the guys who still were congregated around the mail table. "Don't worry, boys. Even the mailman can't take care of his own mail when the skipper starts a-howlin'!" Vinnie then held up a letter that he had written to his family and exclaimed, "I didn't even get a chance to throw this here letter into the batch heading back to the world. Gotta hold on to it for a bit longer . . . the Saint ain't gettin' no perks here!" Vinnie then emphatically thrust the letter into his flak jacket's inner pocket and resumed walking to his forlorn jeep.

*   *   *

The Vietcong soldiers in the trees used complex hand gestures to communicate to their comrades down below what they were viewing through their powerful binoculars, courtesy of China. The Americans were milling about the hill, completely oblivious to what was transpiring on the other side of the DMZ. The attack was about to be carried out.

*   *   *

A loud *CRACK!* reverberated through the thick air. A few of the Marines jumped and instinctively reached for their rifles before realizing that they weren't being attacked. Instead, it was that goddamn jeep backfiring as Vinnie put it through its paces as he tried to address its failing engine. The hood was propped open by a wayward, burned tree branch and Vinnie's thin frame was hunched over the front of the roaring, belching, hot engine.

"This engine is running loud and hot," Vinnie screamed as the ear-splitting volume of the engine made it hard for Vinnie to hear himself.

LeRoy approached Saint and screamed out, "What?"

Vinnie didn't see LeRoy approach him, as his head was still concealed under the hood, and he didn't hear LeRoy. "*SAINT! SAINT! SAINT?*" LeRoy was screaming at the top of his lungs from about five feet away.

Vinnie didn't even flinch.

Goddamn, it's hot as all hell, Vinnie thought to himself as he meticulously manipulated the innards of his jeep. Copious amounts of sweat streamed liberally about his head, face, and neck. *Shit, I hope I don't sweat through that letter that I wrote to Lil, Ma, Pa, and Joseph*, Vinnie thought to himself as he wiped a flood of sweat from his brow for what seemed like the fiftieth time in the three minutes that he was working on the jeep. Vinnie's thoughts were interrupted by a hard jab to his left flank. He peered up through the sweat that stung his blue eyes to see LeRoy standing no more than two feet from him. LeRoy's mouth was moving but all Vinnie heard was the not-so-subtle purr of his jeep.

Vinnie straightened up in front of the jeep ad turned his attention to LeRoy. "Sorry, sir. What were you saying? I couldn't hear you over the engine."

"I was saying that you're lucky it's daytime or your ass would be in bad shape. Hurry up and fix that goddamn jeep so that you can finish being Santa Claus to these guys!"

"Yes, sir!" came Vinnie's obedient response. "If anyone's looking for me, I'll be looking at the carburetor under the chassis, okay?"

"Sure, Saint, sure. Just hurry the hell up, already." Vinnie then slid himself under the jeep to continue treating it with surgical precision.

LeRoy marveled at the work Vinnie was doing. *Anyone else would've junked that piece of shit a long time ago,* LeRoy thought to himself, *and this sonofabitch is gonna turn it into a Rolls Royce before he's done with it!*

"Hey, Captain! C'mere for a minute, I gotta show you something hilarious." Doc Nunn never disappointed when it came to hilarity, so LeRoy left Vinnie under the jeep and walked over to Doc's position near the perimeter of the camp. The closest Marine to Vinnie was Morris. He was about ten yards away, fully enraptured by the fragrant letter from his girl back home.

The guys were milling around. Some were throwing a football, others were smoking cigarettes, and the rest were either catching some fleeting rest or bullshitting. Red was farthest from the perimeter from the camp, walking toward the lake with the intention of wetting his hands to wipe his perspiring brow. He was sweating in the late-morning sun while dividing up the mail and goodies that Vinnie'd left behind minutes earlier. He'd sauntered away from the bounty there to cool off in the nearby lake.

It was another day in paradise.

And then the Marines heard one of the most dreaded sounds in 'Nam, but one that the guys heard in their nightmares.

"TUBING! TUBING! TUBING! FUCKING TUBING! INCOMING! INCOMING! INCOMING! COVER! TAKE COVER! TAKE FUCKING COVER!"

Tubing was a call that every Marine dreaded. It meant that the enemy was attacking and that mortars soon would be crashing down. Tubing meant that a mortar round was rapidly exiting its tube with violent velocity and deadly intention. The Marines knew that if they could hear the tubing they would soon feel its wrath. The Marines began to scatter with a purpose. They knew that milliseconds meant the difference between life and either instantaneous—or painfully drawn-out—death. Men grabbed their rifles and leapt into their foxholes.

Paradoxically, the Marines clutched their rifles at the same time that they clutched religious items such as crucifixes, rosaries, or Stars of David. The Marines in the foxholes squatted as low to the ground as possible and counted off the seconds in their heads, knowing roughly how long before the mortars of death would touch down. They pulled their helmets low over their heads, as if such an act would protect them against an unfortunate direct hit with a mortar inside of the deeply entrenched foxhole.

"Oh, fuck . . . Vinnie!"

LeRoy uttered those words after he nestled into his foxhole. The last time he saw Saint, he was lying underneath his loud jeep, trying to get it to live beyond its allotted nine lives. LeRoy's mind traveled instantly to that moment, a few months earlier, when he'd tested Saint to see if he could hear screams of warning. Vinnie'd never heard the screaming LeRoy and the pit that settled into LeRoy's gut that day had never completely dissipated.

LeRoy knew the mortars were seconds away and that he was too far to run to the jeep and get Vinnie to the relative safety of a foxhole. Nonetheless, the captain poked his head up from the foxhole like a groundhog furtively scanning his surroundings for predators before exiting with trepidation.

Through the dust and scrambling Marines, LeRoy's soul filled with the dread of a thousand deaths: Vinnie was still underneath the jeep, working on it, completely oblivious to the hellfire that was about to descend upon the camp.

"SAINT! VINNIE! SAINT! GET THE FUCK OUT OF THERE AND INTO A FOXHOLE! VINN-NNIE!"

LeRoy quickly realized the futility of his efforts, for he barely heard himself over the roar of the engine and the increasingly louder, sickening sound of incoming artillery whistling through the humid air.

Mike Reagan knew, too.

When he'd heard the tubing, he'd been on the opposite side of the camp, equidistant from Vinnie as was LeRoy, a few yards away from the candies, liquors, and letters that Vinnie had perched on the table for their buddies. He'd instinctively jumped into a nearby foxhole and poised himself for a fleeting moment before he suddenly thought to himself:

VINNIE!

Red was sharing a foxhole with two other men, including Tex. He angrily spat out, "Fuck, fuck, fuck!" and then lifted himself from his defensive posture, startling Tex.

"The fuck you doing, Red?" asked Tex.

"Vinnie's still out there!"

Tex's heart sank. He, too, suddenly realized that Vinnie was last seen under the deafening jeep that he seemed to love so. "Mike, wait . . ." Tex couldn't finish his sentence because Red already was scaling the foxhole in an effort to run to his friend.

"Saint! Vinnie!"

Mike's voice was raspy and halting; a combination of dirt from the foxhole and dust in the air had invaded his trachea made speaking quite laborious. Of course, the palpable fear was causing Mike to find *thinking* to be a difficult chore. The sky was growing dark and Mike's upper torso was completely above the plane of the foxhole. He cleared his throat and coughed up a wad of filthy sputum before screaming as he had never screamed before.

"SAINT! FUCKING INCOMING! VINNIE! TAKE COVER! SAINT! GET OVER HERE, QUICK! VINNIE! FUCKING VINNIE! GET OVER HERE, YOU SONOFABITCH!"

Mike didn't know it but he was crying uncontrollably. He began to climb out of the foxhole but Tex grabbed him by the waist, refusing to permit his friend and brother Marine to walk right into the afterlife.

Mike grabbed a nearby large stone and he flung it as hard as he could, toward Vinnie's jeep. Mike watched the stone hurtle through the air, as if in slow motion. He had trouble following the arc of the stone, and he hoped that it would be as fortuitous as the grenade that he'd flung in the battle to overtake the hill a few months earlier. As Red watched the stone approach the jeep, he looked to the northern horizon and he saw the rapidly approaching rockets and mortars.

"VINNIE! VINNIE! VINNIE! FUCK!"

Mike desperately tried to get his beloved friend's attention. However, the air was becoming thick and the ground was shaking. Tex pulled Mike down into the foxhole, but not before Mike saw what he believed to be movement: Vinnie's legs, which were exposed beyond the undercarriage of the jeep, appeared to be moving out from underneath the doomed vehicle.

Back within the foxhole, Mike crouched down, trying to make himself one with the Earth as he braced for impact. He had not stopped crying. Tex was weeping, too. However, unlike many times in the past when the Marines had cried in terror, unsure if they were experiencing their last moments of life, these two Marines cried for their beloved friend and brother.

They were crying for the Saint.

*   *   *

CLANG!

Vinnie heard a loud banging sound, followed by a painful stabbing sensation to his right thigh. *Fucking Doc Nunn,* Vinnie thought, *only that clown would think that throwing a rock at me is funny!* Vinnie's eyes still stung with sweat. The pain to his leg heightened his senses and he realized that the roar of the engine was unusually loud.

The engine is revving louder than it should, Vinnie thought to himself. *I better check the engine to see if something is going wrong.*

With that, Vinnie propelled himself forward from under the jeep by grabbing the underside of the driver's door and pulling himself out from under it. Vinnie envisioned the boys standing around the camp as he emerged from under the jeep, enjoying the morning heat and the relative solitude of inactivity. He also fully expected to see a playful expression on Nunn's mug after deliberately pelting Vinnie's leg with a heavy stone.

Vinnie emerged from under the jeep and instantly noticed that it was darker than it had been when he had gone under it seconds earlier. Vinnie saw a stone at the side of his jeep and then looked around. The ground was shaking and nobody was around. Aghast, Vinnie immediately realized that the jeep's loud engine prevented him from hearing death as it hurtled unforgivingly through the sky, directly toward him.

Saint looked up and the reflection of streaking mortars and rockets corrupted his icy blue irises. Unadulterated dread overcame Vinnie in the next three nanoseconds as melancholic thoughts dominated his psyche.

How the fuck didn't I hear this shit coming toward me?

Where the hell did everyone go?

Was the rock someone's attempt to get my attention?

How the hell can I escape this?

Where's the nearest foxhole?

Where's my rifle?

In the subsequent nanosecond, resignation took over.

I am gonna fucking die.

I can't believe that I am gonna die in this fucking shithole, so far from home.

I can't believe the gooks attacked us during the day!

In the final nanosecond, terror and abject regret.

I have to be Lilly's best man!

Mama is gonna be devastated!

I gotta wish on Lilly's star tonight!

Me and Rosalie are supposed to finish paying off our engagement ring when I get back home!

Tears clouded Vinnie's vision of the coming firestorm of death. His jaw slackened and his eyes widened as the reflection of the rapidly approaching artillery grew more prominently in his gentle, placid, blue irises.

Approximately one-tenth of a second had passed since he'd seen death coming with a fury.

Vinnie thought of Rosalie and then heaved. He took a sudden, dust-choking breath and then screamed out, "I'M SORRY, ROE! I LOVE YOU, MA, POP, AND JOSEPH. LILLY, I AM SO SORRY THAT I DIDN'T GET TO WISH ON YOUR STAR TONIGHT! I LOVE YOU, SIS!"

No one heard Saint's heart-wrenching, desolate cries. He didn't even hear the words and, as he grabbed the underside of the jeep and began to furiously pull himself under it, he wasn't sure if he actually uttered those words or if they were simply his tragic thoughts. Vinnie rued the fact that he had no time to try to get to the relative safety of a foxhole.

He knew that his only shot was to get under his jeep and pray.

The Saint scrambled to pull himself under the jeep as he simultaneously clutched for the lucky golden crucifix necklace that had adorned his neck for most of his tour here. He became flummoxed when he realized that the cross wasn't there. His thoughts immediately went to the letter in his flak jacket pocket. He heard and felt death coming and his final coherent thought was how sad he was that his letter wouldn't make it to his family if he were to die in this ambush.

His head now was underneath the jeep.

He desperately pulled with his arms while simultaneously kicking furiously with his feet to get the hell under the jeep. The sound of the mortars screaming through the air actually drowned out the loud roar of the engine that was inches from Vinnie's angst-ridden, tear-strewn face. Just then, the Saint's weathered boots, kicking as strenuously as a duck's webbed feet in a pond, slipped in the dusty terrain as his sternum made it under the jeep.

The Saint's trusty jeep then began to rock and wretch violently.

Suddenly, the pounding in his chest was replaced with the stomping of happy feet. The pit of dread and abject terror was supplanted by unbridled joy and tranquility. The acute sense of profound loss was replaced by an eternal togetherness. The innumerable missiles of relentless pain and doom were replaced by shiny, blinking colors of warmth and festivity.

For Vinnie was no longer in Vietnam. He was back home in Jamaica, Queens.

The teenaged, angst-driven, family-first-and-always, man-child now was but a young boy, maybe four or five years old, running aimlessly around a beautifully lit Christmas tree inside of his house, watching his young, strong dad construct a festive landscape of miniature people, all smiling and wearing overcoats, mittens, hats, and earmuffs. This happy collection of his father's miniatures knew not of pain, loss, death, or destruction. They only knew of eternal smiles and cuddly warmth and that made young Vinnie happy at that moment. He looked at the wrapped gifts under the tree and

276

there, to his right, was his older sister, Lilly, equally bouncy with delight and anticipation of seeing what joy Santa had brought them.

Just then, Vinnie's senses were overwhelmed with a familiar aroma. He turned his head to track the scent and he saw his beloved mother, Rose, smiling in the kitchen, as she labored over the stove. Vinnie looked out of the kitchen window and spring now was in full bloom. He could see the cherry blossoms on his favorite tree in the back and the pears beginning to grow on the tree on the other side of the yard.

"Mama, can I taste the cookie dough before you place the chocolate chip cookies in the oven, please?"

"Wow, what a well-mannered boy you are. You sure it ain't because you want to eat all the cookie dough?"

"Aw, shucks, Ma. I'm almost ten years old and I ain't a little kid no more. I just love your cookies; they're the best in Jamaica!"

Rose laughed and capitulated to her son's wishes. She snagged a piece of the cookie dough and reached toward Vinnie with the delectable morsel in hand.

Vinnie reached out . . . and grabbed a can of Coke from his best pal, John Chang.

The thirteen-year-old Vinnie and his pal were in the basement, watching Vinnie's dad create another work of art on his carpentry table.

"Golly, Mr. Santaniello," marveled John, "how do you make such incredible things from wood and nails?"

Carmine laughed and mussed John's hair with his large, sinewy hand. Carmine's hands were those of a carpenter, strong and somewhat misshapen. The nail beds were pockmarked with scars from wayward nails and hammers over the years.

Carmine had a vice grip and he playfully clawed John's head as he looked him in the eye and said, "Son, I've been making houses since I got out of the service back in the '40s. I see the creations in my mind and then I have to use my hands to make those visions a reality."

Vinnie glowed with pride in the aftermath of his dad's revelation. Vinnie revered his dad and strived constantly to make him proud. "Hey, Pop, that's exactly how I feel when I get under the hoods of cars. I know exactly what needs to be done to get 'em up and running again!"

Carmine smiled with great pride at his young boy, for he was a prodigy with cars. The teen had a knack for servicing friends' cars despite his youth. "You're a carpenter like your old man, Vin, but you use cars instead of wood to work your magic!"

Carmine then placed his paw of a hand around Vinnie's shoulder and gave him a hug while jostling him playfully to and fro with his inordinate strength. Vinnie returned the hug and smiled, feeling exceedingly content that he had pleased his father and hero.

"Vinnie? *Viiiiinnnnnnnieeeee!*"

Vinnie, his father, and John all smiled, while Vinnie cringed, playfully mocking the shrill voice of the girl calling him. It was Lilly.

Vinnie turned around to address Lilly. The fifteen-year-old Vinnie had just gotten home earlier than usual from Thomas Edison High School because he was taking midterms and his seventeen-year-old sister likewise had gotten home earlier than usual from Jamaica High. Lilly wanted to know if Vinnie wanted to go to the movies with her and her best friend, Marie.

"Are there gonna be any chicks for me at the theater?" Vinnie smiled after he asked the question but the look in his blue eyes made it clear that he was not kidding.

Vinnie looked in the mirror to confirm that his hair was perfectly greased down. This was 1963, after all, and the look from the '50s had not yet faded.

"Okay, ugly, I think I'm ready to go to the movies with yous gals, but you better hold the chicks back, because these baby blues are gonna work their magic!"

The weather wasn't too cold for this late in November, so Vinnie thought about wearing a nice sweater with a pair of jeans.

"Give me a few minutes to get ready, Lil. What time's the movie start?"

"Two-thirty, so we gotta be ready to leave because it's almost 1:30 now. Do you have any mon—"

"Oh, my God! OH, MY GOOOOOOD!" Blood-curdling screams filled Vinnie's ears. He ran past Lilly into the living room to find his mother, Rose, rocking back and forth on the couch in front of the diminutive black-and-white television that was perched neatly on a table a few feet away from her. Her face was streaked with tears. She repeatedly mumbled in between sobs: "Oh, dear God!"

Confused, Vinnie peered at the TV and didn't immediately comprehend the chaos on the grainy screen.

Lilly ran into the living room. "Mama, what's wrong? What happened? Are you okay?"

Rose absently pointed at the screen with her right hand before pulling it back and cupping it over her mouth. Her muffled, grief-stricken voice was barely audible, but the pronouncement left Vinnie numb: "President Kennedy was killed! Someone shot him during the parade in Dallas! The President is dead! Oh, my God. The president is dead!"

Vinnie and Lilly were numb. They knew that President Lincoln had been shot dead about a hundred years earlier, but they thought that such actions remained behind, in the nineteenth century. The human race had come a long way from such senseless violence, hadn't it? The blood drained from Vinnie's face. His knees felt weak and he was nauseous, but he knew that he had to take action to assist his grief-riddled mother.

"Lil, we gotta help Ma. Lilly? Lil?" Vinnie turned to Lilly to see why she didn't respond. He observed his sister, transfixed before the terrifying images on the television.

"Are you deaf, Lil?"

"No, I'm not deaf, you big dummy!" Lilly sneered at her seventeen-year-old brother and sarcastically continued, "I'm only nineteen, ya know. Maybe I can't hear you over that damn engine that you're fixing!" This mid-April Saturday morning still had the crispness of the stubbornly lingering winter but it was comfortable enough for Vinnie to agree to check out his buddy George's 1961 Chevy Impala. George told Vinnie that the car was backfiring and lurching when he shifted it into gear and he couldn't figure out why.

Of course, Vinnie agreed to help his old friend out, but not without a little friendly ribbing: "Georgie, you know I'd never say no to a friend, but we both know that the real reason that you're coming to me is because you're too goddamn cheap to go to a mechanic, right?"

George Boss feigned betrayal and, with a mock pout, responded, "I'm offended, you greaseball sonofabitch. Don't you know that your *eye-talian* ass is the best mechanic in Jamaica, despite the fact that you ain't even graduated yet from high school?"

The long-time chums laughed and Vinnie told George to bring the car to his house after school.

Vinnie had just removed his head and upper torso from under the hood of George's vehicle and he'd proceeded to ask his nearby sister for a glass of water three times, without a response. Vinnie became agitated. Lilly saw Vinnie's perturbed look and asked defensively, "How did you expect me to hear you over that roaring engine, baby brother? Whatcha need?"

"A glass of water would be nice," Vinnie responded, "and maybe one of Mama's oatmeal raisin cookies!"

"You know, Vinnie," Lilly remarked, "there's more food on this planet besides Mama's cookies!"

"That may be the case, ugly, but there ain't nothing quite as delicious as 'em!"

Lilly laughed and then remarked, "You're lucky that the commies don't decide to nuke us while you're fixing Georgie's car, Vin. You'd never hear the bombs coming."

"That's okay I got you to protect me, Lil," Vinnie remarked. "You'd never let the commies get me, right?"

"Yeah, you're right, ya horse's ass. Mama's gonna be a nervous wreck until the day you come back from Vietnam."

Lilly was celebrating her twentieth birthday, five days after Vinnie's eighteenth birthday.

Sunday, September 25, 1966. It was a seasonably warm day in New York, with the temperatures hovering in the low sixties. For years, Rose and Carmine had held very modest joint birthday celebrations for the close siblings—Lilly was born on September 25, 1946 and Vinnie was born practically two years later, on September 20, 1948. Five days earlier, on his eighteenth birthday, Vinnie had enlisted with the USMC and that meant that he'd be heading to Vietnam soon.

Rose didn't want her son to enlist. She'd have preferred that he try his luck with the draft. But she knew that this had been her son's wish for quite some time and she believed that it wasn't her place to tell her eighteen-year-old son what to do. He was a man now, despite the fact that he'd always be her sweet little boy. Rose promised herself and Carmine that she wouldn't make Vinnie feel guilty about joining the service. After all, the majority of their blue-collar neighborhood believed that all red-blooded American boys should serve their country with dignity, grace, and valor. And that they should serve without fear or remorse, at least according to Carmine, a WWII veteran of the U.S. Navy who had been stationed in the Philippines for much of his tour.

"Rose, don't question Vinnie's decision and don't make him doubt that he made the right decision," extolled Carmine the day after Vinnie had formally enlisted with the USMC. "It ain't easy to serve your country in a foreign land, so the last thing a man in the service needs is the guilt of knowing that his mama did not support his decision to enlist. Vinnie needs your complete support, understand?"

"Yes, Carmine," Rose responded, "I understand."

But I ain't got to like it. I hope to God my little Vinnie comes back home to me, Rose thought to herself before turning her back on her husband and proceeding to the bathroom, where she began to weep silently, yet forcefully.

Carmine heard the abrupt heaving coming from the bathroom and knew that Rose was distraught. He also knew that no words would bring her solace. *Vinnie's gonna be alright over there,* the hardened veteran and grizzled carpenter thought to himself. *He'll make it home and Rose will realize that she was nervous over nothing.*

If Carmine was honest with himself at that juncture, he would have admitted that this thought was made with more aspiration than conviction. With that, Carmine gently rapped on the bathroom door before speaking into the aged wooden surface, "Vinnie ain't gonna get hurt over there, Rose. He's gonna be comin' home."

The handsome forty-six-year-old gentleman rested his forehead against the door to await Rose's response. It was not forthcoming. Carmine craned his neck and looked upward in a desperate gaze toward the heavens before he walked out of the door of the first-floor residence of the modest two-story home, through the hallway, and out the front door to the porch, where he lit a cigarette and took a long, angst-ridden drag on it.

He held the smoke inside of his lungs for an extended time before he exhaled a voluminous cloud of smoke to the heavens in a forceful fashion. Carmine, who had a well-earned reputation for having rock-steady hands when constructing homes with his brother, was taken aback when he noticed that his hands were shaking when he lit up. "Goddammit," he muttered to no one in particular.

"Hey, Vin, is it true? Didja really sign up with the Marines?" Little Joseph, then eleven years old, nervously approached his older brother with both heightened anticipation and building dread.

Joseph had heard about all of the craziness in Vietnam on the radio and he saw updates on the evening news that scared him. "Are ya really gonna leave us for that crazy place, Vin? Can't you just stay here and not go to war?"

Vinnie saw the fear in his little brother's eyes and exercised his paternal instincts to assuage the young boy's fears.

"Don't worry, bookworm, your big brother is gonna be the grooviest Marine in Vietnam! I ain't gonna let nothin' happen to me, I promise. You better write to me when I'm away," Vinnie remarked. Then, in a nod to his younger brother's prodigious artistic talent, he demanded in a lighthearted fashion, "you better send me lotsa your swell drawings, too, y'hear?"

Joseph proudly replied, "I promise, Vin!"

Rose's homemade birthday cake was a delicious combination chocolate-and-vanilla pound cake, with extra blue-tinted icing, just like the kids liked it. Rose yelled from the kitchen, "Lilly, call down Grandma."

Lilly walked out of the first-floor living space, past Rosalie Vitale, Vinnie's girlfriend, and toward the hallway to call her grandmother.

Rosalie was an attractive young lady with shoulder-length, dark-brown hair. Roe, as Vinnie called her, had a very light complexion that accentuated her dark-brown eyes. Rosalie was a petite young woman, maybe a hair over five feet tall, with high cheekbones that sloped down into a narrow, dimpled chin. Like most young ladies of the era, Rosalie had very thin eyebrows that accentuated her eyes.

Rosalie and Lilly were friends, and they wore similar makeup styles. So, like her friend, Rosalie applied a modest amount of bright eyeshadow, usually pink or some hue of bluish purple, that made her eyes stand out in even starker contrast to her light skin tone.

"Hey, Lil," Rosalie asked in her raspy Queens accent, "where ya going?"

Lilly replied, "I hafta get Nunu to come down and celebrate Vinnie's and my birthday."

Lilly then proceeded into the common hallway that extended upward into a staircase that connected the second floor to the first, where the Santaniellos lived. Lilly went to the base of the steps and peered up into the hallway located directly overhead. "Nunu? *Nuuuuu-nuuuuuu?*"

The elderly, silver-haired Sicilian native, a slightly hunched-over, relatively plump woman who stood a few inches short of five feet tall, emerged from her room at the end of the hallway on the second floor. Nunu's skin was olive-tinted, although not nearly as dark as Lilly's complexion. Nunu had a round face lined with wrinkles. Further, her eyes sunk into her ample cheeks and this obscured their hazel color. Nunu had permanent bags under her eyes that reflected the baggage of her decades of experience as a woman who'd come of age in Sicily in the early twentieth century. Indeed, her eyes spoke of the hardships that were intertwined with the pathway of her life. Nunu's cheeks hung from her cheekbones like small pouches, which gave a full, slightly bulging effect to her jowls. She also had a slight goiter that hung below her chin.

Nunu shuffled out of her room and into the narrow hallway that was framed by a wall to the left and a freestanding banister to the right. The four-foot-high, wood-spindled banister overlooked the staircase. One could peer over the banister and see the hallway directly below, which led to the entrance to the downstairs living space. Nunu traipsed to the middle of the bannister and rested her hands upon the railing. She then looked over until she saw Lilly standing in the hallway, approximately fifteen feet directly below her. Nunu's thick bifocals rested on her ample nose as she focused on Lilly.

Using a hybrid of Italian and broken English, Nunu questioned why Lilly was beckoning her.

Lilly did not understand everything that Nunu said, but she assumed that she was inquiring as to why she was being summoned, so she responded, "Birthday-cake time, Nunu. Come down and sing with us!"

The family matriarch, then in her mid-seventies, slowly navigated the steps down as Lilly retreated back to the first-floor living room.

A few moments later, as per family tradition, Rose began to sing "Happy Birthday" to her two oldest kids, with Rosalie, Carmine, and Joseph joining in after Rose sang the first few bars terribly off-key. Nunu sang mostly in Italian. Vinnie and Lilly playfully chided each other, in between singing, over the fact that their parents cheaply combined their birthdays. Rose carefully walked the cake into the living room from the oven in the adjoining kitchen. She placed it on the small, round, cast-iron table that served as a dining room table.

Vinnie and Lilly made birthday wishes after the Santaniellos and Rosalie finished warbling "Happy Birthday." The two siblings and best friends then proceeded to blow out the candles that Rose had liberally strewn about the top layer of the cake's frosting. Rose carefully sliced equally sized pieces for everyone while saving two extra-large slices for Lilly and Vinnie.

"Rose," Carmine noted with a big smile on his face, "you've outdone yourself with this cake! It's better than anything we coulda bought at the bakery on Hillside Avenue!"

"I agree, Mrs. Santaniello," Rosalie added, "the cake is delicious!"

Vinnie swiped at the frosting on his cake with his right index and middle fingers and gestured as if he was going to lick them only to swipe at Lilly's face, leaving a large swath of frosting on her nose. He roared with laughter and commented that the blue frosting matched his eye color, as well as the color of Lilly's and Rosalie's ample eye shadow.

Rose was less impressed. "Oh, Vinnie, what would you go and waste perfectly good frosting by wiping it on your sister's pretty face?"

"Pretty? Mama, are we talking about the same chick? I did the ugly duckling here a favor!" Vinnie laughed at his own humorous comment and Carmine chuckled under his breath.

Rose scrunched her face and pursed her lips before exclaiming, "Keep it up and you ain't getting your birthday gift, young man!"

"Oh, c'mon, Mama. You know I was just goofin' around. Dontcha hold back my birthday gift!" Vinnie pretended to whine like a little kid while Rosalie and the family laughed at his pleas.

Rose played along, too, by telling her oldest son, "You want your birthday gift, big boy? Well, then first tell me the magic words to get it."

Vinnie chuckled at his mom's humor as he harkened back to his youth, when his mom would withhold his guilty pleasures—toys, gifts, and, of course, her amazingly delicious cookies—until he said the *magic words*: "pretty please." Vinnie deliberately and playfully remained silent and scrunched his face up while feigning a temper tantrum. "No gifts until you say the magic words, young man," Rose exclaimed.

Vinnie stayed mum as the everyone's muffled laughter persisted in the background.

Lilly asked, "Don't ya know the words, Vinnie?"

Vinnie peered at Rosalie, who was getting a kick out of Lilly's and Rose's keen senses of humor.

His girlfriend then joined the fray. "What are the words, you big brave Marine?" Lilly chuckled as Roe inquired, "Don't you know the words, Marine?"

Vinnie looked momentarily at Rosalie, smiled, and thought, *She's a good woman. I'm glad we put money down on that engagement ring. It'll be good to marry Roe after I get outta the service. She's gonna be a good mom and aunt.* He then turned his attention to his mother, to finally answer her query. He fixed his gaze on his mom's loving face to answer her question.

Saint squinted to see the face of his inquisitor. The sweat of his brow stung his eyes as the unforgivingly hot sun bore down on him. Vinnie's vision adjusted to the bright sunlight and the question boomed once again in his head.

"What the fuck are the words, you maggots? What are the words that no United States Marine wants to hear, EVER?"

Franklin A. Black, the Camp Lejeune boot camp drill sergeant who barked out the question, was pacing furiously amongst the USMC recruits at the sprawling training base in Jacksonville, North Carolina. The forty-five-year-old leatherneck was a veteran of the Korean War and had served multiple tours in Vietnam during the early 1960s. The NCO stood six-foot-three and had a chiseled physique, with his barrel chest protruding through his uniform. The white man, who hailed from Chattanooga, Tennessee, spoke with a pronounced drawl and an intimidating snarl. His uniform, decorated with myriad medals, was impeccably pressed and his boots shined like black crystals on his feet.

The drill sergeant's face was lined with the stress that came courtesy of having served in two intense wars, and with multiple tours during each conflict, to boot. Black's forehead matched his neck: It was red, leathery, and deeply creased. The crow's feet around his eyes were more like hawk's talons. They were heavily pronounced and exceptionally intimidating, giving his steely gray eyes a sinister, squinting appearance. Black's face was of the prototypical Jarhead: His face was impeccably shaven and his jaw jutted out, proud as a peacock. The drill sergeant's nose was jagged, obviously had been broken in the past—likely on multiple occasions—but that was the only thing that was seemingly out of place on the physique of this man's man.

Black walked with an angry purpose. When he spoke, the USMC recruits jumped to attention. He was one part revered and three parts feared. The recruits joked privately that the *A.* in *Franklin A. Black* stood for *Asshole*. Black tore the recruits down. He belittled them, he questioned their manhood, and he talked afoul of their mamas, all with the intention of building them back up into ruthless, courageous Marines.

The men believed that the contemptuous Black harbored significant enmity toward them and many of the recruits reciprocated the feeling, albeit surreptitiously. In fact, a good number of the recruits quit within the first two weeks of the execrable boot camp.

Black opened the third week of boot camp with the following proclamation: "You see how those motherfuckers left, men? Well, you should be damn pleased that them pansies left here because you wouldn't want such useless assholes at your side when you're deep in the shit and mortars are exploding all around you. You want MEN at your sides, grunts! REAL MEN who will be loyal to you. Men who are willing to die for you!"

Black hesitated and then pointed to a young recruit. "What's your name, boy?"

"PFC Jones, *SIR!*"

"Well, Jones, you maggot. Are you gonna hesitate to lay down your life for that grunt to your left?"

"Sir, no, *SIR!*"

Black looked pleased. "That's right, Jones," Black exclaimed. "Semper Fi, boys. *SEMPER FI!*"

The unforgiving July 1967 sun was beating down on the quivering Marines, many of whom were amazed that not a bead of sweat appeared on the brow of the berating leader as he bore down on the men, all of whom were perspiring quicker than their bodies could generate sweat.

Black, marching purposefully through the lined-up Marines, repeated his query. "What are the words that you maggots never want to hear, EVER?"

All but one of the USMC recruits were hesitant to answer the maniacal drill sergeant. Unfazed, a skinny kid from Jamaica, Queens raised his head and bellowed, "*Corpsman up, SIR!*" Vinnie was surprised at how timid his voice sounded. He then repeated the phrase again, in an effort to connote strength and confidence. *"Corpsman UP, sir!"*

The drill sergeant barked, "Who said that?"

Vinnie straightened his back, glanced down quickly to ensure that his feet were aligned, and then tugged gently at his cap to assure himself that it was in a perfectly aligned position on his head. He then yelled out, "PFC Santaniello, SIR!"

"San-tan-yella?"

"Sir, yes, SIR!" came Vinnie's quick response.

Black speed-walked to Vinnie's position, coming within centimeters of the recruit. Vinnie stood roughly five-foot-eight, so the much-taller drill sergeant bent forward, impeccably straight from his waist, until his eyelashes nearly brushed Vinnie's. "You know what that phrase means, right, maggot?"

Black's spittle splashed across Vinnie's face, but he didn't flinch. Vinnie said without hesitation, "It means a brother Marine needs medical assistance, SIR!"

Black bellowed in a bellicose fashion, "And what does a Marine do if a brother needs help?"

Vinnie looked directly into Black's steely gray eyes and barked in a controlled rage, "Anything and everything to save his brother, SIR!"

Black was pleased. *This one's good. He's a fucking leader,* Black thought to himself. *I gotta remember this maggot's name.* The drill sergeant walked back to the front of the lines of men and asked again, "What does no Marine want to hear?"

"Corpsman up, SIR!" yelled the recruits in unison.

"What?"

"Corpsman up, SIR!"

"What?"

"Corpsman up, SIR!"

"WHAT?"

"CORPSMAN UP! CORPSMAN UP! DOC NUNN . . . DOC MILAZZO . . . CORPSMAN UP! CORPSMAN UP!"

No one was responding to Mike Reagan's desperate, pain-stricken cries. He had emerged from his foxhole two seconds earlier and surveyed his platoon. The carnage before him caused his eyes to widen in an otherworldly fashion.

Seconds earlier, the impact had been gruesomely loud and violent. The unholy sound of crashing mortars and exploding rockets caused many an eardrum to burst. Cam Lo Hill heaved and struggled against the concussive forces of the unyielding maelstrom of enemy fire before it figuratively surrendered to the onslaught and was split open by the relentless ambush of thousands of pounds of firepower.

The foxholes bled rock, clay, dirt, insects, leeches, and larvae, all of which rained down on the prone Marines, lying at the bases of their protective cocoons. One foxhole that contained two Marines had an unfortunate direct hit from a mortar, which instantly killed the brother Marines.

Seconds earlier, Doc Nunn, realizing that Vinnie was oblivious to the ambush, had spat out his cigarette and began to utter the *Our Father* before he broke into a dead sprint into the ambush, toward Vinnie.

He took five strides before the concussive force of mortar meeting rock and clay lifted Nunn off his feet and hurtled him twenty-five feet into a billowing cloud of soot, shrapnel, and searing heat. Doc Nunn was unconscious before he hit the ground.

The men, many of whom were crying and all of whom were praying, remained in prone positions in their foxholes, fingers dutifully pressed against the triggers of their weapons of choice, waiting for the ground to stop shaking, and for their ears to stop ringing. They knew that they'd have to jump out of their foxholes to engage in a firefight with the unseen enemy. They realized that they likely were going to be outnumbered and that a slaughter was all but inevitable, as the surprise ambush completely blindsided the Marines and left them absolutely shell-shocked. Still, they were Marines, and they would go down fighting like the warriors that their training taught them to be.

The blasts, explosions, and concomitant tremors of the Earth finally ceased. Did the ambush last five minutes? Twenty minutes? More? It seemed to last for an eternity. In actuality, the deadly maelstrom had lasted approximately twenty-five seconds. The Marines quickly plowed themselves out of their compromised foxholes and rose from the ground like zombies from a foggy graveyard. The air was thick with soot and dust. The smell of fire, gunpowder, and, yes, death, permeated it. The men struggled to survey the landscape, searching for the blurry profiles of enemy gooks who were expected to be moving in to complete the job of the mortars and rockets.

Mike Reagan emerged from his foxhole with a significant gash across his forehead. Blood was streaming down his face but he was determined to simultaneously kill the enemy and account for his brothers. Red was muttering under his breath in a barely discernible whisper, "Vinnie. Vinnie. Vinnie. Vinnie. Vinnie."

He scanned the landscape and was shocked by what he did not see. There was not a gook to be found. They had ambushed with long-distance firepower but didn't follow that up with an ambush on foot.

"Fucking pussies," Mike uttered loudly to no one in particular. It was then that he envisioned a sight that would haunt him for decades to come. A sight that begat the expression that no Marine wanted to hear, but a phrase that had become as commonplace as the word *fuck* for the Marines here in the shit.

Red called for corpsmen because twenty feet in front of him were the mutilated remains of Peder Armstance. A disturbingly large segment of his head was missing. Gerry Morris's body was a short distance from Peder's. A few minutes earlier, Gerry had been smiling like a kid on Christmas morning after getting the perfumed letter from his sweetheart. Now, his lifeless body was grotesquely bent on the ground behind the same tree stump that he had been sitting on minutes earlier while reading sweet nothings from his babe.

Mike observed another dead Marine a mere ten feet from where he was standing: Francis Z. Platts, a nineteen-year-old from Pensacola, Florida who'd arrived in the company a few weeks earlier. This was Francis' first—and last, thought Mike ruefully— live combat. Red saw multiple holes in Platts's head and one where his left eye used to be. Mike was disgusted by his remorseless, matter-of-fact reaction to the fact that Platts's right eye remained open.

There remained only one unaccounted-for Marine: Saint.

Mike's eyes scanned the terrain nervously, with a gnawing in the pit of his stomach that grew more intense with each passing second. *Where the fuck is Saint?* Mike thought to himself.

His eyes came to rest on Vinnie's jeep. It was on its side, on the passenger side, and the tires were spinning furiously on their axles. The last time Mike had seen the jeep, it was on its tires, with Vinnie underneath it, his legs jutting out in a classic mechanic's pose.

Mike was now standing on the smoking terrain outside of his foxhole, struggling to see what was around the perimeter of the jeep located roughly twenty-five yards north of his foxhole. The jeep was smoking and flames were beginning to cascade in an eerily silent manner from the driver's side, which was facing the skies.

The company driver's side door is facing Jesus in Heaven, Mike thought ominously as he began a slow, unsteady walk to the flaming jeep.

As Mike got closer, he saw what he recognized to be a leg in front of the vehicle. The gnawing in the pit of Mike's stomach doubled down, causing him to gag as he forced down bile.

292

Red froze in his tracks.

"That has to be V . . ."

Mike couldn't bring himself to say the name, as if saying Saint's name would be more sinful than wishing the worst fucking death imaginable on the men who had planned this dastardly daytime ambush.

Suddenly, all of the noise cascading around Mike ceased. He no longer heard the radio man calling in coordinates of their location to the command center; he no longer heard men crying for help; he no longer had to block out the code words being screamed into the radio for airstrikes.

Mike heard nothing because he saw movement. The leg that Mike had observed moments earlier twitched, fell still, and then twitched again.

He's alive! Saint's alive!

"CORPSMAN UP! CORPSMAN UP! DOC NUNN . . . DOC MILAZZO . . . CORPSMAN UP! CORPSMAN UP!"

The calls for help initially dripped out of Doc Nunn's ears like thick pus from badly infected jungle rot. The calls then became a low drone, almost like a distant whisper. The fog in Doc Nunn's head was jungle thick but the words, nay, the desperate pleas that were harkened by a familiar voice became more pronounced and slowly took on special meaning.

It was as if a Marine was cutting through the thick elephant grass and fog of the jungle with a machete: Nunn's head cleared and he realized that Red was calling for him. Doc Nunn tried to lift himself up from his prone position. He was befuddled as to where he was and why he was lying face down in rubble. Nonetheless, Doc wobbled to his feet, but the searing pain in his head caused him to stumble to his hands and knees. However, Red's repeated cries for help caused him to cast aside the symptoms of his concussed brain and keenly focus on Mike's location.

Doc Nunn managed to stagger to his feet and listened intently. "CORPSMAN UP! CORPSMAN UP! DOC NUNN . . . DOC MILAZZO . . . CORPSMAN UP! CORPSMAN UP!"

Okay, thought Nunn, *Mike is calling from the north.*

With that, John Nunn summoned the strength to begin sprinting toward the sound of Mike's voice, despite blurred vision. Doc Nunn began to visualize the jeep and wondered why it was so orange before he realized that it was flipped on its side and ablaze. Doc picked up his pace, only to find himself hurtling through the air again and landing face-first in a pile of soot.

"What the . . . "

Doc Nunn got up on all fours, like a rabid dog, and peered angrily behind him to see what had caused him to unexpectedly trip and fall.

It was a torso. No head, no legs, no arms, just the bloody, grisly remains of a Marine's chest. Doc knew it was a Marine because he recognized the remnants of the uniform, congealed and attached to the blood-strewn chunk of mutilated flesh and broken bones that once was a human being. Doc had tripped over it while running toward Mike.

Fuck, Doc Nunn thought to himself before he made a mental note of the location of the torso—for no Marine, nor the remains of any Marine, is ever left behind. He then resumed sprinting toward Mike's voice.

Doc Milazzo was tending to a couple of badly lacerated Marines on the other side of the platoon when he heard Mike's cries. Milazzo had run to his wounded brothers in the midst of the ambush. Mortars and rockets exploded around him as he heroically ran, unfazed, to those in need. Stone, as Vinnie had nicknamed him, asked the Marines to whom he was rendering aid if they were stable enough for him to run to Mike to see what he needed.

One Marine's bleeding was stanched sufficiently for him to nod groggily that he was okay. The other Marine, whose left arm was badly broken, and who was missing part of his left foot, was high enough on morphine to not even comprehend Milazzo's query. Tony then hugged each brother, told them that he'd be right back, and began running to Mike's painstaking cries.

"CORPSMAN UP! CORPSMAN UP! DOC NUNN . . . DOC MILAZZO . . . CORPSMAN UP! CORPSMAN UP!"

Doc Nunn arrived first. His first impression of seeing Mike and Vinnie harkened to the image of the Virgin Mary holding her broken Son under the cross. Stone arrived seconds later and he audibly gasped.

Mike was on his knees, covered in blood, cradling the head and torso of the fallen Saint.

"No, no, no, no . . . noooooooooo!" Mike repeatedly pleaded in a low roar, with tears staining his filthy face as he rocked to and fro. Mike's arms were gently crossed around Vinnie's neck and upper torso. Vinnie was taking short, irregular gasps of air, and each breath echoed and sounded hollow, as if air was escaping from a tire. Saint's face was immaculate, as was his neck and upper chest. The rest of his body was awash in blood, as shrapnel and searing shards of metal had rendered the rest of him nearly indistinguishable. He was missing his right leg, beyond mid-thigh.

Vinnie peered up at Mike. "Red, I just . . . *mmmmphmfffmmmff.*"

"What Vinnie?"

Vinnie gasped, choked up blood, and began anew, "I just wa– *mmmmmpffff.*" More blood escaped from Saint's mouth.

"Fucking Docs, please! Do something! Save him, goddammit, please save him!" Nunn cast aside his palpable grief and did what came naturally. He furiously jabbed Vinnie with syringes of morphine while Milazzo used gauze and pieces of his own uniform in an effort to stanch the blood that was pouring effusively from the gaping wounds in Saint's abdomen and what remained of his right thigh.

The creases of worry and pain slowly dissipated from Vinnie's brow. He glanced toward the Docs.

"I . . . love . . . you . . . fucking guys."

Vinnie's left leg stopped quivering but Red's lower lip did not. Between tears and gasps of heart-wrenching sorrow, Red shouted with such visceral anger that both Milazzo and Nunn were stunned.

"Vinnie? Saint? You are NOT going to die here, brother. Do you understand me? Saint, you are NOT fucking dying on me. Do you fucking UNDERSTAND ME, brother?"

Vinnie looked up at the man, holding his broken body like a doting dad would hold his newborn son shortly after birth, and seemed to smile.

"Corpsmen up, Red," Vinnie whispered and then paused momentarily before uttering, "Corpsmen . . . up, Sergeant . . . Black."

Mike was hysterical. The movements of Nunn and Milazzo, which were furious and exceedingly rapid in actuality, became slowly trance-like and methodical to Mike. The syringes in Doc Nunn's crimson-stained hands were jutting in and out, in and out, slowly and methodically, into Vinnie's gaping wounds. Milazzo's steady hands, covered, too, in the spilled blood of their Saint, was shoving gauze in an ungodly gaping wound in Vinnie's abdomen while pressing a tourniquet into a wound that was now oozing blood, an ominous sign that spoke of the copious amount of blood that Vinnie was losing, and the speed with which the blood was exiting Vinnie's depleted body.

Mike saw Milazzo looking at him and saw his mouth moving, but he heard no words.

Milazzo was saying that Vinnie was dying.

Mike then peered down at Saint.

"Mike?"

"Yes, Saint?"

"Mike, I . . . just . . . I just . . ."

Mike no longer could control his sobbing. "What, Vinnie?" Mike forced his question through ample tears and heaving cries.

"Mike . . . I . . . love . . . you . . . brother."

Mike's head fell. His chin collided with his upper chest as he tried to control his sobbing, for fear of hurting his vulnerable brother.

Vinnie's wheezing was worsening by the second. There were long pauses between words and longer pauses, still, between breaths. Doc Milazzo placed his blood-soaked gauze on the ground, gently released the tourniquet about Vinnie's thigh and lovingly took Vinnie's right hand in his hands.

Doc Nunn likewise released the pain-numbing syringe from his bloody hands and his eyes followed the needle's death spiral down, toward the crimson pool beneath his fallen brother, before it crashed to the ground amidst a splatter of blood and came to an abrupt stop. A bewildered, defeated, yet indefatigable Nunn then clasped Vinnie's left hand.

Mike placed his hands, which also were congealed in blood, gently upon Vinnie's irregularly heaving chest. Vinnie, still for a matter of seconds, suddenly heaved and choked up more blood. The dazed Marine blinked his eyes rapidly and then locked his steely blue eyes onto Mike's.

"Red . . . tell my family . . . and Roe . . . that I . . . love them."

Another seemingly eternal pause.

"And . . . please . . . tell Lilly . . . that I'm . . . sorry . . . that I . . . failed her. I, I . . . love you . . . Lilly." Vinnie's face contorted in a sense of forlorn, eternal regret. "Mike?"

"Yeah, Saint," Mike whispered, "I'm here for you, Vinnie. I'm right here."

"Mike," began Vinnie in a haltingly breathless tone that belied the strong, determined look in his sad eyes.

"Mike . . . I . . . just . . . want . . . I just want . . . to . . . go . . .

"Home."

And with that profound utterance, Vinnie fell still for all eternity.

Saint's eyes remained locked on Mike's as the mortally injured Marine's pupils dilated. Mike didn't move, he didn't breathe, and he refused to let go of his broken friend. The three Marines—John Nunn, Mike Reagan, and Tony Milazzo—remained on their knees, transfixed and afraid to move because that would confirm what they all knew subconsciously: that their beloved friend was no more.

They waited.

An audible whimper broke the silence. Doc Milazzo, without moving and without releasing Vinnie's hand, glanced up and observed Tex, blood strewn across his face as a result of Earth and gravel angrily descending upon him in the foxhole during the attack, shaking and crying uncontrollably.

Still not a movement.

Vinnie spoke no more, yet his final six words reverberated in Mike's mind.

I just want to go home.

Mike, just twenty-one, didn't know how to respond, but it was immaterial, as Vinnie had breathed his last breath following those words.

At that moment, Heaven welcomed its newest Saint.

"Mike," Doc Nunn gently said, "he's gone, Red. He ain't in no pain anymore. We did all that we could for him and we were there for him 'til the end. He ain't died alone in this fucking shithole. He died in the arms of his brothers."

With that, Doc Nunn gently and lovingly placed Vinnie's hand onto the ground. He gave a knowing glance to his fellow corpsman, Doc Milazzo, who likewise released Vinnie's opposite hand after gently placing it on the ground.

The two heroes knew that they had other injured Marines to tend to and, as much as it broke their hearts, they knew that they had to leave their fallen hero. Both Docs told Mike that they loved him and off they ran, disappearing into the soot, flame, and omnipresent dust, to try to salvage other men who desperately needed their help.

Yet, there remained Mike, with his feet under his haunches, slumped over the lifeless body of the man that was the life of the company. Kilo Company lost its Saint, along with three other men, that morning.

Mike clenched his teeth after he noticed a familiar object jutting out of Vinnie's blood-stained flak jacket. It was a Saint's letter to his family. The letter was dated March 28, 1968 and it was stained with sweat and blood. Mike shook his head, wiped fresh tears from his eyes, and then removed the letter and Vinnie's dog tags by pulling them up and over his dead brother's miraculously untainted head.

Mike knew what had to be done with these prized possessions.

"Tex!"

"Yes?"

Mike, with Vinnie's prone body still propped on his lap, turned to face Tex. Mike's stern, rage-filled gaze caused Tex to visibly flinch. He then stated in a monotone voice, "Make sure these get sent home to Saint's family, you understand?"

"Y-y-yes, Red. Of course."

With that, Tex took the dog tags and the blood-stained letter and somberly walked through the throng of mourning men. The magnitude of the attack was hitting the men. There was great angst and crying amongst these combat-hardened men, for their Saint, and three other brothers, were dead.

Mike, still teary-eyed, gingerly and lovingly closed Vinnie's eyelids over his blank blue eyes. Prior to that, the deceased Saint's eyes seemed to have been staring beyond Red and into Heaven itself. Next, Mike nudged Vinnie's lower jaw upward so as to eliminate the wide-mouthed look of death that Mike and his brothers had seen all too often.

Mike stayed with Vinnie's body until the Hueys arrived and the two young Marines responsible for wrapping Vinnie's body and the three others descended from the bird. The greens dutifully went about their solemn duty of gently and respectfully placing the remains of their dead brothers into black canvas body bags and escorting them onto the Huey for the first leg of the somber journey back home.

The Marines from the Huey took their time with the first three Marines who were KIA in the surprise mortar attack. When they encountered Vinnie's body, they noticed what seemed to be the entire platoon come to attention. The Marines of Kilo Co., many of whom remained dazed, bloodied, and angry, stopped milling about and talking amongst themselves. Even the radio man ceased communicating with HQ as the Marines from the Huey attended to Vinnie's body. The young greens had no idea who Vinnie was, but they ascertained that he was a pretty important member of this platoon given the eyeballs that were upon them.

They noticed a red-headed Marine, with blood crusted across his forehead, watching them especially closely. He looked really, *really* angry.

"Hey, greens," Mike yelled with a maniacal tone, "you guys are gonna take special care of the Saint until he gets back to HQ, right?" Mike's tone made the query more rhetorical statement than

300

question. The two Marines realized immediately that Mike actually was *demanding* special treatment for Vinnie, and they answered affirmatively.

Mike stood at attention and maintained a salute during the entire time that the two Marines loaded Vinnie's body onto the Huey, but his eyes followed every step that the nervous Marines took while transporting Vinnie's body onto the large helicopter.

Mike couldn't stop replaying his final exchange with Vinnie from a few moments earlier.

I just want to go home.

The Saint's final six words, none of them more than a syllable, reverberated in Mike's soul. He couldn't shake the surreal nature of the spiritual exchange with his fallen buddy.

Saint was looking right at me when he died, Red thought. *I'm the last person that Vinnie saw, and the last person that he spoke to, before he died.*

Mike shivered at that thought and marveled at the strength conveyed by Vinnie's blue eyes, even as his soul was escaping his mortal body.

That look in his eyes, Mike continued introspectively. *He looked pissed. He looked angry that he was not gonna go home and take care of his family, starting with being the best man at his sister's wedding. He looked devastated that he wasn't gonna be able to marry his gal, Roe. He fucking asked me to apologize to Lilly for . . . for dying.*

Mike was overcome with emotion yet again.

Red exclaimed, "Fuck," before fresh tears commingled with the dirt that already was streaking his face.

He ain't going to the wedding. He was so proud to be Lilly's best man and he was looking forward to that wedding so fucking much.

More tears.

Mike watched the Huey take off with his Saint stuffed inside of a black canvas body bag. The thought of the bloodied and broken

Vinnie stuffed inside of that bag brought a wave of claustrophobic nausea to Red, causing his knees to buckle and resulting in him involuntarily falling, only to steady himself with his right hand against the ground.

Tex cautiously approached the grief-stricken Marine. "Red, are you al–"

"Leave me the fuck alone, Tex. I ain't in a talking mood."

Frantic, Tex persisted, "But Mike, I foun–"

"GODDAMMIT, TEX, GET THE FUCK AWAY FROM ME!"

Startled, the young Marine surreptitiously slipped the item that he was holding back into his trouser pocket and slinked away from the enraged, grief-stricken Michael Reagan. As Tex walked away, crying, he jingled the item in his pocket.

After Vinnie's body was removed earlier, the younger Marines in the platoon were charged with carefully removing the ammo from Vinnie's jeep, which, miraculously, was not ignited by the morning attack. First, the boys quickly doused the flames that were jutting from the jeep's engine, for that could have been disastrous. Next, they removed the boxes of ammo that remained bungee-corded to the rear of the vehicle.

Tex was one of the young Marines entrusted with this critical task. He had removed a couple of boxes and had returned for another round when a glistening object, near where the hood of the jeep used to be, caught his eye. The jeep still was on its side and the shiny object appeared to be snagged in a part of the engine of the badly damaged jeep. Tex's eyesight remained blurry from the earlier events, so he repeatedly blinked in an effort to focus on the strangely enticing, sparkling object.

As Tex drew closer to the object, his sight cleared and his breath abruptly deserted him.

Holy shit! Oh, my God, Tex thought. Gasping, Tex extended a quivering hand toward the object that had caused him such consternation.

It was Vinnie's gold necklace and cross.

Tex gingerly unsnagged the portion of the popped gold chain from the engine by using his Ka-Bar to pry away the portion of the jeep engine that stubbornly refused to surrender the golden bounty. Amazingly, the broken chain was snagged in such a way as to prevent the crucifix from falling to the bloodstained, scorched Earth a few feet below. Tex stood mesmerized by the item in his hand. Less than an hour earlier, the effervescent Saint was bringing a much-needed morale boost to the platoon and this very cross glistened as it hung from his neck. And now, this was all that was left of the departed Saint of the Thundering Third.

Tex stood, head bowed and shoulders slumped, staring blankly at the small, gold chain and cross in his hand. Suddenly, the young Marine heaved and he began to cry out loud, with his shoulders hitching violently, forward and back, as young Tex mourned his friend, leader, and idol.

None of the other boys dared approach Tex, as they remained numb from what had transpired that morning. Thus, Tex was left to mourn his loss, alone with his angst-riddled thoughts and a gold cross that had sparkled around the neck of a Marine who'd shined even brighter than the gold—before the light of his presence was snuffed out by a wayward mortar.

After a few minutes, Tex composed himself and then noticed Mike by the LZ. *I gotta get this cross to Red,* Tex thought. *He'll know what to do.* It was then that he approached the downtrodden corporal, only to be unceremoniously dismissed by the enraged young man.

As Tex walked away from the distraught Red, he fingered Vinnie's gold chain in his pocket. Tears welled again in his eyes as he wondered — albeit irrationally — if Vinnie still would be in their midst had the chain not inadvertently popped off his buddy's neck while he was fixing his jeep.

Vinnie must not have felt the chain rip off his neck while he was fixing that goddamn jeep, Tex thought as tears cascaded down his face. *He definitely would have removed the cross from the engine and put it in his pocket if he had known.*

Confused and distraught, Tex removed the chain and cross from his pocket, kissed it, replaced it in his pocket and then resolved that he would return this holy grail, along with Vinnie's dog tags and final letter, back to Saint's family in New York.

*   *   *

Red straightened up and looked around, noticing that a number of his brothers were trying hard to make it seem that they were not watching his every move. The stunned Marines knew that Mike was one of the most senior Marines on Cam Lo Hill and did not want to address him after such a palpable loss. Therefore, they merely stood, transfixed, watching his every move but saying nothing.

Red, with Saint's blood still fresh on his hands, arms, and most of his filthy shirt, pants, and boots, became enraged. The frustration of losing his dear friend, and the perceived shame of losing his composure in the company of the men that looked to him as a leader, caused his frustration to boil over.

Red quickly pivoted and sprinted toward his foxhole, causing the surrounding Marines to stumble out of his path of fury. Mike retrieved the rifle that he'd dropped when he saw Saint's leg jitter what seemed like a lifetime ago but what was, in actuality, less than an hour earlier. He released the safety, unleashed a primal scream, and proceeded to spray automatic fire in the direction of the distant DMZ, the direction from which the deadly mortars and rockets had descended, taking out the unsuspecting Saint in the process. The men jumped in horror initially and then, realizing what was transpiring, simply let nature take its course.

"GODDAMN YOU, YOU FUCKING MURDEROUS BASTARDS! FUCK YOU ALL!"

Mike emptied the entire magazine of his rifle, dropped the weapon to his side, and returned to the ring of blood that was all that remained of Saint. Mike dropped to his knees and cried. It was 1300 hours and the warm sun peeked through the scorched remains of the trees on Cam Lo Hill. The rays of sun, visible as virtual dust beams that streaked across the platoon, stood in stark contrast to the melancholic darkness and searing cold that was suffocating Mike's very being.

*   *   *

"Sir, we missed the vehicle, but it was overturned as best I can tell. It appears that we have four confirmed bodies." The Vietcong soldier remained on surveillance, up in the tree with the binoculars. He watched the entire attack from his perch and reported to his superior officer in his native tongue.

The office replied, "I am disappointed that we did not detonate that heavily fortified jeep. That easily would've killed the entire squadron of men stationed in Cam Lo."

The man in the tree frowned; it is never a good proposition when one's superior officer is disappointed in one's work. "Yes, sir. I am sad that we missed such an opportunity, too. However, based on the reactions of the men on the hill, it appears that we killed a very important GI."

"That is all well and fine," came the curt reply, "but we wanted to kill ALL of the GIs on the hill. We cannot call in an ambush with the small group of men that we have near that area. They would be slaughtered by the GIs there and by the back-up that they must already have called in."

The man in the tree knew that there would be hell to pay for this failure.

He purposely neglected to inform the superior officer that one of the men who had fired the deadly mortars at the GIs was struck and mortally wounded by the unexpected torrent of artillery fired by the angry man with the hair that looked as if it was ablaze.

CHAPTER 18

THE AFTERMATH

K ilo Company had lost many men in the year since Mike had arrived as a grunt in the shit. He and his brothers had seen their share of death—enemy and brethren, alike. Enough to last multiple lifetimes. Mike and the boys of the Thundering Third thought they were hardened to the notion of death in a land that figuratively and literally was awash in the blood of untold scores of young Vietnamese and American men. However, Saint's death was different.

Saint's death struck their core.

For, in a world where the men knew to not get too personal and friendly with the man next to you, for obvious reasons, Vinnie vitiated that requirement. The cult of Saint's personality permeated the group. It was impossible not to love him. He was the company driver who would bring the boys their fixings from home, but he was so much more than that.

Other companies had drivers who took advantage of being in the rear and out of harm's way. That wasn't Vinnie. Saint was out with the guys. He fought side-by-side with the boys and risked his life for them. He personified Semper Fi, especially in the manner in which he died.

Worse yet, the guys knew that Vinnie was not even supposed to be at Cam Lo on March 28th. He was sick and he had had the benefit of convalescing in the rear. In fact, he was *told* to stay in the rear, to take advantage of his time there and not return until he felt one-hundred-percent better.

Every Marine knew that, if a superior were to ask, he would say that he'd do the same thing that Vinnie had done, even if it meant dying in the process. After all, that was the way of the Corps. Each man understood that this was what he had signed up for. However, in a quiet moment of confidential introspection, many of the men lamenting Saint's death on Cam Lo Hill were haunted by both his death and by a simple fact that gnawed at them in the pits of their stomachs: Many of them, if they were to be given the choice, would stay behind in the comfort of the rear. For some Marines, the pain of this admission did not subside until they themselves breathed their last breaths.

On Monday, April 1st, Daniel King returned from a week in which he'd volunteered to serve in a platoon up in Khe Sanh that was low on experienced men. He survived a minor skirmish there and was returned to the Thundering Third with the commendations of the platoon commander who had requested the reinforcements. Daniel arrived on Cam Lo Hill at approximately 0600 hours. He didn't immediately see any of his buddies, so he made it a point to look for Red. Daniel bounced from one corner of the platoon to the next and didn't see Mike. However, what he did see was a palpable difference in the faces of his brothers. Daniel was a combat veteran and he sensed that something terrible had happened.

The men who did greet him were subdued in their salutations, if they even acknowledged him at all. Tex, who was quite affable and always willing to help, made pained eye contact with Daniel before quickly looking to the ground while sharing the perfunctory, "Good morning." Tex merely turned away, without waiting for Daniel's response.

That shocked Daniel and left him uneasy. "Hey, Tex," King inquired, "where's Red?"

Without looking up, Tex jutted his chin out and gestured eastward, in the direction of the man-made lake, along the outskirts of the camp. Daniel peered in that direction and there, roughly fifty yards from where he was standing, he saw three men who he instantly recognized to be Red, Doc Nunn, and Doc Milazzo.

Daniel, flush with dread, slowly walked toward the three men. Nunn was puffing furiously on a cigarette, Red was using his Ka-Bar to whittle down a charred tree branch, and Milazzo was skipping stones off the lake while forlornly staring ahead. The men were within inches of each other, but they may as well have been on separate continents, given the lack of interaction among them. It was as if each man was unaware of the presence of the other two.

Fuck, thought Daniel, *this ain't gonna be good.*

Daniel approached the three Marines but not one even flinched or looked his way. The realization that the men didn't react to the loud, crunching sound of heavy boots meeting soot and charred remnants of jungle life all but confirmed Daniel's dread. As Marines, Daniel and his brothers were trained to hear even the faintest of sounds dozens of meters away. It was a basic lesson of survival. Of course, these trained senses were heightened further by the hysteria that every Marine develops and perfects in combat.

In Marine jargon: You hear shit that ain't even there.

Three feet away and still nothing.

"Goddamn it, fellas," King stated, tongue in cheek. "If I was a gook, you'd all have been dead five minutes ago."

No reaction. King's heart sank.

"What the hell's going on, guys? It's like a fucking morgue around here. We were hit, weren't we?"

Dunn exhaled and released a monumental smoke ring while Milazzo hurled a stone across the span of the lake, apparently forgetting to skip it in the water. King heard the stone crack against multiple trees as it disappeared into the thick brush that lined the perimeter of the "pool" that he had swum in many times in the past. King kept his eyes on Red, as he was the wise old head who was about to head to Japan for the final month of his tour of duty.

Red was the pensive thinker and cool customer amongst Kilo Company. When Mike spoke, the men listened. An interesting comparison to Vinnie, Daniel thought. For when Vinnie spoke, his charisma was such that the men couldn't help but listen.

King's voice cracked as he muttered, ". . . Red?"

Mike peered up at King with an icy stare that would freeze even the most brazen of gooks dead in his tracks. The dread bore deeper into Daniel's psyche.

"Wh-where's Saint? Did he return from the rear yet?"

King heard an exaggerated exhalation but he wasn't sure if the culprit was Nunn or Milazzo. Red's eyes squinted into nearly imperceptible slits in response to the question and King immediately regretted asking it. Red released a slow breath without taking his hard, narrow stare off of King.

"Daniel," began Red in his customary gruff, grizzly voice, "about that question."

Daniel knew. He didn't need Red to utter another syllable.

Red looked away from Daniel, as he realized that tears were welling up in King's eyes.

"The fuck happened?" King choked the question out.

Nunn finally became engaged. He cleared his throat and spat a wad of phlegm to the scorched Earth to his left before saying matter-of-factly, "Fucking surprise morning ambush by the gooks."

King heaved and gasped as he tried to regulate his ability to breathe, an instinct that suddenly had abandoned the young man.

"They got him, Dan. The gooks fucking killed the Saint."

Red's succinct response was deadlier than any sniper's bullet could've been. Another audible gasp, followed by the embarrassment of being unable to control the tears.

"It's alright, Danny," Milazzo exclaimed as he stopped throwing stones long enough to gently pat his brother's shoulder before continuing, "the platoon's been crying over this bullshit since it happened."

King's mind was processing this terrible, shocking news too quickly for his mouth to ask questions. He was dumbfounded. *Saint? Dead? But he was gonna wear dress blues to Lilly's wedding in a couple of months. This can't be right. He wasn't even supposed to be here.* The thoughts swirled rapidly through Daniel's mind.

"Wait a goddamn second, fellas," Daniel shouted. "Vinnie wasn't even supposed to be here. He was sick and in the rear, right? Did these cocksuckers make him come back to the shit against his will?"

Red shook his head before Nunn interjected, "You know Saint, Dan. He ain't one to shy away from being with us. He could've stayed in the rear but he voluntarily came back early because he wanted to be with us."

Daniel's shoulders slumped and his head dropped straight back, with his moist eyes peering up at the heavens. He sighed heavily, and then sighed again before bringing his chin to his chest, tightly and rapidly blinking his eyes to squeeze out the tears.

"At least tell me that he went peacefully, fellas. Tell me that it was a sniper that got him, quick and easy." Dan was speaking through heaving cries now. He knew that every Marine's wish was that if he had to die, he'd die quickly and painlessly. And intact. Nobody wanted to be sent home with parts missing.

Red instinctively looked at his pants. Vinnie's blood remained caked on both of his trouser legs. Milazzo peered at his shirt: The left sleeve was jaggedly torn from about the elbow down, a reminder that he had torn it off to use as a makeshift tourniquet for the gaping wound of Vinnie's thigh. Doc Nunn recalled seeing what he believed to be Vinnie's right leg about twenty feet away from where they were working on him. He told the greens from the Huey to retrieve the leg and keep it together with Vinnie's body.

"Danny boy," began Doc Nunn, "what can we say? It was fucking messy, man. Vinnie was under his jeep when the rockets and mortars and shit came flying toward us. Everybody that heard the tubing took cover. Vinnie never heard the tubing—" Doc Nunn suddenly stopped talking as the emotion of reliving that fateful event proved to be too much for the ever-stoic Marine.

Embarrassed, Nunn muttered to himself, "Fucking shit!" before he continued, "Vinnie never heard the tubing because he was under his fucking jeep, fixing his government-issued piece of shit for the bazillionth time."

Red took over the story from there. "I tried to get him, Daniel. I was in my foxhole before remembering that Saint was under that goddamn loud jeep. I tried to run out to get him but Tex pulled me back in the foxhole because the shit was coming in hot already. I took a rock and threw it at the jeep, hoping to get his attention, but I don't know if the rock hit him. I'll never know."

"Next thing I know, the ground is shaking like a sonofabitch and the explosions were louder than anything I've heard since I've been out here. I jumped up after the explosions stopped and the ground stopped shaking. I expected to see ambushing gooks but there weren't any. Instead, I saw three dead Marines, and Vinnie, who still was alive at that point. Vinnie's jeep was on its side, with the driver's side facing Heaven. Man—"

Now it was Mike's turn to have painful emotions steal the breath from his larynx, causing his voice to expire suddenly. Yet he collected himself enough to continue with his voice unsteady and wavering with emotion. "The jeep was filled with ammo but it didn't blow, miraculously enough. We all would've been blown to kingdom come if that jeep had exploded because it was fucking loaded. The jeep got thrown onto its side and it was on fire, but none of the ammo ever detonated. It was the Saint's final gesture to us, I guess."

"Can you believe that shit, Dan?" Mike asked before taking a few seconds to collect himself. "Vinnie, the Saint, our company driver. His goddamn driver's side door was facing Jesus in Heaven." Mike exhaled and then forged ahead in recounting the story.

"When I got to Vinnie, he was pretty bad, Dan. His face and upper chest looked perfectly normal. Those parts of his body probably were under the jeep when the mortars hit. But his belly was ripped wide open and he . . . he . . . *FUCK!* He was missing most of his right leg, god-*DAMMIT!*" More tears descended from the eyes of four men who had genuinely believed until now that Marines weren't supposed to cry.

Dan looked toward Nunn and Milazzo, who were both grimacing and shaking their heads. Milazzo cleared his throat before saying, "Saint was bleeding from everywhere and me and Doc Nunn couldn't stop the bleeding fast enough. This here torn sleeve was because I ripped off that part of my shirt to create a tourniquet for his leg. Doc Nunn did everything he could to save Vinnie. We both did. We—we didn't want him to—to die."

"He wasn't in pain, Danny," said Doc Nunn. "We made sure that he wasn't suffering in his final moments on this Earth. He died at peace and with his brothers around him. The Saint was always there for us, so we were with him until he left us and met his maker."

Mike vigorously rubbed his eyes and faced Dan. He, Nunn, and Milazzo were in a half-circle around their brother Marine. Mike had his back to Dan while the Docs spoke because their words brought him back to March 28th and the pain of reliving that moment was unbearable. In Mike's mind, turning around so as to shield the men from his weakness preserved some modicum of honor. However, he summoned the necessary strength to turn and face his friend before sharing some critical information.

"Dan," Red began, "Saint's final words before he died were, 'Mike, I just want to go home.' He was looking right into my eyes with those goddamn blue eyes of his. He said those words and then he died, Dan. The Saint died in my arms but goddammit, he wasn't in any pain when he passed."

Red gestured toward Doc Nunn and Doc Milazzo, both of whom had pained looks on their faces, before he continued, "These here guys did everything they could to save Vinnie. Every-FUCKING-thing. Vinnie being Vinnie—he's bleeding all over the goddamn place, he's dying, and he KNOWS he's dying—and he still takes the time to tell us that he loves us."

Mike paused. He couldn't speak at that moment. The raw memory of Vinnie bleeding everywhere, with a gaping hole in his gut and a missing leg yet still telling his brothers that he loved them, was way too much for him to bear. Mike fought like hell to suppress the tears but the effort was futile. Red's face was burrowed in unadulterated anguish. His eyes scrunched into slits and the creases on his forehead doubled down and exerted immense pressure upon his brow. His mouth curled instinctively into a frown and he clenched his teeth to muzzle the primitive cries that were rising from the recesses of his soul. The bile rose into Mike's throat and the combination of nausea, absolute anger, and hopeless desolation took its toll on Mike's psyche and his body. He quickly turned and took a few steps toward the lake before he doubled over and vomited what little food he had in his system.

Doc Milazzo hurriedly approached Mike to ensure that he was okay and Red, still doubled over and wiping his mouth with his left sleeve, held up his right arm and extended it behind him in an effort to gesture to Tony that he was as good as he was going to be before he was able to leave this hellhole, preferably alive. And intact.

"Daniel," Doc Nunn began, in an effort to complete the narrative, "Vinnie is . . ." John sighed heavily, realizing what he had done. "Vinnie *was* a great fucking guy. There was no reason at all for him to be there when the shit began raining out of the sky. None. He could've and should've been back in Shangri-La, eating grapes and sipping martinis, not giving a single shit about us down here in the jungle. But that was not Vinnie's style and we all were joking and making bets about how early he'd be back.

"Y'know, Danny, we all joke around and poke fun at each other about the brave Marines *OORAH* bullshit. We remember the crazy drill instructors from boot camp and how they live, breathe, sleep, and shit that stuff! Well, you know what? Saint really did live the Marines' motto. Now, he ain't gonna be the type of guy to yell and scream in your face, that wasn't his style—unless someone pissed him off, of course—but he definitely took his responsibilities as a U.S. Marine seriously. He took his commitment to you and me—and all of us—damn seriously."

Nunn sighed again as he slowly shook his head left and right before he concluded, "Saint was one of a fucking kind, fellas. We were damn lucky to have him here as long as we did."

Red had rejoined the boys halfway through Nunn's soliloquy. He was proud of Nunn, who had shown great resolve in summoning the courage to share those words. Milazzo nodded at the conclusion of John's impromptu eulogy and said, "John, you hit the nail on the head. Vinnie and I shared a common bond because we weren't only struggling to survive here in country, we also both came from the East Coast back in the world. I grew up near the Jersey Shore and Vinnie grew up in Jamaica, Queens, a stone's throw from the Empire State Building. We used to laugh and make fun of each other, saying, 'You have a funny accent!' to each other. The funny thing is that we both denied that we had an accent while laughing at each other's clear accent!"

Nunn interjected, "The both of you motherfuckers sound like you tripped and fell outta the mob, ya greasy *eye-talian* bastards!"

Leave it to Doc Nunn to bring some much-needed levity to an increasingly depressing setting. All four young men, each of whom was ensconced in a cloud of melancholy seconds earlier, began to laugh quite heartily. Tony roughly patted John on the back and leaned over onto his knee to catch his breath, as he was laughing so hard. Milazzo then wiped tears from his eyes, under the pretense that the tears were precipitated by his laughter as opposed to the depths of the pain in his soul. When the laughter died down, Milazzo resumed his own unprompted stream-of-consciousness speech about Saint.

"When me and Saint realized that we practically were neighbors, we became pals and best friends out here. We promised each other that we'd get together after we got back home to visit our favorite beaches. Vinnie was gonna come to the Jersey Shore and I promised to go to Rockaway Beach in Queens. Vinnie kept telling me that the Rockaways were the best beaches on the East Coast and I smacked him over the head because the Jersey Shore and Wildwood blow everything away!"

The boys laughed again. "He began to call me *Stone* because he said that I looked like a stone-cold Italian mobster."

"So *that's* where that nickname came from," remarked Nunn with a laugh.

"Yup," continued Stone, "that's where it came from! Saint was good at giving everyone nicknames that stuck. For example, do any of yous guys know what Tex's real name is?"

The remaining three Marines each shrugged their shoulders and peered at each other. No one had a blessed clue!

"My point exactly," remarked Tony.

"Saint was a cool customer and a really good pal. He was just one of the guys, despite the fact that the guys thought so highly of him. He coulda been one of those assholes who walk around like their shit don't stink, but he wasn't. And the guys loved him for that." Tony glanced down, his voice cracking. He pinched his lips tight, so as to not allow the air of despair to escape from his mouth. Milazzo, the grizzled corpsman who had remained hardened despite having seen more death and broken bodies during his tour than was seemingly possible, somehow was not impervious to the pain caused by this one particular death. Stone realized that Saint's death transcended the deaths of so many other Marines because

Vinnie had made the Marines open their hearts to him. They couldn't help but take a liking to this wise-cracking, exceptionally loyal, brave, funny-talking kid from New York City. Tony was no exception.

Upon hearing each brother bear witness about Saint, Daniel absent-mindedly walked a few steps away from Red and the two corpsmen and toward the lake. Daniel thrust his hands into his trouser pockets as he stepped to the precipice of the gentle wake of the water breaking innocently against the scarred, war-torn shoreline. The water gently cascaded up and around the raised toe of Daniel's boot as he shrugged his shoulders, hands still in pockets, and peered through squinted eyes at the blinding reflection of the sun off of the lake's surface.

Myriad thoughts coursed through the young man's mind, but only one phrase was able to make the journey from his mind to his mouth. "Gee whiz, I can't believe that Saint really is dead. He had a plan and purpose for his life. More than most of us did, that's for damn sure. Goddamn, remember how often he said that he couldn't die because it would devastate his family? His mama is gonna be devastated. And what about his sister, Lilly? Shit, they were constantly writing to each other about her wedding in August and how he was gonna be the best man in his dress blues." Daniel paused and shrugged again before remarking, "You know what I'm saying, fellas?"

Silence.

"Fellas?"

More silence.

Daniel turned around to face the guys. "Boys?"

Red and the corpsmen were overcome with emotion yet again.

Finally, Red summoned the strength to continue the painful soliloquy. "We gotta get Saint's dog tags and his final letter to his family. That would've been what he wanted and, even though it may cause some pain, it is absolutely right for Vinnie's family to have his final words."

"Hey, Mike," Nunn interjected somewhat apprehensively, "there's something else that we gotta send back home to Saint's family."

Perplexed, Red cocked his head toward Doc Nunn with a quizzical look on his weary face. "What's that, Doc? What else do we have to return to the Santaniellos?"

John hesitated and snuck a furtive glance toward Milazzo. Stone knew what John had in his pocket and he subtlety nodded affirmatively in response to Doc's glance.

John slowly reached into his pocket and pulled out Vinnie's lucky cross. Mike's eyes widened and he became slack-jawed. He stammered, "Wha . . . how. . ." before his brain fell victim to his stunned senses and rendered him inarticulate.

"Red," Milazzo interjected, "Tex found the chain stuck in the engine of Vinnie's jeep shortly after he was killed. Him and the other greens were cleaning up after all the shit went down. He said that he tried to give it to you later that day but—"

"—But I cut him off and dismissed him like a total asshole." Mike closed his eyes, lowered his head into the palm of his hand, and sighed in an exasperatingly slow and painful fashion. He bellowed, "God, I gotta apologize to the kid. But first things first: We have to get all of these prized possessions back to Vinnie's family."

Each Marine agreed, so they ended the impromptu funeral and sought out Tex for Vinnie's dog tags and final letter. Mike couldn't bring himself to touch Vinnie's lucky cross, much less look at it, so Doc Nunn held on to the relic as they tracked down Tex for Vinnie's remaining keepsakes. The boys couldn't imagine the pain that they were going to cause Lilly and the rest of Vinnie's family when they received this package but they knew, as Marines, that they didn't have a choice.

No Marine gets left behind.

And neither do any of a deceased Marine's belongings.

*   *   *

Monday, April 1, 1968. It was another unseasonably warm day in New York. Lilly was at work and Carmine was on another construction job. Rose had gotten Joseph out of the house that morning to begin another day in eighth grade at Presentation of the Blessed Virgin Mary School before she returned to her daily routine of picking up after the kids and tidying up the house. Rose went upstairs to chat a bit with her mother after she'd finished cleaning her modest home. Rose spoke in her native Italian with her mother.

"Mama, do you notice how much cleaner the house was when Vinnie was home?"

Nunu smiled and replied, "Yes, that Vincent of yours is such a good boy. He's like having a second man around the house, even though he still is a baby!"

Rose and Nunu shared a laugh.

The forty-six-year-old Rose's short black hair, sprinkled with noticeably more gray since Vinnie's deployment in Vietnam, was neatly parted to the right on her head, with the longer portion of her hair curling slightly over her left eye before cascading over the left side of her head. Nunu's hair—pulled back gently, yet neatly, into a conservative bun befitting her age—was akin to a blanket of freshly fallen snow. The waves of her curly hair rippled toward the back of her head like the waves of the Atlantic Ocean. Her soft, hazel-colored eyes were covered by octagon-shaped bifocals that made her eyes appear larger than normal and also served to accentuate her crow's feet. Nunu was dressed in her omnipresent plain blue dress with a thin white sweater that she seemingly wore throughout the year, irrespective of the weather. Rose was wearing powder-

318

blue polyester pants and a flowery blouse that complemented her pants. Rose was a woman of modest means and, like many women of her generation, tended to neglect herself for the sake of her children. She lifted her black, horn-rimmed glasses from her eyes and perched them atop her head before turning to her mother to continue their conversation.

"Mama, Easter is April 14. It's so late this year. I hope that we actually can enjoy some warm weather during the holiday for a change. I'm going to run to *Woolworth* to buy Easter baskets and candy now. We'll make baskets for the kids and then we'll make a special basket to send to Vinnie. I'll include extra licorice and Tootsie Rolls because he loves them so much. I'm also going to include a lot of extra candy so that Vinnie can share them with his nice friends over there."

Nunu smiled and responded in her broken English, "That's-a nice, Rose," before continuing the conversation in her native Italian. "I'm sure that Vinnie and his friends must love you very much because you send them so many sweets!"

Rose chuckled and said, "I'll be right back, Mama, do you need me to get you anything?"

The doorbell rang before Nunu could answer.

Rose wasn't expecting company and she wondered if her neighbor, Ann Graves, was stopping by to brew some coffee and gossip for a spell. Rose enjoyed Ann's company, but she couldn't do that today because she had to mail Vinnie's Easter basket the following morning if there were to be any chance of him receiving the basket of goodies in time for the holiday. The bell rang again and Rose found that odd because Ann never rang twice.

Saint's mother turned from Nunu's room and traversed the very narrow hallway with the adjacent banister on the right that overlooked the staircase that led to her modest residence.

As Rose proceeded past the banister, her mind wandered to memories of Vinnie and Lilly playing silly games at this very spot when they were kids. One such game entailed the kids taking turns dropping their action figures and dolls through the spindles of the banister on the second floor while one of them tried to catch the descending toys while standing directly below in the narrow first-floor hallway. There was very little space in the area in which the toys descended, so it took some skill and a lot of luck for the falling toys to descend unimpeded into the waiting hands of the sibling downstairs. More often than not, the toys' trajectory would be altered—it repelled off the handrail of the banister or propelled off of the high wall beneath the banister, causing the toys to smack the hands or the face of the child below, much to the delight of the mischievous sibling on the second floor.

The kids wailed with delight when they caught the plummeting toy in the hallway below.

I miss those innocent days, thought Rose, a*nd I regret yelling at them to stop playing that silly game. Oh, what I wouldn't give to have Vinnie home, playing that game with Lilly now!*

The bell rang a third time.

Rose no longer was whimsically reminiscing about Vinnie and Lilly as kids. Instead, she was wondering who the hell was impatiently ringing the doorbell. Nunu called out, "Who is it?"

Rose walked down to the base of the steps before stopping to say, "I don't know, Mama." She bent over the banister on her right and looked through the thick glass that encompassed the top half of a heavy foyer door. She saw an ominous gentleman standing on the porch.

Rose turned around and yelled toward Nunu, "It looks like a police officer. I hope everything's alright!"

Rose became exceedingly nervous—her heart rate was hastened and her breathing occurred in short bursts—as she opened the foyer door and walked into the very small area between it and the front wooden double doors that led to the porch. Rose's dilapidated metal shopping wagon was folded up alongside the wall and a few pairs of winter boots haphazardly lined the floor adjacent to it. The double doors, one of which was bolted down and permanently closed, had full-length, shelved panes of glass that were situated behind long, narrow screens in each door. The family always cranked open the glass panes during the warmer months to allow cool breezes to cascade into the house.

On this day the glass panes were closed to keep out the chill of winter and early spring, although Rose had contemplated cranking them open this day, given the unseasonable warmth, and keeping the heavier foyer door open to allow for the breeze to cool the house.

Rose pulled down the glasses that were perched above her forehead and peered through the double doors, giving the once-over to the uniformed man who stood erectly behind them.

Suddenly, she realized that he was not a cop. Instead, he was USMC.

Immediately, Rose was overcome with a wave of absolute, unadulterated dread that no parent should ever experience, much less the parent of a teenaged boy with his whole life ahead of him. She looked to the right of the USMC official and saw, for the first time, a second, much shorter, uniformed gentleman.

Saint's mother knew why the Marines were at her door as she extended her trembling right hand to unlatch the lock to the front door. She knew before she could utter any words.

The forlorn Rose knew that she was about to welcome the grim reaper into her home.

"C-can I help you, gentlemen?" Rose's voice was as shaky as her hands. The larger Marine who stood directly in front of her, albeit behind the front door, asked in a forced, yet gentle tone, "Are you Mrs. Santaniello, ma'am?"

The questioner, Major Terrence O'Brien, at six-foot-three and 220 pounds, was a mountain of a man. His impeccably pressed uniform was as crisp as the air of an autumn morning and the myriad medals that adorned his left chest shined with the radiance of a thousand suns. The bars on the sleeve of his left shoulder spoke of his high rank. Major O'Brien wore the traditional Marine's cap atop his head and Rose could see a shock of very closely-cropped red hair in the space above his ears left bare by his cap. The major had very pale, almost pasty, white skin and the serious nature of his dark, black eyes pierced Rose to the core. O'Brien's thick, bushy red eyebrows were unkempt when compared to his standard military buzzcut and their appearance made his brow appear to slope well over his eyes, giving them a sullen, sunken effect. It was quite an intimidating presence to Rose, whose neck was craned simply to get a glimpse of this unwelcome stranger.

"Y-yes, I am, sir. How may I help you?" Tears already were welling in Rose's eyes and her voice was getting weaker with every syllable and every labored breath. Major O'Brien removed his cap and his head was ablaze with short, thick red hair. He held his cap over his heart and said, "Mrs. Santaniello, my name is Major Terrence O'Brien, U.S. Marine Corps. Is there anyone else home, ma'am?"

Rose's head was spinning and she felt faint.

"My mother is here, but she doesn't speak English too good. Who's here with you, Major?" Rose recalled that Carmine once told her to always address a military man by his rank only, without his name, and she put that advice to use during this exchange.

"Ma'am, this here is U.S. Marine Corps Chaplain Reverend Chandler Keeney."

Chaplain Keeney stepped out of Major O'Brien's considerable shadow and removed his cap before saying, "Good morning, Mrs. Santaniello. May God's blessings be upon you and your family on this day."

As Rose's lips uttered the words, "Thank you," in response to the chaplain's blessing, her mind was racing uncontrollably. *Oh, my God! My poor baby! My poor Vinnie! I knew that he shouldn't have enlisted! My son . . . my son . . . my son is . . . he is . . .*

The grieving mother could not get even her mind to formulate the D-word, but she unlocked the door to the misery that would haunt her for the rest of her days.

Major O'Brien and Chaplain Keeney respectfully entered the home and stepped aside in the foyer to allow for Rose to lead them to a place to sit down. However, Rose had not moved from the front doorway. Her gaze was transfixed on the military vehicle parked so ominously in front of her home.

Every mother's and wife's nightmare, she thought.

Rose peered across the street and saw her neighbor, Randy, standing in front of his home, shaking his head back and forth. She then peered at the house of her additional neighbor, Buford, who lived next door to Randy. Buford was known to survey whatever was transpiring outside by peering from a perch at his second-floor window. Rose saw the profile of Buford's face in the window and she could've sworn that he was crying.

Rose then craned her neck over to peer to her left, at the adjoining porch of the Graves's home. The adjoining porches were separated only by a three-foot wall. As kids, the Graves and Santaniello kids used to straddle the wall and pretend to ride horses. Other times, they would simply hop the wall to visit the home of their best friends. Rose and Carmine often chatted with the Graves over the wall, as they were very close friends. Rose observed Ann standing on her porch, perched at the base of the short wall.

The faces of Rose and Ann, who were decades-long friends, were etched in agonizing hopelessness and knowing pain as they stared into each other's watery eyes, communicating their mutual sorrow without expressing a single word. The two mothers felt the profound depravity of the situation in their very souls and they each began to cry, for they were mothers of young adults and teens that were far too young to be referenced in the past tense.

Major O'Brien gently cleared his throat and deferentially murmured, "Ma'am?"

Startled, Rose wiped the tears from her eyes and then circled to her right, turning her back on Ann Graves before re-entering her home. The distraught mother of three absent-mindedly left her front door open and proceeded past the respectful gentlemen into her narrow hallway. She then flatly, yet loudly, called out in Italian as she walked past the men, "Mama, come down!" before she trudged toward the door that led to her residence.

Rose paused at the door that led into her residence and looked toward a second door situated immediately to her right, which led to the basement. Rose's mind wandered to the countless times that Vinnie raced down the basement stairs to be with his father. Amidst her all-encompassing grief, Rose harkened back to the time when she had observed her son, maybe ten years old, using a thick black magic marker to write his name onto the low ceiling over the basement stairs.

VINNIE

The name was written horizontally along the downward-sloping ceiling in Vinnie's distinct style of neatly formed, capitalized block letters. Rose saw that V I N N I E in her mind's eye and realized that she'd never be able to hug and kiss that fun-loving, fiercely loyal young man again.

Rose entered her home with the two Marines closely behind and Nunu completing the funeral procession behind them. Rose gestured toward the small couch where she often sat with Vinnie as he watched his Saturday morning cartoons and the two gentlemen sat down. Rose noted mentally how uncomfortable and cramped the behemoth O'Brien appeared on her very modest couch. She wondered if he'd fall through the couch and land amidst a pile of wood shards on the floor. Rose and Nunu then sat upon the adjoining couch, positioned perpendicular to the couch upon which the notification officers were seated.

Rose introduced her mother, "This is my mother, Mrs. Buffa," and Nunu then offered feint, dainty handshakes after the officers extended their right hands toward her. O'Brien then meticulously began his prepared speech.

"Mrs. Santaniello, Mrs. Buffa." The experienced officer knew to look into each woman's eyes as he stated their names. "Chaplain Keeney and I are here to offer you our most sincere condolences on behalf of President Lyndon B. Johnson, the United States, and the United States Marine Corps. Your son, Lance Corporal Vincent Benore Santaniello, was killed in action at approximately 12:30 p.m. on Thursday, March 28, 1968, in Cam Lo, Vietnam. Ma'am, our information is that Vincent was killed instantly by a mortar as he was tending to his government-issued jeep. It was a surprise morning attack by the enemy and your son was one of four men killed that morning. While no parent should have to endure the loss of a child, we hope that you and your family can take solace in the fact that your son was killed instantly.

"He never knew what hit him."

Rose was fairly certain that the major continued to speak but the last thing that she heard was, *He never knew what hit him.*

Conversely, Rose knew *exactly* what hit her.

The emptiness began deep in her soul before it began to overwhelm her. It was a pain like no other pain, yet it didn't feel like an earthly pain. Rose had given birth to three children and the pain of having a child tear through one's body did not compare to the pain that was encompassing Rose's very being as Major O'Brien continued to speak.

Rose felt as if her body was rotting from the inside out.

Vinnie was dead. Her beloved son, Vinnie, was dead.

It didn't make sense, yet, paradoxically, it made perfect sense. The sense of rotting moved to her brain. So bizarre, really. Trying to articulate this sense of rotting is like trying to explain what silence looks like.

The neurons in Rose's brain were firing furiously and the resulting adrenaline rush made her knees buckle. Thankfully, Rose was seated. Otherwise, she would have collapsed. Her thoughts vacillated between absolutely nothing and overwhelming dread, from *OH, MY GOD! VINNIE'S REALLY DEAD!* to black silence.

Rose felt as if she was Jesus on the cross, delivering up His soul as His life passed. Indeed, the sense of rotting gutted Rose and, while her eyes saw the major's lips moving, her brain only processed the vision of Vinnie—her beloved son—being blown apart by a terrible hail of bullets and bombs. She saw her son's blue eyes filled with tears as blood poured from his gaping wounds. She saw his broken body on the ground of same strange land, in some strange, desolate jungle, alone and without his loved ones there—without his mother there, for God's sake—to comfort him in his final moments.

My God, Rose thought, *even Jesus had Mary with Him during His final moments!*

Rose knew her son and she knew that he damn well knew what hit him. He slept with one eye open, for crying out loud. He knew what hit him. There was no doubt in her mind about that. Rose's final coherent thought, following her realization that—contrary to Major O'Brien's reassurance—Vinnie knew what hit him, was this mind-numbing and soul-searing fact: He had to have thought of his mama as he came to realize that he was going to die out there in the middle of nowhere, thousands of miles from home.

Rose suddenly was incapable of normal, involuntary breathing.

The shriek of pain began as a low, nearly imperceptible murmur.

Rose's black eyes proceeded from barely perceptible slits to eyes that resembled those of cartoon characters, so big that they exceed the size of the cartoon character's head. The shriek became exponentially louder in a matter of milliseconds. Her mouth was stretched to its physical limits and her hands began to spasm uncontrollably. Rose had been seated but she shot up, causing the chair upon which she was seated to bolt backward, repel off of the wrought iron legs of the dining room table, and roll awkwardly toward the kitchen.

Nunu tried to control her daughter but she was no match for the rage that had overcome a mother that had just lost a child.

Major O'Brien, initially stunned at the sudden and absolute metamorphosis of this devastated woman, instinctively rose from his perch on the couch and tried to grab Rose's flailing hands, in an effort to get her to sit down on the couch that was way too small for his extra-large frame. Chaplain Keeney was transfixed by this display of unadulterated agony and did not move from his seat on the couch. Rather, he began to pray for Vinnie's soul, and for Vinnie's mother.

The sound that emanated from Rose's mouth had its genesis from her core. The sound resembled the word *no* but it was a long, pained syllable:

"Oooooooooooooooooo . . . nooooooooooooooooo . . . ooooooooooooooooooooooooooooooo!"

Rose made this sound at an ear-splitting octave until her breath ceased. She gagged and dry-heaved as her body lurched. Her survival instincts kicked in and forced her to take a lung-infusing breath. Rose then resumed howling in agony.

This process repeated itself for an indeterminate period of time and neither Nunu nor Major O'Brien was capable of getting Rose to control herself.

Rose felt that she was neither alive nor dead at that moment. Indeed, she felt as if she was relegated to purgatory.

Rose's neighbors—Randy, his wife Betty, and Ann Graves—all heard the shrieks of unadulterated horror coming from within the Santaniello home and they ran through the open front door to try to help the inconsolable Rose. They all knew the news without having been present for its formal delivery. The military vehicle parked in front and the presence of uniformed men spoke volumes. The scene inside the house resembled the chaos of war as a soldier tried valiantly to control the wild aggression of another, while three others struggled simultaneously to calm their compatriot.

Amidst the hysteria, Chaplain Keeney turned to Betty and asked her if she knew the name of Rose's local priest. "Father

James McLaughlin," Betty replied between her own tears, "from Presentation of the Blessed Virgin Mary, about a half-mile straight up 89th Avenue, on Parsons Boulevard."

The chaplain scanned the room for a telephone and, upon finding it, dialed 911. The 103rd precinct of the NYPD was only three blocks from Rose's home, so the police arrived within minutes of the call and they, too, bore witness to the painful saga within the Santaniello home.

Unsurprisingly, Rose continued to shriek in agony, but Major O'Brien and the neighbors convinced her to lie down on the couch. Her head was on Nunu's lap and Nunu, while crying, stroked Rose's hair, as she had once a long time ago when Rose, then a young girl, was crying over the loss of her grandmother. Rose's voice was terribly hoarse but she continued her rhythmic cries of pain and futility. Reverend Keeney asked the officers to drive to Presentation and endeavor to bring Father McLaughlin back to the home. The cops obediently set off for the church's rectory. A short while later, the cops and the priest arrived.

Father McLaughlin, a regal man in his late fifties, was tall and thin, and his salt-and-pepper, thinning hair was combed neatly to the right. His bushy sideburns obscured the rims of his thick black glasses and they accentuated the very long, thin face that sunk behind the spectacles perched atop his rather prominent nose. The priest knelt in front of Rose in the overcrowded living room and took her hand. Rose's voice was absolutely wrecked, as the continuous shrieking had taken its toll, making her barely audible. She remained numb and incoherent from the realization that her Vinnie was no more.

"Mrs. Santaniello? Mrs. Santaniello? Dear sister, speak to me, please," Father McLaughlin gently beseeched the grieving mother. Rose's eyes cleared slightly, but she did not respond. The priest, who had baptized Vinnie nearly nineteen years earlier, brought his face closer to Rose's and said in a soothing, barely audible whisper, "Mrs. Santaniello, sister. I know of your pain, my dear, I know. Nothing that I say will make you feel any better. You must open your heart to God's mercy and know that His only begotten Son, who Himself sacrificed His life so that we may have eternal life—so that Vincent would have eternal life—will bring you mercy if you believe in Him."

In response, Rose merely blinked, while Nunu repeatedly crossed herself. Father McLaughlin removed a rosary from his pocket, intertwined the blessed relic between his and Rose's right hands, and began to repeat its litany of prayers. Rose, still laying on her side with her head turned toward the priest, continued to moan while Father McLaughlin repeatedly prayed the *Hail Mary*.

Major O'Brien turned to Randy. "Sir, do you know where Mr. Santaniello is?"

"Why yes, I do. He's at a job site in Flushing. Do ya want me to get him, sir?"

"Please."

Randy squeezed Betty's hand and said, "Please help her," before he walked toward the front door. Betty wet a towel and gently wiped it across Rose's forehead, face, and neck, while Ann gently caressed Rose's left hand. Meanwhile, Father McLaughlin prayed the *Our Father* while Major O'Brien and Chaplain Keeney thanked the officers and advised them that they could leave.

*   *   *

Randy jumped into his truck and drove twenty-five minutes to Flushing, where Carmine and his brother Angelo were working on a house that they had built. Upon arriving, Randy observed Carmine perched on a ladder against the new house, painting its exterior. He parked his truck about a hundred yards from the construction site, exited his vehicle, and leaned against its hood.

Randy was befuddled. How was he supposed to tell his best friend that his beloved son had been killed in the war? He paced nervously for a few minutes before forcing himself to approach the worksite. Seconds later, he was standing directly below Carmine, whose back was to the agitated bearer of terrible news. The fifty-year-old gentleman had no idea what he was going to say to his long-time friend.

Randy and Carmine had been friends since the mid-1940s, after Carmine returned from World War II. Randy, two years Carmine's elder, also was a veteran of World War II, having served in the Army. Randy and Betty were already living in their home when the Santaniellos moved in across the street. Randy was very handy and when he saw his new neighbor painting and doing all kinds of odd jobs around the house, he knew that he'd found a lifelong friend. Shortly thereafter, Randy and Carmine became inseparable. They shared war stories when they were out of earshot of their spouses and kids, they enjoyed cigarettes in each other's back yards, and they performed small construction projects in each other's homes.

Randy thought, *For twenty goddamn years, I never had a situation where I didn't know what to say to Carmine. And now here I am, standing right below him, and I ain't got a clue what to say.*

The knot in the pit of Randy's stomach caused him to feel ill.

Disheartened, Randy cleared his throat and practically spat out the words, "Hey, uh, Car? Carmine, come down here for a second."

Carmine's olive skin was darker than usual as he toiled under the unforgivingly strong spring sun. He wore a long-sleeve t-shirt that was streaked with paint and a sweat-soaked red bandana around his head. As he painted, a hammer swung from a leather tool belt fastened to his paint-smeared, well-worn canvas carpenter pants.

Carmine looked down from the ladder after hearing a familiar voice.

"Randy? What the hell are you doing here?" Carmine quickly descended the ladder and removed the bandana from his head to reveal his thick black hair, still slicked back in a uniform fashion. "What the hell's wrong, Randy? Did something happen to Rose? Did Nunu fall down?"

Carmine's eyes were wide with consternation, as he deduced that something terrible had to have happened to precipitate Randy's presence. "Is Betty okay?"

Randy looked down and guiltily muttered, "Yeah, yeah, Car, nuttin's wrong with Betty, or Rose, or Nunu, for that matter."

Carmine looked confused for a few seconds before his eyes suddenly widened. His forehead creased and his jaw tightened, causing him to speak through pursed lips.

"Vinnie?"

The question was more whisper than utterance and Randy didn't answer immediately, as his eyes remained fixed on the ground. Carmine, never one to control his temper in the most docile of times, became enraged that Randy would not look up into his eyes.

Carmine roared, "RANDY!" before violently grabbing his best friend by the arms, causing Randy to flinch in pain.

"What happened to Vinnie, goddammit? Is he injured? Is he—"

Carmine caught himself and suddenly, like Rose, he was frozen in abject terror. Carmine hadn't cried since the Great Depression forty years earlier, but the forty-eight-year-old man recognized the familiar lump in his throat. The fiercely proud man composed himself because showing emotion would constitute a concession to weakness. He blinked in rapid succession and began to question Randy again in a direct manner, but with a tone that was much less confrontational.

"Randy, look at me and tell me what happened to my son." Carmine already knew that his son was dead but he needed confirmation from his lifelong friend.

"Carmine, ah, I'm really sorry. You know that Vinnie was like a son to me, too. I loved that kid." Randy was equally stubborn, so he was trying his damnedest not to cry. The tears didn't cascade from his moist eyes but the weakness of his voice was an indicator of the effort that he was expending to avoid breaking down.

Carmine dropped his head, put his hands on his waist, and released a long sigh. The veins in his muscular forearms, triceps, and biceps began to bulge and pulsate, as Carmine's heart rate began to escalate quickly. He then began to mutter under his breath, "Goddamnit, goddammit, goddammit." As he continued to repeat the pained expression, his voice began to rise in volume and in exasperation until he was literally yelling it at the top of his lungs.

"GODDAMMIT! GODDAMMIT! GODDAMMIT!"

Angelo came running from the back of the house, thinking that his brother was injured. "Car, what the hell is wrong? What happened?" Angelo suddenly noticed his brother's neighbor. "Randy? What the hell are you doing here?"

Carmine looked up and the look in his eyes shook his unflappable brother.

Angelo thought, *I haven't seen that look in Carmine's eyes since our brother, Vinnie, di*– Angelo caught himself, immediately became crestfallen, and whispered an anguished "Oh, no ..."

"Ang, I've lost my son. I've lost my son to the goddamned war."

Carmine was forlorn, Randy was sullen, and Angelo was shocked. Everyone loved Vinnie; they knew of his fierce loyalty to his family and they fully expected him to be a fantastic father and uncle one day soon. At nineteen, he had his whole life ahead of him, a life of promise and honor. And now here were three men, in their late forties and early fifties, talking about this inspirational kid in the past tense.

"Ang, I gotta get home. Rose is in a bad way."

Angelo looked at his brother and said, "Go. And let me know if there is anything I can do for yous."

With that, Carmine ran toward Randy's car and into his new, unwanted life of pain, anger, sorrow, desolation, repression, and depression.

As Randy sped off toward Jamaica, Carmine, deathly silent and alone in his empty thoughts, resigned himself to the notion that his life, and the lives of his entire family, would never again be the same. Carmine reminisced about when he lost his kid brother, Vinnie, decades earlier. That death, while somewhat expected, still sucked the life out of his parents and siblings. Carmine's parents never recovered from that death and now Carmine found himself in that identical, unenviable position. The overwhelming ache in his heart confirmed that sad reality for him.

Carmine slumped into Randy's passenger seat, placed his right hand over his forehead, and repeatedly rubbed his temples. He closed his eyes and silently wished that this all was a nightmare. Indeed, he said a prayer asking God to make all of this terrible news disappear as soon as he ceased rubbing his temples, as the pain was overwhelming. Alas, he removed his hand from his eyes and peered over at his friend, Randy, who was wiping tears from his eyes. Carmine returned his hand to his forehead and obscured his eyes. This really was a nightmare, albeit a permanent one from which he would never awaken.

As Randy turned his car onto the block that they shared, Carmine peered out of the passenger side window to see the military vehicle parked in front of his house. The grieving father also saw his neighbors congregated outside of their homes, quietly murmuring amongst themselves. However, when Randy pulled up and Carmine exited the vehicle, the neighbors stopped talking and avoided making awkward eye contact with Vinnie's dad. All of the neighbors knew how close Vinnie was to his father and they also knew that Carmine was going to be absolutely devastated by the loss of his oldest son. Thus, while the neighbors felt great compassion and sympathy for the Santaniellos, a majority of them likewise felt that it would be best not to speak to the grieving family right away, so as to respect their privacy.

Carmine exited Randy's vehicle and walked briskly with his head down toward his house. The front door was unlocked and ajar and Carmine overheard a cacophony of voices as he entered his home. A potpourri of familiar and unfamiliar sounding individuals. He entered the living room that overflowed with humanity and saw two uniformed men—*Notification officers*, he thought—amongst Father McLaughlin, Nunu, Betty, and Ann, standing around his wife, who was rocking on the couch in a fetal position while mumbling indecipherably.

Carmine noticed that Rose's tired voice sounded very pained and hoarse as he made his way to her through the sea of humanity, without acknowledging the company in his home. Carmine knelt until his face was inches from Rose's and he whispered, "Rose, Rose. I'm here, Rose." He took Rose's hand and continued, "I'm sorry, Rose, I'm sorry. I really believed that Vinnie was gonna make it home. Vinnie is a strong kid and a leader. There's no way he's gonna get hurt . . . or killed." Carmine's mind was racing so fast that he did not realize that he was speaking of his dead son in the present tense.

Rose looked into Carmine's eyes. She spoke not a word and the emptiness of her glance was so jarring that Carmine thought that it was as if Rose was in Vietnam, looking at their son's dead body.

Carmine stood up and faced the two notification officers. Carmine recognized the bars on the uniforms of the notification officers and instantly knew their ranks. "Major, chaplain. Good morning, sirs." Carmine then gestured to the kitchen area behind them. Before walking into the kitchen, however, Carmine turned to Ann and Betty. "Please take care of Rose while I talk to the officers." The women nodded silently and Carmine joined the officers in the kitchen.

CHAPTER 19

WHAT CAN YOU TELL ME?

C armine began the somber discourse with the notification officers. "So, gentlemen, what can you tell me about my son?" Major O'Brien extended his right hand to Carmine, who respectfully extended his right hand out in response to the major's gesture. One firm handshake and salute later, O'Brien introduced himself and Chaplain Keeney to Vinnie's father. Keeney offered the blessing of Jesus to Carmine, who respectfully thanked him. However, internally, the blessings infuriated Carmine. *How the hell was God blessing my son in Vietnam?* he thought. *Where was Jesus then?*

The chaplain observed the consternation in Carmine's face and he retreated into the recesses of the kitchen in a gesture of deference to Major O'Brien. Distraught, Carmine returned to the living room and sat on the armrest of the couch where Rose lay.

"Sir," began O'Brien, "on behalf of the President of the United States of America, the U.S. Marine Corps, the citizens of our great country, Chaplain Keeney, and myself, I extend the sincerest of condolences to you, your wife, your mother-in-law and, of course, your children. Your son served our country with valor and bravery and he will be greatly missed not only here, but by the men he called brothers back in Vietnam.

"Sir," continued Major O'Brien, "our intelligence reported that your son was struck by a mortar while tending to his government-issued jeep. He never knew what hit him."

Carmine grimaced and peered at the floor and thought, *Vinnie died doing what he loved: fixing a goddamn car.* Carmine, cognizant of the fact that he was not looking at the major, silently scolded himself for disrespecting an officer and returned his eyes to meet Major O'Brien's. He cleared his throat and asked with surprisingly little conviction in his voice, "Was he in any pain before he–"

Carmine caught himself. He paused and cleared his throat again before continuing, with his dignity intact. "Was he in any pain before he passed?"

Major O'Brien did not hesitate: "No, sir. Your son was not in any pain."

Carmine was furious at the irony of finding solace in the fact that his son had died pain-free. "He's a good boy, Major O'Brien," remarked Carmine, once again lapsing into the present tense to describe his deceased son. "Vinnie did everything for everybody and he never expected anything in return. He told me in his letters that his Marine buddies called him 'Saint.'" The grieving father smiled ruefully.

"'Saint' sounds about right when talking about my Vinnie, Major." Carmine placed his paw of a hand over his eyes and rubbed them vigorously before repeating somberly and in the midst of a pained sigh, "Sounds about right."

Major O'Brien knew that Vinnie had returned to his platoon on March 28th instead of staying in the rear for a few more days to recover from his asthma attack, but he chose to not divulge such devastating information to the Santaniello family. Instead, he picked up on the theme established by the father, who was visibly struggling to maintain his composure. "Yes, sir. Saint surely was an appropriate nickname for your son."

Carmine leaned forward and said in a hushed tone so as to not incite Rose, "Sir, what is being done with my son's body?"

"Mr. Santaniello, your son's body was preserved and delicately transported to Japan, where it awaits flight to San Francisco, then to Delaware, and, finally, up to here in New York." The thought of Vinnie's body being contained in a body bag sickened Carmine.

He gasped before continuing, "Sir, my son's body cannot fly across the world alone. He was always there for anyone, be it friend or family. I can't have him fly back here alone."

Major O'Brien was befuddled and didn't know how to respond. Carmine saw the uncertainty in the major's face and immediately reassured him, "Don't worry, Major. I have an idea. My son's best friend from this neighborhood, John Chang, is a corpsman in Vietnam and his tour is ending next month. Vinnie told me that John was spending his last month in Japan. Major O'Brien, I am a veteran of World War II and I need a little courtesy here, sir. I need you to coordinate having John accompany my son home. I can't have Vinnie packed like a goddamn piece of meat on some airplane."

Carmine paused. His voice was exceedingly loud and aggressive. He cast a furtive glance around the room: Randy had a mortified look on his face, Father McLaughlin looked chagrined, and Chaplain Keeney appeared downright distressed.

Carmine sighed and looked to the major, who remained stoic. "I apologize for the disrespect, sir, but this is too much to bear. I loved my son, sir. I loved him more than my own life. Vinnie was more than my son; he was one of my best friends. We did everything together and the neighbors all loved him, too. This ain't easy for anyone in this room, sir. My son enlisted in the Marines; he wasn't drafted. He felt an obligation to serve his country and he did that honorably.

"I know from Vinnie's letters that the boys over there thought as highly of him as the boys back here did. I gotta explain this somehow to his sister, Lilly, who loved him as much as I do. Then I gotta explain this to his kid brother, who's only thirteen. And if that's not bad enough, I hafta tell his girl, Rosalie, who he probably was gonna marry soon after he got back from the war. This is gonna kill them, sir. Kill them all. We ain't never gonna get over this loss, sir. Never.

"Vinnie was gonna be the best man in his sister's wedding in August. Now, what the hell are we supposed to do? What do we do now? Vinnie was the rock of this family, sir. The goddamn rock. And now that rock ain't here no more. He was gonna carry the family name with pride and be a great husband and father. He was supposed to come back here after this here war and be the man that he was destined to be. He was supposed to come back home after Vietnam and be the respected young man that everyone here in our neighborhood looked up to.

"Ya see, Vinnie wasn't just another nineteen-year-old knucklehead. He had a good head on his shoulders and he . . . he was gonna be the man that led this family going forward. And now, all that hope, all that promise, all that greatness, is . . . is done. Over! He ain't here no more. He was killed. And now his body is in a goddamn canvas bag halfway across the world, waiting to be flown home."

"Carmine," interjected Randy, hesitantly and softly, "Carmine, we ain't gonna get Vinnie back alive, but we can get him back with his friend watching guard over his body. Ain't that right, sir?" Randy turned to Major O'Brien and was looking him in the eye when he asked the question.

O'Brien nodded and turned again to Carmine, who was trying his damnedest to not hyperventilate. "Mr. Santaniello, sir, what can you tell me about your son's friend, Chang?"

With that, Carmine proceeded to provide the major with all of the details about John, as he had learned from Vinnie. He even called the Changs and, after audible screams of despair could be heard over the line, the grieving father obtained even more pertinent information about John "Doc" Chang. Over the course of the next hour, Major O'Brien and Carmine discussed how they would coordinate getting John to accompany Vinnie's body on its long journey to its final resting place.

Carmine was pleased that his son would be honored in such a way. And he was so grateful that Vinnie's best buddy from home would be there. *Vinnie would have liked that. John's presence will bring Vinnie's tortured soul peace,* he thought. Once the tentative plans were hashed out with Carmine and the major, the notification officers bid the family adieu. Carmine walked the gentlemen out and saluted each man before shaking their hands and opening the doors to the military vehicle for each officer.

As the chaplain began to enter the vehicle, Carmine placed his right hand on the chaplain's shoulder. Chaplain Keeney was shocked at the tension and sheer strength of his vise-like grip. Carmine leaned over and whispered, "I'm sorry for cursing in there, Father. Please forgive me for my sins. And forgive me for the hatred that is in my heart now. That hatred ain't never leaving my heart, Father. I'm gonna die with that dark anger and hatred in my soul. Please forgive me for that, okay, Father?"

Chaplain Keeney was taken back, yet he understood completely. "God bless you, brother. May the Lord give you strength to overcome this terrible tragedy."

Carmine wasn't satisfied. "Chaplain, I'm filled with rage and anger right now. My son is dead as a result of this war that makes no sense. This ain't World War II, Father. This is Vietnam. *Vietnam!*" Carmine emphasized before choking back tears. He was frustrated and defeated, yet he drew a deep breath and forged on.

"My wife and I don't have our oldest son no more because of this goddamn war. I ain't never going to stop hating the sons of bitches that killed my son. I'm never going to stop hating them. I need you to forgive that sin, Father, because I know that, as a

Roman *Catlick*, I ain't supposed to hate people. I ain't a religious man, but I believe in Heaven and Hell and I want to see my son again in Heaven one day. That's why I need your forgiveness, Chaplain Keeney."

The fire in Carmine's eyes underscored the dire nature of his pleading to the chaplain.

Chaplain Keeney had witnessed much grief over the years in his role as a notification officer for the USMC, but he had never witnessed the sheer unadulterated passion displayed by Carmine Santaniello. He both feared and respected this heartbroken father. Chaplain Keeney pondered his request for a second, silently asked Jesus for strength, and then turned his face to meet the grieving father's pleading eyes.

"Your sins are forgiven, Mr. Santaniello. I pray that your soul may find peace before you meet the Lord on the last day."

And with that, the military vehicle pulled away, leaving Carmine, his silent anguish, and his eternal torment in its wake.

Carmine stood outside well after the military vehicle disappeared out of his sightline. The proud World War II veteran diligently tried to remain stoic but his stomach was burning as if a hole bore into his gut. He swore that day that a piece of his soul joined Vinnie's in the afterlife. He felt alone, empty, cold, and absolutely enraged. Alone and confused, Carmine re-entered his home with balled, tense fists, never to be the same until he breathed his last breath twenty-three years later.

Devastated, Carmine walked through the narrow hallway toward his first-floor residence. He paused by the basement door and placed his right hand gently upon the rickety door. Moments later, he rested his forehead against his hand and in the solemnity of the moment, he swore that he heard Vinnie's voice joyously joining his dad in one of their many basement carpentry adventures.

"He's . . . gone . . . gone . . ." Carmine muttered in a hushed tone before he entered his home to console his wife.

"Rose? Rose, c'mon. We have to be strong for the kids, Rose. This ain't gonna be easy for them and we hafta be strong for 'em."

Rose had summoned the strength to rise from her fetal position on the couch. She was seated on the couch, with her mother by her side. Nunu was gently massaging Rose's neck and shoulder as the distraught mother continued to sob while she rocked back and forth.

Rose peered at her husband but she was having difficulty comprehending him. "What did you say?" Rose asked weakly.

Carmine repeated, "We have to be strong for the kids. This is going to be very difficult for them."

Rose exhaled as her shoulders slumped and her head sunk down toward her upper chest. "How . . . how can I be strong for them when I can't even be strong for myself, Carmine? Vinnie . . . my beloved Vinnie—" Rose's sobs became much more forceful and pained.

The beleaguered mother fought through her grief to continue. "My beloved Vinnie is gone—he's . . . he's DEAD!—and you want me to be calm? CALM? How can anyone be calm now?"

Carmine gritted his teeth and swallowed his rage. "Don't worry about it. I'll take care of this." With that, he turned and walked past Ann, Randy, and Betty, through the kitchen, and out the back door. Carmine lit a cigarette and took a long, measured drag as he peered up at the sky. Strangely, he had the following thought pass through his mind:

My God, my God, why have you forsaken me?

Carmine remembered this expression from the story of the Passion of Christ, which was read during Palm Sunday Mass. Carmine hadn't been to church in years but he recalled that, as a child, he was stricken by the boldness of Jesus as He chided God for allowing Him to die such an excruciatingly painful death on the cross. Carmine was always confused by this moment and he remembered being a little upset that Jesus had the temerity to question his Father. However, now, as he peered up at the vast blue sky, he understood Jesus's exacerbation at that moment.

Carmine knew.

As he looked up at the heavens, searching for a sign that his son was at peace, he said aloud, "My God, my God, why have you forsaken me?" Carmine then looked longingly at the sky, hoping against hope that he would be given a sign that his son was at peace.

And then the phone rang.

Carmine re-entered his house. Rose had not moved and she did not even acknowledge that the phone was ringing. He proceeded to the telephone. Randy, Ann, and Betty were seated around the small dining room table. Carmine cleared his throat and answered the telephone.

"Hello?" Silence. "Hello?" More silence. "Hel–"

Carmine heard rustling, followed immediately by, "Is this the Santaniello residence?" The strange voice sounded like a young man, likely not much older than Vinnie.

"Yes, yes it is," replied Carmine. "Who's this? How can I help you?"

"I saw a military vehicle in front of your house this morning. Was your son in Vietnam?"

A chill spread slowly through Carmine's body. "Yes, yes he was. Who the hell is this?" His voice became louder and angrier as he questioned the unknown caller.

"Is your son dead, sir?"

The question tore right through Carmine and actually caused him to wince in pain. "Wha–what was that?" Carmine was befuddled and agitated.

"Your son, sir. Was he killed in Vietnam?"

Pain streaked across Carmine's brain like a wayward missile. "Yes, yes he was."

Randy gestured toward his friend, as he could see the discomfort on his face. "Car, who is it? What's going on?"

Carmine could not even begin to register a response to Randy's question before the voice on the other end of the call bellowed in an ear-piercing, crazed manner: "I'M SO GLAD THAT BABY-KILLING, MARINE DOG IS DEAD! HE WAS A NO-GOOD PIECE OF SHIT! FUCK HIM AND FUCK YOU! I HOPE HE ROTS IN HELL!"

The line went dead.

Carmine clenched the phone receiver in his hand and gulped hard. He had barely processed the notion that his nineteen-year-old son and best friend was dead and now he was thrust into dealing with such a terrible, anonymous call. Carmine peered around the room and saw that everyone—except Rose, who remained oblivious in her own cocoon of dread—was looking at him. They had all heard the callous, dastardly words of the manic caller and they were stunned.

Carmine, whose heart was pumping rapidly, smashed the phone receiver down on the cradle, causing everyone—even Rose—to jump, startled. He then turned and retreated again toward the yard. Randy began to follow him but Carmine thrust his left arm behind him and held up his hand, without breaking his stride, to silently advise Randy not to take another step. Randy stopped dead in his tracks as Carmine continued into the backyard, leaned against Vinnie's favorite tree, the cherry tree, and reflected on what had transpired. Irrepressible rage was overcoming him.

The phone rang again.

Carmine's rage and profane thoughts were so overwhelming that he did not hear the shrill ring of the telephone from where he stood in the back yard.

Rose answered the phone.

"Hello?" Rose's voice was weak and distant.

"Is this the Santaniello home?" The voice sounded very serene and respectful to the despondent Rose.

"Why, yes it is," she replied. "Who is this, please?"

"THAT PIECE-OF-SHIT, BABY-KILLING MARINE SONOFABITCH SON OF YOURS GOT WHAT HE DESERVED! I HOPE HE ROTS IN HELL!"

Rose gasped and fainted into Randy's arms, who had been running in from the kitchen in a vain effort to get to the phone before Rose answered it. Randy caught Rose and simultaneously grabbed the plummeting receiver, roaring into it, "Who are you, you goddamn coward?"

Randy heard a man snicker, followed by a click. The line was dead. "Goddamn piece-of-shit hippies," Randy muttered. He handed the phone to his wife before laying Rose on the couch, next to her distraught mother.

Carmine walked in shortly after this incident, oblivious to what had occurred. No one dared tell him, for fear that his rage would cause him to react in a manner that would worsen an already-terrible situation. Randy surreptitiously walked to the phone, removed the receiver from the unit, placed it in such a manner as to make it appear that the phone was hung up while it was, in fact, off the hook. Randy knew that Carmine would not be able to tolerate another cowardly, anonymous person calling to revel in the profound misery that had engulfed the Santaniello home.

Rose had come to and had a wet rag on her forehead. Nunu, Ann, and Betty were seated around her on the couch, each taking turns consoling the grieving, heartbroken mother. Carmine stared at the clock. It was 2:00 p.m. and he knew that his younger son would be home from school in less than an hour. Lilly worked at an office in New York City and the subway ride from Downtown Manhattan back to Jamaica, Queens was an hour under optimal conditions, so she wouldn't be home until 6:00 p.m. at the earliest.

Carmine pulled a chair to the front of the couch and he sat on it before leaning forward to draw closer to his devastated wife. "Rose, we gotta try to be strong for our children." Rose nodded, but Carmine knew that she was going to be a mess. He turned to the people in the room. "Would you mind staying here until after we tell the kids? I'm gonna need your help." Everyone immediately pledged their assistance and remained seated amidst the suffocating despair.

Shortly before 3:00 p.m., everyone within the house heard the voice of Vinnie's twelve-year-old brother. He entered the home after saying goodbye to the friends who had accompanied him on their walk home from Presentation of the Blessed Virgin Mary, the small Catholic school on Parsons Boulevard.

Joseph was an eighth-grader and he was set to graduate in June. He was a handsome young boy with slick brown hair that was neatly combed and parted on the left side. Similarly to Lilly, Joseph had dark-brown eyes and a slightly olive complexion. The youngster entered the house in his school uniform: a white collared shirt, a burgundy tie emblazoned with the yellow vertical initials *PBVM*, brown pants, and his well-worn Buster Brown shoes.

Joseph ran into the house and was taken aback by everyone in the small living room. He smiled nervously as he peered around the room. He noticed that his mother would not look up at him and then he was surprised to see his father—Carmine never got home from work before 5:30 p.m. For a second, Joseph feared that his grandmother had died earlier in the day, but then he observed Nunu tucked behind Randy and Betty in the corner of the packed living room.

Joseph nervously asked, "Pop, why are you home so early? What happened?"

"Joseph," began his father, "sit down, son." The youngster obediently sat on the small loveseat perpendicular to the couch where his mom was sitting. He snuck a peek at his mom's face, which was mostly concealed with her hands, yet he still observed that she was crying. Joseph felt all of the eyes on him and that overwhelmed him. He peeked again at his mother before he was overcome and began to weep.

Nervous and confused, Joseph looked to his father and said between sobs, "Pop, please tell me what's wrong."

Carmine walked over to his younger son and placed his hand on his son's shoulder. "Joseph, it's your brother, Vinnie, son. He . . . he . . . he–" Carmine's voice suddenly quit on him and he couldn't finish his sentence. He coughed a couple of times to clear the lump in his throat and then swallowed hard before divulging the heartbreaking news.

"Son, Vinnie died in Vietnam last Thursday. Your big brother is in Heaven now, with his Uncle Vinnie, looking down on us."

Joseph couldn't breathe.

The twelve-year-old child began to cry and Carmine wrapped his muscular right arm around the shuddering shoulder of his confused, devastated son. Rose sighed loudly and snuggled her nose into the side of her boy's face, kissing him repeatedly as she continued to cry. Randy patted Joseph's head, messing up his immaculately greased hair. Nunu sat ashen in the corner of the far couch while Betty and Ann stood in the periphery of the cramped living room, silently weeping.

Carmine, Rose, Nunu, and the neighbors all took turns consoling the youngster as he asked a series of questions for which no one had an answer. Vinnie was dead and no one could explain to him why or how. Sadly, everyone in the room shared Joseph's questions.

The clock was ticking closer to the moment that everyone in the room dreaded: Lilly's arrival from work.

Carmine advised his neighbors that they should leave; there was no need for them to linger for what promised to be a terrible occasion. Everyone assured Carmine that they wanted to stay to lend support to Lilly, who was the oldest of all of the neighborhood kids and therefore viewed as every kid's honorary oldest sister. The sharp, stern glance of rebuke that Carmine shot in the general direction of the well-meaning neighbors convinced each of them that their presence, kind-hearted though it may have been, was not desired. Each of the somber visitors filed out quietly, but not before

346

respectfully patting, hugging, and kissing the forlorn Santaniellos who remained huddled on the couch.

Lilly unlocked the front door and traipsed into the hallway, as per her custom, at 6:35 p.m.

*   *   *

"Ma, Pa, I'm home! Ma, what's for dinner?"

Nunu was upstairs in her bed. The stress of the day had taken a terrible toll on her and, not wanting to witness Lilly's heart-wrenching reaction to the tragic news, she retreated to her bedroom minutes before Lilly's anticipated arrival. Everyone heard the familiar *CLUMP!* of Lilly dropping her bag to the floor in the hallway, which was followed immediately thereafter by the muffled sound of her steps as she approached the door to their home. Lilly also customarily kicked off her high-heeled shoes and slipped her feet into the slippers that she left adjacent to a free-standing mirror perched in the middle of the small hallway, just beyond the foyer area.

The twenty-one-year-old Lilly had an extra bounce to her step on this day. At Vinnie's request, she had shared one of his letters with her officemates and everyone had agreed to chip in for a nice care package that would be mailed to him the following morning. They put together a box of candy, gum, newspapers, comics, a few months' worth of *Playboy*s, letters from a few workers, and various trinkets that were scrounged up from the office. One young lady who found Vinnie handsome inscribed her name and phone number on a scrap of paper and sprayed it with her perfume as an added bonus.

Lilly had laughed at this woman. "Sandy, you're such a jackass. My brother ain't gonna be interested in you. He's goin' steady with a local gal and they're probably gonna end up hitched!"

Undeterred, Sandy rolled her eyes and exclaimed in a hopeful voice, "Ya never know, Lil!"

The thought of this spontaneous show of love and affection for her little brother and best friend still was fresh in Lilly's mind when she dropped her bag, kicked off her high heels, and stopped to stare intently at the mirror in the hallway. Rose used to give Lilly a hard time about this habit because she mistakenly believed that Lilly was gazing at herself. However, Rose came to learn that Lilly had shoved into the corner of the mirror—at eye level—a Snoopy doodle that Vinnie had drawn for her when he was home last. Lilly placed the drawing in the mirror when Vinnie left for Vietnam to ensure that she'd see it every day and therefore stop and think about her brother as soon as she got home from work.

Lilly gazed at the drawing and gently rubbed it with her right hand as she thought, *I miss you so much, Vin. I can't wait 'til you come home in a few months for my wedding. You're gonna look so handsome in those dress blues!*

Lilly's thoughts were interrupted by the sound of . . . nothing. The house was too quiet. Usually, she'd hear the radio or television blaring or she'd hear her parents talking loudly. She heard absolutely nothing now and that alarmed her. She hoped that nothing had happened to Nunu. She reached for the doorknob to enter her residence.

Carmine was sitting with his head in his hands, wondering how the hell was he supposed to tell his daughter that her best friend was dead. Rose remained in a stupor, so she wasn't going to be of any assistance in this endeavor. Their youngest child was in his room with his blanket over his head so that Lilly wouldn't hear his cries when she got home. Carmine dreaded the looming creak of the turning doorknob. It would herald an overwhelming gloom that would linger for the remainder of their days.

The doorknob creaked.

"Goddamn it," Carmine muttered.

CHAPTER 20

AN EMPTY SOUL

April 1, 1968. At 6:30 p.m., Lilly exited the E train after an hour ride on the subway from her job in Lower Manhattan. She emerged from the subterranean labyrinth of tracks and hot, overcrowded subway cars that creaked and jostled with humanity and, after scaling the staircase up to the corner of Hillside Avenue and 169th Street in Jamaica, Queens, she realized that the unseasonably warm sun had completed its descent into the depths of the blood-red western sky and that the moon had risen in its wake. The sky was enveloped in a thicket of black and the coolness of the night air had suppressed the hope of the day's warmth. The heavens glowed with the glimmering remnants of stars that were long gone, yet still shined brightly on the Earth that was light years away from them.

During Vinnie's time in Vietnam, Lilly had a habit of looking up at the stars on her daily evening walks home from the 169th Street subway station. She imagined that he simultaneously was looking up at the very same stars. She often asked Vinnie in her letters to look up at the stars in the smoky Vietnam sky and feel comfort in knowing that his beloved sister may well be looking at that very same star, at that very moment, halfway across the world. Of course, Vietnam was eleven hours ahead of New York time, but that didn't stop the young siblings from imagining this possibility. Vinnie advised his sister that it began to get dark in Vietnam at approximately 5:30 p.m., so she'd have to look at a star early in the morning if he had any shot of peering at the same constellation halfway across the globe.

Indeed, there was one such letter in which Lilly picked a date and time, four weeks into the future to allow ample time for the letter to arrive in Vietnam. Lilly advised Vinnie that she'd go to the backyard at 6:30 a.m. on the date specified, look up in the sky, and make a wish on the first star that she saw. She instructed Vinnie to do the same thing at 5:30 p.m. in Vietnam. Lilly wrote that she believed that God would make sure that they made a wish on the same star at that time.

Vinnie chuckled out loud when he read this letter. *That Lilly,* he mused, *she's a real hoot!* The bemused younger brother wrote back to Lilly, "Don't worry, ugly. I will make the wish on that date. I ain't gonna miss it, even if I have to dance between incoming arty! It would be really groovy to wish on the same star, you knucklehead! I wouldn't miss this opportunity for the world."

Lilly picked *March 28, 1968* for the mutual wish.

The twenty-one-year-old peered up into the still-dark morning sky at precisely 6:30 a.m. and she immediately marveled at what she felt was the brightest star she'd ever seen in her life.

That star is so big and so bright, Lilly thought. *I bet that Vinnie can see it all the way over there in Vietnam.*

Lilly had then wished for the same thing that she prayed for every night before going to bed: Vinnie's continued safety in a faraway, scary place. She went to work that morning with a smile on her face, happily believing that Vinnie had simultaneously wished upon that same star.

*　　　*　　　*

"Pop, why is everyone so quiet? Why is it so dark in here? Why are Ma and Joseph crying? Where is Nunu? Oh, my God, is she okay? Did something happen to Nunu?"

Lilly's forehead creased and the pupils in her dark-brown eyes widened in their struggle to overcome the darkness that enveloped the small home. Lilly shot a furtive glance toward her mother, who was weeping, and Joseph, who had a blanket over his head so as to not expose his palpable grief. His face was obscured from Lilly's careful glance, but she could see the rising and falling of his shoulders, which she interpreted to mean that he was crying.

The pit in Lilly's abdomen worsened and she began to tremble. She walked into the dining room area and stopped a few feet from her father.

"Pop, please . . . what's going on? Is Nunu okay?" Lilly blinked rapidly and cast a scared look at her dad, a look that pierced his very soul.

"Lilly," Carmine began before abruptly stopping. He got choked up. Carmine cleared his throat and began anew the arduous task of delivering such life-shattering news.

"Come 'ere, sweetheart."

Lilly approached Carmine and he placed his right arm around her shoulder.

"Nunu's fine; she's just upstairs. Lil–" resumed Carmine, before he was interrupted by another impromptu, pregnant pause. *Goddammit*, he thought.

Carmine tightened his grasp of Lilly's shoulder. He inhaled and after a long, solemn breath, he pursed his lips and began to speak.

"Li–"

"It's Vinnie, ain't it?" Lilly interrupted her father in a breathless whisper that even she barely heard.

Carmine, the absolute rock of the family and a proud man, winced and began to silently weep, all the while maintaining a firm, loving grasp on his daughter's shoulder.

"Vinnie ain't comin' home alive, right, Pa?"

Lilly's voice remained barely audible yet absolutely resolute.

"That's right, sweetheart. Your brother," Carmine cleared his throat, "your brother was killed in the war."

Lilly's knees buckled and her chin descended into her bosom as she began to weep.

She asked between sobs, "When?"

Carmine kissed his daughter's forehead and struggled to say, "Last Thursday, March—"

"Twenty-eighth?" Lilly completed her father's sentence in an exasperated fashion. She stopped crying and the pain in her shattering heart was temporarily supplanted with unadulterated scorn.

She asked again, "Vinnie was killed on March 28th? What time?"

Carmine looked puzzled and said, "I don't know exactly when, but the chaplain who came to the house earlier told us that he was killed by a mortar right around noon, Vietnam time."

Lilly suddenly felt weak and dizzy. Bile assaulted her throat as she struggled to breathe. Lilly realized that Vinnie never got to wish on the star that evening, even though he promised that he would.

Lilly's mind wandered back to the morning of March 28, 1968, when she looked up and was immediately drawn to the biggest, brightest star she'd ever seen.

Oh, my God, he was dead before I wished on the star here.

Lilly tensed up, so much so that Carmine was startled.

"Lilly, you alright?"

No reply.

"Lil?"

The devastated young lady bent her knees so as to free herself from her father's loving grasp and she walked briskly toward the front door.

"Lilly!" Carmine bellowed, "Where are you going?"

No response.

Carmine pounded the dining room table with his fist, causing the table and the nearby china cabinet to rattle loudly.

"Goddammit, answer me!" Carmine was at his wit's end and Lilly's sudden unwillingness to engage infuriated him. Rose snapped out her fog at the sound of Carmine's angry tone and she shot him a look of consternation.

"Lil," Carmine asked in a much more soothing, parental tone, "talk to me, sweetheart. How are you feeling?"

Lilly stopped but did not turn around to face her father. She took a deep breath, exhaled, and replied in a low, raspy voice, "How am I feeling? My brother is dead. He was supposed to make a wish upon a star with me a few hours after he was killed. He was supposed to be the best man in my wedding this summer. He was supposed to be the godfather of my first child. He was supposed to always be there for me—for us!"

Lilly gasped. Her voice no longer was low and raspy. Conversely, it rose as she spoke, like a crescendo in a riveting operatic performance. Tears streamed down and shrouded her pain-stricken face in streaks of dark mascara and eyeshadow. Her beautiful face was transformed into a ghoul-like, ominous appearance that befit such a horrific occasion.

She shrieked loudly, "I was supposed to be there for him. Instead, he died alone, somewhere across the damn world, and I wasn't there for him."

Lilly cried uncontrollably before mustering the courage to continue.

"I wasn't there for him," she repeated. "When he was dying out there, he probably was thinking of his family and . . . and . . . we were half a world away from him. What if he died alone, Pa, and his last thoughts were about us?"

The question pierced Carmine's heart and caused him to wince.

Lilly's mind was going a thousand miles an hour and suddenly she thought of the star that she'd wished upon on March 28th. It was the biggest, brightest star she'd ever seen in her life. The sky was full of stars that morning but when she looked up, *that* star was the first one that she saw. It was the first and only star that caught and kept her attention.

"Oh, God," she whispered, "that was him. That was no star; it was Vinnie. He was looking down on me from Heaven."

Lilly heaved and her knees buckled as the realization that her beloved Vinnie really was dead began to sink in. Lilly thrust out her arm and leaned her hand against the closet door, to steady herself. She exhaled as a fresh stream of salty tears cascaded down her flushed cheeks.

The forlorn young lady peered over her shoulder, toward her unsuspecting father. The darkened hollows around her eyes and the spiraling sinews of black mascara and eyeshadow that stained her face stood in stark contrast to her pale complexion. Lilly's ghastly appearance startled Carmine. He thought that she resembled a corpse.

"How am I feeling, Pa?" Lilly repeated her dad's inquiry with a hint of scorn, but in a low and steady monotone. "How'm I feeling? I feel like my soul is empty, Pa. I feel dead inside. My soul died with Vinnie. That's how I'm feeling."

With that, the downtrodden older sister turned her head and reflected upon how the rest of her life would now lack meaning and purpose. Lilly walked into the hallway and past the now-dreaded hallway mirror. She stole a glance at Vinnie's artwork—more tears erupted from her eyes, causing Vinnie's Snoopy character to morph into a blurry sea of despair—before running through the doors and out of the house. She needed to talk to her best friend and next-door neighbor: Ann Graves's twenty-one-year-old daughter, Marie.

Left behind in Lilly's wake were three confused mourners: Rose, who'd been in a stupor the entire day; Joseph, who was struggling with the notion that his big brother was gone; and Carmine, who was resisting the urge to go absolutely fucking berserk.

Lilly ran into the Graves home, which adjoined the Santaniello residence, and Ann Graves burst into tears when she saw the profound agony in Lilly's face. Ann thrust out her arms and Lilly didn't hesitate to nestle into them. Ann was a second mom to the bereaved Lilly and her warm hug was greatly appreciated.

"Oh, Lilly," Ann struggled to exclaim through her own tears, "I'm so sorry, sweetheart. Losing Vinnie like this hurts all of us so much!"

"What am I gonna do, Mrs. Graves?" Lilly asked rhetorically. "I'm so empty. I'm lost without my brother. He was my best friend. What am I gonna do now that he's gone . . . *forever?*" Lilly accentuated the last word and let out a grief-stricken shriek.

Vinnie, Lilly's bright beacon of hope, was snuffed out so cruelly and suddenly. Vinnie, her beloved big-little brother. What was she going to do without him?

Ann kissed Lilly on her forehead and the young woman proceeded to run into Marie's bedroom. Ann wanted to follow her into her daughter's bedroom but the cacophony of painful wails that began an instant later forestalled Ann's efforts.

The two lifelong friends proceeded to cry and curse the world until late into the night. Shortly after midnight, Lilly retreated to the Graves's backyard and she climbed over the short dividing fence to get into her own yard. The chill of the night air caused Lilly's teeth to chatter as the howling wind stung her tear-streaked face. However, she refused to surrender to the cold and retreat inside. Instead, shivering and undeterred by the overcast night sky, Lilly slumped down against the trunk of Vinnie's erstwhile favorite, the cherry tree, and, between tears and chattering teeth, peered at the heavens.

"Where are you, Vinnie? Where are you, goddammit?" Lilly muttered as she gazed across the great expanse of sky.

Seconds melted into minutes, and minutes elapsed by the dozen, but the beleaguered woman remained steadfastly perched against the tree trunk, like a night owl scanning a field for prey. By 2:00 a.m., Lilly was fighting exhaustion and fatigue.

"Carmine, please go out there and get Lilly in here," beseeched Rose, looking out of her bedroom window from the edge of her bed in their darkened room. Carmine was leaning against the warm radiator adjacent to the window as he, too, was watching Lilly. He knew that Lilly was cold and tired but he also knew that she was determined to accomplish whatever it was that she intended *alone*.

"No, I can't disturb her, but I will keep an eye on her to make sure that she's okay. Close your eyes and rest, Rose. It's been a terrible day for all of us. I'll let you know when Lilly's back inside." Carmine had never stopped looking at Lilly while he spoke to Rose and the nestling sound that followed assured him that his grief-stricken spouse had taken his advice.

"Vinnie," Lilly whispered in a shivering voice, "please show me a sign that you are at peace. Please help me know that you are okay. I can't believe that you're actually gone. I can't imagine living my life without you.

"You promised that you'd be okay in Vietnam when you left us last summer and I believed you. You always sugarcoated what was *really* happening over there in your letters and, even though I wanted to believe you, I knew that you were full of shit. All the news reported was death and destruction and yet you made it sound like you were on an extended recess in school."

Lilly bowed her head and cultivated yet another round of tears. Nonetheless, she forged on in her painful soliloquy. "I even tried to delude myself into believing that you were telling the truth about Vietnam and that I had nothing to worry about.

"I'm angry, Vinnie." Lilly sighed and exclaimed the following, with pauses between each word as she struggled to define the sorrow in her heart: "I am angry . . . betrayed . . . confused . . . hurt . . . terrified . . . and devastated. My soul is empty, Vin. We were inseparable and we needed each other.

"Now, all I have are your letters, your tapes, and your pictures. They will fade and yellow but I will never allow your memory to fade from my heart, soul, and mind. Vinnie, I love you. I will always love you and I'll never forget you for so long as I live. You'll always be my big-little brother, and I'll always be your stupid, little-big sister." Lilly gestured with her hands as she spoke to her brother, whose spirit she believed was high above her, intermingled with the vast darkness of the cloud-riddled night sky.

"All I need is one thing." Lilly held up her right hand and thrust her index finger toward the sky as she said this. "Please show me a sign that you're okay. Show me that you're at peace. Please." Lilly wiped her eyes as she spoke to the vast heavens.

Carmine continued to watch from the bedroom window. Although it was dark, he deduced from Lilly's gestures that she was "talking" to Vinnie.

That's it, he thought. *I gotta get her.*

However, at that very moment, he observed the moon emerge from behind the clouds and suddenly Lilly was aglow with moonlight. Carmine was transfixed at the window.

Lilly blinked rapidly as her eyes remained fixed on the brightening sky. A smile slowly emerged as Lilly saw something else besides the moon emerge from behind the clouds. Indeed, adjacent to the full moon was a bright star. And not just *any* star: It was the same one that she had observed back on March 28th. It was the largest and brightest star that she had ever seen.

Lilly smiled.

"Hi, Vin. Thanks for letting me know that you're at peace and still with me. Now I know why I saw that big star back on March 28th. It was you, trying to let me know that you were in heaven and at peace. I love you, Vinnie, and I will ALWAYS love you, more than anything in my life. You will always be the brightest star in my life, big-little brother. The pain will never go away, but I will take comfort in knowing that you are at peace now . . . and forever.

"I love you, Vinnie. I love you, I love you, I love you, I love you, I love you. And I will miss you for as long as I live. God bless you, Saint.

"Please keep watching over me and don't ever forget about me."

With that, Lilly propped herself up from the ground at the base of Vinnie's cherry tree. Oddly, she was at peace as she opened the back door and re-entered her home at 2:45 a.m. The bright moonlight illuminated the kitchen and Lilly saw the profile of her dad, standing in the dark, just a few feet away.

"Hey, Lilly," Carmine said in a low, reassuring tone, "come here." Lilly walked toward her father and began to weep as she sunk into his warm, comforting, and strong arms.

"I know, sweetheart, I know," Carmine said as he gently stroked Lilly's hair.

"It ain't fair, Pop. It ain't right that Vinnie was killed over there," Lilly exclaimed. "What are we gonna do without him?"

Carmine was stumped. He instinctively opened his mouth to speak. However, the words escaped him. "I . . . I don't know, Lil. I just don't know."

With that, Carmine escorted Lilly to her bedroom, with an arm draped around her shoulder. Lilly thanked her father and kissed him goodnight. Carmine began to leave the room but turned around and walked back to his daughter, who was sitting on the edge of her bed. He bent over to meet her eyes with his.

"I love you, Lilly."

"I love you, too, Pop. Good night."

Carmine rose, turned his back to Lilly, and walked out of her room while wiping tears from his eyes.

*   *   *

Lilly woke up the next morning and realized that she had two calls to make. First, she called her workplace. Her friend, Sandy, the receptionist, answered the telephone. This, of course, was the same young lady who had written her phone number on a piece of paper and then sprayed her perfume on it before placing it in the office's care package for Vinnie. Lilly advised Sandy of the terrible news and the ensuing shriek pierced Lilly's ears something fierce. Twenty minutes later, Lilly hung up and dialed Rosalie's phone number.

"Hello?"

Lilly was relieved that Rosalie answered the phone. She began, "Hey, Ro, it's Lil, how ya doin'?"

Rosalie peered at the clock and saw that it was 8:30 a.m. "Why are you at work so early, Lil? You usually don't get there before a quarter to nine."

Lilly replied, "I'm not at work today, Roe. I stayed home."

"Why, are ya sick?"

Lilly hesitated. "Rosalie, why don't you come over my house this morning?"

The nineteen-year-old Rosalie was dumbstruck. She and Lilly were good friends, but the request—out of the blue, no less—was weird. "Lilly, what's wrong?"

Lilly cleared her throat and simply repeated, "Come over, Roe, okay? I gotta go now. Uh, the dogs need to go outside. See ya soon. Bye."

Rosalie exclaimed into the receiver, "Hello? Hello? Lil?" A dial tone ensued.

Vinnie's girlfriend nervously ate breakfast, washed up, and told her parents that she was going to the Santaniellos. Rosalie's parents did not flinch at the pronouncement—their daughter spent ample time at her boyfriend's home despite the fact that he was away at war. Her parents knew that the Santaniellos were quality people and that Vinnie was a great kid. In fact, Rosalie's mom hoped that her daughter would marry Vinnie after he returned from Vietnam.

Thirty minutes later, the doorbell rang at the Santaniello home. Lilly ran to answer the door and she actually walked out and greeted Rosalie on the porch. The crisp morning air was pleasing. The weather wasn't nearly as warm as the previous day, but the coolness was comforting.

"Hey, Roe," said Lilly, "thanks for coming by."

Rosalie noticed an ominous change in Lilly's demeanor. Her friend seemed distracted and sad. "Lilly, please tell me what's wrong. I've been a nervous wreck since you called me out-of-the-blue this morning and told me that you weren't going to work."

Lilly diverted her eyes from Rosalie and turned her back to her friend. "Roe," she said without turning around, "I . . . I have bad news."

Confused, Rosalie placed her hand on Lilly's shoulder and asked, "Did Ralph break up with you? Are you calling off the wedding?" Lilly noticeably flinched but did not otherwise react to Rosalie's questions.

"Lilly!" Rosalie's voice was forceful and loud. The young lady's confusion was replaced with consternation. "You made me come here and now you're ignoring me. What the hell is going on?"

Lilly sensed the rancor in Rosalie's voice and turned to face her friend. Rosalie was stricken by Lilly's tear-streaked face and the empty look in her eyes.

She knew before Lilly could open her mouth.

"Roe," Lilly began in a pitiful monotone, "Vinnie was–" Lilly cleared her throat and turned around again to glance toward the corner where Vinnie used to hang out and sing with his pals. After a few seconds of awkward silence, she continued. "Vinnie was . . . he was killed in Vietnam last Thursday, Rosalie.

"He ain't with us no more."

"No. *No!* NOOOOOO!" Rosalie collapsed, shrieking, on the porch.

Ann and Marie ran out of their house next door as Carmine ran out of his own house. They all witnessed Rosalie in a fetal position on the porch, retching in an uncontrollable fit of rage and despair.

"Oh, God, not Vinnie! Not Vinnie! How could he die?" Rosalie thought of the engagement ring that she and Vinnie had picked out before he left for boot camp. "He was gonna be my–" Rosalie caught herself but the tears did not relent.

"Oh, Mr. Santaniello," she said as Carmine helped her up off the porch and embraced her in a fatherly fashion. "How could this happen, Mr. Santaniello? There's gotta be some mistake here! He can't be dead! Oh, my God . . . Vinnie can't be dead. He can't be!"

Rosalie looked at Carmine through a torrent of tears and the look in his eyes confirmed that the love of her life—the man of her dreams, her future husband—would be seen only in her dreams for the remainder of her days.

Carmine turned and re-entered his home. Rosalie turned to Lilly and asked, "How can I ever read all the letters that Vinnie wrote to me from Vietnam, Lil? They are all I have left of him and I don't know if I'll ever have the strength to look at them ever again."

Lilly looked directly at Rosalie and said, "I have dozens and dozens of letters from my brother that I will cherish forever. It'll hurt like hell, but I'm gonna save 'em in a special place."

Rosalie was nearly delirious and these words befuddled her. "How can you do that, Lil. How? They will be a constant reminder that Vinnie– that he . . ." Rosalie gasped and choked out the remainder of her feelings amidst heaves and snorts, "Those letters will be a constant reminder that Vinnie is dead!"

Lilly stared at her distraught friend and replied, "Roe, Vinnie's letters are more important to me than anything else in my life because . . . because . . ." Lilly stammered and began to cry. However, she grew angry at her weakness, so she cleared her throat and completed her thought with conviction.

"I'll always cherish and read Vinnie's letters 'cause they are a saint's letters from the depths of Hell.

"Vinnie'll always be alive and well in those letters!"

With that, Lilly walked defiantly into the uncertainty that was the rest of her life.

Conversely, Rosalie remained on the porch, numb and resigned to the fact that she intended to get rid of the letters and pictures that Vinnie had sent her. They would only serve as a constant reminder of his absence. Sadly, she knew that maintaining such artifacts would drive her mad.

*   *   *

Thursday, April 4, 1968. Rose, Carmine, Lilly, Joseph, and Nunu were seated around the dining room table, finishing up dinner. The table was eerily silent during dinner, just as it had been for the last three days since everyone had learned of Vinnie's death. Once again, Rose barely ate. Instead, she poked a fork at the food, peering absently at her plate and then at Vinnie's empty chair on the opposite side of the table. Lilly became increasingly uncomfortable with the morbid silence; her unfettered mind imagined what Vinnie's final moments must have been like and the images that she conjured up were disturbing.

"Ma, Pa," Lilly respectfully asked, "since we're all finished up with dinner, ya mind if I turn the TV on?"

"Go ahead, Lil," responded her father. "We could use a little distraction from what's been going on here."

It was 6:30 p.m. when Lilly walked over to the thirteen-inch, black-and-white TV in the living room and pulled a knob to turn it on. Next, she adjusted the antennas situated atop the small box until the picture on the screen was relatively static-free. She twisted the channel knob until she came to channel two and then turned a separate knob to increase the volume.

The news anchor was somberly recounting something that had happened in Memphis, Tennessee. Lilly adjusted the antennas again so that she could clearly hear what the news anchor was saying and her mouth became agape.

"Ma, Pa . . . Martin Luther King was shot on a balcony a few moments ago and the news is saying that he is . . . dead."

Rose lowered her head and asked rhetorically, "What's going on with our world?"

Lilly observed, "Too much death and hatred, if ya ask me."

CHAPTER 21

DOC CHANG AND THE GODDAMN BABY KILLER

*M*onday, April 15, 1968. Okinawa, Japan. John "Doc" Chang, Third Class Petty Officer HM3, arrived at the USMC base in the early evening to ride out the final days of his tour in Vietnam. Having been in the throes of active combat only hours earlier, Chang now was in a state of nirvana.

Upon arriving at the clean, quiet base, John marveled at his good fortune. *I made it. I fucking made it out of the shit, alive and in one piece. Holy shit, what luck. I do a month here and then I get to go back to my family in the real world, get a job, and start a family of my own.*

John didn't know what to do with himself and his newfound freedom. So, at 1900 hours, he took his first hot shower in almost a year. Refreshed and clean, John eyed the huge bunk that he had in his quarters. Chang hadn't slept in a real bed since he'd left home for boot camp, and the sprawling bunk was too tempting to resist. The corpsman eschewed chow and instead dove onto the enticing bed.

Golly, I haven't had a bed this comfortable EVER! John thought. *I could get used to this!*

John nestled his head into the comfortable pillow and fell into a deep sleep within seconds. For the first time in what seemed like forever, John slept comfortably and without interruption. It was too soon for the PTSD nightmares to become entrenched in John's psyche—that torture was yet to come. For now, Chang slept like a baby and actually relished an experience he had forgotten: silence.

Unfortunately, the solitude was fleeting.

"Doc, Doc? Wake up, Doc, quick!" A young Marine corporal, equal in status to John, nudged Chang's shoulder. Initially, John did not move, as he was in a deep sleep. John was so lost in his dreams that the corporal initially feared that his colleague had the terrible misfortune of having survived Vietnam only to die in the solitude of Okinawa.

A flinch of the slumbering Doc's shoulders alleviated the corporal's trepidation.

"Doc, Doc? C'mon, WAKE UP!"

"*Mmmmmmmppphhhh* . . . huh? Wha–?" John suddenly snapped upright. "Where's the body? Who's hurt? Where's my morphine drip and needles? Get the gauze and tubes for the tracheotomy, quickly!"

"Doc," reassured the corporal, "the war's over for you. You ain't in the shit no more. You're in Japan now. Remember?"

John shook the cobwebs—and the early seeds of his forthcoming PTSD—from his head and regained his bearings. "Oh, yeah, I forgot I was here. I was just sewing up a Marine's gut about twenty-four hours ago, so you'll hafta excuse me if I forget that I ain't there anymore!"

The corporal nodded his understanding. "Understood. But you still have to get up and get dressed on the double because the commanding officer wants you in his office right now."

John nearly fell out of his bunk.

"Holy shit!" John exclaimed. "The full bird wants to see me? Get the fuck out of here! There must be some mistake; I ain't done nothing wrong!"

Vietnam made the guys so paranoid that, when something out of the ordinary occurred like getting called into the commanding officer's office, a Marine expected the worst, even if the Marine practically knew that he had done nothing wrong. Chang was no different.

"Shit," Doc Chang continued, "I just got here and I sure as shit don't want Uncle Sam to find a reason to send me back to combat! They got the wrong guy, pal. I ain't done shit and they are gonna try to pin some shit on me." Chang sighed. "Goddammit!" Chang spat out his reaction and then slowly retrieved his hat, tucked in his shirt, and traipsed toward the rear, to the full bird's opulent office.

As Chang came upon the entrance to the office, a familiar nausea set in his abdomen and he swore that he could smell burning, rotting flesh wafting through the air again.

"Good morning, Colonel, sir. Corpsman John Chang, Third Class Petty Officer HM3, here." John did not salute the superior officer because they were indoors, but he stood erectly.

"At ease, Chang. Have a seat." John sat down and tried to project a demeanor that belied his apprehension at having been summoned to the commanding officer's office.

"Listen, Chang, we got a call from a Mr. and Mrs. Santaniello from back in New York."

Chang's mind instantly began to race, even as he observed the full bird's mouth continuing to move. *Why would Carmine and Rose be calling? Oh, man, did Nunu die? Did someone get hurt back home?* John thought before refocusing on the colonel. He was staring at John as if expecting a response. *Oh, shit,* he thought. *The full bird just asked me a fucking question and I have no idea what he said! I'm heading back to the shit for sure now.*

The poor bastard, thought the colonel. *He must be in total shock over this.*

John was in full panic mode. *What do I do now? What the fuck do I say?* "I'm sorry. Could you repeat that, please?" John winced, expecting to bear the brunt of the superior officer's wrath for having the gall to ask him to repeat himself. The full bird rose his right hand and slightly arched it back. *Holy shit! He's gonna punch me in the face!* Startled, John braced himself for the oncoming assault.

The colonel instead gently placed his hand on John's shoulder and said, "I'm sorry, Chang. I was told that you and Lance Corporal Santaniello were very close. You were childhood friends and you both served in Vietnam at the same time. Will you honor his parents' request?"

Chang was beside himself. *Request?* He thought, *A request for what?* John began to speak, "I–"

The sympathetic colonel interjected, "Chang, I know you saw a lot of terrible things during your time in country and you went through a lot of tough shit as a corpsman, but nothing can be more hurtful than learning that one of your best friends has been killed in action. I'm sorry for your loss, Chang, but Mr. and Mrs. Santaniello asked that you bring the body of their son, Lance Corporal Vincent Santaniello, home. Will you honor your friend's parents' request?"

John got weak and dizzy. His knees buckled. The room suddenly became very dark. He repeatedly blinked, as if to awaken himself from what surely was a nightmare. His throat burned and tears welled in his eyes.

Oh, no! Oh, my God, no! Vinnie? Oh, please, not Vinnie! John thought as the gravity of the situation finally dawned on him.

"Wha–" John choked out as he was struggling to breathe, much less to remain upright and actually speak. "What happened to Vinnie?"

The superior officer repeated himself. "KIA, Chang. 28 March in Cam Lo. Mortars in a surprise morning attack. We believe he was killed instantly and didn't suffer. Again, I am sorry for your loss, Doc."

Initially, the young corpsman, at twenty only a few months older than Vinnie, was in denial. "No, no. Vinnie can't be dead. I just got a letter from him yesterday. He was telling me about how excited he was to be the best man for his sister's wedding in August. He told me that we were gonna go get a couple of drinks in a bar back home, to celebrate my getting out of Vietnam and his sister's wedding. This can't be . . . it can't be true!"

The look in the full bird's eyes told John everything that he needed to know. Flabbergasted, John thrust his hand out to steady himself on a nearby table. "I can't believe it. I can't believe that Vinnie is . . . is . . . dead." John's voice trailed off to a barely discernible whisper as he uttered the word *dead*. He lowered his head and bit his lower lip. Thirty seconds elapsed, all in awkward silence, as the colonel waited for an answer from John, who continued to struggle with the distressing news.

John proceeded to the next stage of grief. He was enraged. "Those gook bastards killed a good man. Vinnie was the pride of the company; the men loved him. He did so much for those guys in the Thundering Third. They adored Vinnie and called him Saint. I hope the sonsabitches who killed my buddy were fucking mutilated!" John suddenly came to, and realized that he was venting and cursing in the presence of a superior officer. John's face softened and his voice took on a more conciliatory tone. "I'm sorry. Please excuse my language."

Oh, damn, Chang thought. *I haven't given the full bird an answer yet!* "It would be an honor to accompany Vinnie home to Jamaica. But I have another three weeks left in my tour. How—"

The colonel interjected. "Don't worry about finishing your tour here in Japan. You take care of your buddy and honor him. We will pull a few strings to make this happen, Chang." With that, the colonel extended his right hand toward John. Still weak-kneed, John lifted his right hand from the table and gave his superior a firm handshake.

"Thank you. What is the next step?"

The colonel released Chang's hand and explained, "We get you fitted for new uniforms and shoes and you're on the next plane to El Toro, California at 1700 hours this afternoon. You'd better get moving." John nodded respectfully and then turned to leave, but the colonel patted John's back. "Your friend was a hero, son, and you're doing an honorable thing for his family. God bless you, Chang."

"Thank you," John stated sheepishly. "Semper Fi." With that, the heartbroken corpsman exited the colonel's office and walked into an uncertain future.

* * *

In the span of ten hours, John shaved, received a fresh military haircut, and had his seabag located, cleaned out, and re-packed with fresh gear. Of course, John remained grief-stricken at the news that his childhood buddy was dead.

John boarded a U.S. military transport plane with a heavy heart and a nervous disposition. *How do I greet the Santaniellos? Carmine and Rose are like parents to me and Lilly and her little brother are like my siblings.*

John slept during the twelve-hour flight but his thoughts were haunted by the proposition of seeing the lifeless form of his once-vibrant pal while simultaneously trying to calm the grieving Santaniello family. John conceded that he'd rather run through hot arty to aid an injured brother than deal with this painful reality.

John's plane touched down in El Toro, California at 11:45 pm. He had orders to proceed to Dover Air Force Base at 1300 hours the following day, but there were things to be done before he boarded the flight to Dover.

First, John had to be fitted for new USMC uniforms and that took a couple of hours. Next, he had to eat. He hadn't eaten in twenty-four hours and that had taken a toll on him. He could not wrap his head around the fact that he had been tending to someone's grievous head wound less than two days earlier and now he was hours away from being back home in New York. However, his elation at having survived the insanity of Vietnam was subdued by the fact that his best friend didn't share in his good fortune. John struggled to sleep that night in El Toro. Visions of Vinnie, and of John's imagined version of his friend's gruesome death, plagued his every waking moment.

*   *   *

At that very moment, over three thousand miles away, Carmine received a call from the local USMC headquarters. Unfortunately for Carmine, this call immediately followed yet another anonymous caller who had blasphemed Vinnie's memory with the usual assortment of vulgarities and false accusations. The Santaniellos had been besieged with such calls multiple times per day since Vinnie's death and the occurrences were severely stressing them. The elder Carmine was absolutely livid when he hung up the phone, only to have it ring again ten seconds after he'd slammed the receiver down.

"HELLO, GODDAMMIT!!"

The exasperated voice caused the heart of Colonel Maynard Tapp, the USMC official on the line, to skip a beat. Unnerved, the official's senses re-engaged and he responded to the unorthodox salutation. "Mr. Santan—"

"I said hello, goddammit. Who the hell is calling now?"

The delay in long-distance calls was very pronounced so, although Colonel Tapp began to greet Mr. Santaniello, Carmine only heard crackled silence. Carmine immediately realized his error as the familiar voice came over the line. It was the voice of the San Francisco-based Colonel Tapp, with whom Carmine had spoken a few days after learning of Vinnie's death.

The colonel had taken a liking to Vinnie during the then-green Marine's tenure in San Francisco before Saint was shipped out to Vietnam during the summer of 1967. The colonel even made it a point to reach out to Carmine and Rose after Vinnie's deployment to let them know what a fine Marine they had raised. Carmine developed a rapport with Colonel Tapp after telling him about his service in the U.S. Navy during World War II, and the colonel had asked Carmine to stay in touch.

Unfortunately, the next time that they spoke was when Carmine called the colonel to let him know of Vinnie's death. The colonel's sadness was palpable. Carmine asked Tapp during that call if he could arrange for Vinnie's body to have a special military escort home. And Carmine didn't want just any escort. He wanted Vinnie's childhood pal and fellow serviceman, John Chang, to do the honors. Colonel Tapp made no promises but he ensured Carmine that he would do everything in his power to fulfill the request. Carmine had hung up cautiously optimistic that Colonel Tapp would come through for Vinnie.

Now, two weeks later, the colonel called Carmine back to let him know that his request had been granted and, in turn, Carmine had greeted him with a vulgar (yet unintentionally so) salutation. The beleaguered father smacked his forehead and covered the phone mouthpiece with his hand as he uttered in an exasperated fashion, "Jesus Christ!"

"Colonel? Colonel Tapp? Are you still there, sir?" Carmine understood that he would have to silently wait for a number of seconds before he would hear the colonel's reply. Staticky silence ensued. *Goddammit,* he thought. *I scared the colonel away.*

Suddenly: "Hello? Mr. Santaniello, sir? Can you hear me?"

"Colonel Tapp? Yes, sir, I hear you and I am so happy to hear from you. I'm sorry for the way that I answered the phone, but losing Vinnie has been real difficult for all of us here. And to make matters worse, we get calls at least five times a day from cowards who tell us how happy they are to hear that Vinnie's dead. We've also received anonymous letters since Vinnie's death, making him out to be Satan.

"And if that ain't enough, we've had ten funeral homes reject us because Vinnie's a Vietnam Marine. We ain't got a place to hold Vinnie's wake yet, sir. It's a goddamn disgrace and it's been hard for everybody."

That sobering information made Tapp despondent. "That's a damn shame, Mr. Santaniello, but I do have some news for you and your family. The USMC has authorized John Chang to accompany Vinnie back home. He has orders to fly into Dover Air Force Base and to then accompany Vinnie in the hearse ride up to New York."

This was music to Carmine's ears. It was the first good news that he had received in the terrible two weeks since learning of Vinnie's death. "Why, thank you so much, sir! My family will be thrilled to learn that John has been granted permission to bring Vinnie home!"

Carmine, overcome with emotion, continued, "My son has to be treated with respect on his final mission and there's no one that I trust more with such an awesome responsibility than John, sir. Vinnie loved John like a brother and me and my wife and kids didn't want Vinnie to come home alone. We wanted him to be with his brother on his lonely trip home. Sir, please make sure that Vinnie's respected and not thrown in a goddamn box in the cargo wing of a jet, sir . . . please."

Colonel Tapp was shocked at the desperate, weak nature of the last *please* of Carmine's plea. The tone in Carmine's voice saddened the colonel. "Mr. Santaniello, please know that I am not merely paying you lip service when I tell you about my admiration for your son. I only had the opportunity to be in his presence for a few weeks last summer, but I knew right away that he was one hell of an American and one hell of a Marine. God bless him and God bless you and your family in your time of grief. It will be an absolute honor to ensure that your son arrives home with the love and dignity that he deserves."

"Thank you, sir," replied Carmine. "My whole family thanks you. I will never be able to thank you enough for this, sir. You have no idea how grateful we are." Carmine stopped and held the phone as far from his mouth as he could. He was crying and he perceived this as a great sign of weakness. Carmine quickly composed himself and hoped that Colonel Tapp had not heard him whimpering like a baby. In turn, the colonel, himself emotional, replied, "You're welcome, sir. I promise that we will honor your son."

The two veteran servicemen proceeded to discuss the protocols of how, when, and where Doc Chang would guard such precious cargo during a long, solitary trip across multiple bodies of water, vast expanses of land, myriad cultures, and innumerable ethnicities. The trip from the wasteland that was Vietnam to the hardscrabble concrete jungle of Jamaica, Queens.

Upon hanging up the telephone, Carmine actually smiled, ever so slightly, for the first time since he'd held Lilly during the early morning hours after his family had been dealt the crushing news about Vinnie.

"Rose, Vinnie ain't gonna be shipped home like some goddamn luggage. Johnny Chang is gonna take him home. Ain't that good news, Rose? Vinnie ain't gonna be alone when he returns to New York. His best pal from here is gonna be with him. Ain't that swell, Rose?"

Rose, who had slept terribly in the nearly three weeks since she'd learned of her son's death, mustered the strength to reply, "Yes, Carmine, that is wonderful. I'm happy that Vinnie won't be alone when he comes home."

Rose's demeanor suddenly changed. "I just wish that he was alive during the flight home. I just wish that I could hug him one more time, tell him that I love him one more time, give him—" Rose began to hyperventilate.

"Rose, ya gotta calm down. Killing ya self ain't bringing Vinnie back. Slow down and breathe." Rose's constant meltdowns were taking a toll on Carmine. He had to be the unflappable rock of the family during this horrific ordeal and his inability to vent, in conjunction with the anonymous phone calls and letters, was bringing him to a boiling point.

"Rose, I think we oughta—"

The phone rang. It was 10:30 a.m.

Lilly, seated on Vinnie's bed in the adjoining room, flinched at the sound of the ringing phone due to the anxiety that the anonymous callers were causing the family. In fact, the calls had gotten so ruthless and unnerving that Rose, Lilly, and Joseph were not allowed to answer the phone. Carmine and Rose peered at each other before Carmine reached for the telephone. He took a deep breath and exhaled before he cradled the phone against his ear.

"Hel—"

"FUCK YOU AND FUCK YOUR BABY-KILLING, COCK-SUCKING, PIECE-OF-SHIT MARINE SON, SANTANELLA! WE HOPE THAT GODDAMN BABY-KILLING BASTARD MARINE GOES TO HELL FOR HIS TERRIBLE MURDERS IN VIETNAM! THE BLOOD OF THE INNOCENT KIDS YOUR SON KILLED ARE ON YOUR HANDS, POP, AND ON YOUR WIFE'S, TOO! ROT IN HELL, GI SCUM!"

"Who the hell is this? Answer me, you commie, pinko bastard!" Carmine was irate. This call was the straw that broke the camel's back and Carmine's increasingly loud voice underscored that fact. "YOU THINK YOU'RE SO GODDAMN TOUGH OVER THE PHONE, DO YA? WELL, YOU HAVE MY ADDRESS, RIGHT?"

Lilly came running into the living room after she heard her father shouting in such a frightening manner.

"COME ON OVER AND TALK LIKE THAT TO MY FACE, YA YELLA BASTARD! C'MON, TOUGH GUY, YOU TOUGH PIECE OF SHIT, COME OVER HERE NOW! MY ADDRESS IS ONE SIXTY-EIGHT DASH—"

The caller interrupted Carmine. "I ain't gotta come over there to hurt you, Pops. I'm doing just fine from where I'm at, daddy-o!"

Click!

"Hello? HELLO? *HELLO, GODDAMMIT?* THAT'S IT, I'VE HAD IT. I'VE *FUCKING* HAD IT!"

Rose and Lilly were startled at Carmine's use of the F-word, as he never used it in their presence. Instead of replacing the receiver on the telephone, Carmine yanked it extremely hard, causing the cord to rip from the phone base and bungee wildly at him, narrowly missing Lilly's face on its recoil. Rose, keenly aware that Carmine's rage would not be curtailed, instinctively placed her arms around her children's shoulders and huddled them close to her, akin to a mother bird placing her wings around her chicks in an effort to thwart a predator's primal urges.

Carmine's face was taut and his brow was creased. Spittle flew from his mouth and his eyes, squinting and ablaze with unadulterated rage, were moist. The phone remained in his hand with the cord hanging limply from it, like the motionless tail of freshly killed prey in the unforgiving clenches of a predator's jagged teeth. Carmine flung the receiver, with the cord gyrating wildly, mightily toward the kitchen, where it exploded against the wall adjacent to the back door. The receiver disintegrated into shards that went in multiple directions, akin to an exploding grenade. Its impact with the wall left a large hole in its wake.

Carmine's lust for vengeance had yet to be satiated. He turned his sights on the source of his venomous disdain for humanity at that very moment: the receiver-less telephone. Carmine stomped toward it and, over the din of Rose's exclaimed pleas for calm, he grunted loudly as he aggressively grabbed the base of the phone and jerked it off the side table that was farthest from his huddling wife and kids. The cord that extended from the rear of the phone down the side of the table and into the wall fell limply behind the side table, as the force that Carmine utilized to snatch the phone caused the cord to snap out of the jack. Carmine held the phone like a bowling ball and turned around to face the kitchen and back door. He then marched the short distance to the door, opened it, and took a few steps before he violently spiked the phone to the ground. Once again, there was an explosion of phone shrapnel in myriad directions.

Still, Carmine's unadulterated rage was not quelled.

He stomped back inside the house, passed through the kitchen, and made a hard right turn into his bedroom. Carmine slammed the door shut. Dresser drawers opened and slammed shut. Rose and Lilly heard what appeared to be shuffled paper. The bedroom door swung open and Carmine emerged from his bedroom with a canvas satchel filled with stuffed envelopes, photographs, and tapes.

"Carmine, *NO!* Don't do it!"

Rose cried as she spoke, for she knew what Carmine intended to do with all of the letters, pictures, and tapes that Vinnie had sent to them from Vietnam. Carmine ignored his wife's desperate pleas and continued through the kitchen and out the back door. The irrational, livid man then placed the canvas bag, filled with nearly a year's worth of Vinnie's Vietnam memories, letters, recorded talks, and trinkets, onto the ground, commingling them with the remnants of the shattered telephone. Carmine, crying tears of unadulterated rage, then removed a book of matches from his pants pocket.

"'GODDAMN BABY KILLER,' HUH? DON'T WANT TO ACCEPT MY VINNIE'S BODY FOR A WAKE, DO YA? GLAD THAT MY SON IS DEAD, ARE YA? WANNA WISH PAIN AND DEATH UPON MY FAMILY, DO YOU? WELL, TO HELL WITH ALL OF YOUS, YA GODDAMN SONSABITCHES!"

Carmine poured turpentine on the canvas bag and then lit five matches simultaneously. Rose gasped in horror and her "NO!" was but a faint, throaty whimper. Lilly's eyes grew wide and her jaw was agape. She wanted to plead with her father to try to think before he embarked upon an act that he'd surely regret, but she was frightened of what her dad was capable of doing at that moment.

Lilly opted to remain silent, a decision that she'd rue until her last moments on Earth.

"FUCK ALL OF YOU MISERABLE INGRATES! MY VINNIE WAS TOO GOOD FOR ANY OF YOU YELLA BASTARDS! YOUR LIVES AREN'T WORTH HIS SACRIFICE! I'LL NEVER ALLOW HIS MEMORY TO BE SMEARED BY YOU HATEFUL SONSABITCHES!"

With that, Carmine lowered the five lit matches to the bag. Flames began to rise, slowly at first but then with sickening speed and efficiency. The pile of Vinnie's invaluable artifacts quickly congealed with the melting phone shards and created a thick, black plume of smoke that wafted skyward. Lilly's best friend, Marie, watched the terrible events unfold from her second-floor bedroom window next door.

Oh, my God, Marie thought, *Carmine is burning all of Vinnie's letters and pictures!* Marie wept as she watched the last vestiges of Vinnie go up in smoke.

As Carmine stood over the dancing flames, cursing in an indecipherable fashion, Lilly dislodged herself from Rose and ran upstairs to her room.

I've gotta get the letters and pictures that Vinnie sent to me before Pa gets to them, Lilly thought. For the first time since Vinnie had left for the service, Lilly didn't stop at the mirror to glance at Vinnie's Snoopy as she passed it on the way to her room. Instead, the young woman, crying profusely, sprinted up the stairs and into her small, second-floor bedroom. She reached under her bed and removed a dusty old Buster Brown shoebox. Lilly, still on her knees, opened the box and lovingly touched the dozens of letters and pictures that Vinnie had sent to her from boot camp and Vietnam over the previous year.

"Oh, Vinnie," Lilly exclaimed through her tears, "please forgive Pop. He doesn't know what he's doing." Lilly gently stroked the letters and held up one picture of her brother, holding a very large rocket launcher in his hands while standing on a bridge, explosions visible and frozen in time in the photo's background. Lilly's tears descended from her cheeks as she struggled through her watery eyes to focus on her favorite picture of Vinnie from over there.

"I love you, Vinnie." Lilly gasped and struggled to continue, "Why did you have to die?" She brushed her hands over the letters one more time, as if touching Vinnie's writings were akin to touching her brother. She then lifted the prized photo up to her lips and planted a gentle kiss upon the brave man-child who stared back at her. Lilly then replaced the photo in the shoebox, closed the cover, and tucked it under her arm before she ran back downstairs and out the front door.

Lilly hopped over the porch divider and ran into the Graves's home. She ran up to Marie's room and startled her best friend, who remained seated at her bedroom window, fixated on the flaming carnage that raged below.

"Marie? Marie? You have to do me a favor!" Marie turned to Lilly, her mascara-stained face and quivering lips incapable of producing a discernible sound. Lilly extended the Buster Brown shoebox to her best friend and desperately said, "Whatever you do, don't ever let my father know that I gave this to you."

Marie recognized the box immediately, as she and Lilly often read Vinnie's letters and looked at his pictures together in Lilly's room. Marie mustered just enough courage to spit out, "Oh, my God, Lilly. Vinnie's letters?"

Lilly nodded. "You have to hide them here and don't ever tell anyone that you have them here. Promise?"

Marie gasped before responding, "I promise, Lilly. I ain't ever gonna tell anyone that I have Vinnie's letters and pictures."

With that, Lilly glanced over Marie's shoulder and out of her bedroom window, into her own back yard. Her father was stomping out the flames as he doused them with a hose. With every step, Carmine stomped on Lilly's fleeting spirit and broken heart.

What was once a mosaic of the promise of a beloved young man, the pride of his friends and family, now was but a congealed conglomerate of ash and grotesquely misshapen plastic. Like Vinnie, his letter, pictures, and tapes—once full of great promise—were brutally destroyed for all eternity.

With the fire extinguished, Carmine retreated back into his house. With no phone and no letters or recordings from his beloved son, Carmine's house now was silent. Lilly was not there and Rose's face was as ashen as the memories that had been snuffed by flames moments earlier. Indeed, the house was perfectly silent. Yet the torturous agony that screamed in Carmine's soul proved to be more caustic than any devious anonymous caller could hope to be.

Carmine realized that he had committed an egregious error in judgment. Indeed, a millisecond of unadulterated rage had spawned an eternity of arduous regret and shame.

Carmine turned and walked ashamedly back to the backyard. He kneeled over the ashes of his son's legacy and wept. *Oh, my God, Vinnie. I'm so sorry. I failed you and I failed those that you left behind. I'm so sorry, son. I love you, Vinnie. I love you, son.*

With that, Carmine rose and took the first step into his new reality: A life of constant regret and gloomy, melancholic guilt.

*   *   *

Lilly woke up the following morning and waited on the corner of her block for the mailman. She needed to make a deal with the letter carrier. The weary young woman, still devastated by the loss of her best friend, was ever-mindful of her father's destruction of Vinnie's letters and tapes a few hours earlier. In fact, she refused to go to sleep after she returned home from crying into the wee hours of the night with Marie. Instead, Lilly sat awake in the darkness of her bedroom, haunted by a thought that she could not eradicate from her mind no matter how hard she tried: What if Vinnie sent letters home in the days preceding his death but they had yet to be delivered? Surely, she thought, her father would angrily snatch them and burn them as he had her brother's other keepsakes. Lilly thought, *I can't let that happen again. I gotta think of something.*

And so, Lilly devised a plan.

The mailman arrived at his customary time, 8:15 a.m. Lilly approached him and asked if he had any overseas letters from her brother. The mailman told her that he did not. Lilly quickly looked around to ensure that no one was within earshot, then stepped toward the mailman and whispered, "Listen, ya gotta do me a favor. If you ever have any letters from my brother in Vietnam, you canNOT deliver them here."

"Why not?" queried the confused mailman.

"Because my brother was killed in Vietnam a few weeks ago and my pop is in a bad way. He burned all my brother's letters and pictures last night and I just know that he'll burn anything else that comes from Vietnam."

The letter carrier was befuddled and scared, equally.

"Whatcha want me to do, then, young lady?"

Lilly looked the mailman directly into his eyes and stated, "Ya gotta promise me something: If you get any letters from my brother in Vietnam, you gotta deliver them to my next-door neighbors, the Graves family. My girlfriend, Marie, will hold on to the letters and get them to me without my father knowing. Now: PROMISE, please!"

The mailman gazed at the tear-streaked, pained face of the young woman, sighed, and exclaimed, "I promise."

*   *   *

Wednesday, April 17, 1968. Vinnie was coming home. As cruel fate would have it, this day also was the twenty-first birthday of

380

Vinnie's good friend, a man who had desperately tried to save his life a few weeks earlier: John "Doc" Nunn. Vinnie's body arrived in Japan that morning, cleaned and dressed impeccably in the Marines' dress blues. It was the very uniform that Vinnie had hoped to wear on the altar of his hometown church, Presentation of the Blessed Virgin Mary, during his best friend and big sister's planned August wedding. Instead, the uniform draped the broken remnants of what once was a vibrant, promising leader.

And a now-forever nineteen-year-old young man.

It was roughly 9:15 p.m. in Okinawa when Vinnie's body was set to fly to El Toro, California for the first leg of the trip to his final resting place. At that very moment, across the world in Jamaica, Queens, it was 8:15 a.m. on that Wednesday morning and Lilly performed her new ritual: She checked to see if the mail had been delivered. She observed letters in her mailbox, so she hopped the short wall between her porch and Marie's to peer inside of her neighbor's small mailbox, located next to their doorbell. Lilly nervously opened the top latch of the burgundy mailbox and instantly recognized an airmail military envelope, the kind that Vinnie used to mail letters back home. Lilly's trembling right hand clumsily gestured toward the letter. The grief-stricken young woman was sickened by the notion of receiving a posthumous letter from Vinnie.

Upon removing the letter, Lilly observed Vinnie's distinct cursive upon the envelope: *The Santaniello Family*. The envelope was very different from the dozens of others that Vinnie had mailed home. For starters, it appeared filthy and worn. Lilly wondered if the letter somehow had been trampled or otherwise mishandled on its trek home. Lilly cast aside her thoughts and carefully placed the envelope into her pocketbook. She then effortlessly hopped the dividing wall. She was back onto her porch, entered her house, and immediately ran upstairs to her room, where she sat alone. Lilly took a deep breath before she slowly removed the weathered envelope from her pocketbook.

Lilly was bewildered as she held another letter from Vinnie, albeit one that was drastically different. The envelope in her trembling hands contained a saint's letter that had been written from Hell but sent to her from Heaven. Lilly was having difficulty wrapping her mind around the fact that Vinnie had been alive when he wrote this letter and now, upon its delivery, he was dead. The young woman had a lump in her throat because she held in her hands the last vestiges of her brother.

Lilly carefully unsealed the envelope and slowly removed the letter from within. She became angst-ridden when she saw that the condition of the letter was identical to that of the envelope: weathered and tattered. Physically, this letter was unlike any of Vinnie's previous mailings. For starters, the parchment was not the soft, white paper on which he had written dozens of other letters.

Why is this paper so hard and yellow?

Something on the bottom of the letter caught Lilly's eye. Lilly's initial confusion was replaced with abject terror as her eyes quickly filled with tears. The young woman instinctively cupped her hand over her mouth as she gagged.

The letter's got blood on it!

Lilly tried to convince herself otherwise, but there were flecks of dried blood on this letter. She carefully opened the letter that was folded into thirds, looking for the date of the letter to solve the mystery bloodstains.

"Oh, no! Ohhhhh, no, no . . . nooooooo . . . " Lilly muttered in pain.

The young woman looked away before looking back at the top of the letter.

"That date. It can't be . . . oh, my God! My poor, poor Vinnie. Oh, God!"

Lilly wept uncontrollably as she tried to read Vinnie's final letter through her tears.

Dear Mom, Dad, Lil & Joseph,

Hi! I got 4 more letters from you today. 2 of them from you, 1 from Joseph and 1 from Lillian. So here I am again. I'm just fine. I'm going to answer a few of your questions real quick before I forget them. Sending letters with a six-cent stamp takes the same amount of days as airmail does. And if the mail's running smooth, it's 7 to 10 days to get here. The [photo] negatives [are of] me, Richie Williams, and B.J. O'Hare; we all went through boot camp, I.T.R. [Infantry Training Regiment], and came over here together. And we'll all go home together. O'Hare lives in Florida. Richie Williams lives in PA. We're the Unholy 3. Ha Ha. You should have already received the few pictures I sent you. Plus you should get some more the same time (give or take a day) that you get this letter. I'm really glad that my album is getting bigger. I can't wait to see it. I bet I probably won't remember half the pictures because I've only seen the ones I sent you.

I know those two girls and mother that live next to John's house. I believe their name is Kosnickle or something like that. When you see them again, tell them I said hello. Also, tell my old buddy "Joe" that when I get home me and him will have a few beers together. He's such a nice man. He's just like a grandfather. Also tell him that I send my best regards to him and his wife. If I had his address I'd like to write him a letter.

So the neighborhood has changed. I bet I probably won't recognize half the people when I get home. Do those nuts (the Monster family) still live across the street? They'll probably be outside this summer making scenes if they still live there. It's a shame. I can remember when that neighborhood was a very nice place. Now you can't even leave a bicycle on the porch without it getting stolen. Man, that's really a shame. Now Joseph's out of a bike. Do you remember all the bike parts I used to have scattered all over the back yard, front yard, and in the basement?

I just came back from Cam Lo Hill and on the way back I took some real nice pictures for Joseph to try and draw. I took a picture of a church and a school building that were all damaged by the fighting that took place there. If he can draw it, he'll really capture the way of war. Also I took a picture of a woman selling bananas and stuff. I'm going to shoot this whole roll just for Joseph. It's a shame that it's only black/white but that was the only kind I could get my hands on.

Mom, you can count on me on going swimming in the pool if it's up. And Pop can stand by because it will be just like it was last time when we used to fight to see who will push who into the pool. I remember one time I pushed Pop and Pop pulled me in with him. Ha. But Pop had all his clothes on. Ha Ha. We sure had fun then. Having a pool like that in your back yard sure is a great pleasure.

I remember when the summer used to come. The back door would be opened and the screen door would take its place. And when I came home from school everyone would be sitting on their porches or in the back yard working on their gardens.

I haven't decided yet whether or not I'm going to sneak up on you like I did the last time I came home on leave. Or if I'll let you pick me up. I think you enjoyed it much more when I sneaked up on you. Ha Ha. I remember Pop and Joseph were in the front. Boy, did Pop get surprised. Ha Ha. I just stood there and waited for Pop to look up. He was picking weeds from the front garden.

And then I remember when my leave was up and I had to go to Calif. I'll tell you, between Mom and Lilly, you almost had me crying. Boy, you women! I just don't know. The only person who acted cool was little Joseph. Ha. I had a great time in California. The short time I was there I enjoyed myself. I never got to see San Francisco though. I was in San Diego for almost 2 days. That place is all squids. I saw a couple of my buddies from boot camp that were stationed at Diego. I saw Hogan, Schultz, and a few other guys. Did I send you many pictures from Calif.? Did I send you any pictures of Disneyland? Let me know. I'm just curious. OK. Well, I got to be going now. Oh, before I forget, I have enough tapes and the tape recorder is holding out. Well, take care.

Love, Your Son & Brother
Vinnie

P.S. Don't forget to tell all those other people what I said and give my Love & Regards to both grandmas in our family. Is Robert Baas out of the service yet? Let me know.

Vinnie had written this letter shortly before he was killed. That explained the bloodstains on the letter, but the condition of the parchment and the bleeding ink stains on the letter remained a mystery to her. The explanation, one that Lilly would never come to learn, was that Docs Nunn and Milazzo had been wielding cocktails of narcotic pain medication, in a frenetic attempt to stanch Vinnie's terminal bleeding a few hours after he had written his final letter and put it in his flak jacket. The cocktails spilled as Nunn and Milazzo desperately tried to administer them to Vinnie's body. The splashing of the medications was exasperated by Vinnie's involuntary thrashing about, in response to his overwhelming trauma. Additionally, the corpsmen poured water on Vinnie in an effort to clean him up as they tried to salvage his life and dull his pain. The combination of water and narcotic cocktails spilled onto Vinnie's upper body and drenched the envelope and letter that Vinnie had stowed away in his jacket's inner sleeve roughly an hour before he was killed. Vinnie had intended to bring his letter—and the rest of the platoon's letters—to the Dong Ha HQ mail drop later in the day.

Lilly was beside herself as she struggled to read the letter. It was difficult enough to bring herself to read her brother's final letter, knowing full well that he died with this very letter on his person somewhere. He could've written only *Hello* and that would've devastated her. But this letter . . . Lilly, in her desperate grief, interpreted the letter to be an ironic reflection by Vinnie on his life.

It was as if he knew that he was gonna die, she thought.

Lilly reflected on the content of Vinnie's final letter. She had written to him to report that Joseph had his bike stolen right off the porch—"Boy," Lilly wrote, "was Pop ever sore about that! He wanted to murder the thieves!" She also wrote to ask Vinnie about whether or not first-class mail was slower than airmail. Lilly wiped away tears as she reflected on Old Man Joe, a neighbor from down the block who liked to joke that Lilly, Vinnie, and Joseph were his grandkids and that Vinnie was his favorite.

Joe and his wife were devastated when they learned that Vinnie was killed. Lilly had never seen old Joe, a Word War I veteran, cry, and she was shocked to see the proud old man lose his composure like he did. Lilly decided that she would share Vinnie's letter with old Joe because of how much he loved her deceased brother. She was apprehensive about going forward with this plan, but she resolved in her heart that it was the right thing to do.

Lilly re-read the letter multiple times, despite the torment caused by seeing Vinnie's blood on the parchment. Lilly realized that she had not seen any pictures of war-torn churches or buildings, nor had she seen pictures of people selling bananas. *Where could these pictures be? Oh, my,* Lilly thought, *I hope they come because Joseph would have to draw them to honor Vinnie's dying wish!*

The pictures would never arrive.

The most crushing aspects of Vinnie's letter were his musings about the family pool and the time that he surprised everyone by unexpectedly showing up at home. Carmine built a small, four-foot pool for their small back yard every spring and then disassembled it every fall. The kids adored this rite of passage and their friends enjoyed it even more, as pools weren't commonplace in Jamaica, Queens. The kids' friends often visited the house during the summers, to cool off and horse around in the pool. Lilly recalled her amazement at how many kids fit into their small pool. Carmine took great pride in his pool and he ensured that it always was crystal-clear and clean. Lilly swore that her little pool was cleaner than all of those fancy pools out on Long Island.

Lilly wiped tears from her eyes and chuckled as she recalled the moment when Vinnie tried to push their father into the pool, clothes and all. She reminisced about the summer of '66, which turned out to be Vinnie's last full summer with the family. Her father had come home from work one brutally hot day around the Fourth of July and his shirt was soaked through with perspiration.

"Holy mackerel," Carmine mused, "it's hot as blazes out there today! I thought we were gonna drop like flies in the damn heat!"

Lilly had been seated in the kitchen with a large industrial fan droning loudly in the background when her father walked in. She was drinking a lemonade as she looked out of the open window that faced the back yard. She observed Vinnie and Joseph enjoying some freshly cut watermelon at a table near the perimeter of the pool.

"Hey, Lil," called her father, "wanna bring me a tall glass of that stuff, hon?" Lilly immediately stopped drinking her beverage and tended to her father's request. She retrieved his favorite glass from the cupboard and poured him a tall, cold glass of lemonade. Carmine drank the entire glass in one gulp, and exclaimed, "Ah, that was delicious! Thanks!"

"You're welcome, Pa," Lilly responded. Vinnie looked toward the nearby kitchen window with a mischievous grin on his face.

"Hey, Pa," Vinnie called out, "I think I saw some crap at the bottom of the pool. You wanna come check it out?"

"Ya can't get off your ass to check it out yourself, Vinnie? Am I raising a buncha lazy kids or something?" Carmine asked with a smirk and a disarming tone that conveyed to the kids that he was not perturbed at the request. Indeed, he knew exactly what Vinnie was trying to do, and he played right into the trap.

"Y'know, this pool ain't been the least bit dirty in the fifteen years that I been puttin' it up and takin' it down," Carmine boasted. "I can't imagine there being any crap in it!" He then walked along the deck that he had built, flush to the top edge of a section of the pool, and leaned over in an exaggerated fashion to peer into the crystal-clear water. Carmine then threw up his hands in an I *don't see anything* gesture as Vinnie and Joseph suppressed laughs.

"It's hard to see," responded Vinnie. "Ya gotta lean in and look at the edge of the liner along the wall."

"Oh, of course!" Carmine then bent over even further, figuratively beckoning to be shoved into the pool.

Vinnie silently approached his father like a lion stalking its unsuspecting prey. However, little did Vinnie know then that prey, too, can act as a predator—something that the young man would come to learn a little more than a year later, halfway across the world in the jungles of Vietnam.

As Vinnie stealthily slinked toward his father, Carmine listened intently for the approaching sound of muted footsteps and breathing, all the while feigning obliviousness as he peered into the pool. Suddenly, Vinnie placed his hands upon his father's back and began to push. Carmine, quick and nimble for a man in his late forties, immediately twisted around and, as the momentum of Vinnie's push propelled Carmine into the pool, the agile father grabbed Vinnie's arms and they both plunged, fully clothed, into the coolness of the pool.

Startled, Lilly initially gasped before breaking into a fit of laughter. She left her seat in the kitchen and ran onto the deck of the backyard. Pointing at her drenched father and brother, Lilly exclaimed, "Ha ha ha ha ha, Vinnie! Pop foiled your plans, huh?" Vinnie and his dad playfully laughed and splashed in the pool. Joseph tried to push Lilly in the pool, but the savvy sister would have none of it. "In your dreams, pipsqueak," Lilly exclaimed as she playfully shoved her eleven-year-old brother aside.

"*Caaaaaaw*-mine!" screeched Rose from the threshold of the kitchen door. "What the hell are you doing in the pool with all your clothes on?"

Undeterred, Carmine shouted, "Hop in, why dontcha, Rose? The water's mighty fine!"

"Oh, *Caw*-mine!" With that, Rose returned to the kitchen to resume cooking that evening's dinner. Vinnie and his dad continued to wrestle and laugh in the pool. They were two men frolicking in the pool, enjoying each other's goofiness and feeling content with the knowledge that they were destined to be best friends for decades to come.

*   *   *

Lilly cried hysterically. The more that she tried to control her sobbing, the worse it became. She mused, *How could a memory seem so recent, yet so very long ago?*

Her mind quickly rewound to another painful memory, this one exponentially worse than the pool incident. It was the time that Vinnie surprised everyone by coming home after completing boot camp in August 1967. Vinnie had a few days off before he was to be shipped out West on the first leg of his deployment to Vietnam and he'd decided to take advantage of the rare time off by visiting his unsuspecting family.

Vinnie had previously advised his family that he wouldn't be able to take leave before he left for Vietnam. He fabricated a reason, telling his family that his tour in Vietnam would be extended by a month if he went home that summer.

On that fateful day, Lilly was in Nunu's room, sitting on a chair adjacent to a window that overlooked the front of their house. Lilly was dating a young Puerto Rican named Raul Morales, who was known as Ralph to his friends. It was a not-so-well-kept secret that Lilly and Ralph were contemplating marriage, and Lilly often sat at the window, pondering a life with Ralph. On that warm summer afternoon, Lilly was at the window, contemplating her future. She overheard her dad complaining about the tireless task of removing weeds in the garden below as she gazed up at the blue sky.

"These goddamn things grow as soon as ya pull 'em," he yelled in an exasperated tone.

Joseph was standing next to his father and Lilly heard him ask, "Hey, Pa, wanna watch *Lone Ranger* with me? I'm drawing a really swell picture of him and Tonto and watching the show helps me draw them."

"Sure, Joseph, sure," Carmine responded over the din of car engines and chirping birds. "Just gimme another minute to yank these goddamn weeds outta the garden."

As she looked down at her father yanking weeds from the garden, Lilly was preoccupied with her thoughts about whether or not Ralph was right for her. A thin man walking toward the house appeared in her peripheral vision and Lilly nearly fell out of her chair when the passerby stopped on the sidewalk, a few feet from her father and brother.

There was Vinnie, with a duffel bag slung over his shoulder, standing in his khaki USMC uniform, silently staring ahead with a mischievous grin affixed to his thinner-than-she-remembered face, waiting for his father and brother to look up and see the best surprise this side of Christmas morning. Lilly let out a whoop and turned to sprint downstairs and outside to give her brother a huge hug, but she abruptly stopped and turned again toward the window, for she did not want to miss the reactions of her father and brother.

"These goddamn weeds," Carmine complained again as he closed his eyes and arched his shoulders back from his kneeling position in an effort to relieve the tension in his lower back. Upon opening his eyes, Carmine couldn't believe who was standing right there: Vinnie!

Joseph had his back to the front of the house. He was drawing the flowers that he and his mother had planted in a separate, small plot of Earth closer to the porch. He was startled by his father's sudden exclamation.

"Jesus Christ! Look who's here!"

Joseph turned around to take in what his father was talking about and he saw his father giving Vinnie a strenuous bear hug. "Vinnie!" The young boy squealed with delight.

Happy that she witnessed those priceless reactions, Lilly scrambled from Nunu's room and ran downstairs while bellowing, "Vinnie's home! Vinnie's . . . HOME!" She made a beeline for her brother outside. Rose was cleaning in the kitchen and was about to prepare lunches for her family when she heard Lilly's announcement.

Rose was bewildered, as she mistakenly believed that Vinnie already was in California, awaiting his deployment to Vietnam. Nunu was seated in the living room, knitting a wool sweater for no one in particular.

"Che dice?" Nunu said to Rose in her native tongue.

"She said that Vinnie's here. Our boy is home!" Rose exclaimed in Italian as she threw her cleaning rag down on the washing machine and scurried through the living room, through the hallway, and out the front door, leaving her mother in her wake.

Rose ran outside to see her husband, Lilly, and Joseph all over Vinnie. Rose, with tears in her eyes, uttered, "My Vinnie, look how handsome you are in your uniform!" Vinnie looked up and, while in the midst of hugs and kisses, walked toward Rose and gave her a long, firm bear hug.

"Hello, Mama. I missed you."

*   *   *

Holding Vinnie's final letter in her trembling hands, Lilly recalled how she, Joseph, and her parents had intently listened as Vinnie regaled them with stories of boot camp. She reminisced wistfully about her mom's lament that the service was not feeding Vinnie well enough, because he was much skinnier than when he'd left. Lilly couldn't forget the distinct look of pride in her father's eyes as he surveyed his son.

His son, the Marine.

Heartbroken, Lilly recalled how they'd all made their way inside, where the returning hero was doused with kisses and Italian platitudes by Nunu. Soon, the neighbors came in to hug Vinnie and wish him well. Carmine retrieved his Instamatic camera and took a picture of them in their back yard: Vinnie in his impressive military uniform and Lilly in her favorite faux-leopard miniskirt.

Lilly sniffled before walking to the closet where she stored the family photo albums. She turned to that photo and emitted a sad chuckle as she noticed for the first time that one of the family dogs, Queenie, was caught running in front of them as her father snapped the picture. Queenie's brown coat blended in almost too well with the bottom portion of the photograph.

Lilly stared at her brother's face in the photo, so alive and so vibrant, and thought, *My God, I miss him so much. How am I going to go on without him?*

Lilly returned to her room and caressed Vinnie's final letter. She re-read the part where Vinnie recounted his eventual departure for California. That proved to be the last time that she would ever see him. The entire family had accompanied Vinnie to the airport. Vinnie once again was in his USMC uniform and he was hugging everyone and telling everyone that he loved them. Rose, Nunu, and Lilly were absolute emotional wrecks. Joseph looked sad but he was trying his best not to cry. Lilly stared at Vinnie's face as he said his goodbyes and, knowing him as intimately as she did, she detected a sense of fear and insecurity beneath his rough exterior.

"Mama," Vinnie said for what seemed like the thousandth time, "I promise that I will stay away from trouble. Ain't nothin' gonna happen to me, Mama. I promise." My God, how those words echoed loudly in Lilly's head as her mind's eye traveled back in time.

Lilly recalled getting close to her soon-to-depart brother before placing her lips to his ears and whispering, "You gonna be alright over there, right, you big, ugly dummy?"

Vinnie immediately placed his mouth in front of her ear and whispered in response, "What the hell else am I gonna do over there except be careful? Remember, I'm chickenshit, right?"

The loving siblings then shared a hearty laugh, much to the dismay of the remaining family members who weren't privy to the whispered communications.

Lilly then kissed Vinnie on the cheek and whispered, "I love you, chickenshit. Promise that you'll come back to us."

Vinnie looked his older sister right in the eye and shot her a wink. That was Vinnie's way of saying, "Don't worry about it. I got this!" She had seen that wink thousands of times in her lifetime and Vinnie had always delivered on the promise behind the gesture. Lilly recalled feeling reassured about Vinnie's future. She actually felt confident that he would make it back home to them at some point during the late fall or early winter of 1968.

It was time to say a final goodbye.

Rose and Nunu were bawling uncontrollably. Joseph continued his noble fight to refrain from crying. Carmine was sad to be saying goodbye to his son and pal, but proud that Vinnie was joining the service. And then there was Lilly, Vinnie's big-little sister, best friend, and confidante. The siblings, separated by almost exactly two years, could practically read each other's minds. The word *close* didn't do justice to just how close Vinnie and Lilly really were. Their love for—and loyalty to—each other was undeniable.

While the remaining Santaniellos (and Nunu) repeatedly exchanged *I love you*s, Vinnie and Lilly merely looked into each other's eyes. They knew.

As Vinnie turned to walk to the gate where his flight and an uncertain future were waiting, Lilly called out, "Hey, Vin!"

The young man, seabag slung over his right shoulder, stopped and looked at Lilly over his left shoulder.

"Happy birthday, happy Halloween, happy Thanksgiving, Merry Christmas, and happy New Year!" Lilly called out.

Not missing a beat, Vinnie wisecracked, "Ya missed Valentine's Day, St. Paddy's Day, and Easter, dummy!" He and Lil then simultaneously winked at each other and chuckled at the duplicity of their actions.

Lilly mouthed a silent, "Love you," and Vinnie mouthed the same in response.

Vinnie flashed a thumbs-up sign at his family and yelled out, "Love yous guys!" before he turned and walked forward, growing ever smaller before finally disappearing into the tunnel of eternity, never to be seen alive again.

*   *   *

Lilly struggled to return to the present. Tragically, the memories were much easier on her battered soul than her current reality. She looked down at the closing of the letter:

Love, Your Son & Brother

Vinnie

"Oh, Vinnie, my Vinnie," Lilly exclaimed between sobs, "you were a godsend for the family and for me. We were so lucky to have you, even if it was only for a couple of years. Life is so fickle and cruel, little brother. One minute, you're signing a letter to your family and then the next minute, you're . . . you're . . ." Lilly couldn't bring herself to say the word *dead*. Instead, she plopped down on her bed, lying on her back while still holding Vinnie's letter over her head. She came to a sudden realization.

Pop can never see this letter. The date . . . the blood . . . the content of the letter . . . it'll destroy him. This is the last thing that Vinnie ever wrote to us before he died. I can't have Pa burn this or any of the other things that Vinnie sent to me. I will have to hide this letter with the others in Marie's house and never tell anyone about them.

With that, Lilly perused the handwriting on the tattered pages one final time, as if *the writing* were Vinnie, and then she cried as she gently folded the letter along its creases and slowly placed it back in the envelope. Lilly then scurried next door to Marie's house and deposited the letter into the box that was secreted in Marie's bedroom, never to be revealed to anyone else—or so Lilly thought.

CHAPTER 22

COMING HOME

*A*pril 18, 1968. El Toro, California. Locally, the time was 10:30 p.m. After roughly seventeen hours in the air, Vinnie's body had landed a couple of hours earlier and was being prepared for its final flight to the East Coast in a couple of hours. John Chang had landed in El Toro approximately twelve hours earlier. He was wearing a freshly provided uniform, with perfectly pressed creases in the shirt and slacks.

When John deplaned, he immediately noticed that American civilians were positioned to his right, only a few yards away, albeit behind a flimsy chain-link fence. Upon seeing these people, and before he could process what they were saying, John instantly thought to himself that it seemed like ages since he'd seen an American face that was not in a filthy, blood-stained, and tattered military uniform.

That thought was interrupted by a considerable wad of phlegm that struck John on the right side of his face and slid down his cheek before dripping onto the fresh lapel of his uniform's shirt.

John instinctively ducked and clutched for the nonexistent firearm at his hip after he was struck by the abhorrent "incoming." The young corpsman's reaction shocked himself, as he actually thought that he was back in Vietnam for a split second. Confused by his reaction, John regained his focus, wiped the phlegm from his face, and looked toward the people behind the fence.

"FUCK YOU, YOU PIECE-OF-SHIT SCUM!"

"WHY DON'T YOU GO BACK TO VIETNAM, YOU MURDEROUS TRAITOR?"

"YOU BABY-KILLING FUCK . . . WE HATE YOU!"

"LOOK AT YOU. YOU LOOK LIKE ONE OF THEM AND YOU WERE KILLING THEM! YOU ARE A DISGRACE TO TWO RACES, YOU PIECE OF SHIT!"

"WE LOVE HANOI HANNAH AND WE HATE U.S. SERVICEMEN . . . GO BACK TO VIETNAM, YOU PIG!"

"HERE, CATCH, YOU DAMN KILLER!"

A plastic, white baby doll, its arms and legs jaggedly slit open, presumably by razors, was tossed at John, striking him in the chest. John, unsure what to make of the item, clutched it before it fell to the ground, and examined the small projectile. The fake, blonde hair was matted with what appeared to be red paint, and the naked doll's body likewise was covered in swaths of red paint. One eye appeared to have been stabbed out of the doll's head and the words *FUCK YOU, PIG!* were handwritten onto the doll's buttocks.

"LOOK FAMILIAR, PIG?"

John stopped walking as he locked eyes with the perpetrator of this heinous act. The proud corpsman felt his heart race as beads of sweat populated his brow. His face became taut, his teeth clenched, and his arms flexed. John's right hand balled into a fist as his left hand clutched the doll, which he subconsciously held up to his chest as if it were a child of his.

"YOU GONNA KILL ME, TOO, PIG?"

John again reflexively reached to his waistband for the firearm that no longer was there. John snapped out of his rage, unsure as to why he'd had another fit of unadulterated hatred. He took a few steps toward the fence, never taking his eyes off of the perpetrator, and stopped when there was nothing but the chain-link fence between him and the increasingly nervous protestor. The Caucasian protestor, likely in his early twenties, had long, brown, unkempt hair that flowed generously below his shoulders. He sported a bushy mustache and a long, matted, brown beard. His hair was swept back, away from his face, by a bandana. The man wore a tie-dyed t-shirt, bell-bottom jeans, and sandals.

The protestor's appearance was a stark contrast to the clean-shaven Chinese-American veteran who stood before him. John had short-cropped, neatly groomed black hair that was maintained under a service cap. John stood roughly five-foot-nine and he was thin but very fit. John's facial features reflected his ancestry: His skin closely resembled that of a Native American while his eyes gave a subtle nod to his Chinese heritage.

The corpsman's uniform was freshly pressed and creased to perfection. His black patent-leather shoes shined with the radiance of a dozen black diamonds. John pursed his lips and took a deep breath while never lessening his fiery stare at the protestor. The young man on the other side of the fence, despite having dozens of fellow protestors surrounding him, peered awkwardly downward. He then stumbled slightly backward under the scrutiny of nothing more than John's stern, unforgiving gaze.

"You're really brave to throw a mutilated doll over a barricade at me. You'd last roughly one-tenth of a second in Vietnam, you yellow bastard."

John's heart was beating so hard that it felt as if it was going to tear right out of his chest. Nonetheless, he continued.

"I'm flying home to bury a friend who died so that you'd continue to have the right to express yourself. Unfortunately, you choose to express yourself by showing that you are an absolute asshole, unworthy of my friend's sacrifice. God bless you, sir."

John then snapped to attention and suddenly thrust his right hand up, offering the stunned protestor a mock salute. The corpsman then tossed the doll over the fence into the hands of the bewildered young man. Fittingly, the man dropped the doll and it landed with its ass facing up at the protestor. John, head held high, defiantly walked away. Defeated, the protestor struggled to mount a defense to his wounded pride.

After a few seconds, the man muttered, "Oh, yeah? Well . . . fuck you, pig!"

John never broke stride and didn't acknowledge the man's weak comeback.

Outwardly, John evinced a sense of strength and pride, as well as an iron will that the service had instilled in him. However, that veneer of strength was only skin-deep. Internally, John felt absolutely alone and miscast. He was the enemy . . . within his own country.

John walked through the threshold of the gate, officially on U.S. *terra firma* for the first time since April 1967. The veteran sank into a melancholic state as he reflected on his feeling that he was more welcome in the Vietnamese jungles of blood, charred and mangled flesh, and smoking mortar shell casings than he was in his own unappreciative country.

*   *   *

Vinnie's casket, carefully guarded by local Marine reservists, was escorted down a private ramp at the airport in El Toro and wheeled into a U.S. military facility that contained a makeshift morgue. This facility was responsible for preserving the returning bodies of U.S. servicemen and women who had perished abroad and were making their trek home. As Vinnie's body was wheeled into the morgue, not far away John was returning to the airport gate for his red-eye flight to Dover Air Force base in Delaware, where he would finally meet the lifeless body of the young man who had seemed to be in perpetual motion when John last saw him. Vinnie's body was loaded onto a special military plane two hours later and embarked upon the penultimate part of the trek to its final resting place.

John sat aboard the plane to Dover in a somber mood. The interaction with the heckler from the previous morning left John angry and hurt. The guys in Vietnam spoke about how people back in the world received returning GIs, but the Marines hearing that just assumed that the reports were blown way out of proportion. The men naively believed that there was no way Americans could be so cruel to the servicemen and women returning from the war. The prevailing thought was that the reports had to be some made-up bullshit.

However, upon experiencing the rancor firsthand, John dejectedly thought, *That loon Hanoi Hannah was right! Americans really do fucking hate their own.* This realization hurt John, because he knew firsthand the noble sacrifices that his brothers had made in Vietnam. Like a typical Marine, John didn't think of the great sacrifices that *he* had made in country. No, he had survived, therefore he denied that his own tour had entailed any personal sacrifice. It was those men like his best friend, Vinnie, who'd made the true sacrifice. Men who were coming home in boxes if they were coming home at all.

Goddamn, thought John as the plane lifted off for the east coast of America, *we are fucking enemies over there in the shit, and right here in our own back yards, too.* John lowered his head in resignation and shook it dejectedly.

After all the craziness, all the dying, and all the close calls, we are enemies in our own country. All those fucking deaths, for what? To have fucking bloody, stabbed dolls thrown at us when we get home? What a fucking joke!

John's anger was rising to a fever pitch and he became alarmed at how tense and infuriated he'd become within seconds. He felt an uncontrollable urge to lash out and to maim.

Starting with that goddamn hippie at the airport, he thought.

In John's rage, he believed that if he were to have had his firearm during that confrontation, he would've shot the protestor. That thought both exhilarated and petrified the young returning corpsman. John, mild-mannered and well-reasoned prior to his tour in Vietnam, now found himself struggling with an uncontrollable inner rage. He was especially frightened by the nearly spontaneous manner with which the rage surfaced. His anger was not triggered by any one thing and therefore John did not know how to harness the unbridled aggression.

Frustrated, John closed his eyes and hoped to find peace in his dreams. However, his dreams rudely greeted him with images of broken bodies, the aroma of burnt flesh, and the familiar, blood-curdling cries of grievously injured brothers.

"Johnny, Johnny? Please, Johnny. Please help me!"

It was Vinnie, but John Chang couldn't find him because the air was thick with smoke and thicker with cries and moans for help.

"*Corpsmen up, corpsmen up, corpsmen up!*"

"Doc Chang, c'mere quick, I need you!"

"Doc, Doc, I'm dying, Doc. I can't find my leg and blood is shooting outta my femoral artery like a fucking volcano! Hurry! I ain't got much more time left!"

The calls for Chang were coming from all quarters, from different brothers. Chang struggled to see. The fog of smoke and burning flesh prevented him from seeing the hand that he held in front of his face, much less the broken bodies strewn about the hill a mere dozen yards from his position.

John panicked and began to yell, "Vinnie? *Vin-nieeee-EEE!* Where are you? I want to help you but I can't find you. Where are you?"

"I'm here!"

The response was like an orchestra of dozens of injured and dying Marines. Amongst the cacophony of scared voices was

Vinnie's. John desperately began to run toward his friend's voice, however, he tripped over a body part and fell to the ground. Upon closer inspection, John realized that he had tripped on an arm and it had subsequently grabbed him by the ankle. The body-less arm would not surrender its grip of John's leg.

"Let me go! Let me go, goddammit! I gotta save my friend! Vinnie? Vinnieeeee! Where are you?"

"I'm here!"

It was the same collection of desperate voices, including Vinnie's. Again, John struggled to see and his breathing was labored in the thick, soupy Vietnam air. He repeatedly kicked at the hand around his ankle, in an effort to escape its grip. Eventually, the hand released John's ankle and the corpsman stumbled forward, trying to find his friend before it was too late. As John rushed forward, he encountered a field of faces staring back up at him. The faces extended upwards. John was in a garden of death.

The faces were frozen in varied expressions of pain. Many were missing chunks of skull, eyes, noses, and jaws. A number of others were intact yet badly bloodied.

All were lifeless.

"Holy shit," John exclaimed as he walked through this wasteland of despair, "these are the guys who died on my watch. I failed them! They were crying out to me in pain and afraid to die. They told me that they were gonna miss their mamas and their gals back in the world. They asked me to save them and I didn't.

"I fucked up."

John began to weep tears of blood. He endeavored to wipe the tears from his eyes, but the blood smeared across his face and obscured his vision. John began to panic. He wondered if he'd die before he reached his friend. Or worse yet: If he'd fail again and find his lifelong friend lifeless.

"Vinnie? Vinnie, where are you, pal?"

"I'm . . . here . . . save . . . me . . . *[cough!]* . . . don't . . . let . . . me . . . die . . . John. Don't . . ."

John realized that Vinnie's voice no longer was obscured by the throng of voices that he had heard minutes earlier. Vinnie's was the last audible voice.

"Fuck! Vinnie, please. It's so hard to see out here and the blood in my eyes is making it even worse! Wave something, bang something, throw something. Please, Vinnie, help me find you!"

Silence echoed in John's ears. He trudged onward, feeling the searing heat envelop him and hearing incoming artillery whistle by his head with such ferocity that his helmet quivered and his ears rang in its wake. John bravely humped forward, desperate to find his brother and best friend. However, a mortar exploded nearby and the concussion of its blast lifted John off his feet and threw him like a rag doll through the air. John felt eerily unencumbered from the stressful bondage of war as his arms and legs oscillated wildly through time and space.

John's out-of-body experience was ephemeral. He crashed hard on what appeared to be damp, rocky ground. Dazed, John shook his head to dislodge the cobwebs from the recesses of his mind. He sat up and waited impatiently for his eyes to adjust to the darkness.

Goddammit, hurry and clear up already. I gotta find Vinnie. I gotta save my friend. I can't fail him.

The corpsman relied upon his training and surveyed the land. His eyes adjusted to the darkness. The ground under John's feet shifted unexpectedly. John looked down and a familiar form came into focus.

"You are too late, John. You failed in your mission to save me, old friend. I'm dead."

It was Vinnie. The mortar blast had not thrown John onto a rock pile. Rather, it had flung him atop his friend. Startled, John collapsed onto his knees to survey his companion.

"Vinnie, look at me, pal. I will save you!" Vinnie's body was grotesquely disfigured; he was missing a leg and part of an arm. John pulled out his morphine needles and gauze pads but he didn't know where to begin.

"John, put your kit away, you're too late. Look at me. I'm dead. You're never going to bring me back."

"Vinnie!" John shook Vinnie by the shoulders but he offered no resistance. Shocked, John shook Vinnie's lifeless body again, and the mortally wounded Marine's head bucked violently. John stared at Vinnie's face and, initially, his blue eyes shined like beacons. A bright light shined from Vinnie's eyes, blinding John in the process. However, as quickly as the light flashed in Vinnie's eyes, it was gone. His eyes dimmed and became lifelessly dark.

John held the broken, dead body of his friend as blood cascaded down his arms.

"Vinnie? Vin? No, Vinnie, please. Please don't die," John pleaded as tears flowed from his eyes. "I'm so sorry that I was late! Oh, God, no, no, NOOOO! Vinnie, I'm sorry that I failed you. I love you, brother! Vinnie? *Vinnie? NO! NO!* NOOOOOOOOO!"

"Doc? Doc? Chang? *CHANG!* Wake up! Wake up before you cause this plane to crash!"

Startled, John's eyes flashed wide open. He was no longer in the bloody, stiflingly hot jungles of Vietnam, over the body of his friend.

"Wh-where am I?" John inquired of the uniformed personnel that stood over him.

"You're on a plane to Dover. You're going home." Confused and still not fully awake, John struggled to comprehend his fellow serviceman.

"Dover? But my friend, Vinnie, I was trying to save him but I was—"

"John, please wake up! You ain't in 'Nam anymore. You musta been having a nightmare or something. You're safe and you ain't been trying to save anyone. But you sure as hell have been squirming, waving with your hands, and jerking your head since we took off outta El Toro a couple of hours ago!"

John finally emerged from the fog of sleep and the grasp of terror that was his nightmare. *Holy shit,* he thought, *what the hell kinda nightmare was THAT? I hope it never happens again.* He then murmured under his breath, "I'm so sorry that I failed you, Vinnie, just liked I failed all those other injured Marines out in the shit."

Petrified, John refused to sleep for the remainder of the flight. He did not want to be transported back to the Hell that he had left behind. And so began John's decades-long struggle with PTSD and his struggles with trying to get a peaceful night's sleep.

John watched the sun rise over the East Coast as the plane began its descent. He couldn't remember the last time that he had observed such a peaceful setting. The plane touched down seconds later. A half-hour later, John was at Dover Air Force Base in a special basement office, eating a delicious breakfast of pancakes, eggs, bacon, and sausage. The weary war veteran cried as he ate his first good meal in well over a year.

"Chang? John Chang?" John peered up from his plate and, noticing that an officer was addressing him, leapt to his feet and offered a crisp salute.

"Sir, yes, sir!"

"Relax, Chang. I just want to fill you in on what to expect over the next couple of hours. The body of your friend, Lance Corporal Vincent B. Santaniello, is making its way here from El Toro. He actually took off a couple of hours after you did. The body will be in its casket when it arrives and, if you'd like, you can view your friend's body before it is loaded into the hearse for the drive up to New York."

John stood motionless and could not utter a response. Instead, he was preoccupied with the notion of seeing his lifelong friend in a casket.

"Chang? What do you want to do?"

"I'll view Vinnie's body, sir," John replied impulsively.

"Thank you, Chang. I'll be back when we are ready for you. Enjoy your breakfast, young man." The officer turned as if to walk away, but he stopped after taking a couple of steps and turned back to John.

"Hey, Doc," the officer said in a reassuring, gentle tone, "thank you for your service to your country and to your fellow Marines out in Vietnam. I know you experienced some crazy shit and, in case you ain't noticed, you Vietnam GIs ain't exactly getting a hero's welcome back here.

"Be careful, Doc. Lay low when you get back to civilization. And don't go around bragging that you did a tour in 'Nam, unless you want to be attacked by yellow commie bastards." With that, the officer offered John a hearty handshake and a solemn salute before he retired to his quarters down the hall.

John looked at the floor and sighed.

"Shit. I just wanna get home, get a job, and start working. I ain't looking for any trouble." He then sat down at the table and took another bite of his pancake.

Two hours passed and the officer had yet to emerge from his office. John spent the entire time fretting about seeing his pal in a casket. The young corpsman's earlier nightmare had unnerved him, and he was sickened by this whole affair. In fact, John began to second-guess his decision to do this for Vinnie's parents, because he was scared.

The officer finally returned to Chang's room. "Chang," he stated matter-of-factly, "your friend, Santaniello, arrived. Follow me."

Holy shit. I'm more nervous now than I was when I ran into arty to try and rescue a casualty.

Chang tried to play it cool but he was visibly shaken. As John walked a few steps behind the officer, he felt as if he was humping up one of the notoriously numbered hills of Vietnam; his breathing was becoming labored. The officer suddenly stopped and, without turning around, asked, "You okay, Chang? You sound like you're dying back there!"

John offered a weak *I'm fine* between gasps.

"It ain't too late to back out," the officer said. "We'll make up a believable excuse as to why you couldn't complete this mission."

John momentarily entertained that option before thinking that Vinnie undoubtedly would've done the same for him, and would have done so without hesitation.

"Hell no, sir! I ain't backing away from Vinnie or his family. He was my brother back home and we never deserted each other when the going got tough back home, so I sure as hell ain't desertin' him now!"

"That's good to hear, Chang. The U.S. trained you right," exclaimed the officer. "Now, let's go."

The two men stood before a heavy, metal-framed door. The officer unbolted the door and grunted as he pushed it open. The men were greeted by a *WHOOSH!* of icy air as they entered the morgue for returning bodies. John looked around the ice-cold room and he observed at least twenty bodies lying in caskets or on stretchers. Chang's eyes darted left and right.

And then he found him.

Across the room, roughly twenty-five feet from where he stood, was his friend's casket. John read the tag that hung from the side of the simple casket: *SANTANIELLO, V.B., KIA CAM LO.* The officer saw the pain in John's face and said that he'd leave him alone for a few minutes.

John was overwhelmed at the notion of being alone, albeit with his friend, in a room full of dead people. However, he was committed to fulfilling the promise that he'd made Carmine while he was in Japan hours earlier.

Get it together, man. Vinnie needs you more than ever.

John hesitantly approached Vinnie's casket. As he drew closer, memories of growing up with Vinnie flooded his mind. John harkened back to those carefree days of running down Jamaica Avenue, crossing 168th Street, and heading toward the movie theater with Vinnie and the boys to catch a flick. Next, he reminisced about hanging out in Vinnie's basement and watching Carmine create marvelous structures with his expert carpentry skills. He also wistfully recalled standing outside of the grocery store, singing off-key with Vinnie and their poor-man's barbershop quartet.

Oh, my God, John thought as reality cruelly pre-empted his walk down memory lane, *Vinnie's dead.*

John found himself at the base of the casket and saw something that he'd never seen before at other funerals: The casket was half-open and half-closed. Vinnie was completely visible from his mid-chest up to his head, but John couldn't see anything below Vinnie's chest. Even more confounding was the fact that Vinnie was behind what appeared to be curved, bulletproof glass. The glass extended from the top of the casket, above Vinnie's head, until it met the wooden portion of the casket above Vinnie's chest. The wood comprised the balance of the casket. John wanted so desperately to touch his friend and to whisper into his ear how much he loved him, but the barrier prevented any such contact.

Vinnie was entombed in his casket.

John stared through the glass and into many yesterdays as he peered at his best friend's face. Vinnie was as handsome as ever, despite the fact that his face was skinnier than John remembered. Additionally, despite the heavy makeup that was spread across Vinnie's face, John noticed pronounced crow's feet surrounding the outer rims of his pal's eyes. The hair was immaculately combed and it was darker than he recalled. It was darker than the light-brown-and-blond combination that always caught ladies' eyes back when they were young and carefree. There was something wrong, though, besides the fact that Vinnie was in that goddamn glass-enclosed casket. John wracked his brain to figure out what was missing from, what was off with, the remains of his beloved friend.

And then it hit John.

Vinnie's blue eyes were eternally extinguished. Those eyes lit up every room that Vinnie was in and they also set him apart from his olive-skinned, brown-eyed family members. Vinnie's steel-blue eyes were his secret weapon. John reminisced about the affinity that many young ladies shared for his pal's blue eyes. They lent him a sense of mystique and now, sadly, they were snuffed out. That explained the sensation of darkness that enveloped John as he stood at respectful attention at the foot of his brother's casket. Suddenly, John was overcome with the emotion that he had been repressing.

John peered down at his handsome friend and heartily cried as he observed the crisp dress blues that adorned the dead Marine's body. He despaired at the fact that Vinnie was being buried in the very uniform that he'd planned to wear at his sister's wedding just a few months later.

Chang placed his hands on the glass above Vinnie's cleanly shaved face and perfectly parted hair, and he steadied himself against the considerable weight of the casket.

"No, goddamnit, no! Vinnie, this ain't fair, this ain't right! You were the rock of your family and the rock of our friends. What will we all do now without you, Vin?" John yearned for just one more moment to share with his departed friend.

"VINNIE! We were gonna go have a beer at the bar up on Hillside Avenue and 169th Street, next to the Emigrant Savings Bank, when you got back! We were gonna talk about chicks, R&R, cars, rock and roll, and the shit that we saw over there.

"We were gonna talk about being men, and maybe about getting married soon! Why'd you hafta die, Vinnie? Why'd ya hafta go and fuckin' die on us? You were supposed to make it back, goddamnit. You were supposed to make it back!"

John's voice trailed off into a barely discernible plea as he lowered his head against the glass that entombed his friend. John's tears streamed down the contours of the enclosure and he saw Vinnie's blurred face literally inches away.

Beleaguered, John shouted, "VINNIE? Holy shit, Vin, I'm gonna miss you something terrible. I love you, Vinnie. Thanks for always being there for me, through thick and thin. I'll never forget you, Vinnie. *Never*. You're my best friend right now and you'll *still* be my best friend fifty years from now!"

John rubbed the tears out of his eyes and stood up, over the casket. He realized that he couldn't lose it like this again when he arrived in New York the next morning. He had to be strong for Carmine and Rose, for Lilly and Joseph, for Nunu, and for Rosalie. John lowered his head as he reflected on how devastating the wake and funeral were going to be to Vinnie's family and friends.

He turned to walk out but then stopped and looked up to the ceiling. Slowly, John turned around and walked back to the casket. He gently placed his right hand on the casket and then lifted all of his fingers but for his index finger. John pressed his index finger hard against the glass and recalled that day, over a decade ago, when he and Vinnie had pricked their index fingers and then pressed their pierced index fingers against each other, rubbing the commingled blood against the digit of the other while exclaiming the same expression to each other.

John looked down at the peaceful, expressionless face of his deceased friend and then repeated what he and Vinnie said to each other as nine-year-olds.

"Blood brothers forever."

John slightly smiled through the tears. He was rich with wonderful memories of his fallen brother.

"I love you, blood brother. Vinnie, I will always love you and I will never forget you, for so long as I shall live."

With that, John patted the glass over Vinnie's head and chest, again wiped the tears from his eyes, and slowly walked out of the morgue and back into the office, where he saw the officer waiting for him.

"You okay, Chang?"

"Yes, sir."

"Good. Go get some sleep, Chang. You'll be leaving for New York at 0430 hours tomorrow morning."

*   *   *

0430, April 21, 1968. John was seated next to another Marine in the nondescript black hearse. He had just accompanied Vinnie's casket from the base, along a special tarmac, where five other Marines in their crisp dress blues assisted him in pulling the casket toward the awaiting hearse. These Marines sensed that Vinnie was special to John; they privately expressed their condolences to him before offering very solemn salutes to Vinnie's casket.

John observed the pageantry and thought bitterly, *I can't believe my brother, Vinnie, really is gone. He's dead. He's really fucking dead. Goddamn.*

Vinnie's casket was strapped and secured very tightly into the rear of the hearse, which further saddened John because Vinnie had seemingly been in perpetual motion when he and John used to make their way around the old neighborhood. Indeed, seeing Vinnie so still was jarring to his old wingman. The driver asked John if he had everything and if he was ready to go.

Ready to go.

John couldn't believe that he actually was going home for the first time in what seemed like forever. Yet what should've been the happiest day of John's life was by far the worst ever, for his best friend was lying a few feet behind him. As the hearse pulled onto the northbound interstate, tears began traveling south, down John's cheeks.

410

The driver tried to make small talk with John but he was not in the mood, so he pretended to be asleep. He maintained this ruse for the nearly three-hour drive up north. John peeked periodically and recognized the New Jersey Turnpike, then the Verrazano Bridge. Next, John recognized the Belt Parkway and Brooklyn, and he knew that they weren't that far from Queens. The hearse took the Belt Parkway exit for the Van Wyck Expressway and John got a lump in his throat, for he and his pal were minutes away from home.

The hearse came to a stop and the driver gently nudged John.

"We're here."

John opened his eyes and he instantly recognized the funeral home. They were on Hillside Avenue, mere blocks from Vinnie's home in Jamaica. Tears welled in John's eyes as he saw the very bar where he and Vinnie had been planning to enjoy their homecoming beers with aplomb and relief. Instead, John was preparing to wheel his friend's lifeless body into a funeral home. John dabbed his eyes and turned to the driver.

"What now?"

The driver turned to John and responded, "I will remove the casket on the gurney and then the funeral parlor workers will wheel the casket into the funeral home. You will walk behind the casket, standing guard over it as you march solemnly. Once you're inside, the staff will give you further directions."

John saluted the young Marine and thanked him. He then exited the hearse and watched the process unfold before his eyes. The funeral home's staff exited the rear of the facility as the Marine driver removed Vinnie's casket, affixed to the gurney and draped in Old Glory, from the hearse.

Reflexively, John barked out an authoritative, "CAREFUL! That's not just another dead person. It is the body of a Marine and, more importantly, it is the body of my brother. You will treat him with dignity and respect at all times! Understand?"

Shaken and alarmed at the unexpected, forceful command, the four staffers immediately cowered before stuttering a collective, "Y-y-y-yes, sir!"

The four men gingerly and resolutely wheeled Vinnie's casket inside the funeral home, with John marching behind them while maintaining a salute, ensuring that Vinnie's entrance into the parlor was dignified and respectful.

As John entered the funeral home's rear entrance, he was able to peer into the room where Vinnie's wake was being held and he saw Carmine's profile. Suddenly, a young man who didn't think twice about running full-bore into a firefight in order to render aid to injured brothers while hot incoming artillery whistled about his head became hesitant and weak-kneed at the sight of Vinnie's dad.

Holy shit, what do I do? What do I say? John thought as, to his surprise, he instinctively began to stride toward Vinnie's family. John's heart pounded as he got closer to the Santaniellos.

There's Carmine, Rose, Joseph, Nunu, and Lilly, John thought, *and they don't even know that I'm here.*

"Good afternoon, Mr. Santaniello, sir."

Stunned silence.

"Mrs. Santaniello, Mrs. Buffa, Joseph, Lilly. Good afternoon."

Carmine looked as strong as ever to John, but his face couldn't mask the intense pain he had suffered since learning of his son's death.

"John!" Carmine's eyes lit up upon recognizing John. "C'mere, son," he continued, before grabbing Chang by the shoulders and giving him a bear hug that nearly squeezed all of the oxygen from John's lungs. Carmine did not release his vise grip of John, thus the corpsman was unable to say anything in response. He was struggling for air. John felt moisture about his neck and realized that Carmine was weeping.

Carmine placed his quivering lips millimeters from John's ear and muttered through gritted teeth, "I'm so proud of you, John. Welcome home, son. I will never forget what you did for my son. From today on, you are a Santaniello. You are my son, you understand? I love you like my own son, John."

Carmine released his grip slightly, to allow him to extend his arms while holding John about his shoulders so as to get a better view of the returning serviceman. Chang was dressed in traditional USMC dress greens, but since he actually was commissioned as a corpsman through the U.S. Navy, he wore Navy stripes on the sleeves of his dress greens. His black, patent-leather shoes were buffed and shined to a blinding glow.

John stood erectly and at attention as Carmine looked him over and repeated, "I'm so proud of you, son."

Finally able to breathe, John took a deep breath before responding, "Thank you, sir. I'm so sorry about this, sir. Vinnie was like a brother to me and I love him something fierce. He was a great man."

John then turned to the rest of the family, standing uneasily behind Carmine, and continued, "You all should know that Vinnie was a great, brave Marine who was loved by his entire Company. He served well. I am so sorry about losing him. I loved him like a brother and I consider all of you my family."

That was it.

John's emotions, which he had been able to hold in abeyance, overcame him. He began to cry and, ashamed, he turned and lowered his head into his hand as his shoulders heaved. Carmine and Rose simultaneously approached John, with Carmine taking John's left shoulder as Rose grasped his right hand.

Rose, whose face was ashen, cleared her throat and stated, "Don't cry, John. It isn't your fault. Those sons of bitches took our Vinnie, not you. You served your country and you served Vinnie by bravely bringing him back home. Please don't cry, John. You performed a great service to us and to Vinnie by flying across the world to bring him home to us." Rose then gently kissed John's right cheek and gave him a slight hug before she returned to her mother and children.

Carmine continued to hold John's left shoulder as Lilly approached John from the right. Lilly gently clasped John's right shoulder in her hand. John peered over his right shoulder to glimpse Lilly's face. He smiled at her and she returned a warm smile. John realized that he had no right to break down in front of the Santaniellos, of all people, given the depth of their despair and he apologized to Vinnie's family for his undisciplined act.

The corpsman wiped away the tears and sniffed before he took a breath and said to Lilly, "You look great, Lil. I'm really sorry about . . . this."

Lilly leaned over and kissed John's cheek before saying, "Thank you, John. I know this has been a terrible ordeal for you, too. You grew up with us here in Jamaica and we shared so many happy memories. Thank you for coming home with Vinnie. It's comforting to know that my brother had his best pal at his side for the trip back home."

John was impressed by Lilly's courage and maturity under such duress. "You know, Lil," he said while turning to face her and simultaneously locking eyes with her, "Vinnie absolutely loved and adored you. You were his best friend. He told me so many times that he was gonna take care of you and your family after the service. But, Vinnie being Vinnie, he made me promise not to tell you guys that because he didn't want you, in particular, to call him a square!"

Lilly chuckled at John's impromptu confession and smiling, she responded, "Vinnie was a knucklehead like that. He always tried to project the same tough-guy persona as Pa! We all knew that he was a nerd, though!"

John and Lilly, two kids from the old neighborhood, stood at the awkward precipice of the onset of adulthood, but neither had fully relinquished their not-too-distant carefree times as teens.

Of course, John had suppressed his teenage tendencies for the past year as Vietnam had greatly expedited his process of entering manhood. And Lilly had been abruptly coerced into abandoning her relatively simple lifestyle when she was confronted with the tragic death of a truly loved family member, much sooner than she should have expected to have to deal with such a thing. Yet, there they stood, two erstwhile kids from a much gentler time, briefly smiling and laughing in a manner that belied the great tragedy that was in their midst.

Lilly gave John another hug, and he returned the love with equal vigor. The smile quickly abandoned Lilly's lips. She again lowered her head and walked back to her family, leaving John and Carmine standing alone as Vinnie's casket was being wheeled into the room.

CHAPTER 23

IT IS FINISHED

John felt a palpable chill as the casket was wheeled into the room. He snapped to attention and rigidly paced to the men who were wheeling Vinnie's remains toward the center of the room, where he would lie over the next two days. The funeral home workers were completely intimidated by the stern-faced serviceman and they hesitated and looked to John for directions on how to do the job that they had been doing for years. John gestured with his chin toward the final location and the men completed their grim task.

The casket still had the plexiglass covering the top third of Vinnie's body, with the wooden casket remaining closed from Vinnie's lower torso to where his feet would've been. That portion of the casket was draped in a beautifully crisp American flag. John waited for the staff to leave the casket and then he immediately positioned himself at the head of Vinnie's casket, turned erectly to face Vinnie's body, and offered a solemn, heartfelt salute.

John's eyes began to well up, but he willed the tears away because he did not want to bring shame or additional pain to Vinnie's family. John peered out of the corner of his eyes and noticed that the family was slowly approaching the body. He saw a familiar horror in their faces. The corpsman released his salute and then snapped his body around, arms straight at this side, and looking straight ahead at the oncoming Santaniello family.

Bedlam ensued.

"My baby! My baby! My poor Vinnie! Look at you. They have you sealed inside of a tube. I can't even touch my baby's face one more time! Oh, my God!" Rose then threw herself on top of the plexiglass, over her son's prone body, and John noticed Vinnie's body shift slightly inside of the casket as a result of the jolt.

"Oh, Vinnie, my God, Vinnie! What did those bastards do to you? Why? WHY? *WHYYY?* I didn't want you to go over there. I knew you weren't gonna make it back to me. I *KNEW* it! What am I gonna do without you, Vinnie? I need my baby back. Vinnie, you were too young to die." Rose's face was awash with tears and streaked with red, as she repeatedly used her fingers to thrust the tears from her face.

John flinched as Rose wailed. The scene playing out before him slowed in his mind's eye, as he thought to himself that the pain in Rose's cries reminded him of the panic-stricken cries of otherworldly pain that came from grotesquely injured and mortally wounded brothers out in the shit. John began to sweat as he felt the searing heat of the jungle creeping up his chest and suffocating his collar, making it difficult to breathe. John blinked rapidly in an effort to escape this confusing fog that had been enveloping him all too frequently since he'd left 'Nam, but he couldn't shake it.

He was back there.

Panicked, John's eyes began to dart around what was once an eerily silent funeral parlor, but was now a viper-infested NVA death trap. John heard more cries of pain and he quickly darted his head to and fro, scanning the uneven, dark terrain for his injured brother.

Instead of a brother Marine, John saw Lilly, down on her knees in front of Vinnie's casket, audibly crying and repeating Vinnie's name between sobs. John snapped out of it, away from his internal demons, and was back in the funeral home. Rose was seated on a chair ten feet in front of the casket, with her husband seated to her left, his arm draped around her shoulders. Nunu was seated to Rose's right and she was dressed all in black, with a black veil concealing her grief-stricken face. Joseph was standing on the covered side of Vinnie's casket and peering over toward his exposed upper body.

Carmine rose from his seat and began to walk, ever so slowly, toward his beloved son. He immediately noticed the half-open casket and plexiglass enclosure and the gravity of the situation hit him like a ton of bricks.

Goddamn, the grizzled World War II veteran thought, *my boy's legs were blown off. My poor Vinnie's legs were blown the hell offa him.*

John maintained a stoic appearance as he stood guard over Vinnie's casket. Carmine approached him. The dazed father was trying to distract himself from the realization that his son must've suffered greatly when he died, so he turned his attention to his son's best friend. Carmine's fatherly instincts kicked in. He saw the anguish in the young man's face. With nauseous despair in the pit of his stomach, Carmine turned to the corpsman.

"Johnny," Carmine began, using a nickname that only he, Vinnie, and their closest friends used when addressing him, "relax, son. You're amongst family now. You don't have to be so stiff."

Try as he might, however, the despair in Carmine's heart was too great, and he lapsed into vast self-loathing.

"Johnny, this here," he said as he gestured toward his son's remains with his right hand, "this is my fault, son. See, I encouraged Vinnie to join the service. I made him go. But then when I knew he was being sent to Vietnam, I told him to get out on account of his asthma. He coulda gotten out because of that, and I wrote him many times while he was over there, asking him to get out."

Carmine paused and inhaled in an effort to collect himself and to stall the bile that was invading his throat. His eyes were moist and the sight of this great man in such a weakened state depressed

John. This man who had been his idol as a kid. Carmine was what John had aspired to be as a man and now his hero was compromised and on the verge of crying.

"But he didn't want to leave, Johnny," Carmine looked square into John's eyes and John, nervous as all hell, nonetheless returned the gaze without flinching. "He said that he couldn't leave his guys. He didn't want to let his guys down." Carmine's voice trailed off and became a little pitchy as he recounted this exchange with his heroic son. Vinnie's father looked up toward the heavens and then lowered his head in the direction of the casket. John followed Carmine's eyes as the grieving father struggled to look into the plexiglass. Finally, Carmine's eyes locked on his son.

Carmine found solace in the fact that Vinnie's hair was immaculately combed, his face was clean-shaven, and his dress blues were radiant under the glass.

"He looks so peaceful, Johnny," Carmine whispered absently. "My boy. My boy. I killed my boy, Johnny. I *killt* him."

Carmine placed his hands on the plexiglass and leaned forward slightly, bowing his head until his forehead rested upon the glass partition over his son's chest, which was adorned with a series of pins and medals, including the Purple Heart.

John hesitantly approached Carmine and placed his hand on Carmine's shoulder. "Mr. Santaniello, sir, I . . . I . . . I–" Carmine lifted his head and observed John peripherally.

Carmine cut off John's thought with his own melancholy proclamation. Whispering just audibly enough for Chang to hear, Carmine exclaimed, "There's no need for me to live anymore.

"Johnny," Carmine continued, "my life ain't worth a damn right now. I caused all of this, son. This is all my fault. There ain't no goddamn reason to live no more."

Chang was stunned and momentarily speechless. He couldn't even think, much less formulate what to say to his best friend's father. He could not assimilate the despair in Carmine's admission. This was a man of honor and boundless fortitude in John's eyes, so seeing him this distraught shocked the corpsman.

"Mr. Santaniello, sir. Vinnie would not be happy to hear you say that, sir."

Carmine froze momentarily. He stared into John's eyes and the corpsman realized instantly that Carmine's life was irreparably damaged. Vinnie's tragic death destroyed his father. The sadness in the older gentleman's eyes portended the misery that would persist for decades to come for the defeated shell of a once-proud man.

Carmine pivoted back to his son's casket and as his head descended toward the plexiglass tears splashed down upon the protective barricade. John's reassuring hand slid down, off of Carmine's shoulder, as he continued to sob.

John returned to his post to the right of Vinnie's casket, adjacent to his resting head. He glanced toward Lilly and saw that she was crying uncontrollably. The dark streaks of mascara intermingled with her tears to mar her beautiful face. John saw the pain in her face and immediately recounted all the memories that he had shared with her and Vinnie.

Goddamn, he thought, *Lil's gonna have such a hard time with this 'cause Vinnie took such good care of her. He was a big brother to her even though he was younger than her. None of the neighborhood guys dared to disrespect Lilly because Vinnie and his dad wouldn't tolerate that. And, gosh, did the neighborhood guys fear getting on the bad side of Vinnie or Carmine.*

John's eyes scanned the room, from Carmine to Rose, and then to Lilly, Nunu, and Joseph, respectively. Each was struggling with this terrible loss and their collective pain moved the young corpsman. He couldn't fully comprehend how devastating Vinnie's death would be to the Santaniellos. Surely, he knew that it would fracture what was a very close-knit family. Chang could only hope that the vast divide caused by Vinnie's death would not permanently fracture his surviving family and friends.

John repeated this wish multiple times over the next thirty-six hours, as scores of locals visited the funeral home to pay their respects to Carmine, Rose, Nunu, Lilly, and Joseph. The scene over the course of the two-day wake service was similarly depressing. So many people approached John, who was permanently stationed at the side of Vinnie's casket, and remarked on how wonderful it was to see him. Others commented on how mature he had become since going into the service. Still others said that he was barely recognizable in his dress greens. And nearly everyone extended him a firm handshake or a hug, expressions of condolences and love.

John was composed until the moment his own family arrived to pay their respects to the Santaniellos. John's mother, father, and fourteen siblings entered the room during the early portion of the first day's service. The room already was crowded with grieving friends when the Changs arrived unbeknownst to John, who had not seen his family since his return from Vietnam.

John had called his family the night before, from Dover Air Force Base, and explained that he would be in New York the following morning. John also explained to his family that he was there to serve in his official capacity as a member of the service and, as such, he warned his family that they should not make a scene when they see him in the funeral home. He reminded his mother, in particular, that she couldn't make a scene when she saw him. John sternly reminded his mother that Rose would be there and the last thing that he wanted her to see was a mother rejoicing in the shadow of Vinnie's casket at the return of her son from the Vietnam War.

The Changs, absolutely reserved and completely respectful, had the children sit in the rear of the room, so as to not cause a commotion toward the front, particularly in the first row, where Vinnie's family was seated. Mr. and Mrs. Chang slowly walked toward the Santaniellos and when they arrived at the front row, Carmine and Rose immediately stood to greet them. Mr. and Mrs. Chang had visited the Santaniellos on multiple occasions after they'd learned of Vinnie's death and their classy display of love and respect profoundly impacted Carmine and Rose.

Carmine and Mr. Chang shook hands after Mr. Chang bowed respectfully. The two men then embraced for an extended period of time before Mr. Chang progressed to Rose. Mrs. Chang bowed and respectfully shook Carmine's hand as her husband bowed and gently hugged Rose. The Changs performed the same ritual for the remainder of Vinnie's immediate family, all the while not even acknowledging their son, who was stationed a mere ten feet from where this was occurring. True to their word, Mr. and Mrs. Chang did not outwardly acknowledge their son, despite the great joy and anxiety that they both were experiencing at that very moment.

Carmine and Rose stood and spoke with the Changs briefly. "We will forever be indebted to your son, John, for what he did for our Vinnie, and our family," Carmine remarked solemnly. "He is a wonderful young man and he'll always be a part of our family."

Rose, still adrift in the fog of depression that enveloped her, looked to Mrs. Chang and asked, "Have you had an opportunity to see your son since he returned home?" Mrs. Chang demurely noted that she had not and Rose, shocked, asked Mrs. Chang to go to her son.

"You are blessed to have the opportunity to hug and kiss your son and welcome him back from the war. Please, please go to your son." Rose gestured to John as she said this, but Mrs. Chang politely declined the offer and thanked Rose for her courage.

Carmine turned and looked to Chang. "John, come here."

"No, sir, I must stay with my friend." John was doing his damnedest to fight back the tears that were welling in his eyes.

"John, you've been standing there for hours," Carmine stated. "Please take a break to use the facilities and rest your legs. The bathroom is out the door, to the left."

The look in Carmine's eyes revealed to John that it was okay to leave his post and that further resistance would not be well-received.

John turned and saluted Vinnie and then, in a fluid yet erect fashion, pivoted on his feet 180 degrees and exited the room, all without acknowledging his family. Once John was in the foyer, Carmine turned to the Changs and said, "Please go to your son. Bring your kids and welcome home your son. He is a truly amazing young man."

The Changs thanked Rose and Carmine, bowed again to every member of the immediate family, then walked very slowly and respectfully to their obedient, quiet children. Without fanfare or any undue noise, the entire Chang clan walked out of the room.

The funeral director, who had realized when John exited the room that a family reunion was about to transpire, ushered John into a private room in the basement of the facility. He then returned to the main foyer, where he greeted the Changs and directed them to the basement. Once outside of the view of the Santaniellos and grieving friends and family, the Changs quietly, yet tenderly, greeted their heroic son back into the fold.

There were seventeen sets of tear-soaked eyes in the room as the Changs hugged and kissed their returning warrior. "Oh, son," remarked Mrs. Chang, "I am so relieved that God blessed us with your return. I was so scared that I was going to become one of the grieving mothers that I saw on the news every night. We missed you so much! Thank God you are home, my beloved son."

"John," began a forthright Mr. Chang, "what you did for the Santaniellos was very noble. Your actions have brought great honor to the family. I am so proud of you and so happy that you are back home."

John's siblings all repeated similar refrains as the Changs became whole again.

"I must go back," John remarked a few minutes into the heart-wrenching reunion. "I must comply with my orders and stand guard over our friend."

The Changs stepped aside, as if they were a human sea that was parting, and John stepped through the middle of the family, out of the room, and back upstairs, where he resumed his post next to Vinnie. John made eye contact with Carmine and he nodded discreetly toward Vinnie's father, which Carmine rightfully interpreted as a *thank you* from the emotional young corpsman. Carmine nodded in return.

Two veterans, heartbroken and forever impacted by the Vietnam War in overlapping yet radically different ways, were communicating with each other with nary a word being spoken between them.

The funeral was held the following day in the nearby parish of the Santaniello family, Presentation of the Blessed Virgin Mary, located at the corner of 89th Avenue and Parsons Boulevard, in the heart of Jamaica, Queens. Vinnie's casket, draped in an American flag, was escorted into the Roman Catholic church by six Marines dressed in their crisp dress blues, including pristine white pants, shiny black patent-leather shoes, and USMC-issued white-trimmed hats.

The Marines marched in somber unison into the church and, once Vinnie's casket was in its appropriate location in front of the altar, the Marines, in perfectly rehearsed fashion, carefully and respectfully removed the flag from its perch atop Vinnie's casket, folding it perfectly as it was removed.

Father McLaughlin presided over the funeral and the task proved very difficult for the priest, as he knew the family and had had the opportunity, a decade earlier, to celebrate several Masses with Vinnie serving as an altar boy. Of course, Father McLaughlin also had paid a very difficult visit to the Santaniello home on the day that the family had learned of Vinnie's death. The family's cries of despair that day haunted the priest in the days that followed.

The Santaniello family filed somberly into the church behind Vinnie's casket. Rose looked as if she was being dragged into the church by Carmine; she leaned heavily upon Carmine's right arm and shoulder as she trudged with hesitant, unsure steps into the church. Rose was dressed all in black, with a black veil obscuring her head and face. Carmine was dressed simply in a black suit, white shirt, and black tie. He felt as uncomfortable in such attire as he looked—it was not his typical wardrobe. The faces of the grieving parents were ashen and their jaws were taut with overwhelming grief. Further, their foreheads bore the anxiety-ridden hopelessness that one would expect of parents who have lost a child much too young to die.

Nunu, dressed identically to Rose, walked behind the grieving parents, and, like her daughter, she was propped up by the arm of her grandson, Joseph, who was clad in a dark suit and tie. Nunu's face, streaked with tears, was obscured by a black veil, and she was muttering prayers in Italian as she proceeded up the aisle, behind her family and Vinnie's casket. Joseph looked confused, perplexed, and sad. His eyes were red and his mouth was wound tightly into a frown. Clearly, Joseph was experiencing the wave of emotion that any twelve-year-old would have when trying to process the unexpected death of an older sibling.

Next in the progression of despair was Lilly.

Unlike her grandmother and mother, Lilly chose to walk into the church alone. She refused her fiancé Ralph's offer to walk her in. The oldest of the three Santaniello siblings wore a long, black skirt and her hair was pulled up into a bun. She wore conservative makeup and did not wear a veil to conceal her face. The combination of Lilly's olive skin, black skirt, sheer black stockings, and black heels gave her an ethereal presence as she walked unescorted into the church. Lilly's coal-black eyes were weary yet determined, almost angry in their appearance. They stared straight ahead in an unwavering fashion. Her lips, colored by in a muted red lipstick, were slightly pursed in a frown while her jaw was fixed by her clenched teeth.

Unbeknownst to everyone in the church, Lilly had brought Vinnie's final letter with her. It was still within its envelope and lovingly maintained in the purse that draped over her shoulder. In her hands was clasped an absolute treasure: The picture from the previous summer of her and Vinnie in their back yard, just before Vinnie was deployed overseas and into eternity.

Lilly held the last picture of them together tightly, yet carefully, in her hands. She had promised Vinnie the night before that she would not cede control of the photo to anyone, no matter what.

And that meant her father, too.

To his credit, Carmine had observed the photo in his daughter's hands as they entered the limo outside of their house earlier that morning, and he suppressed his initial urge to take the photo from her. Truth be told, Lilly's icy stare as she entered the limo convinced Carmine that it was a battle not worth waging.

As Lilly walked up the aisle, behind her grandmother, Joseph, Rose, her dad, and the Marines who wheeled Vinnie's casket up to the altar, the throng of friends and family seated in the pews to her left and right marveled at her grace, strength, and amazing fortitude. Everyone knew that Lilly and Vinnie were best friends and, as such, the congregation was stunned and driven to tears themselves by Lilly's proud march up the aisle. She was heartbroken, to be sure, but she'd promised Vinnie the night before that she'd be the strongest person in the church that day.

I ain't gonna cry, Vinnie. I promise you: I ain't gonna cry. I'm gonna be strong for you, like you were strong for me all these years. I love you, Vinnie.

True to her promise, Lilly walked with poise and a stern gaze past her family and friends. She passed Ralph and his family—including his brothers and sisters, with whom Lilly was friendly—without flinching. Ralph's mother, Matilda, lovingly reached into the passing progression of family and managed to caress Lilly's left hand. Lilly glanced toward Matilda and respectfully smiled and bowed her head as she continued walking toward the front of the church.

Lilly next saw Rosalie and her family. Of course, Rosalie had been a fixture at the funeral home during the wake and she had visited the Santaniello home quite often after Lilly broke the terrible news to her. Lilly felt great empathy for Rosalie; it had seemed like a foregone conclusion that she and Vinnie were going to be married.

As Lilly passed Rosalie and her family, her mind wandered to how Vinnie's and Rosalie's children would've looked.

Strange what kinda thoughts go through your mind when someone dies, Lilly mused.

Lilly peered through the space between Nunu and Joseph, in an effort to see the casket being wheeled ahead of her—as if she needed validation for this nightmare—but the presence of her parents obscured it. Lilly's attention turned to the pews to the right of the altar. The first row was reserved for the Santaniello family and the rows behind it were filled with aunts, uncles, and cousins from both sides of the family. They all looked devastated. Vinnie had been as popular with his extended family as he had been with his brothers in Vietnam. And speaking of brothers: There was John Chang, sitting in the fourth row with his enormous family, right behind the Santaniello and Buffa contingents.

Lilly's razor-sharp focus was broken momentarily by the sight of John, who was wearing civilian clothes, as opposed to the military garb that he'd worn during the wake.

Now that's the Johnny that I remember from the old days, before he and Vin were sent off to Vietnam.

John was wearing dark shades. However, he removed them after he realized that Lilly was looking at him, revealing moist eyes and a tear-stained face. John was not embarrassed by the tears, despite the notion that they were unbecoming for a Marine. Lilly's stoicism was nearly broken at the sight of John's vulnerable face and she heaved to suppress an outburst of unadulterated pain.

The somber procession suddenly came to a stop.

Vinnie's casket had reached its designated location before the altar and, as fate would have it, John was standing in his pew, adjacent to Lilly when she came to a stop. Suddenly, Lilly's despair overcame her and the color drained from her face as her knees buckled, causing her to lurch unsteadily to her right. John sprang to action and clasped Lilly's right hand and shoulder.

"You okay, Lil?" John was a USMC corpsman again and Lilly was his most important patient.

Lilly forced a smile before placing her lips a few inches from John's ear and whispering, "No, I'm not. My brother should not be in that casket up there, Johnny." The pain in Lilly's eyes broke John's heart. "My brother should not be dead, right?"

That question pierced John. He stammered, cleared his throat, and whispered in his friend's ear, "You're right, Lil. He shouldn't be dead. He was a great fella. I loved him like a brother.

"He was family, just like you, Joseph, Nunu, Rose, and Carmine all are family. I'll always be there for all of you. If you ever need anything, know that your brother Johnny is just a phone call away."

Lilly regained her composure upon John's encouraging words. The color returned to her face and as her family began to be ushered into their pew, Lilly smiled at John and mouthed, "I love you."

John responded in a slightly more pronounced whisper, "Love you, too, Lil. I love you, too." He gave her hand a gentle squeeze and she resumed walking to her designated pew, located to the right of Vinnie's flag-draped casket.

John sighed and muttered under his breath, "Goddamn it, Vinnie. What are we gonna do without you, buddy? How are we supposed to go on without the one that was everyone's rock?" John then peered at the casket and recalled the surreal scene a few days earlier when he'd observed Vinnie during the wake. The memory caused John to shudder. It served as another cruel reminder of the unforgiving consequences of war. John despondently shook his head as the funeral Mass began.

Father McLaughlin began to solemnly greet Vinnie's friends and family. Suddenly, the realization that Vinnie really was dead hit John and hit him hard. He grasped the pew ahead of him, lowered his chin, and began to weep. The Saint, once proud, strong, and loyal, was now but a memory, never to be seen or heard again.

John's mother placed her arm around John's shoulder and kissed the back of his head. John lifted his head and, with moist eyes, swallowed hard and focused on the kind words of a priest who had known Vinnie quite well.

Lilly had courageously agreed to recite the first reading of the funeral Mass. Father McLaughlin gestured toward Lilly when it was time to read the scripture and she stood up, walked to the center aisle, directly in front of Vinnie's casket, and genuflected toward the altar. As her right knee came into contact with the marble floor, Lilly hesitated and thought, *Vinnie, this is for you. I wouldn't be able to do this if it weren't for your spirit being with me to get me through this. I love you.*

With that, Lilly crossed herself, got up, and walked confidently—almost indignantly—to the lectern, where she proceeded to read from the Book of Wisdom, 2:23-3:9. It was a section that she chose, with Father McLaughlin's assistance, especially for her brother.

> *For God created human beings to be immortal, He made them as an image of His own nature; death came into the world through the devil's envy, as those who belong to him find to their cost. But the souls of the upright are in the hands of God, and no torment can touch them. To the unenlightened, they appear to die, their departure was regarded as a disaster, their leaving us like annihilation; but they are at peace. If, as it seemed to us, they suffered punishment, their hope was rich with immortality; slight was their correction, great will their blessings be. God was putting them to the test and has proved them worthy to be with Him. He has tested them like gold in a furnace, and accepted them as a perfect burnt offering. At their time of visitation, they will shine out; as sparks run through the stubble, so will they. They will judge nations, rule over people, and the Lord will be their king forever. Those who trust in Him will understand the truth, those who are faithful will live with Him in love; for grace and mercy await His holy ones, and He intervenes on behalf of His chosen.[2]*

Lilly read this scripture with great purpose. Every word was enunciated, and every sentence punctuated with heart-wrenching

---

[2] https://www.catholic.org/bible/book.php?id=27&bible_chapter=2

emotion and steadfast love. Lilly was not one to read in front of people, yet she was uncannily calm during this particular instance. Indeed, she would say for years afterward that Vinnie was up on the altar as she read, holding her hand and keeping her calm.

The congregation was captivated, not only by Lilly's performance but by the power of the Scripture that she read so eloquently. So powerful was the Scripture that many in the church sat mesmerized by its clear parallel with Vinnie's life and death. The young man's untimely passing was regarded as a disaster by everyone in the church. Indeed, Vinnie's death was akin to an annihilation of their collective hope in humanity's greater good. Yet their faith taught them to believe that Vinnie nonetheless was at peace. As much as their hearts were in their throats, the faithful who attended this funeral were called to believe that there was great peace amidst this suffocating tragedy.

For many that day, including Carmine, Rose, and scores of others, this peace proved elusive, as the cloud of despair was too overwhelming. However, a handful of the faithful who filed out of the church at the conclusion of the funeral were surprised to feel an ember of hope amidst a great blaze of despair.

John was struggling between the two realms. He was utterly devastated by the loss of his best friend and brother, but he felt some warmth in his heart as he reflected on the tenor of Lilly's reading. John considered himself a good Catholic, and the sentiment that resonated within him was this: "The souls of the upright are in the hands of God, and no torment can touch them."

Yet John struggled with trying to convince himself that Vinnie's soul was in the hands of God and that, as such, he could not be tormented. Additionally, John lamented, *Vinnie's soul may not be tormented, but the reading didn't say anything about the torment that his death is causing me.* Indeed, John was tormented about many aspects of his service in Vietnam, and this torment would take up residence in John's scarred psyche for decades to come.

At the conclusion of the funeral Mass, Father McLaughlin beseeched the angels and the saints to accompany Vietnam's Saint through the gates of Heaven and into eternal paradise. Following that invocation, the six Marines who had escorted Vinnie's casket into the church returned to escort the casket to the rear of the church, where Father McLaughlin stopped at the doors leading to the exit from the church. The priest turned and, with moist eyes, gestured to the Marines, who snapped to attention and meticulously unfolded the crisp American flag before perfectly draping it over Vinnie's casket. Father McLaughlin then sprinkled the covered casket with holy water. He placed incense in a golden thurible and swung the instrument to and fro as he walked deliberately around Vinnie's casket—the circulation of incense around a casket during a funeral Mass is an ancient Catholic custom of blessing. The priest then turned and walked toward the throng of family and friends lined up behind Vinnie's casket and he swung the thurible toward the crowd in a symbolic gesture of blessing them, too.

The priest then returned to the rear of the church and stopped at the head of Vinnie's casket, returned the chained thurible to the altar server, and bestowed a final blessing upon Vinnie and his survivors before he formally ended the Mass and walked out into the seasonably warm April sunshine. The six Marines holding Vinnie's casket marched in unison behind the priest and respectfully placed Vinnie's casket into the hearse for its drive to his final resting place at the Long Island National Cemetery in Farmingdale, New York.

The priest shared hearty hugs with the Santaniello family and with John Chang before they filed into the limo that would take them to the cemetery. Carmine had told John before the funeral Mass that morning that he wanted him to travel with the family to the cemetery. John considered respectfully declining the offer until he looked into Carmine's eyes and realized that resistance would be futile.

The Santaniellos and John graciously stood at the doorway to the limo and thanked all the family and friends who had come down to the funeral to show their respects for the fallen Marine. Many tears were shed during these exchanges before the Santaniellos— and the honorary Santaniello—finally retreated to the limo, mentally fatigued.

The hearse proceeded slowly through the streets of Jamaica until it came to a stop in front of Vinnie's house. The block was very small, so only the limo and the first two cars that followed were able to visualize the ceremonial stop. Lilly, realizing that this was Vinnie's last trip to the old house in Jamaica, finally succumbed to her emotions and released a primal scream, followed by heaving sobs and copious tears. John Chang also was crying, but he had the wherewithal to place his left arm around Lilly's shoulder and give her a reassuring squeeze.

"He's here, Lil," John said. "He's here with us to help keep us strong."

As if on cue, the hearse resumed its slow progression to the Long Island National Cemetery in Farmingdale, New York by traversing the streets of Jamaica, and a series of highways before reaching Vinnie's final resting place.

Once at the cemetery, a squadron of Marines was present to present the colors before performing "Taps" and carrying out a twenty-one–gun salute. The Santaniellos were mesmerized by the pomp and circumstance of the military burial ritual, but they greatly appreciated the wonderful respect and love that the servicemen showed their fallen hero. Next, Father McLaughlin, who had accompanied the Santaniellos in their limo, again blessed Vinnie's casket before the Marines once again performed their rehearsed, beautifully choreographed ritual of removing the flag from Vinnie's casket and impeccably folding it before presenting it with gentle love and reverence to Vinnie's shaken mother.

Rose accepted the flag in her unsteady hands and lowered her head toward it in profound grief. "You are an American hero, Vinnie," the bereaved mother whispered to the flag as her head remained lowered toward it, "but you will always be my little boy and beloved son. I love you, Vinnie."

Her husband, Carmine, overheard this invocation and bit his lower lip so as not to let his emotions escape in the presence of so many. Nonetheless, the forlorn Carmine reached over and gently caressed the flag, in a deferential sign of love and respect for his brave Marine son who had made the ultimate sacrifice on behalf of his country. As a World War II vet, this meant a great deal to the grieving father.

Next, the cemetery staff, with the Marines' collective assistance, methodically lowered Vinnie's casket into its final resting place amongst a sea of uniform lines of the white tombstones of past fallen heroes and, in some instances, their deceased spouses. The sense of dread in the air was palpable as the finality of the situation struck each member of the Santaniello family as well as the forlorn John Chang. Carmine, Rose, Nunu, Lilly, Joseph, and John all huddled together in an impromptu group hug, with Vinnie's flag serving as the nucleus of this familial cell, and their tears intermingled on the grass and Earth at their feet.

The sobs were only partially drowned out by the barking of orders of the Marines as they came to attention with rifles on their shoulders, a show of respect to their brother as he was lowered into the Earth. John separated himself from the Santaniello throng to stand at attention and offer a crisp, respectful salute to his eternal brother, as tears flowed unimpeded down his cheeks and onto the dirt that ultimately would be thrown atop Vinnie's casket.

Lilly walked over to the freshly dug, tremendous hole in the Earth that swallowed up Vinnie's casket. She peered into the great hole through her tears and gazed at Vinnie's casket. The older sister then removed a beautiful, silky lily from a bag and held the flower over the threshold of Vinnie's eternal resting place.

"Now you will always have your best friend with you, Vinnie."

With that, Lilly released the lily and watched as it gently swayed through the air and came to rest directly on the portion of the casket that was closed over Vinnie's face.

"I love you forever, Vinnie, and I'm never, ever gonna forget you. You were my life . . . and you always will be."

Vinnie's father approached the casket as Lilly retreated back to the family. Carmine rubbed his eyes and drew his moist hand up, across his tension-creased forehead, and across his greased-back hair. He peered down at the dirt-streaked casket and flinched at the sight of the lily. Carmine clenched his teeth and shook his head in disbelief. John Chang walked over to Carmine, placed his arm around the despairing father's shoulders, and gave a reassuring hug to the man he revered. Carmine turned his head slightly so that John could see his right eye over the bridge of his nose.

Carmine immediately looked back down at his son's casket, inhaled deeply, and opened his mouth to speak.

"I am dead now. I can't wait to be in there with you, Vinnie."

Carmine did not wait for Chang's response. Instead, he kicked at a stone with unbridled ferocity, causing it to ricochet off of the dug-out walls and onto Vinnie's casket. He then turned toward his family and gestured toward Rose, Nunu, and Joseph. The remaining Santaniellos approached Vinnie's final resting place, with Carmine holding Rose by her shoulders while Lilly held Nunu firmly by her arm.

"Oh, God, my baby! My baby! My baby! My Vinnie, my son! Why? Why? WHY?"

Rose's pained cries of despair echoed throughout the cemetery and seemed to unnerve the men preparing Vinnie's plot. The distraught mother's knees buckled and Carmine caught her before she fell into the large hole. Nunu repeatedly prayed the rosary in Italian, frequently bowing her head and crossing herself in the process.

Finally, Joseph approached the hole in the ground and apprehensively peered over its precipice. He reached into his pants pocket and pulled out a piece of paper that contained an exquisitely drawn rendition of Snoopy, flying on his dog house, in a bitter battle with the elusive Red Baron.

Vinnie was quite fond of this scene out of the popular *Peanuts* comic strip and he always joked with Joseph that he could draw the scene better than the youngest child of the family.

"This is for you, Vin. I hope you like it. I know that it'll never be as good as the one that you drew."

With that, the twelve-year-old boy released the drawing into the plot and, with tears streaming down his face, returned to his family.

John Chang had remained at the corner of the hole in the ground throughout this sad procession and he realized that he now was alone with his buddy. The Santaniellos had retreated toward the tree-lined roadway about sixty yards away.

Chang refused to look down again at the casket, as he had visualized it more than he cared to over the previous seventy-two hours. Instead, he looked up, into the expansive blue sky.

"Hey, pal, please do me a favor up there. Please watch over your family, especially your Pop, as he is taking this very, very hard. Thanks for being my best friend, Vin, and thanks for always being there for us boys all those times we hung out on Jamaica Avenue. I love you, Vin.

"I promise that I will do all that I can to be there for your family, just like you always intended to be there for them after you got out of the service. Rest in peace, brother. Until we meet again in paradise, please know that I will always love you and always honor your memory.

"I ain't ever gonna forget you, you tough sonofabitch! God bless you, Saint. Now, go hang out with the other saints up there."

With that, John quickly peered one last time at the casket, which was rapidly becoming obscured by descending Earth, before he turned and walked toward the Santaniellos.

As John approached the family, he noticed Carmine, gesturing purposefully in front of one of the trees that lined the curb by the road nearest to Vinnie's gravesite. Upon getting closer, John realized that Carmine had a carving knife in his right hand and he was carving letters into the tree that stood roughly ten feet high.

435

The trunk of the tree was of moderate size in diameter, roughly twenty inches wide. After a few minutes of work, Carmine stood up and reviewed his handiwork. John peered down and realized that Carmine had carved Vinnie's name into the tree.

V   I   N   N   Y

Carmine always had spelled Vinnie's name with a -*y*, despite Vinnie's insistence on ending his name with -*ie*.

"Now," Carmine noted, "we'll always know how to find Vinnie's grave when we return here."

The Santaniellos, mentally, physically, and spiritually exhausted, all paused and viewed the carved tree with an odd sense of satisfaction before they retreated to the limo for a surreal ride from the rural countryside of Long Island back to their broken lives in the concrete jungle of Jamaica, Queens. As the limo departed the cemetery, more than a few of its inhabitants found it rather odd that a hardened city kid like Vinnie would be buried in the peace and quiet of the country out on Long Island.

As the limo sped along the westbound Southern Parkway on the way back to Jamaica, John reminisced about Vinnie: He often said that real city kids never went to Jones Beach during the summer because those beaches were reserved for the privileged, rich kids of Long Island. Instead, the groovy city kids went to the Rockaways out in Queens. John recalled Vinnie's brash proclamation as the limo approached an exit sign on the parkway that read *Wantagh Parkway South-Jones Beach.*

John smiled at the cruel irony: Vinnie, the quintessential tough city kid, now was an eternal Long Islander.

CHAPTER 24

A NEW
BEGINNING

O ver the ensuing weeks, Lilly struggled with the idea of postponing her wedding. Vinnie was supposed to be her best man, and his death cast an immense pallor over the planning. Originally, Lilly told her parents that she didn't feel right about celebrating anything with Vinnie's death so fresh in everyone's minds. She believed that proceeding with the wedding would be a slap in the face of Vinnie's memory. Rose, to her credit, advised Lilly that, as much as they all loved and missed Vinnie, they couldn't give up on life.

"Life goes on," Rose reminded her depressed daughter, "whether we'd like it to or not." Lilly appreciated her mother's input but she remained torn at the prospect of proceeding with the wedding.

Her father remained very withdrawn and dark in the weeks following Vinnie's death. He rarely spoke to anyone and got into the routine of getting up early for work without interacting with the family and then later eating dinner by himself, followed by a brief respite for a couple of cigarettes either in the back yard or on the front porch before disappearing into his bedroom for the night.

He had become a recluse.

One day, Lilly summoned the courage to interact with her father. "Pop," she began, "can I ask you a question?" Carmine looked in her general direction and nodded affirmatively. "Look, Pa, I know what happened to Vinnie is unfair and terrible, but you can't check out on us forever."

Carmine looked vacantly again at Lilly and asked, "What's your question?"

Lilly shot a look of consternation at her father before sighing and replying, "I'm thinking of putting off the wedding, Pa. It ain't right to celebrate on one hand while mourning Vinnie's death on the other. I feel terrible doing this."

"Lilly, sweetheart," said Carmine, "we all miss Vinnie. We all wish he was still here with us and we all know that he loved us fiercely and that he'd do anything for us.

"Lil, as much as I feel like my life is over and as hard as I find it to go on with my daily routine, even I know that life goes on. Ya gotta move on with your life because that's what Vinnie woulda wanted."

Carmine put his arm around Lilly and pulled her toward him. The loving father then gave Lilly a prolonged hug before kissing her on the forehead.

"If you feel in your heart that you should go forward with your wedding in August, then do it."

Lilly smiled as tears welled up in her eyes. "You're the best, Pop. Thanks!" With that, Lilly retreated back to the family room, looking for her youngest brother. "Hey, Joseph? Joey? Where are you? I got news for ya."

Carmine retreated back into the dark, unforgiving recesses of his guilt-ridden mind.

The wedding proceeded as planned on August 24, 1968. Lilly was a beautiful bride and her husband, Ralph, was a handsome groom. Joseph, then thirteen years old, served as Lilly's best man and everyone, including John Chang, marveled at how amazing he did in filling Vinnie's considerable shoes. Rose, Nunu, and Carmine all were rather subdued, but cordial. The day was a happy occasion, although there was an undeniable pallor cast over the entire event. Lilly was married on the very altar where she'd stood a few months earlier to read that powerful Scripture in Vinnie's honor. Father McLaughlin, the officiant for Vinnie's funeral, presided over the wedding. The family and friends in attendance—to a person— remarked that the day was a joyous occasion. However, the joy was far from unbridled.

After all, the Saint, who was to have been there and impeccably attired in his impressive dress blues, was absent. The sheer glee that his smile and charisma would have brought to the event was eternally extinguished. And that unfortunate reality permeated everyone's psyche that day, whether consciously or subconsciously.

The beautiful, tough-as-nails Lilly finally was married, a few weeks before her twenty-second birthday and what would've been Vinnie's twentieth birthday.

Tragically, Vincent Benore Santaniello, Lilly's best friend and fantastic younger brother who was to have served as the best man, could be present in spirit only for the blessed event.

*   *   *

Thursday, November 28, 1968. Thanksgiving Day. Lilly drove out to the cemetery early that morning, as she had done so frequently since Vinnie's funeral and burial. In fact, Lilly had made it her custom to visit Vinnie's grave every Sunday morning, as soon as the cemetery opened, rain or shine. As Lilly sat amidst scattered, crunchy autumn leaves before Vinnie's freshly lain, immaculately white tombstone on that brisk, windy Thanksgiving morning, her mind wandered back to the first time that she had seen Vinnie's gravestone: Friday, September 20, on what would've been her brother's twentieth birthday. Lilly asked her boss if she could report to work at noon that day so that she'd have time to travel out to Long Island to visit her brother's grave. Lilly's boss not only said yes, but he gave Lilly the day off, with pay, out of respect for the suffering that she and her family had endured since that April.

Lilly arrived at the cemetery by 7:30 a.m. that warm September morning and she had to wait a half-hour for the gates to swing open for the public. Lilly drove dutifully to Mall Drive East in the cemetery, toward section 2H, site 2554, and she parked in a familiar location. Lilly exited her car, taking a bouquet of flowers with her, and looked for the "Vinnie tree." Within seconds, Lilly encountered the omnipresent VINNY on the tree trunk. She then walked in a straight line from the tree until she came to the spot where Vinnie was buried. However, much to Lilly's surprise, the small, nondescript marker that had held Vinnie's grave had been replaced with a small, simple-yet-elegant, white gravestone.

The beautiful young lady's eyes widened as she perused the arch at the top of the stone. She choked back tears as she observed the simple cross that was etched into the top center of the stone.

Her eyes then scanned the engravings upon it.

VINCENT B
SANTANIELLO

NEW YORK

L CPL
US MARINE CORPS

VIETNAM

SEP 20 1948
MAR 28 1968

PURPLE HEART

Lilly became disheartened as she read the engravings.

Every time that I think that I'm used to Vinnie being dead, something happens that surprises me and serves as a screwed-up reminder that my little brother ain't here no more, she thought.

The despondent older sister gently placed the bouquet of birthday flowers at the base of the freshly placed stone. Next, Lilly closed her eyes and sighed deeply before she rubbed her hand gently across the face of the stone, feeling the alternate smoothness and roughness of the engravings upon her fingers. Lilly imagined that she was gently caressing Vinnie's face as her hand traversed the perimeter of the stone. An abrupt breeze struck her face in the midst of this moment, blowing her black hair about her face.

Lilly reflexively removed her right hand from the stone to remove the hair from her eyes and when she was able to again see clearly, she realized that she was looking directly at the tree into which her dad had carved Vinnie's name.

"Hi, Vinnie," Lilly said instantly. "That's pretty groovy how you can control the wind now. I miss ya, Vin."

A cold breeze ended her flashback to a few months earlier and brought her back to the present.

This was the second Thanksgiving without her best friend, but the first one for which she knew that she'd never see him again, at least not in this life.

She leaned against the cold stone and imagined that she was leaning against her brother as he sat in his bed. Lilly often playfully plopped herself next to Vinnie as he sat on his bed and she'd always try to nudge him over. She smiled at the fleeting nature of this silly memory and she gently whispered, "Good morning, Vinnie. Happy Thanksgiving, little brother.

"I have good news for you today, Vin."

Lilly then reached into her purse and removed a small notepad and a pen. Lilly never got over the fact that Vinnie died with his last letter to the family in his pocket. Her heart still throbbed with despair each time she recalled receiving that March 28, 1968 letter weeks after Vinnie's death.

She resolved that such a fateful scenario was so cruel that it nullified any efforts to rationalize or rectify its patently unfair nature. Thus, Lilly decided that, out of respect to her brother, she would write letters to Vinnie at his gravesite every time that she visited the cemetery. When Lilly finished writing the letters, she taped them, initially to the nondescript grave marker and later to the gravestone. Of course, the letters never were there when she'd return the following Sunday. Alas, Lilly comforted herself by imagining that angels came down to retrieve the letters and deliver them to Vinnie in Heaven after she left the cemetery.

This was Lilly's way of trying to lessen the sting of Vinnie probably dying with the thought that his last letter to his family was in his shirt. Lilly just *knew* that Vinnie died despairing the notion that his family was going to receive a letter from him posthumously.

Lilly squinted her eyes tightly and shook her head rapidly in an effort to dislodge that terrible thought from her mind.

"Focus, Lil," she reprimanded herself out loud, "this is Vinnie's time, not yours."

"Vinnie, you're gonna love the good news! Remember the letter that you wrote to me about how excited you were to be an uncle one day? Well . . ."

With that, Lilly sat down on the soft Earth and crunchy autumn leaves strewn about the perimeter of Vinnie's stone, leaned against her big-little brother just like old times, removed a pen and pad from her purse, and began to write.

11/28/68

Dear Vinnie,

Hey there, big-little brother, how are you doing up in Heaven? Things down here haven't been the same since you left us. Ma and Pa haven't been the same since you went up there and Joseph seems quieter, too. Nunu is Nunu! I still don't understand a damn thing that comes out of her mouth! Ha Ha! The gang at work all says hello. I actually told a few of them that I write these letters to you and they think that I'm off-my-rocker crazy. Do you think I am? I think that doing this keeps me close to you, so the hell with everyone who thinks this is crazy!

442

Rosalie and John Chang still come by the house a lot. I feel terrible for Roe, she really was preparing herself to be Mrs. Vincent Santaniello and she is really sad and lonely now. Poor girl. I'm like her big sister now and I'm trying to keep her positive. Johnny is a really wonderful fellow, he stops by nearly every day after work to see if Ma needs help with anything. He also tells Pop that he shouldn't hesitate to ask for help with anything. Johnny is A-1 in my book.

Married life is going swell. After you went up there, Ma and Pa didn't want me and Ralph to move into the apartment that we had chosen, even though it was just a couple of miles away. So, as you know from my last couple of letters, we've been living upstairs. Nunu doesn't seem to mind that she now lives in a little room that used to be a closet in the upstairs hallway. Pop and Uncle Angelo fixed it up real nice for her.

Pop also fixed up the room that was next to that closet for Ralph and me. My new bedroom is really groovy. Ralph's still looking for a job, and we hope that he can get something soon. He can't be a bum forever, right? Just kidding, we'll be fine. Too bad he couldn't become a professional fighter. I bet them heavyweight boxers make some good money and Ralph was a Golden Gloves champ, as you know! I'll let you know when my hubby gets a job.

Okay, little brother, that is all for now. You take care of yourself up there in Heaven. Did you say hello to Jesus for me yet? Tell Him and Mary that I really will stop cursing one day! Ha Ha! I love you, dear brother of mine. "Talk" to you again real soon!

Love always, your big-little sis,
Lilly

P.S. I bet you thought that I wasn't going to share the big news with you. I didn't forget. Are you ready? You better sit down on one of those clouds up there, brother of mine! Guess what? You're going to be an UNCLE! That's right: I'm pregnant and the baby is due in July of next year. Now, I know if you were down here, you'd make some awkward, uncomfortable joke about how I became pregnant, so just keep that smart talk to yourself, ya hear me? 'Uncle Vinnie' . . . that has a nice ring to it, don't it? I really hope that I have a boy because we definitely would give him your name as his middle name. See . . . I'm never going to let you leave me! Don't worry, if the baby is a girl, we'll just have to name her Vincenza! A boy would have to take Ralph's name as his first name, but he'd have your name as his middle name. Ralph Vincent Morales . . . that don't sound half-bad, right?

I love you, Vinnie, and I miss you more each day. You would have been a great uncle and my kid is gonna miss out on a really groovy fella in you. Let's just say that I have a boy: Little Ralph Vincent Morales will have a LOT to live up to if he wants to be like his Uncle Vinnie. Ha Ha Ha! The poor kid don't have a chance, right? I know what you're saying right now: He ain't ever going to be as handsome as you, right? I just hope he comes out smarter than you! You know I love you, stupid. Now, go back to being with all the saints up there. I'll see you in my dreams, Vin. I love, love, love, love, love you and I miss you with all my heart. And your little niece or nephew loves you bunches too! Happy Thanksgiving! Make sure that you don't eat all of Jesus' stuffing and be sure to save Him a turkey leg!

With that, Lilly took out her trusty Scotch tape and she lovingly fastened the letter to Vinnie's gravestone. Next, she leaned over and kissed the cross on the stone, as she had done since the stone was set in place. She then traced her finger over the cross before making the sign of the cross over Vinnie's name.

"I love you, Vinnie. You may have died a lance corporal but you'll always be a loving big-little brother to me."

Tears suddenly sprouted from Lilly's eyes and splattered across the stone and even moistened Lilly's letter a bit. Lilly rubbed her eyes and sniffled a couple of times before she regained her composure. She stared at the engraved name again on the stone and shook her head, still dismayed that her brother and best friend in the entire universe really was gone. Leaving the cemetery always proved difficult for the young woman, for she felt guilty about leaving her brother alone, especially now that it was getting colder.

"I gotta go now, Vin. Happy Thanksgiving. I will see you in a few days, on Sunday morning. Take care, brother. I love you and I miss you something fierce!"

Lilly then patted the top of the stone and planted another kiss on it, just for good measure. She then stood up, winked at the grave, and rubbed her belly while saying, "I hope it's a boy!"

Lilly then turned and began to walk toward the Vinnie tree, where her car was parked. As she walked, a strong gust of wind swirled behind her, rustling the leaves into a furious funnel. Lilly's hair blew from back to front and the fervent gust nearly knocked her over as the pace of her steps was hastened by the wind.

Upon arriving at her car, Lilly looked back toward her brother's grave. The funnel of wind seemed to be right behind his stone and the leaves were whipping upward in a display of nature that amazed Lilly.

"Geez, Vin," Lilly exclaimed over the howling wind, "calm down, already. I got another eight months before your little nephew or niece says hello!"

Lilly entered her car and began to slowly drive away from the Vinnie tree. However, something caught her eye peripherally. Lilly stopped her car and looked toward Vinnie's grave. Amazingly, high above the ground and whipping around in the leaves which seemingly extended to the heavens was what appeared to be a piece of paper. Lilly exited the car and clumsily ran toward Vinnie's stone.

Once there, Lilly noticed immediately that all that was left of her letter to Vinnie was two pieces of flimsy Scotch tape, flapping desperately in the wind. Lilly swept her hair out of her face and looked up, repeatedly blinking as she did so to clear the blowing debris from her eyes.

Lilly saw the letter, whipping amongst the leaves, getting higher and higher above her head.

On its way to Heaven, thought Lilly as a broad smile overtook her face.

Still smiling and looking up toward the heavens, Lilly chuckled as she shook her head in amazement at what she was experiencing. After a couple of seconds, the letter seemingly disappeared in the clouds.

Astonished, Lilly lowered her head and began to slowly walk back toward her car. However, she stopped after a few steps. Her back was to Vinnie's grave, but she turned her head and glanced up to where she'd last seen her letter ascending to its angelic recipient. After a few seconds, she peered down at her beloved Vinnie's grave. Lilly blew a kiss in the direction of her brother's final resting place and then placed her hands over her heart. Next, Lilly turned to completely face Vinnie's grave.

Lilly smiled and opened her mouth to express a final sentiment before returning to Jamaica for her first Thanksgiving without Vinnie.

"I love ya, Saint."

Afterword

The genesis of this book began shortly after my family and I buried our mother, Vinnie's best pal and "little-big sister," Lilly, on my eighth wedding anniversary, of all days: July 31, 2002. Lilly was fifty-five years old when she died suddenly on July 26, 2002. My two younger brothers, Vinnie (yes, my brother also was named after Uncle Vinnie) and Tony, and my younger sister, Rosina, and I were in Mom's apartment in Rego Park, Queens in early August 2002 to gather up her belongings. I came across an old box that was unfamiliar to me. This mystery box contained dozens of letters—perfectly preserved but for one—that Vinnie had written to his sister from his time at Camp Pendleton and, of course, his tour in Vietnam.

I'd never known about this treasure trove of history and, naturally, I felt immense angst at having been deprived of the opportunity to discuss these amazing letters with my mother. My younger siblings and I grew up in Vinnie's old house in Jamaica, Queens. I remember the story of Vinnie as more myth than reality during my childhood. I recall thinking as a child that he was an old guy who died in some strange war. I had no idea how old Vinnie was when he died but I surmised that he was *really old*, like forty-eight—my age as I write this afterword!

447

There were a couple of pictures of him in my grandparents' house, downstairs from where I grew up, as well as one pretty good drawing of Charlie Brown and Snoopy done by my late uncle, but nary a word was spoken about him. My grandparents rarely, if ever spoke about Vinnie and if they did, it was in reverent, albeit truncated tones. Likewise, my mother and her younger brother rarely spoke about Vinnie. Nunu, my great-grandmother who lived in our house until her death in 1979, didn't speak English, so she was more like the silent, loving great-grandma who shuffled around the house and spoke in Italian to my grandparents.

I do have memories of driving out to the cemetery with my grandfather, Carmine, who we affectionately called *Dada*, and my grandmother, Rose, and I remember marveling at the "Vinnie tree." I also recall Dada telling us that he'd carved the tree to help him find Vinnie's stone and that was understandable, given the vast sea of identical white stones that dominate the landscape of the cemetery to this day. As a child, I was more interested in the Vinnie tree than I was in the gravestone. I didn't understand what Vietnam was at that age, and I sure didn't comprehend or appreciate the incredible significance of the countless white stones. Sadly, I had no context for what was so important about the mythological figure known as Uncle Vinnie, so I didn't give it much thought.

Of course, I'd see Uncle Vinnie's distinct handwriting every time that I entered our basement—one of my favorite pastimes as a kid—to watch my grandfather work on one thing or another. Vinnie's name was written in what appeared to be a black marker on the ceiling leading down to the basement. That ceiling was angled down—it was the underside of the stairs that led to where I lived with my father, mother, and three siblings. I remember thinking that it was cool to see the handwriting of an uncle that I never met. As a kid, I equated that handwritten name with getting the autograph of one of my baseball idols from the Yankees, namely Reggie Jackson, Thurman Munson, Mickey Rivers, or Lou Piniella.

VINNIE

I remember thinking that that name up on the ceiling was so cool.

448

In hindsight, I regret that I failed to take more of an interest in my late uncle. I wish that I had asked questions of Rose, Carmine, my uncle, and my mother about Vinnie. My ambivalence about Uncle Vinnie ended rather abruptly when I read all of his letters to my mother. The box also contained myriad pictures of Vinnie, and I was equally mesmerized by them. I recall how astounded I was when I realized that Vinnie was just a kid when he died in Vietnam; a nineteen-year-old kid who wrote about his life in Vietnam to his twenty-year-old sister.

I was thirty-two when I read these letters for the first time and I vividly remembered then what *I* was doing as a nineteen-year-old: I was a sophomore at Georgetown University in Washington, D.C., just figuring out who I was while attending class with nary a care in the world. Conversely, Uncle Vinnie had been in Vietnam, living literally second-to-second, just trying like hell to avoid getting his head blown off by an incoming mortar. I was flabbergasted by the realization that, while in Vietnam, Uncle Vinnie was closer in age to writing letters to Santa Claus than he was to my age when I began reading his letters to Lilly.

I knew as I read those letters that I would write a book based on them, but there was one significant obstacle to realizing that ambition: I knew next to nothing about him. My mom was dead. My grandfather, Carmine, had died in 1991. My grandmother still was alive at the time (she died in 2013), but I didn't want to have her relive such dark times, especially given the fact that she wasn't in the best of health. So, I set out to try and find people who would have known my uncle in Vietnam.

I posted on multiple military websites, including those that were both USMC- and Vietnam-specific. After more than a decade, I only had very marginal results to show for this endeavor and I was losing hope in my dream to honor Vinnie's memory—and my mom's memory, too—with a book based upon the hallowed letters. However, my despair ended with an amazing, unexpected telephone call in January 2014.

Angel Canales, an ABC News reporter at the time, called to ask if I was the nephew of Vincent Benore Santaniello. Predictably,

I was shocked, but I advised the reporter that I was before I asked him to identify himself. Mr. Canales told me that he'd just done a piece on a celebrated personality out in the Pacific Northwest who would be able to share some information with me about my uncle. That person's name was Michael Reagan, a former Marine who served a tour in Vietnam.

Now, since 2002, I had spoken to approximately a dozen former Marines who'd known Uncle Vinnie, but their memories were too faded and ultimately did not help me with my goal of writing about my late uncle's experiences in Vietnam. Mr. Canales provided me with Michael's phone number and I went into the telephone call with this gentleman with minimal expectations.

"Hello?" The voice was soft, warm, and inviting. I immediately felt at ease.

"Hello, may I speak to Michael Reagan?"

"Speaking. Who is this?"

"Hello, sir, my name is Ralph Morales. A reporter named Angel Canales gave me your name and number and asked me to call you about an uncle of mine who was killed in Vietnam."

"Are you Vinnie's nephew?"

That question caught me off guard, and I swallowed before responding with an affirmative, "Yes, sir."

"You need to understand something, Ralph. Your uncle was in no pain when he died."

My heart began to pound. "How do you know that, Mr. Reagan?"

"Because I was holding Saint in my arms when he died."

I couldn't believe my ears. Did this gentleman just say what I thought he said?

I practically was numb for the remainder of that conversation. I actually was talking to someone who'd known Vinnie over in Vietnam and was with him when he died.

Amazing.

Equally amazing was the fact that Mike actually referred to Vinnie by his nickname, Saint, the name that Vinnie himself proudly used in his letters to my mother.

I realized immediately that I had to meet this man.

Mike and I spoke for well over an hour that evening and I learned from him that he was an artist and founder of the Fallen Heroes Portrait Project (www.fallenheroesproject.org), which he began in 2004 after a Gold Star widow who had seen Mike's amazing artwork asked if he would be kind enough to draw her late husband, a corpsman who served in the USMC in Afghanistan, and Mike agreed to do so. Upon seeing the vivid likeness of her husband in the portrait, the widow told Mike that she was able to sleep through the night for the first time since her husband had been killed in action, because he was now back home.

Mike realized immediately what his life's calling was and he abruptly retired from his job at the University of Washington. He committed his life to drawing portraits of members of the U.S. Armed Forces who were killed in service to our nation, for their surviving Gold Star families.

Michael has since expanded the scope of his project. He has drawn portraits of military members of foreign nations, of the victims of the Sandy Hook, Connecticut school shooting, of the victims of the shooting in a Charleston, South Carolina church, of members of law enforcement killed in the line of duty, and of countless others.

Nearly seven thousand portraits later and Mike still has not charged a nickel for his amazing work. Yet the love, admiration, respect, and gratitude expressed by the recipient Gold Star families have enriched Mike far beyond what any currency could.

I learned from Mike that 2014 was the tenth anniversary of his labor of love and that he was planning a tenth-anniversary celebration of the project for the forthcoming Easter weekend. I was fortunate enough to fly out to Edmonds, Washington for the gala celebration and I was privileged to meet Mike, his wonderful wife Cheryl, and their three exotic cats.

Mike took me down to his studio and we talked for hours.

"Do you know what the impetus was for the Fallen Heroes Project, Ralph?"

"No, sir."

Mike looked directly into my eyes and proclaimed, "Your uncle is the reason why I decided to give up my career and devote my life to this project."

Yes, I was floored by his response, too.

Mike explained that, as he'd held Vinnie back in Cam Lo, Vietnam on March 28, 1968, he'd realized that the grievously injured young Marine was not long for the world. Thus, Mike did what he could do to comfort Saint while Docs Milazzo and Nunn tried in vain to save him. Vinnie's last words on this Earth inspired Mike, nearly forty years later, to start the Fallen Heroes Portrait Project.

"Mike, I just want to go home."

Those words resonated in Mike's soul for almost four decades before they took on a profound meaning to him. Mike decided that he had to send Vinnie's brothers- and sisters-in-arms home to their grieving Gold Star families.

The tenth-anniversary celebration of the Fallen Heroes Project was a night that I shall never forget. I was able to meet a great number of esteemed Gold Star family guests and friends of Michael.

I also had the distinct honor of meeting the irrepressible John "Doc" Nunn. John and Mike spoke with me for hours over the course of that weekend and I made myself a sponge, soaking in as much as these two esteemed gentlemen were able to share. Doc

Nunn told me the account, which I included in this book, of how he and Doc Milazzo tried to save Vinnie.

Doc was a hardened veteran. Indeed, he was a man who came home from Vietnam broken, physically and mentally. However, he struck me as a profoundly proud man, with old-school USMC toughness exuding from his pores. John had a tough exterior and he wasn't afraid to tell me his opinions of the Vietnam War.

Mike presented me with a special portrait of my uncle at the tenth-anniversary celebration and, after Mike and I said some words to the gathering about the significance of my uncle and his eternal role in the project, I walked back to my seat at the table that I shared with Doc Nunn. Doc asked if he could hold the portrait and I obliged, of course.

Doc looked at the amazing portrait and the battle-hardened, grizzled veteran began to cry.

"I'm so sorry that I couldn't save you, brother! I'm so sorry that I failed you, Saint!" John, with tears streaming down his weathered face, then kissed the portrait. What a palpable, poignant moment.

John put me in touch with Tony "Doc" Milazzo, still a Jersey Shore guy all these years later, and I had the great honor of meeting him. Tony shared his memories of my uncle, and he, too, expressed regret at his "failure" to save my uncle.

What is amazing to me is that there literally are thousands of people walking the face of the Earth at this very moment who owe their very existence to the valor, courage, and life-saving skills of corpsmen like Doc Nunn, Doc Milazzo, and Doc Chang.

These men walked into firefights with absolutely no regard for their own self-preservation. They were razor-focused on saving the lives of their injured brothers. And they saved scores of lives in the process. The lives they saved were of folks who were able to make it back home to their loved ones. Many of them eventually started families; families that would not have existed but for the indomitable spirit of the corpsmen.

Yet, John and Tony lamented the fact that Vinnie died on their watch.

The humble men did not want to hear about the myriad lives that they saved. They could only express intense regret and sorrow about the one life that they could not save. Neither hero can accept the fact—even more than fifty years later—that Vinnie's injuries were so grave that no one short of Jesus Christ was going to save him.

The kinship and love that I developed with and for these men, each old enough to be my father, was fervent. Indeed, I forged relationships with them that I shall cherish for the remainder of my days.

Importantly, Mike, John, and Tony shared myriad stories with me about their experiences with Vinnie in Vietnam leading up to that fateful day and I was able to incorporate them into this book. I also had the opportunity to meet Daniel King, thanks to my friendship with Doc Nunn, and Daniel shared some amazing stories of his memories with Vinnie, too. John also told me that Ned LeRoy, the captain who actually wrote a condolence letter to Vinnie's parents, still was alive. I spoke to Captain LeRoy and he graciously shared his memories of Vinnie with me.

Finally, I reacquainted myself with John "Doc" Chang, a childhood friend of Vinnie who served concurrently in Vietnam. I actually have childhood memories of John visiting our old house in Jamaica, and I recall my mom and grandparents being quite fond of him. John patiently recounted many of his happy childhood memories of Vinnie, which I gratefully included in this book. John's memories of growing up in Jamaica in the 1950s and early-to-mid 1960s were both uplifting and inspiring. Further, his wonderful memories provided me with invaluable context for the life and times of my uncle, which had been foreign to me.

More than anything else, John humanized Vinnie. He breathed life into this amazing story and transformed Vinnie from myth to man in my eyes. Of course, John eloquently shared the hardest time of his life: When he accepted my grandparents' request to accompany Vinnie's body home. I cannot begin to put into words the palpable pain that seared through John's voice as I spoke to him about his tragic memories.

John frequently began to cry but, when I apologized for having him delve into the long-repressed, eternally painful recesses of his mind and told him that he did not have to revisit such terrible memories, John eschewed the notion of not forging ahead. It was similar to how he'd overcome the doubts that had crept into his mind about fulfilling my grandparents' request and bravely proceeded with the noble task of accompanying my uncle's body home.

John would not succumb to the anger, the fear, the pain, and the confusion that plagued him for decades in the form of the ever-pervasive PTSD. Indeed, John said that he *had* to share these memories with me in order to honor his friend, a young man that he *still* considers his best friend despite not having seen him alive for more than a half-century.

John sacrificed himself and endured the pain of revisiting such terrible times in order to honor his deceased buddy. I owe John a debt of gratitude, which I can never repay, for his invaluable assistance. More importantly, I owe John an abundance of thanks for being there for Rose, Carmine, and their children in their times of unbearable pain and relentless sadness.

Meeting these American **HEROES** provided me with the context and inspiration that I needed to write this book. Without them, I never would have been able to write this tribute to Vinnie. Sure, I could have written a completely fictitious account of the young man that I never knew, but I concluded that such an endeavor would have been absolutely vacuous and devoid of purpose. I knew that the best way to honor my uncle was to do so through the eyes— and the hearts—of the people who knew him best and loved him unconditionally.

I realized after speaking to these heroes that the book was about them, too. Indeed, this book took on a life of its own and it became a tribute not only to my grandparents, my mother, and my late uncle, of course, but an important tribute to these heroic Marines. They set aside the pain of reliving an era that had scarred them for decades to valorously share their memories of Saint with me. I realized as I was writing this book that it was to serve as a tribute to all of the men and women, living and deceased, who have served our nation with valor and selflessness in the armed forces.

I'm sure that some of the memories that I heard from these heroic servicemen aren't one-hundred-percent accurate. Indeed, how could they be, after the waters of a half-century have washed over the shores of their minds? Yet the fervor with which they shared their stories and the unconditional love that they expressed for their fallen brother were undeniably genuine.

These men loved Vinnie and surely Vinnie loved them back with the same loyalty and ferocity that he reserved for his own flesh and blood. Vinnie likely entered the Corps as a wise-cracking, street-wise boy, but he died a battle-hardened man and a warrior Marine. My uncle was able to make that transformation thanks to Mike Reagan, John Nunn, Tony Milazzo, Daniel King, John Chang, Captain LeRoy, and hundreds of other unknown Marines who served with him in the Thundering Third between 1967 and 1968. *Semper Fi!*

Fittingly, I shall conclude this book with a reference to the woman without whom I absolutely would not be the person that I am today: my late mother, Lillian Santaniello Morales. The pain of losing my mother in the inexplicable and sudden manner that I did, back on July 26, 2002, remains in my heart to this day. My mother was my best friend. I trusted her implicitly and I shared everything with her.

Lilly was far from perfect. Indeed, she never took her brother's advice not to curse and to "speak more like a lady." She cursed so ferociously that I'm sure that hardened men like Red, Doc Nunn, Doc Milazzo, Daniel King, and Doc Chang would've blushed and cowered at Lilly's unquenchable tenacity and fiery tongue!

Lilly was brutally honest yet she was funny, kind, warm-hearted, and, most of all, loyal. Fiercely loyal. She loved her four children and she would do anything for us. She shielded my brothers Vinnie and Tony, my sister Rosina, and me from so much during our childhood.

I still can't believe that she repressed the pain and terror of losing her brother and best friend, and that she never opened up that window of her soul to us.

I often wonder what happened to all of the letters that my mom wrote to Vinnie. Mike Reagan and Doc Nunn told me that the USMC firmly believed in sending a fallen brother's belongings back home with the body. It was their way of showing respect for their brother Marine. So, Vinnie's brothers in Cam Lo very likely collected all of his belongings—including his letters, pictures, and tapes—and placed them in a seabag that then was provided to the appropriate officials to ensure that the seabag made it back home.

I can only surmise that my grandfather burned these treasures in the fit of rage that Marie Mattia (formerly Marie Graves), my mom's lifelong best friend, described to me. That is so sad because I really would have loved the opportunity to get to know the twenty- and twenty-one-year-old Lilly in much the same way that I came to know the eighteen- and nineteen-year-old Vinnie.

Mom, this book is as much about you as it is about Vinnie. The story of one is incomplete without the story of the other. You so often were a light for me in times of vast darkness and I forever shall be indebted to you for your unwavering love and support. I wholly believe in my heart that you would've been very proud of this book.

Rest easy up in Heaven, Lil, and be sure to say hi to Vinnie, Dada, and Grandma for all of us down here. Your kids and grandkids love you, Ma.

Thank you, Mom, for the inspiration that permitted me to posthumously bring honor to your brother: a great kid, a fiercely loyal and loving family member, a valorous Marine, and someone who is so much more than simply a name on the Vietnam Veterans Memorial Wall in Washington, D.C. Indeed, thanks for helping me to honor a previously unsung American hero: Vinnie "Saint" Santaniello.

Oo-rah.
Semper Fi.
I love you, Uncle Vinnie.

Glossary of USMC slang, abbreviations, and jargon

Arty: Artillery.

The Crotch: Marine slang for the USMC.

C-4: Composition C-4 plastic explosives.

C-rats (C-rations): Thin, cardboard boxes that contained rudimentary meals for Marines.

Charlies: Slang for the Viet Cong enemy.

CP: Command post.

Coors: Radio code for dead Marines.

Dee-dee: A play on the Vietnamese expression *didi mao*, which means "go away." The Marines adopted this phrase and used it when the enemy deserted a fight and endeavored to leave quickly.

DMZ: Demilitarized zone.

The Five: The executive officer, or second-in-command, of a specific USMC company.

Frag: A grenade—also known as an M-26 or Mike twenty-six.

The full bird: Nickname for a commanding officer, as he wore the full-eagle insignia on his chest.

Getting short: Marine slang meaning that a veteran's tour was winding down to its final weeks.

Gook: A slang term that was used to describe the enemy combatants in Vietnam.

Green: A Marine with no combat experience.

Grunt: A term used by Marines to describe those infantrymen that are in the midst of combat.

Gunji: Marine slang used to describe someone who was overly zealous.

HEs: High explosives.

H&S: Headquarters and Supply.

Hanoi Hannah: A female Vietnamese radio personality who made propaganda-filled English-language broadcasts that were spearheaded by the North Vietnamese in an effort to disenfranchise the American military personnel who were based in South Vietnam. Many of Hanoi Hannah's broadcasts were aimed at deflating the morale of the American military members.

The head: Marine slang for bathroom.

Hooch: Marines' tent-like structures, often nothing more canvas sleeves, propped up by poles, sticks, or other jungle materials.

Huey: A military helicopter, also called a *bird* or a *gunship*.

Jarhead: A slang term for Marines.

Ka-Bar: Also known as a K-Bar, this was a knife that typically had a seven inch blade and a leather handle.

LZ: "Landing zone," a small strip of land in the jungle that served as a precarious area for U.S.-helicopter take-offs and landings.

LP: A listening post; usually consisted of two Marines who were dispatched at night, on the outskirts of the defenses. They were equipped with a radio and their job was to listen for potential enemy movement so that they could warn their brother Marines of a possible ambush.

NCOs: The USMC non-commissioned officers responsible for the lives of their men in combat situations.

Numby: A new Marine; see *green*.

Oley: A Marine wounded in action.

Ordnance: Weapons; ammunition.

Px truck: A post exchange vehicle where Marines could buy basic items like cigarettes, writing materials, food, and drinks.

RPD: "Ruchnoi Pulemet Degtyarev," a machine gun that used the same ammo, a 7.62-mm round, as the more-prominent AK-47.

RPGs: Rocket propelled grenades.

Rubber lady: A Marine's bed—USMC-issued mattress or, more often than not in Vietnam, just sheets strewn about the jungle floor.

Seabag: A Marine's duffel bag that contained basic necessities.

Seabees: United States Naval Construction Battalions. Shortened to CBs and better known as Seabees, they had many responsibilities, including grading airstrips, building barracks, and conducting soil tests for an amphibious landing zone.

SP pack: Packages that typically contained toiletries and cigarettes that were donated by people back in the U.S.

Squid: Slang for Navy members.

The Three: Battalion operations officer.

Tubing: The sound of the explosion that propelled an armed mortar shell from a mortar tube. Marines knew that a deadly mortar round was seconds away from potentially deadly impact when they heard the distinct tubing sound.

The Two: Battalion intelligence officer.

Ralph Vincent Morales

R alph Vincent Morales was born sixteen months after the death of the uncle whose name he carries, Vincent (Vinnie) Benore "Saint" Santaniello. Vinnie was killed in action on March 28, 1968, in Cam Lo, Vietnam, as a nineteen-year-old USMC lance corporal. Ralph grew up in the same house in which Vinnie was reared in Jamaica, Queens, New York City. Ralph was determined to overcome the challenges of his childhood and he did just that by graduating from Georgetown University in Washington, D.C. in 1991 before moving back to New York. He worked full-time during the day, attended class at night, and graduated from St. John's University School of Law in 1996.

Ralph went on to become a successful, highly respected prosecutor in Brooklyn, New York, where he developed a reputation as a fair-but-tough prosecutor and a terrific trial attorney who accepted any case, regardless of its inherent challenges. As an assistant district attorney, Ralph was regarded as a formidable adversary and a compassionate advocate for those seeking justice. Ralph eventually moved on to private practice, where he further enhanced his reputation amongst his peers as a respected trial attorney.

Ralph also is a highly regarded member of his community in Farmingdale, New York, where he has volunteered countless hours as an elected Board of Education trustee. He has served as president and vice president during his tenure on the Board of Education. He also is an Executive Board member of the Farmingdale unit of the Nassau County Police Activity League. "Coach" is second only to "Dad" on Ralph's shortlist of favorite titles. Last, but certainly not least, Ralph is wholly devoted to his family, including his wife, Joanne, and their five children: Mark, Luke, Rebecca, Gianna, and Mateo.

When Ralph is not in court trying significant matters before juries throughout New York City or in Nassau and Suffolk Counties, he can be found giving inspirational talks to the children of his school district or coaching children of all ages in various sports. And if he is not selflessly tending to the needs of his community, Ralph is upholding the one tenet that was of paramount importance to the uncle that he never got to know and love: He is undyingly loyal to the loves of his life who serve as the very foundation of his soul: His family. Semper Fi!

3/28/68

Dear Mom, Dad, Sis

[illegible] I got 4 more letters
from you today. I [illegible]
from you. 1 from
[illegible] I'm
[illegible] I'm going
to answer a few of your questions
real quick, before I forget them.
[illegible] letters with a 6¢ stamp
takes the same amount of
days as air mail down here
if the mail is running smooth.
It's between 7 to 10 days. Forget
[illegible] negatives is me, Richie
Wilde and B.J. Odom. We all went
through boot camp, I.T.R. and came
over here together and we'll all
go home together. Odom lives in
Florida. Richie Wilde lives in
[illegible] the San Poly [illegible] 3 [illegible]
You should have already received
the [illegible] pictures I sent you. Plus
you should get some more the

Vinnie's final letter dated March 28, 1968.

Vinnie's final letter dated March 28, 1968.

Vinnie's final letter dated March 28, 1968.

Vinnie's final letter dated March 28, 1968.

③

I was trying to remember when the summer used to come the back door would be opened and the screen door would take its place. And when I came home from school everyone would be sitting on their porches or in the back yard working on their gardens ... weather was not ... I'm going to sneak up on you like I did the last time I came home on leave. Or I'll let you pick me up. I think you enjoyed it much more when I sneaked up on you. Remember Pop were in the front. Boy did Pop get surprised ... understood ... and waited for Pop to look up. He was pulling weeds from the front garden ... and then I remember when my leave was up. I had to go to Calif. I'll tell you between from ... you almost had me crying.

Vinnie's final letter dated March 28, 1968.

Vinnie's final letter dated March 28, 1968.

④

those other people what I said
And give my love + regards to the
both grandma's + our family. Is
Robert Boas out of the service yet?
Let me know.

Vinnie's final letter dated March 28, 1968.

COMPANY "K"
3rd Battalion, 4th Marines (-)
3d Marine Division (Rein), FMF
FPO San Francisco 96602

30 March 1968

Mr. and Mrs. Carmine J. Santaniello

Jamaica, New York

My dear Mr. and Mrs. Santaniello:

It is difficult for me to express the regrets and sorrow felt by the
Marines in this company over the recent death of your son, Lance
Corporal Vincent B. SANTANIELLO, U. S. Marine Corps, on 28 March 1968
in Quang Tri Province, Republic of Vietnam.

Vincent, as you know, was our company driver. Our company has been
standing the defensive perimeter of Cam Lo District Headquarters since
22 March 1968. On 28 March 1968 our company came under enemy mortar
fire, and it was at this point that Vincent was seriously wounded
throughout the body by fragments from a mortar round. Vincent was
immediately treated by a corpsman and evacuated to the helicopter
landing zone, but failed to respond and died of wounds at 12:10 p.m.
on 28 March 1968. The last rites of the church were received by
Vincent from Lieutenant Commander D. F. FOGARTY, U. S. Navy Chaplain
Corps.

A Mass will be celebrated in honor of Vincent in the near future.

Vincent was one of the finest Marines I had ever known. His exemplary
conduct, leadership, and singular determination to do every job well
were qualities that all of us respected. We will miss him and hope
you will find some comfort in knowing this.

If there is anything I can do, please feel free to write me.

Very sincerely,

Edward O. Le Roy
EDWARD O. LE ROY
Captain, U. S. Marine Corps
Commanding

The USMC notification letter to Mr. and Mrs. Carmine J. Santaniello.

Michael "Red" Reagan's 2014 hand-drawn portrait of Vinnie. Portrait
used with permission and pursuant to copyright, Michael G. Reagan,
Artist/President; The Michael G. Reagan Portrait Foundation.

www.ingramcontent.com/pod-product-compliance
Lightning Source LLC
Chambersburg PA
CBHW060758030726
47503CB00002B/298